My Circus,
My Monkeys

by Phil Trum

Text copyright © 2016 by Phil Trum

Printed in the United Kingdom

First Printing, 2016

ISBN 9781520143323

Black Glass Books
167 Buxton Road
Stockport
SK2 6EQ

blackglassbooks@gmail.com

My Circus, My Monkeys Facebook page:
www.facebook.com/MyCircusMyMonkeysNovel/

[1] Bass, Red and Johnny

"Cello," grunts Bass. Crumbs of Toffee Crisp fly into the warm, late June afternoon air. Red and I scan the crowd of shoppers and schoolkids. Bass wipes his mouth. "Cello, definitely."

"Where?" asks Red.

I spot her. Short blonde hair. Crop top. Cut-off denims over bright purple tights. I've seen her around. I think she's in my sister's year. She'll be sixteen, a larva for sure. A few top notes, but nothing in the lower register. She's exactly Bass's type. "The honey in front of The Zone." I screw up my empty crisp packet and toss it into the waste receptacle on my right.

Bass's eyes glaze over. "Victoria," he mumbles, naming her. "She is definitely ready to play the cello."

Red snorts derisively. "What? The one with the zit on her cheek?" He removes his glasses and begins wiping the lenses on the bottom of his tee-shirt. "You mean you'd like her to play *your* cello."

"What does that even mean?" I scoff.

"You know precisely what it means," says Red. "Anyhow, she's too skinny for my liking. She wouldn't make it past the first audition."

Bass turns to look at Red. "Not even 'The Demon VII: Further Adventures of the Demon'?"

I chuckle. We pass The Demon on the way to school each morning. We've no idea what breed it is – probably a cross between a Staffordshire Bull Terrier and a troll. It is, without doubt, the ugliest dog in the world. It stands there, behind a black wrought-iron gate, watching us pass, its tongue dangling from its ugly, misshapen mouth

3

and its tiny, bright red penis sticking down. I don't know if it lives out its pathetic existence in a permanent state of arousal or whether it just gets an erection at the sight of us three.

Red screws up his face and squints at Victoria. "I don't know. What do you think, Johnny?"

OK, let's pause there, shall we? Yes, I know, we're barely into the first chapter. Don't complain. I'll try not to make a habit of it, but this is important. Crucial.

I need to make *one* thing absolutely clear before we go any further. I am only interested in older women. And by older women, I mean older than *me*. So that's any woman 18 and over. OK, there's an upper limit, but let's not go there. And yes, I know this is purely hypothetical. Believe me, I am fully aware that there are no crowds of women – older or younger than me – trying to lure me, siren-like, into their clutches. However, for the sake of argument, from a purely conjectural vantage point, I just want to make it crystal clear that I have no interest in girls younger than me. I might be *weird* but I'm not *sick,* OK? I might, on occasion, *look* – purely for research purposes – but that's as far as it goes.

I could explain this in more detail – and may well do so later – but, for now, suffice to say that I am uninterested in members of the fairer sex until they are fully, um, *developed.* Sure, I can shake hands with the argument that younger women – girls my age or younger – can show a certain level of *potential,* but I can't embrace it. No *bro hug* from me with that one.

So, we clear? Excellent. Can't have you thinking ill of me. Not yet. Once you've read chapter four you can hate me.

Oh, and I lied back there. That bit about not pausing to explain very often? Complete nonsense. Big fat lie, dripping in maple syrup. I'm going to pause to explain, suspend the narrative to clarify, if you will, regularly. If that kind of thing puts you off, you'd better cut your losses and bail now. See ya!

Still here? Cool. Right, where were we? Ah, yes, of course. Hot summer weekday afternoon, early June. It's after school and I'm chillin' with the homies, sitting with my two best mates – Red and Bass – watching the world go by. Or more specifically, watching the girls go by. And we've got a 16-year-old girl, 'Victoria', in our sights. Red wants to know what I think of her...

"Let me see," I say, staring across the street. "Fast forward three years for a start. You how I like my steak cooked." I close my eyes for a second. "Silver metallic slip dress, sheer tights, maybe a pair of those weird Irregular Choice courts with the funny characters on the heel. Maybe Justin Bieber's head or something."

Bass chuckles. "I feel you."

"Not a pink wet-look mini-skirt?" asks Red.

"Nah," I mutter, losing interest a little. "Gotta ring the changes."

Bass and Red grunt in unison. They think I'd fancy my gran if she was wearing a PVC mini-skirt. They're wrong, of course – the thought disgusts me – but I will admit to firmly believing that nothing flatters the female figure more than something tight and reflective. Hey, we all have our peccadillos. Some of us, I guess, as you'll see, have them more than others.

We stare at Victoria for a minute or so. Bass finishes his Toffee Crisp. Victoria smiles at a boy in a Nike track-suit as he walks up to her.

5

"Here comes Dick," says Red.

Victoria and Dick put their arms around each other and stroll off down the street.

"Tart," murmurs Bass.

"Ho," grunts Red.

"I've still got to get my sister a birthday present," I say, watching Dick slip his hand into the back pocket of Victoria's cut-off denims.

"What's the hurry?" asks Bass. "I thought you said her birthday wasn't for another couple of weeks."

"Anyway," says Red, "why don't you just buy her the new album by you-know-who?"

We all cross ourselves solemnly. Spectacles, testicles, wallet and watch.

"Very funny," I say, "and, as you well know, she's already got it. She downloaded it the day it came out. She's even got the CD."

"How retro," mumbles Red.

"Do you have to get her anything?" asks Bass. "Rosie's, what, sixteen now? The only thing she'll want is cash, or a voucher, or something. Get her a twenty quid Topshop gift certificate. I don't know why you're stressing."

I shrug. I've asked myself the same question innumerable times over the last couple of weeks. Usually I spend less time deciding what to buy Rosie for her birthday than I do deciding whether or not to buy *Kerrang!* each week – and that takes about a nanosecond. I can't even remember what I bought her last year. Probably a copy of Teen Girl Monthly. 'What your boyfriend is REALLY doing in the toilet!!!' My wit really does know no bounds. This year, though, for her sixteenth birthday, I've got this feeling that I need to make more of an effort, that I need to get her something meaningful. Man.

"What about a violin?" asks Bass. "I've always thought of Rosie as a violinist – you know, something high-pitched and grating on the ear."

"Sixteen," murmurs Red absently. "The age of consent. How about something about ten inches long, two inches wide, and with a little electric motor inside?"

And there, in a nutshell, is what can happen to a teenage boy after he's spent thousands of hours watching internet pr0n. And also the reason why Dominic Killington, one of my two best buddies, is nicknamed 'Red'. After his favourite website. Google it. NSFW.

It crosses my mind to call him out on this one. There are lines, you know. Blurred at times, for sure, but there are lines. But I can't be arsed. It's too warm. We're lolling on a bench on one of the backstreets in the Home Counties commuter town in which we live and go to school. And hang out, and waste time, and plot world domination, and watch girls.

We watch Suzana Comănici-Jenkins walk past, by far the strangest girl in our year. Among her many weird attributes is her aloofness. It goes well beyond detached, several motorway exits beyond unsociable. It's as though she's not actually *here,* as though her presence in this world is an anomaly, a side-effect of some spooky rift in the time-space continuum. As though she's actually in some distant part of the galaxy where she spends twenty-four hours a day watching bizarre, sub-titled, Swedish films. All we see is a ghost, a shade.

Or maybe she's just shy.

But my money's on cold-hearted bitch.

Bass pulls out his phone and checks the time. "Gotta run soon."

He has a trumpet lesson every Tuesday at five o'clock.

Trumpet? Did you read that right? You thought he was called 'Bass'. Well, you did read that right, and he is called 'Bass'. More anon.

Although he pretends otherwise, Bass loves playing the trumpet and never misses a lesson, even though Grade 8 came and went (Distinction, if you must know) a couple of years ago. Red thinks it's because of Miss Moore, his teacher, who Red thinks he once saw in some pr0n flick – *Drooling Secretaries 5,* probably. I've never seen Miss Moore. Or *Drooling Secretaries 5,* I hasten to add. All Bass will say is that she's got 'great lips', and Red, as one would expect, finds this extremely amusing.

Red draws in a deep breath between his teeth. "T'n'A, three o'clock. *Candy*, methinks."

Red always picks names like that. Candy, Brandy, Bambi, Tammy and Melody are his favourites.

Bass and I survey the crowd for Candy. Being Red's type – think bargain basement working girl (if you catch my drift) – she isn't hard to find.

Candy is probably twenty but looks forty-five. Medium length hair, in very poor condition from what I can see from this vantage point, pulled back severely into a scrawny pony-tail. It's bleached yellowy-white, with two inches of dark roots. Too much makeup, badly applied. Tatty, yellow, scoop-necked tee-shirt. Denim mini-skirt. Bare, blotchy legs and scuffed white court shoes. One of the heels – which aren't nearly high enough for my liking – is worn down half an inch. She looks like she needs a good

8

meal. Every day for a year. I feel sorry for her. Which is magnanimous of me.

"Hotel domestic," says Red hoarsely, "definitely. 'Do you mind if I clean your room now, Sir?' Then she comes into the room, pulling the cleaning cart behind her. 'Oh, I see you've just had a shower, Sir. Do you need some help drying off?' Hooded eyes straight into camera. The camera pans down...."

We watch Candy walk past. She has a tattoo on her right calf. I can't make out what it's supposed to be but it looks like a dog vomited up some grape juice and she couldn't get rid of the stain.

"Viola," says Bass. "Third desk, where we can't really see her very well."

It's obviously my turn, though my heart's not quite in it. As noted, I suspect Candy would be best served with a home cooked meal and the love of a decent man, but appearances need to be kept up. "White satin corset, black trim, half cups, six suspenders. Headlights peeping over the top. White stockings. Black patent leather court shoes with-"

"-six-inch heels," say Bass and Red in unison. They smirk.

"Dog's dinner," says Bass.

"I wouldn't say no," says Red, staring at Candy as she moves off down the street.

I laugh. Red wouldn't say no to an armadillo.

"What am I going to get Rosie?" I ask again as Candy disappears into a newsagent's.

Bass resumes his scrutiny of the passers-by. "How much do you want to spend?"

"Thirty? Fifty max. Less, if possible. Something like that."

"How about a tattoo?" suggests Red. "A little red rose at the top of her thigh, or a butterfly."

"Great idea," I say, "or maybe a deck of cards on her upper arm."

"Three dots by her eye," says Red, warming to the idea, "or '1488' on her forehead."

"You drongo!" I grunt, punching him hard on the shoulder. I love him like a brother but he really can be an idiot. "Wherever the line is, we can always be sure you'll be standing five metres on the other side of it."

"I thought you said you only wanted to spend thirty quid," says Bass.

Red and I look at him. He's thinking our tattoo suggestions are serious.

"That's right," I say. "I could probably only afford 'L-O-V-E' tattooed across her knuckles. I could get her 'H-A-T-E' next year."

"Or..." says Red, moving another few metres away from the line, "you could get her a W on each buttock so when she bent over it'd say WOW."

I turned and shove Red so hard he has to grab the bench-seat to stop himself from being pushed off.

"Pack it in, Johnny!"

"You deserve it. She might be a bloody larva, but she's my sister."

Bass is ignoring our tussle. "Look, here's one for Johnny."

I see her, about twenty metres away, walking towards us, pushing a stroller. OK, I admit it, I've got a bit of a *thing* for young mums. Not *really* young mums, like fourteen-year-olds, which is sick, but young mums like this one. I'd guess she's in her early twenties. She's wearing white and green Converse high-tops, white, pink and green floral leggings and a loose green vest. Her dark brown hair – which is in excellent condition, you'll be pleased to hear, glossy, lustrous – is tied loosely at the back of her head with a white ribbon. She has dark eyes and full lips. As she walks, her breasts sway gently beneath the vest.

"Cressida," I mutter.

What? Too upper class? So sue me.

"Hmmm, once she's back home, and little Tarquin is down for the night, I think she'll be wanting to change into something a little more exotic. Black glued rubber vest dress, polo neck, ankle length. Jimmy Choo Romy 110s. Navy and silver coarse glitter degradé pointy toe pumps. That's 4.3 inch heels, round metallic."

"You what?" asks Red under his breath as Cressida draws nearer.

"An expression of her individuality."

"Flute," says Bass.

"For which she could find an alternative use," says Red.

As Cressida passes, we look down at the pavement, as though a crack has suddenly demanded our undivided attention. I steal a quick glance at her face to find her looking at us. I'm not surprised by her expression of faint disgust – a common reaction to the sight of three seventeen-year-olds with major hormone problems – although I am, as usual, slightly injured. It's hardly my fault that I can't look at a female between the ages of fifteen and fifty without imagining her as a possible sexual partner, is it? I suppress my guilt and stare at her buttocks, picturing them sheathed in that black glued rubber vest dress.

"I've got to go," says Bass, standing and picking up his trumpet case.

"Give her some tongue for me," says Red.

The flush in Bass's cheeks darkens. "Are we doing anything tonight?"

I shake my head. "I've got a chemistry test tomorrow. Heads down, no nonsense, mindless boogie."

"Oh, yeah. See you tomorrow then."

Red and I watch him walk down the street. He passes two girls, friends of my sister, Rosie: Dawn Ferner and Mamta Malhotra. The two wenches look at each other conspiratorially then start giggling as they walk into New Look.

"What about this weekend?" asks Red.

I'm busy imagining Mamta Malhotra in thigh length boots. "Eh?"

"This weekend. Anything happening?"

"I think Blunt Instrument might be playing The Black Hole."

"Are they metalcore?"

"Throwback thrash, I think."

Red reaches into his bag and pulls out this week's *Kerrang!* He finds the gig section and runs his finger down the listings. "The Suppurating Sores on Friday and The Androids of Doom on Saturday."

"Must be the weekend after, then."

"Isn't one of your brother's friends in The Suppurating Sores?"

"Most of my brother's friends have *got* suppurating sores."

Red rolls up the magazine and shoves it back in his bag. "I'm going to see if they've got that Squat 12" single in yet. You coming?"

We cross the street and enter The Zone. *King For A Day* by Pierce The Veil is playing. Red walks over to the rack of metal 12" vinyl singles while I absently flick through the large selection of second-hand CDs. Red quickly finds what he's looking for and moves to the counter at the rear of the shop, behind which *she* is standing – she being Apollonia Wallace, the most desirable woman in the entire world.

[2] Apollonia Wallace

If I were to devote the entirety of this overblown novella to the subject, I could do no more than scratch the surface of the extraordinary entity that is Apollonia Wallace. If I were to expand it into a tract of Proustian proportions, I would still be unable to do her justice. It's impossible to compare her to any other woman, living or dead. If I were the editor of the OED I could never find the words to describe her astonishing physical beauty. If I were the poet laureate, I would be utterly unable to describe the strength and depth of her personality. If I were the most gifted artist in the known universe...

All of which is, of course, something of a cop out. I *know* that. Really, I do. The thing is, I've got zero confidence in my ability to describe Apollonia Wallace – either her external appearance or what I know of her personality. Without doubt, I would only be able to do half the job – or less – especially with my lumpen, turgid prose style. It would be like describing a Ferrari as a 'fast, red car' or heavy metal as 'a particularly loud, simple and repetitive form of hard rock'. The latter example is lifted directly from the first Google hit – make of that what you will.

So, basically, even though I'm painfully aware that it does little more than highlight the deficiencies of my literary ability, I'm not even going to try to describe her. Instead, you'll just have to paint your own portrait of Apollonia – something Pre-Raphaelite would be a good place to start. What I can do, though, is provide a few biographical details which you can use as you see fit.

Apollonia's parents are William D Wallace, one of the most distinguished barristers in the country, and

Patricia Wallace, an obstetrician and gynaecologist at our local hospital. Mr Wallace won a gold medal at the Moscow Olympic Games – some track event, I think – and after that his career only got better. Dr Wallace also won a gold medal but that was for something to do with a medical examination of some sort. I know all this because my dad's a GP and he knows Apollonia's mum, Dr Wallace, quite well.

Apollonia, who's 20 or 21, has two older brothers. William Jr. is in his late 20s or early 30s, something big in the city. Greg is a couple of years older than Apollonia. I can just about remember him at school although no one could ever forget that he attended St. Michael's School (or St. Mick's, as we ingeniously refer to it) because his name's on every sporting trophy displayed in the cabinet that greets you as you walk through the front doors. No Wallace could ever be just an anabolic, though. Greg went to Oxford to read marine biology, or something like that, and now spends his time fishing for plankton or snorting coral somewhere off the Great Barrier Reef.

Apollonia, however, is the most impressive star of the family – a supergiant in the Wallace quadrant, where each member seems permanently on the brink of supernova. I'm not convinced that the stellar metaphors are working here, but you'll just have to take my word for it that, compared with Apollonia, her parents and brothers seem like under-achievers.

Academia, music, sport, drama, it doesn't matter. She excelled at, and continues to excel at, anything to which she turns her perfectly formed hands. She passed grade 8 piano while she was still in junior school. She got to the finals of the Young Musician of the Year competition. You'll have seen her on the box if you like that kind of thing. She plays clarinet and saxophone. She was in the National Youth Orchestra and the National Youth Jazz Orchestra. Someone told me she played sax with Jamie Cullum at Ronnie Scott's when she was just seventeen.

She got all A*s at GCSE, it goes without saying, but they only let you take ten GCSEs at St. Mick's. That didn't stop Apollonia taking several others outside of school. I think the final tally was fifteen, or something insane. She passes exams with less effort than it takes me to squeeze a zit, or so it seems.

Apollonia was hockey captain the year St. Mick's won the regional finals. Netball captain as well. Lead role in the school plays for her last three years. DoE Gold award. Head girl, *obviously*. She went up to Cambridge two years ago to read Economics & Management. Last I heard, she was editing a university journal in which some publisher had expressed an interest.

OK, OK, I hear you groaning, the clever tart's a combination of Marilyn Monroe and Albert Einstein – beauty and brains in one perfectly-formed package. She's probably got an ego to match, hasn't she?

Nothing, thankfully, could be further from the truth. Apollonia doesn't know the meaning of the word arrogance, and she wouldn't know conceit if it bit her on the tit.

Yeah, yeah, you mutter, so she's Bambi's mother as well, is she? So, what's she doing working in a back-street music shop, then?

Well, I've left the most awe-inspiring facet of Apollonia Wallace's personality until last: she loves metal! None of the ultra-extreme stuff – as far as I know, she's not into Darkthrone or Circle of Dead Children – but the more mainstream stuff like Killswitch Engage and Funeral For A

Friend. She's not averse to some old school classic rock – Maiden, Leppard, AC/DC, that sort of thing – and (be still my beating heart) she seems to have something of a penchant for 90s rock. The first time I heard Soundgarden was when she slotted Badmotorfinger into the player in The Zone.

I have sufficient neurones to acknowledge the fact that not everyone is into metal and therefore not everyone is going to accept that Apollonia's appreciation of things metallic ices her three-tier personality cake, so I'll have to put things into context a bit.

Imagine you're a male accountant. Every day you put on your grey suit and drive in your grey car to your grey office building. The only thing that gets you through the day is thinking about motorcycles. Your dream is to ride across the States on a Harley – the wind in your hair, insects in your teeth, and so on. One day, you're in the pub at lunch-time with your grey friends, sipping a half of mild. You spy, sitting on a stool at the bar, the most incredible woman you've ever seen. She's wearing a short skirt and a loose cardigan, and, although she's facing away from you, you can see she's got legs from there to there, an arse as firm as a firm thing, a trim waist and hair the colour of spun-gold tied up in a loose knot.

Your pulse quickens and sweat beads on your grey forehead. For reasons unknown, she swivels on the stool so that you can see her profile. Her face makes you want to whimper like a puppy. She reaches up and undoes a clasp, allowing her hair to fall down over her shoulders. Soft golden rain. As she says something to the woman sitting next to her, her teeth sparkle.

The blood vessels in the side of your neck are throbbing so forcefully, you fear an imminent cerebral

17

haemorrhage. The woman of your wildest dreams then slips off her cardigan, revealing a short-sleeved silk blouse. Your brain suddenly becomes immune to all external stimuli as your gaze zooms in on her forearm, the skin of which has been tattooed. Surrounding a grinning skull are the words: *Live To Ride, Ride To Live.*

Get the picture? Clear as? I hope so. I wouldn't like to think I'd wasted an hour of my time thinking up that long-winded analogy. However, I also hope that you now have a rough idea of the magnitude by which Apollonia's metallic interest enhances her appeal – to me, anyway.

As you'd expect, though, Apollonia's not your average metal aficionado. One of Greg Wallace's buddies, Buzz, works for some kind of promotion company and knows most of the big metal bands. Buzz went out with Apollonia once upon a time – although I prefer not to think about Apollonia *going out* with anyone – and thus Apollonia knows at least half the megastars in the metal firmament on a first-name basis.

The reason that Apollonia works in The Zone is that another one of Greg's chums owns the place and, as a favour to him, Apollonia helps out for a couple of weeks during the holidays. As I understand it, the turnover goes off into orbit whenever she's working there. I know I buy a lot more albums when she's there, as does everyone else I know. Sure, we can all download or stream everything ever but that doesn't get you a few minutes breathing the same air as Apollonia Wallace.

How do I know so much about Apollonia? Well, clearly, it's not because of the numerous heart-to-heart conversations we've had over the years. It will come as no huge surprise, I'd wager, to learn that I've never spoken to her. I doubt she knows I exist. No, much of what I know about her is public knowledge. At least in this town and at St. Mick's. Plus, as noted, my dad knows her mother, so I've picked up a few extra nuggets of information there. Add countless hours spent lurking in The Zone, listening in on her conversations with other people, and the end result is my encyclopaedic knowledge of Miss Apollonia Wallace.

I know I'm droning on a bit here about Apollonia but there's just one more thing I think I ought to clear up. I should imagine you're wondering how I can deify Apollonia Wallace while I spend hours sitting on the bench outside The Zone with Bass and Red degrading practically every female that passes.

I can see why you'd be wondering that. I sometimes wonder myself. As far as I can tell, it's not something peculiar to over-sexed, upper middle class, seventeen-year-olds. I've heard it said that men like to either look up to women on a pedestal or down at them in the gutter – so they can look up their skirts or down their blouses. This makes sense to me. I'm not saying it's right. Not at all. I'm just offering it as explanation, and suggesting that I'm not particularly unusual. Or that what goes on inside my head isn't more than two standard deviations from the mean. I hope.

[3] Larvae On The Loose

So, Red is waiting behind another couple of boys, his Squat single clutched in his sweaty paw. Apollonia's face looks a bit like that of the Madonna of the Streets by Robert Ferruzzi – you know, *pure*, emitting a golden glow. Red and the other two boys are trying to look at her while appearing not to look at her, if you know what I mean. It's not as if I'm not doing exactly the same thing, mind you, holding up a grubby second-hand Anthrax CD in front of my face and affecting intense concentration while stealing glances at Apollonia.

The first boy, Billy Gibson, who's in my physics class, hands over a tenner and I can see his hand almost shaking as he receives his purchase from Apollonia. I nod at him as he passes me on the way out but he doesn't acknowledge my presence. His eyes are glassy and he looks as though he's under the influence of a drug well known in these parts, a legal high, if you will – a drug of frightening addiction called Apollonia Wallace.

I look back toward Apollonia for a second or two but then I have to look away again. Sometimes, she's almost too beautiful to look at for too long. It gives me an odd aching sensation. Not in my groin, though. Or, rather, not *just* in my groin. Not even specifically in my heart. More sort of all over, kind of like someone who stands outside a Lamborghini showroom every weekend, staring at a gleaming Aventador LP 750-4 Superveloce Roadster for half an hour, knowing he'll never be able to afford much more than a Fiat 500.

I want her, but I know I can't have her. I know I'll never be able to have her. So standing here, staring at her forever would be more than acceptable. But I know I can't do that either.

Slightly dazed, I leave The Zone then pause and lean against the window. Sitting on *our* bench are a couple of Sharons. Red would love them.

One of them really *has* purple blotches over her white legs. The other has her hair done up in an immense bun which is nearly as big as her head. Very odd. They're both wearing fairly standard Sharon gear – dirty canvas flats, knee-length mini-skirts one size too small, tee-shirts from the market and about five times as much gold jewellery as is acceptable in all but the most down-market nightclubs. Then there are those podgy, blotchy, fading spray tan legs. I scan my enormous mental clothing inventory for something which might improve matters.

Sharon #1, with the leg blotches – let's call her Shaz, I'm sure her friends do – is definitely heavy-set, but she needs to make more of her ample chest and less of the elephant in the cellar. She wouldn't look bad in one of those 50s dresses, halter top, big skirt, maybe even with a petticoat. Red with small white polka dots might suit her colouring. Get rid of the fake tan. Some statement shoes. Fussy platforms. Bows, ribbons, whatever.

Sharon #2, with the immense bun, is more of a challenge, with her apple shape. I'm going to go with a trapeze dress, in a plain, dark colour, maybe dark grey, and luxuriant fabric, something which hangs beautifully. I'm not sure her arms can be improved, so a lightweight long-sleeved cardigan would be helpful. Perhaps some bold pattern tights and plain, black flats. A simple, chunky necklace, if she can be persuaded to wear her hair down. If she insists on the Godzilla bun then maybe some bold earrings instead.

21

I am shaken from my reverie when I realise that my sister's friends have reappeared and one of them is actually talking to me – the temerity of the little slug.

"Are you going to be at the party on Saturday?" asks Mamta Malhotra.

"Rosie says *everyone's* going to be there," says Dawn Ferner, looking at me in a way I find hard to decipher. It's either lust or disgust. Probably – preferably – the latter.

"What party?" I ask, looking away, hoping that nobody I know will see me talking to girls from my sister's year.

"*Your* party," says Mamta.

The sky darkens. There's a deep rumble of distant thunder. Lightning spider-webs across the sky. A bolt shoots down and strikes me squarely on the top of my skull. A deafening crack of thunder splits the air. At least that's what I think happens. Mamta means my parents' party, which I'd completely forgotten about. *Very* Freudian.

For as long as I can remember – and the ritual pre-dates my appearance on God's green earth, apparently – my parents have held a party every June. But this is no dinner party for six. Oh, no. It's not even a house party for a couple of dozen of their closest friends. If only.

No, this is an invite-everyone-and-their-dog event of epic proportions. Mum and Dad rent a marquee for the garden – *two* of them last year. The house is over-run by adults getting progressively tanked up, by teenagers skulking around the place, by younger kids tearing around like demented meerkats.

And I'm not joking, they really do invite *everyone*. I could probably cope if I had some say in who was invited but no, every noob and jock in my year seems to turn up,

22

plus those in my siblings' years – which all makes for an event which becomes, year on year, an ever-deepening chasm of utter horror.

To make matters even worse – is that even possible? you cry – this year my father has had the absolutely brilliant idea that Bass, Red and I will be tending the bar. OK, sure, that means we'll have easy access to as much ale as we can stomach, but it also means that we'll no longer be able to slope off to my bedroom, to hole up until the dreadful event nears its conclusion.

"Oh, yeah, that," I say, glancing back over my shoulder and into The Zone to see Red almost imploding with happiness as Apollonia takes his card and pushes it into the card-reader.

"Mamta and I are coming," says Dawn. The timbre of her voice forces me to scan her pubescent face for a microsecond, long enough to spy the smudge of chocolate near the corner of her mouth. Or maybe it's a very dark mole. Or a malignant melanoma.

"Super," I say.

Where's Red? I've certainly got far better things to do than stand here talking to two of my sister's larval friends. Opposite, one of the Sharons is lighting a cigarette. She's puts her lighter away then sucks hard, as though her life depended on it. Unbidden, a vision of her sucking hard on something else pops into my head. It is not a nice image. What is wrong with me?

Shuddering, I turn and look into The Zone again. For some reason, Apollonia's having a problem with the machine. She gets Red to enter his PIN again, then she twists the reader around and inspects the display. I watch her lips move as she speaks to Red. She could be telling him that the machine indicates that his penis is only an inch

23

long, but he won't care. He's utterly enraptured, as anyone of sound mind would be if allowed to stand so close to Apollonia for so long.

"We were looking for something to wear, weren't we, Dawn?"

Shit! Are they still here? I assume an air of utter disdain as I return my attention to them. "Really?"

If I were in a comic strip I would have an arrow pointing at me with the word 'sarcastic' written by it. Dawn and Mamta seem to think there's a sign hanging around my neck saying: 'No Friends. No Life. Please Talk To Me.'

"What do you think we should wear, Atticus?" asks Dawn.

Atticus is my real name. Red and Bass call me Johnny because I once spent the best part of a week looking at very little else other than the huge range of rubber stockings on eBay. My pals are, without doubt, a very witty pair.

"Black latex vest dress," says Red from behind me, answering Dawn's question.

I watch their larval faces as he speaks and I'm barely able to stop myself from laughing. Mamta looks as though Red has just blown chunks all over the pavement. Dawn looks as if she's going to have to eat it.

"Fishnet stockings," continues Red, seemingly unperturbed by the larvae's reaction to his appearance. "Oh, and don't forget the six-inch heels. They're Johnny's favourite, aren't they, Johnny?"

For a moment it occurs to me that if Dawn bit down on her lower lip any harder she would draw blood.

"Black," I say.

Dawn switches her gaze from Red to me.

"Patent, if possible," I add.

Dawn's expression dissolves slowly into one of incomprehension. Mamta grabs her arm.

"C'mon," she urges, pulling Dawn away.

"What did *they* want?" asks Red as we watch them hurrying away. Dawn's arse isn't perhaps as non-existent as I remember. Another few years and maybe.

"They're coming to my parents' party."

"When's that?"

"Saturday."

"*This* Saturday?"

"Yeah, so The Androids of Doom are going to have to do without us." I turn and look down at the vinyl single. "You got it, I see."

"There was an import album as well that I fancied but it was a completely double decker price."

I smile. Red's parents are loaded, seriously. Unless that album was north of a ton he could have bought it if he wanted. Whatever.

"'Shameless girlfriends amuse each other in the open air'," says Red, spotting the Sharons.

He really does spend far too much time looking at pr0n websites. I groan.

"Girlfriends Tina and Cindy relax after a hard day at the office. It's a hot summer day. They roll up their skirts to catch more of the sun. The ice-creams they're licking aren't cooling their temperatures at all. A passing policeman stops to chat. Tina tells him his she's never seen such a big truncheon. The copper looks at her sternly then tells her he's going to have to ask her to accompany him back to station. Ice-cream drips onto her exposed thigh. She scoops it up on her finger then puts her finger in her mouth. 'Yes, Constable,' she says, 'but can my friend come with me?'

Close up on the copper's face as he says: 'This way, ladies.'"

Red pauses for breath, staring at them.

"Finished?" I inquire. "I'd better be getting back to Dawson's Creek."

"And miss this once-in-a-lifetime opportunity to observe a brace of prime specimens such as these?"

[4] Atticus William Blake Childress: Testosterone King

That's me. Bit of a mouthful, isn't it? Still, it's not my fault. Blame my parents. I do.

Atticus was my father's choice – my mother wasn't too keen, apparently. My father, rather obviously, loved To Kill A Mockingbird. My mother's main counterargument was that she thought I'd get called 'Atty'. To date, no one's ever called me 'Atty'. I've been called many other things, but not that. So, as my mother had got her way when they named my older brother Zach, my father got his way with me. Atticus it is.

William is simple to explain – that's my paternal grandfather's name. Blake, however, is a little more difficult. My father would have me believe that it's in honour of William Blake, the eighteenth century 'Author & Printer'. He was a bit of a head-case, you know – kept getting visions and stuff like that. In my father's study, there's a poem by Blake hanging on the wall – *The Tyger*. The first verse goes like this: 'Tyger Tyger. burning bright, In the forests of the night; What immortal hand or eye. Could frame thy fearful symmetry?' Anyone who reckons that *eye* and *symmetry* rhyme has got to have a few screws loose, don't they?

Anyway, the reason why I'm somewhat reluctant to accept my father's explanation is that my mother had a boyfriend named Blake before she met my father. This information is all from my maternal aunt Frannie. She's my mother's youngest sister. At 23, she's only six years older than me, and younger than my big brother Zach, who's 24.

A bit of an afterthought on my grandparents' part. Or a mistake.

I digress. Which is unusual for me. In case you hadn't noticed yet.

Frannie told me that my mother was head over heels for this Blake character for ages and was an emotional cripple for months after he emigrated to Canada. If you believe things the way Frannie tells them, my father wouldn't have had a chance with my mother had this Blake still been around. Fascinating stuff, eh? Still, if Blake hadn't buggered off to Maple Syrup Land then I wouldn't even be here.

To some people, Childress might seem like an odd name. Obviously, not to me, as I've had it for, oh, a while now. Google tells me it's derived from the Old English word 'cildra-hus', which means children's house or orphanage. Tough to say something witty about that, isn't it?

So, with matters of nomenclature out of the way, let's get down to the nitty gritty. Let's wipe away the dust and grime and take a look at *the real Atticus Childress.*

I suppose the first thing you'll want to know is why am I obsessed with women's fashion, with particular – some might say *worrying* – interests in latex and heels.

One word.

Catwoman.

More specifically, Catwoman as portrayed by Michelle Pfeiffer in the 1992 Tim Burton Movie *Batman Returns.*

Oh, there have been many other Catwomen, before and after Pfeiffer, and nearly all of them have their merits, but it was that one, it that movie, with that actress, that did it for me.

28

If you're short on time, just Google "Catwoman Michelle" and look at the *images* results for two minutes. Got it? Cool. Feel free to skip the next few paragraphs.

If you haven't just been Googling – and welcome back if that search triggered a cascade of equally fascinating website visits – then you'll probably still know what I mean. You can picture her, can't you? All slinky and sensual in sheer, black, wonderful latex. How come all the good words start with *s*? Slinky. Sensual. Sheer. Stockings. Suspenders. Sex. See what I mean?

Anyway, I'm sure that's how it started. I've no idea when I first saw that movie. It's old now. I think my parents had a VHS copy, and then a DVD box set arrived one Christmas, or birthday, for someone. My Dad? Zach?

When I first saw it, when I first saw Catwoman, I can't have been affected by it as I am now. I was only a small kid. Six? Seven years old? At most I would have registered that she was *naughty,* or that she was *attractive* to men.

Like most lads, from a young age, I was very keen on superheroes – games, comics, movies, clothing, duvet covers. Batman probably wasn't one of my favourites. I still have a soft spot for Spiderman. Tobey Maguire era, if you must know. But that Batman DVD box set was around, and I would watch all those movies regularly.

But it wasn't until I was older, once the seeds had been sown by repeated exposure to Pfeiffer's Catwoman, when my hormones were doing the volcano and earthquake thing, that the planets came into alignment, that my hormones and neurones started jumping to that disco beat, and it started.

I can remember it quite clearly, actually. It was about a month before my sixteenth birthday. Until that time, my mental image of a sexually desirable women was drawn from the usual sources: celebrities on TV and the internet, music videos, glossy magazines, movies. I'm sure most males will know what I mean.

Being the son of a doctor, knowing where the old textbooks are stored, and therefore having access to several books with full-colour photographs of female genitalia, explicit pornography held no particular attraction for me. Peer pressure, on the other hand, demanded that I show at least a passing interest.

Some of my friends, Red in particular, have yet to pass through this stage. He can cruise the pr0n sites, watching the mating rituals (and variations thereof) of the human race for hours on end, or so it seems. I worry about that boy.

So, there I was, on my phone or my laptop (can't recall which now) looking on eBay, for radio-controlled airplanes or Spiderman underpants, when I happened upon the women's clothing section. Well, you can't really avoid it, can you? There you are, looking for a deleted album by some obscure Portuguese ambient death metal band, and up pops some scantily clad vixen in a 'sexy nurse' uniform, or whatever. This time, though, the photo was of a lithe lady in a tight, black catsuit.

Some sort of alarm bell went off inside my head. At the time, though, I had no idea why there was such a racket going on within my skull. I stared at it for ages, then moved on, looking for those radio-controlled airplanes, but always came back to *that* photo. I saved it, copied it to my phone, and just kept looking at it. As noted, much more graphic material is easily available, and, no disrespect (hollow laughter) to the model but there are a lot of photos of much more attractive women to look at. I did not know why it consumed me as it did, only that it did.

One thing led to another. Searching the Women's Clothing section of eBay for 'latex' and 'rubber' certainly kept me busy for some time. As you'll know, with the internet, the world, as they say, is your oyster, and there is a *lot* on the internet to ensure amusement for a young man with certain tastes and interests.

I spent a lot of time – too much, no doubt – on a website called *Sultry Nights* – the name itself sufficient to send a hormonally-over-endowed teenage boy into fits of apoplexy – that featured a bevy of beautiful models (well, about half a dozen) wearing various items of lingerie. There were no exposed headlamps. No Brillo pads were visible (not that you see many of those *anywhere* these days) – except on one model wearing a lacy body-suit. None of them was staring into the camera with that sexually ravenous (or smashed out of their heads on Columbian marching powder) porn-star look. I was, nonetheless, enraptured.

I studied every page of that site, scrutinising the models' faces and bodies, examining each article of lingerie with obsessional diligence. I poured over every description, the fabrics, the cuts. I became *au fait* with materials such as satin, ciré and *wet-look PVC*. As I said, I lived and breathed that site for weeks – well, two or three – until I discovered the next one.

I went back to that first site – *Sultry Nights* – a few weeks ago. Looking at it again after more than a year, I was shocked to find that almost nothing held my interest for more than a second or two. Except for the one photograph that sparked off my interest in all things rubber. I can describe the picture for you in minute detail, because it is forever etched on my mind.

Tiffany is about twenty-two and five foot nine. She has an immaculate figure – you know, curves in all the right places and other assorted clichés. She's lying on her stomach on a tiger-print rug, side on to the camera, so we can see every inch of her stunning figure. Her long, dark blonde hair cascades in a fountain of curls down her back. Her make-up is perfection in a glamour-shoot sort of way: black eye-liner, grey eye shadow, twin streaks of blusher slashing across her cheeks like gaping wounds, bee-stung lips painted deep red with liner one shade darker. You get the picture (yes, we see!). She's wearing a black wet-look PVC bustier with lace-up front which accentuates her full breasts. Or maybe makes less-than-full breasts look bigger. But it's what else she's wearing that catches (and holds for ever) the eye. You've probably heard the expression *painted-on jeans*. Well, whoever thought that one up must have seen (or had in mind) Tiffany in this pair of black wet-look PVC leggings. Photoshopped? Possibly. Probably. But who cares? Waist to ankles covered with black high-gloss paint. The swell of each buttock reflecting the studio lights. The gentle curves of her calves gleaming. One knee bent, lower leg perpendicular, the other stretched out horizontally. And, to complete an already perfect vision of loveliness, a patent leather, six-inch-heeled court shoe encasing each foot. What more can I say? I'm shifting position in my chair even as I type. Sigh.

Anyway, I think that's enough about my fetishes for a while. This chapter's supposed to be concerned with those aspects of my multi-faceted personality which may need explaining early on. I guess I should give you a little information about my personal history. A bit like one of those 'What I did in the summer holidays' sort of things, except it should be called 'What I've done with my life so far'.

Not a great deal, if the truth be told. Go back and read the chapter on Apollonia Wallace. Divide by ten. And you get me.

Let's see, I was born on Christmas Day, seventeen and a half years ago. Any of you who were born in Christmas week will know what I'm talking about when I say it's a real bummer. Big time. I mean, I don't care what anyone says, you do *not* get the same number (or quality) or presents or receive the same amount of attention that you would if your birthday was at any other time of the year. I'm sure your eyes are filling up with tears of sympathy right now, aren't they? Ha! You see? That's exactly what I'm talking about. I can't even count the number of times this relative or that friend of the family has handed over some item of negligible worth with the words: 'We were going to get you [some piece of rubbish worth X] but instead we decided to get you [another piece of rubbish worth X times 1.5].' The whole thing makes me sick. You know, I've heard of some people who have a *second birthday* in June or July, to make up for having a crappy Christmas birthday. Well, not in my family. You think I'm being petty? Perhaps, but just ask yourself if you'd like to have a birthday on Christmas Day.

This is more difficult than I thought, you know, trying to think of what you might find interesting about me. I mean, apart from being able to do a Mr Spock sign with my fingers. I've heard there are some poor unfortunate sods who can't do that. Imagine that! I can crack all five knuckles in each hand. Though not all at once.

Music's a fairly important aspect of my life, so I'll tell you about that.

My parents forced me to have piano lessons from the age of seven. I passed grade five when I was thirteen and, as my parents had always told me I could give it up if I reached that standard, I did just that. I can still play. There's a piano at home. But I rarely touch it.

I really wanted to play the guitar, and I persuaded my parents to part with some cash for some lessons once I gave up the piano. I only had a dozen or so lessons. I was keen on playing the guitar, just not keen on practising. I still play – more of that later – just not well. Good enough for rhythm guitar in a garage band!

I've mentioned that Bass is a keen trumpet player. He's in the school orchestra. First chair, or desk, or whatever they call it. A couple of years ago, he convinced me to join, the percussion section. I wasn't keen. Told him it sounded lame. But he wore me down. And it's nowhere near as awful as I'd thought it might be. All you have to do is count time and hit things. Suits me. Long stretches where there's nothing to do, other than look at all the girls. There's a cellist in the upper sixth, Alina Nash, whose arse was sculpted by Canova. Not familiar with his *The Three Graces?* Google it. Or think of Beyoncé. Doesn't matter. I get to stare at Alina Nash's backside for long periods during orchestra rehearsal. Win.

I'm tiring of this autobiographical shoe-gazing, as I'm sure you are, so let's skip it. I'll chip in with anything else that seems relevant as we go along.

[5] The Handsome Cucumbers

That's the name of our band.
This week.
Last week it was The Liquid Pineapples.
We're going through a bit of a fruit and vegetable phase at the moment. Over the last two or three months we've been The Non-Viable Melons, Chainsaw Strawberry, The Vacuous Gooseberries and, one of my favourites, Pear. Red preferred A Nice Pear. We couldn't agree.
I play, as mentioned, rhythm guitar. Bass plays drums. Hah, no he's the bass player. Red plays drums. When I say *play* I'm using the term loosely, in the same way that you'd call Rhianna a singer. We've had a lot of trouble finding a lead guitarist and we've never had a proper singer, not one who can, like, sing. In the main, Bass does the singing, though he either sounds as though English isn't his first language or as though he's swallowed some bleach.
We play a thrash metal hybrid we call crash metal. OK, it's actually Red that calls it crash metal. If you heard us play, you'd think *crap metal* was closer to the mark. We do plenty of cover versions – mostly covering up anything about the song that would make it recognizable. You should hear our version of Of Mice And Men's *Would You Still Be There?* – it's absolutely stomach-churning. Bass does the 'clean' vocals, while Red does the 'unclean' vocals. I do the 'Where's The Fairy Liquid?' miming in the background.
We've also got a handful of original compositions, mostly written by Bass although I've penned the odd ditty as well. Bass's songs usually bear a striking similarity to

35

those written by Metallica – principally because he learned to play the bass guitar from a music book of their *Ride The Lightning* album – the main difference being that his lyrics are even more gloomy.

Exhibit #1: the first verse of *Steel Through Flesh*:

'Nothing left. No hopes. No dreams.
In the dark, my conscience screams.
You took my heart and stole my soul.
And left within a deep black hole.'

Cheerful, isn't it? But wait, it gets worse:

'My saviour gleams, release at last,
From pain and tears for all that's passed.
In the dark, a bright white glow,
A salve for grief and my sorrow.'

I didn't say he could write a lyric that scanned, did I? He tries, though, which I suppose is something. Mind you, *Steel Through Flesh* is one his more upbeat tunes. You should hear *As My Life Ebbs Away* or *Dark Black Heart*. Bass won't provide an adequate explanation of the suicidal nature of his lyrics. Red and I don't *think* he's planning on topping himself. It seems he just likes writing lyrics about it. Still, we try not to leave him alone with loaded firearms. I think it's just a topic that certain adolescent males find attractive in a navel-gazing sort of way.

My songs tend to be more concerned with traditional metal things like babes, booze and bikes. Not that I'm drawing on any first-hand experiences. *Stiletto Stamina* is probably my best song but I have zero intention of embarrassing myself by reproducing the lyrics here.

You'll have to wait for the 20th Anniversary Deluxe Edition of this book. I will include my song lyrics in the appendices. Let's just say that it's not a song about a boat called *Stiletto Stamina.*

We practice in Red's garage because it's separate from the rest of his house. We make such a racket that neither Bass's parents nor mine will tolerate us anywhere within earshot. Red's house is huge. More like a mansion really. His dad's some sort of wheeler and dealer. *What* he wheels and deals, none of us knows for sure, least of all Red. Bass thinks he's an arms dealer. I'm not convinced but I'd be surprised if whatever he does is totally kosher. Red says he's away a lot, overseas. But I'll tell you more about Red's parents later on, if I feel like it. I'm supposed to be telling you about our band.

The best way to give you an impression of what it's like to be a member of The Handsome Cucumbers is to tell you about our most recent practice session which was last Friday night. Oh, first I'd better tell you that our current lead guitarist is Phillip Dunwoody who's in Bass's economics class. Phil's technique is incredible. He can play, note for note, practically everything Steve Vai and Joe Satriani have written – perhaps not up to speed or always in the right order, but not far off. Also, he's got a pretty good singing voice. In other words, he's not going to last long in The Handsome Cucumbers.

Anyway, when I arrived at Red's house, I could tell, even as I walked toward the garage, that it was going to be one of *those* nights. To judge from the volume of Red's epileptic drumming, you'd think there was a small-scale war going on.

As I open the side door, the noise is ear-splitting. Not content with hammering away at his drum kit without the aid of amplification, Red's hooked up his latest acquisition. Did I tell you that Red's father buys him practically anything he wants? Not unlike my evil sibling, Little Bennie, but more so. I guess some people really *do* have money to burn. I'm not sure Red's father always *knows* what he's buying. Red's always a little cagey about exactly how it works. The PA system in Red's garage is bigger (and louder) than a lot of pro systems I've seen and heard at various club level gigs.

Closing the door behind me, I nod at Bass – who's found the least noisy corner of the garage in which to tune his guitar – then walk up to Red, who's grinning like a psychopath. My teeth are rattling so violently that for a few moments an image from a Tom and Jerry cartoon flits across my mind. You know, one where Tom gets hit on the head with a frying pan or some other object that would patently kill him outright and he stands there, vibrating with the force of the impact, until his teeth start to crack and, piece by piece, they fall out, tinkling to the floor. I bend down and lay my guitar case on the floor then stand up straight again and draw my finger across my throat. After repeating this gesture about a thousand times, Red finally stops. A few seconds pass, during which my hearing returns. The deep throbbing hum of about twenty gigantic amplifiers fills the air.

"Great, isn't it?" says Red, grinning maniacally.

I walk toward the nearest of the monolithic amplifiers and inspect the row of knobs. "This as loud as they go?"

"What do you mean?" he asks and I can tell, without looking at him, that he is crestfallen.

I try to keep a straight face as I turn to him. "If we're going to make it, we're going to have to get something a lot louder than this. I mean, I could hardly hear you outside."

Red scrutinises my face and he's just about decided that I'm pulling his leg when Bass strolls over, his guitar slung across his upper thighs, Sid Vicious style. "Don't encourage him."

"Metal can never be too loud," says Red.

"The point that you seem to be missing so widely," says Bass gravely, "is that it's quite appropriate to pump out a zillion giga-watts from the PA as long as the band are *behind* the PA and not slam bang in front of it. *You* may be quite happy to be wearing a hearing aid by the time you're twenty but I'd quite like to keep my eardrums intact, thank you very much."

Red looks at me for support but there is none forthcoming. "Bloody snapperheads."

"Perhaps a couple of notches," I say to Red, "down?"

I wouldn't mind so much but every single rehearsal starts off in exactly the same way. Red wants to crank everything up, in true Tap fashion, to eleven, then Bass castigates him for wanting to be in the audience and not in the band. Eventually, a compromise is struck and we usually get down to actually playing something after only about a couple of weeks.

Tonight, we manage to get through Metallica's *Welcome Home (Sanitarium)* with no more than six million mistakes. We always start off with that one – it just seems to get us in the mood. OK, I know, Metallica aren't exactly *current* these days, having released, arguably, one good album in the last ten thousand years, but their early stuff, up to Puppets, is unparalleled. And so say all of us.

"Where's Phil?" asks Red, sweat pouring down his bright red face.

Bass and I exchange a glace then Bass turns to Red. "I thought *you* were telling Phil about tonight."

Red glares at Bass. "Why would *I* tell him? He's in *your* economics class. I naturally assumed that you would inform Phil about our little get-together this evening."

"And I wouldn't credit you with anything that might even remotely be called a memory," says Bass, his voice rising in volume as he starts to enunciate very carefully, "so I will remind you that I told you this morning that I did not have economics today and that you would therefore have to tell Phil at lunch-time."

Red looks at Bass for a couple of seconds then turns to look at me.

"I refuse to answer that question," I deadpan, "on the grounds that I don't know the answer."

Red scowls then looks back at Bass. "Oh," he manages after a few seconds. "Shall I give him a ring?"

"That might possibly be the most sensible suggestion you've made this decade."

Red fumbles his phone out of his back pocket. Bass and I walk around the garage, turning off every other amplifier. "Finished those new lyrics?" I ask.

"Decaying Emotions?"

I nod.

"Almost. A bit stuck on the chorus, though. Want to hear the first verse?"

"Later, eh? I'm still feeling fairly cheerful, despite the absence of the fretboard wizard."

"Ten minutes," announces Red. "What about *Satanic Sluts*?"

Red's only attempt at song-writing.

40

"No!" exclaim Bass and I.

Phil arrives half an hour later, after we've played through *Dark Black Heart* three times and changed our name to Dissected Rats, Clitoris, Barry And The Big-Boned Women, The Sexually-Enlightened Hamsters, Clitoris (again), Lump Hammer, and finally Silicone Implants (Red's most printable suggestion – honestly).

Phil plugs in his guitar and lets rip with some Bring Me The Horizon riff I recognise but can't place exactly. Enraptured, the three of us just watch him. I feel as though I really have no right to even touch my guitar, never mind attempt to play it. I give Phil another week as a Handsome Cucumber – a Silicone Implant, I mean. From Bass's expression, I can see he's thinking similar thoughts.

We blast through a few covers, including an almost passable version of Pearl Jam's *Jeremy*. We also try to play *Decaying Emotions*, Bass's new song but, as he hasn't worked out all the chord changes properly we end up playing *Smoke On The Water*. We nearly always end up playing that one. Bass starts the riff then I join in. Even Red can keep the beat. Phil looks at us as if we're three little pigs in shit then, with a sneer and a sigh of resignation, joins in and starts singing. In places, he even sounds a bit like Gillan. Well, sort of.

Finally, about ten o'clock, Phil unplugs his guitar. Bass walks over to him and stands there watching him snapping the catches on his case. "Next Friday, same time?"

Phil looks up as though the thought of another rehearsal had never crossed his mind. "Sure. Yeah."

Man of few words, our Phil. We bid him adieu.

"Better put up a notice for a new lead guitarist," I advise.

41

Red and Bass nod solemnly.

"I've been thinking about a keyboard player," says Bass.

"We're a metal band," says Red.

Bass absently tunes his E-string. "Loads of metal bands have keyboard players. Dream Theater. Children of Bodom. Blah blah blah."

"True," I say then look at Red. "What have we got to lose?"

"Ah," sighs Bass, "the dignity of labour."

Sometimes he says things like that.

[6] Sibling Rivalry

Not in my family. At least, not that I'm aware of. I'd like to think that I have nothing in common with any of my siblings, and therefore nothing for which we could compete. Yeah, right, and the NHS is completely safe in the hands of the Tories.

Seriously, I suspect that the Childress children are more alike than any of us would like to admit. First of all, let's get the demographics out of the way. Zach's the eldest at twenty-four. He's currently *between jobs*, as they say. I'm next, at seventeen and a half. Then there's Rosie who, as you know, will be sixteen soon. Then there's Benjamin who's ten. The four fabulous Childress children. They should make a film about us, or write a book.

Zach went to St. Mick's and got two A levels for his troubles – art and economics. Somehow, he got into one of those 'new' universities, the ones that used to be polytechnics. I forget which one. Somewhere up north. The University of West Huddersfield or something. Amazingly, he lasted a whole two terms. It's never been satisfactorily explained to me whether he left or was pushed. I have my own theories but they're probably best kept to myself. Zach has many strengths – God bless him – but he's never been great at sticking at things. The longest he's lasted in a 'proper job' was when he worked in a local shoe shop for two months.

Now, heaven means different things to different folks but working in a shoe shop comes pretty close to Elysium in my estimation. It would have to be a special kind of shoe shop, mind you. Ladies only. I wouldn't want to sell trainers to anabolics, or shoes with flashing lights to toddlers. And I'd want to be in the high heel section, thanks very much. Hang on, I'm rethinking the 'no kids' rule. OK, there could be a small kids section, to cater for young mums. See, I can think laterally. Anyhow, back to Zach. Wasn't that an Amy Winehouse album?

Recently, he's been a roadie for a band called Forked Tongue. Heard of them? Nope, nobody has. I was going to say: Zach's been *roadie-ing*, but I'm not sure that's a word. In my dictionary it says:

n. **road'ie** *(slang)* a member of the crew who transport, set up and dismantle equipment for musicians, esp. a pop group, on tour.

It doesn't say anything about a verb. I roadie. You roadie. They roadie. We've been roadie-ing. Strange. Sounds kind of funny if you say it over and over. Roadie. Roadie. Roadie. See what I mean? Anyway, that's what he's been doing. Suits him right down to the ground. Although it would give me a bit of credibility at school if he'd roadied for a band of which anybody had heard.

I'm planning on devoting a whole chapter to Rosie later so I'll proceed directly to Ben, my younger brother. Otherwise known as Little Bennie, especially when I want to irritate him, which is most of the time. I'm told that when describing someone, one should start with his or her good points.

Ben brushes his teeth every night before bed.

Right, now I can get on with demolishing his character, for want of a better word. First, what's with that name? Not his fault, granted, but I have to begin somewhere. What got into my parents when they decided to call him Benjamin? Everyone and their dog seems to be

44

called Benjamin these days. If you walked into any primary school playground at lunch-time and shouted out 'Benjamin!' two-thirds of the little tots would spin around to look at you. There are six of them in my brother's class. And the BD (Benjamin Density) only increases as you go down through the years at school. As far as I can tell, there are nurseries where they won't admit male infants unless they're called Benjamin. They're going to start naming girls Benjamina soon, you watch.

Next, he's the ultimate spoiled brat. The epitome of the term. The paradigm. The exemplar. Everything he wants, he gets. Toys, games, sports equipment, everything. It makes me sick. It's not as though he throws tantrums when it looks as though he might not get something he wants. Oh no, he's shrewder than that. When it suits him, he can be 'Mummy and Daddy's Little Angel', all sweetness and light. He knows *exactly* how to get what he wants. But I see the other side of him: his little smirks of self-satisfaction when he's just conned some kiddie consumer durable out of them, his evil little face contorted with concentration when he's planning his next campaign. You know the Kubrick the film *The Shining*? Imagine the character Jack Nicholson plays in it, aged ten, and you've got my brother, Little Bennie, in a nutshell.

Lastly, although I could go on for hours on the subject of my darling little brother, he can beat me at any computer game you care to mention. The little weasel. This may sound rather trivial to you, but it's bloody embarrassing. In fact, I'm not going to mention it again. So there.

He does brush his teeth last thing at night, though. Just probably not very well. But I'll bet he doesn't floss.

[7] The Childress Zit Cream Theory

I wake up to the sound of Rosie's favourite group. Even though her room is on the other side of the house she has her sound system cranked up so high that the walls of my room are practically vibrating with the painful din of those four quavering voices shrieking out the lyrics of their latest hit. A paean to their legions of flat-chested larval fans. What is it with girls like Rosie? Even she, at nearly sixteen, must be getting too old for this crap. What on earth do they see in these manufactured gangs of singing geeks?

I simply don't understand why they've not become extinct. It seemed to be going that way several years ago, only for TV shows like X Factor to bring them back. These gaggles of crooning airheads seem to keeping the traditional music business limping along.

I'm unclear if they even have record company 'scouts' any more. If they do, they're probably locked in dark rooms, doing nothing but watching endless self-uploaded YouTube videos. Otherwise, they probably look at the models in the men's underwear section on the Debenhams website. Perfect skin (or perfect make-up), immaculately groomed hair with just a dash too much gel, whiter-than-white teeth. Everything just perfect. Perfectly false. Or perfectly Photoshopped. What the bimbettes see in them is utterly beyond me. I just don't understand it. Really I don't.

For a few seconds I contemplate switching on my sound system. I downloaded a bootleg live Of Mice And Men album recently. But I'm not capable of facing anything quite so intense at quarter past seven on a Wednesday morning. Instead, I grab my phone and flip to a website I found recently called *Corruption*: 'We specialise in high heels that combine comfort and elegance in a wide variety of styles from plain court shoes to thigh boots.'

After a happy few minutes, I haul my arse out of bed, and stumble across the landing into the bathroom. The room stinks of Rosie's deodorant. I can't blame her really. I think most of us go through that phase when we're convinced that the slightest whiff of body odour is going to send anyone we meet running for cover. Some people never get out of that phase, of course, and some unfortunately never seem to reach it.

I lean in toward the mirror to perform my daily zit inspection ritual. The one on the left side of my nose which appeared a few days ago is just entering the smouldering volcano state. There's one just starting below the left side of my mouth and another one on the right side of my neck. If they were making a film of my life, there would now be some dramatic music (*Carmina Burana* probably) and some histrionic zoom shots. Then there would be a contrived close-up of my mortified expression.

Well, I don't hold with any of that sort of thing. A zit's a zit, isn't it? Given the choice, I'd rather I had a clear complexion, of course. Who wouldn't? But I don't see much point in working myself up into a frenzy over a few stupid spots.

They're funny things, zits, aren't they? Funny-peculiar, that is. I know I'm not the first person in the history of the universe to notice how they seem to have an extremely vindictive sense of timing. You know the score, I'm sure. There you are, looking forward to some kind of social engagement. A party, perhaps, at which you want to

47

make a particularly good impression. Maybe the (intended) love of your life is going to be in attendance. You've been working overtime with the cleansers and scrubbers – defoliants which have removed most of your epidermis. You wake up on the morning of the event and what do you see in the mirror but a monstrous zit, right smack in the middle of your forehead, glowing and throbbing like a glowing, throbbing thing. But I'm not telling you anything new, am I? Been there. Done that.

Two things amaze me about zits. First is the inversely proportional relationship between the size and/or general appearance of them and the actual physical discomfort they cause. There are the ones which I first notice when I scratch my face, pick my nose, or whatever. Even if I prod it as gently as I can, the pain is excruciating. I start to think I've developed some new strain of bubonic plague. At the first opportunity, I locate the nearest mirror only to find that there's nothing to see. In contrast, there are the other sort of zits which cause zero pain and which only come to my attention when I notice this huge pus-filled balloon sprouting out of my chin and I think: 'Jumping jellyfish! (or words to that effect) Have I really been walking around all day with *that* on my face?'

The other thing about zits that really bugs me is the way zit lotions and potions are advertised. I mean, I don't know who's advising these people but they're obviously under the impression that the average teenager loses an IQ point with every zit they squeeze. Just five days of treatment and that pizza face is history? Gonads. Who on earth are they trying to kid? The advert that really deviates my nasal septum is the one where some larva (who doesn't have a single zit in the first place) rubs a cotton wool ball across her fresh little face then holds it up to the camera so we can all see the copious amounts of soil thus removed. Have you ever tried that? I have, on more than one occasion. You can stand there, in front of the bathroom mirror, filling the toilet with one dirty cotton wool ball after another for the rest of your life.

You'll be pleased to learn that I have a theory about zit cream advertising. Did you ever think of comparing cats to acne-sufferers? I thought not. Well, it's exactly the similarities between these two superficially disparate groups that forms the basis of my theory.

When cat-food is advertised on television, it is portrayed in such a way that it looks fairly appetizing to your average cat-owner. I'm not saying that cat-owners are expected to think they'd like to eat the cat-food themselves (although some of those 'meaty chunks' bear a worrying similarity to the stew the serve at St. Mick's) but they are supposed to think that their cat would find it delicious. The cat-food makers have to advertise to the cat-owners and not the cats because the owners hold the purse-strings. Another reason is that cats can't read, of course, so they wouldn't know a tin of *Yummy-Paws* from a tin of pickled gherkins.

So, how does this relate to zit cream, you ask yourself as you contemplate turning the page to see how long this theory of mine goes on for. Basically, just as cat-food is advertised to cat-owners, so cream for acne-ridden adolescents is advertised to owners of acne-ridden adolescents *viz.* their parents. You see, if I've got a fiver in my pocket the last thing I'm going to do with it is pop into my local chemist's shop and blow it on a bottle of the latest wonder lotion. But my mother is very different, as, I suspect, are a lot of mothers. I can't remember the last time she came back from the supermarket without a bottle or five of *Spotzap* or whatever.

49

I haven't quite finished with The Childress Zit Cream Theory because I've yet to explain just how it is that mothers across the land are so easily persuaded to part with hard cash for all these lotions. I think I'll have to bring in The Childress Jeckyl and Hyde Teenager Theory at this point, which is most simply explained by a thumb-nail sketch of Joyce, Mrs Average-Mother.

Joyce gives birth to a baby boy, Sonny. For the first few years, everything is hunky-dory. Sonny is, to all intents and purposes, your average pre-pubescent boy. He does well at school. His behaviour, while not exemplary, is more that acceptable. Then one day, when Sonny is twelve or thirteen, things start to change. He spends an increasing amount of time in his room or out with his friends. Demands for mobile phones, video games, skateboards and other pre-teen consumer durables multiply. He becomes sullen and communication starts to deteriorate. He grows taller, perhaps taller than Joyce. His voice breaks and his face breaks out. He is no longer a child. Perhaps, he gets into a bit of trouble at school. Joyce finds cigarettes in his drawer, or pr0n sites in his browser history. What is happening to good-as-gold little Sonny? He's turning into something Joyce can't understand.

Of course, what's happened is that Joyce has merely forgotten what it was like when she was Sonny's age. But that's part of The Childress Adolescence Amnesia Syndrome and I'll no doubt get around to that, given the time and opportunity, or maybe not. Anyway, what happens is this: Joyce is watching Coronation Street, Britain's Got Talent or Celebrity Hamsters Attack!!! and she sees an advertisement for *Zitrid*. The youth portrayed in said advertisement is clean and wholesome, fresh-faced and innocent with, maybe, an endearing twinkle of well-

50

modulated rebellion in his or her eyes. In short, everything Sonny once was but, sadly, is no more. With enough repetition, the subliminal message locks into place and Joyce thinks if only Sonny used *Pimplekill* he would be just like the wonderful youths in the advertisements. And guess what she just happens to bring home with her next time she visits the local mega-mart.

If, by some unlikely chance, poor media-manipulated Joyce finds the shelves of her friendly zit cream emporium empty, then all she has to do is come by my house. We could re-stock most shops, three times over.

Hold your horses. Grip your gryphons. I've only just now started to wonder if cats can get zits. Now there's a worrying thought.

[8] Dawson's Creek

I absent-mindedly pick at the zit on the left side of my nose for a minute or so until it looks a fair bit worse than it did before I started. There's a welcome silence between songs on Rosie's sound system. Then 4Tune8 start singing again. There! I typed the name of the group, even though my fingers were trembling. I knew I'd have to sooner or later. 4Tune8. What an incredibly stupid name. Thankfully, by the time I've showered and dressed, Rosie has gone down to breakfast and I am spared further torture at the hands – or should I say the thin, reedy voices? – of 4Tune8.

I have to wear a uniform for school. Isn't that pathetic? St. Mick's must be the only school in the galaxy that forces sixth formers to wear a uniform. If I was going to a sixth form college, I'd be able to wear what I wanted. I wouldn't be constricted by paternalistic notions of conformity. I would be able to express myself fully, let the world see exactly what Atticus Childress is all about. You know, jeans and a tee-shirt, that kind of thing.

St. Mick's used to be a boys' grammar school, back in Tudor times, or something. Maybe not quite that long ago. Even though it's been a state school for ages, the names of the years haven't been modernised. What, in most other British schools, would be years 7 to 11 (for kids aged 11-16) are the first to the fifth forms. Confused? You will be.

I know some schools are divided up into upper and lower schools, or the sixth form is on a different site, but at St. Mick's everyone's on one big site, kids from 11 to 18. This means – and I can hardly bring myself to contemplate this – that next year, when I am in the upper sixth, that little weasel, Bennie, my so-called brother, will be at the same school as me. I am seriously thinking of joining the Army.

To get back to the St. Mick's uniform, the only redeeming factor is that it is, for the boys, rather... er... *understated*. This results in all the boys looking like undertakers, or undertakers' children. The uniform for all boys – from first form to upper sixth – consists of: black shoes, dark blue or dark grey socks, dark grey trousers, white shirt, dark blue or dark grey pullover (in the winter and spring terms only), black tie and black jacket. No blazers with flashy striped piping or overly ornate crests on the pocket for St. Mick's. Oh, if you reach the dizzy heights of becoming a prefect you're allowed to wear a blue tie and brown shoes just to show how superior you are.

Such a rigid dress code allows little room for the expression of one's personality. Chiefly, one is restricted to a small number of variations in the type of black tie and, particularly, how one ties the knot. Some boys, usually those with a rebellious streak, opt to incorporate two thirds of the tie in the knot, leaving an inch or two dangling down. When a pullover is worn, the aim is to fill the diamond of shirt formed between the collar wings and the V-neck of the pullover with a solid mass of tie. Myself, I eschew this sartorial option for the thinnest tie I can find, tied into the smallest knot I can manage. I might, if pressed, attempt to assign some kind of psychological meaning to this habit, but I can't be bothered. I'll leave you to draw your own conclusions.

So, by the time I've re-knotted my tie half a dozen times – until it's just right – it's almost quarter to eight. In the kitchen, Mum is standing by the cooker, sipping coffee from the *World's Greatest Mum* given to her by Bennie last Mother's Day. She's watching the television on the counter.

53

The volume's turned down because Dad likes to listen to Radio Four. Don't ask me to explain. It sounds as stupid to me. Dad is sitting at the table, engrossed by the front page of The Independent.

In case you think I've cocked up that paragraph, I assure you that it's 100% accurate. Dad is *reading* the paper, while *listening* to the radio, and Mum is *looking at the TV* (with the sound off), presumably trying to follow what's going on, while *listening* to the radio, or just daydreaming. Adults, eh? *La vida loca.*

Every thirty seconds or so Dad has another spoonful of Bran Flakes. Rosie is as absorbed by her magazine as Bennie is by the game of Pissed-Off Parrots (or whatever has taken his fancy this week) he's playing on his phone. Occasionally, Mum or Dad will berate him for spending too much time on his phone but they mainly seem grateful he's not texting his dealer for a new supply of legal highs or something.

I'm not certain about the title of Rosie's magazine – and I have no intention of asking her – but there is a curious strategy employed by the publishers of women's magazines when it comes to naming their organs. It strikes me that the titles they choose are meant to give the impression that the contents are appropriate for an age-group three or four years older than the age of their actual target readership. Thus, *Seventeen* is read mainly by thirteen or fourteen-year-olds, *Nineteen* is read by fifteen-year-olds or... you get the point? I'm sure that *Cosmopolitan* is not read by anyone over twenty-three.

"Blood transfusion?" inquires Rosie, looking across at me as I sit down. It takes me a couple of moments before I realise the focus of her caustic badinage.

Yes, sister, dear, I am living with acne vulgaris. Please give generously.

"Zit city," says Bennie, crinkling his face in disgust.

I mimic his grimace. I struggle briefly to fling back a witheringly sarcastic retort. Not this time. I'm not really a morning person, in contrast to the rest of my family, apart from Zach, who's as semi-comatose as me until about eleven o'clock. As I pour cornflakes into a bowl I reach surreptitiously into my trouser pocket then dab the nose zit with a piece of toilet paper.

Mum finishes her coffee and stows the mug in the dishwasher. "I hope you've tidied your room."

She is still watching the television so I'm not sure to which of her offspring she is directing this question, although I have a pretty fair idea. Nevertheless, I pretend not to have heard her.

"I swear, Atticus, the time is quickly coming when I'm going to refuse to even go into that tip you call your bedroom. I'm just going to close the door every time I walk past."

Had I not heard this statement of intent a thousand times previously I might feel the urge to think up an appropriate reply. As it is, I continue the tried and tested policy of saying nothing. In our family something else usually happens. This time, it is Dad who comes to the rescue.

"Have you asked Dominic and Oscar about the party?"

Dom Killington and Oscar Clarke, otherwise known as Red and Bass.

I shrug, speech temporarily impaired by a mouthful of cornflakes.

Rosie looks at Dad. "Asked them what?"

55

"I've asked Atticus if he and his friends will tend the bar on Saturday."

It's Rosie's turn to pull a face. "Dom Killington," she murmurs, shuddering melodramatically. "What a creep."

If I said that Rosie doesn't particularly like Red that would be slightly understating the case. Unfortunately for Red, he's not going to win a popularity contest with any demographic. He is – if I were to be charitable – something of an acquired taste. Or maybe Bass and I just have slightly lower-than-normal thresholds for aberrant personality traits in our friends.

It's not that Red is more emotionally/sexually stunted than your average 17-year-old male (myself included) but that he seems unable to conceal from anyone exactly what he's thinking. He's not so much an open book as an open copy of the *Hot 100* issue of *Maxim*.

If I'm visualising one of the dinner ladies at school in a boned satin corset top with eyelet back then I'd like to think that neither she nor anyone else can tell what I'm thinking.

When Red looks at a member of the opposite sex, it's usually patently obvious that she's been stripped naked and dropped into a brothel scene from *Game of Thrones*. His eyes bulge maniacally and he doesn't so much salivate as drool, copiously.

I'm making him sound a bit like a rabid dog, which is something of an exaggeration, but not actually that far from the truth. Suffice to say that most females I know, Rosie included, would cross to the other side of the street if they saw Red coming towards them.

It's a shame, really, because, under all that, he's actually a funny, sensitive guy. When he's not being a sexist pig.

"I'm not sure," I mutter.

Dad looks at me. "Whether Dominic's a creep or whether you've asked him about the party?" he asks, grinning as though he's just wrapped up the Joke of the Year contest. It's sad, really, when the signs of dementia first become apparent.

Behind me, Mum chuckles quietly. They were made for each other.

"I'll mention it today, OK?"

"Please don't," says Rosie.

[9] The Childress Laws of Breast Nomenclature

I watch Bass walking toward me along our street. The term *vacant expression* must have been invented with him in mind. Only when he's a couple of metres from me does his face show any sign of life.

"I solemnly swear that I am up to no good," he quips.

"You'll have to speak up, I'm wearing a towel."

"Phil messaged me last night."

"Let me guess. Musical differences? Considering a solo career?"

"Not quite."

"I know, AC/DC called. Angus has ringworm and they need Phil to step into the breach."

"He said his parents were turning the screws a bit. Must do better at school. That sort of thing."

I kick an empty cola can along the pavement. "And you believed him? I think he last failed a test when he was a foetus. Shame he didn't Facetime you. His nose would have grown so fast he'd have cracked the screen on his phone."

"I'm just telling you what he said."

"I know. Not exactly 'Sam Smith Announces Engagement to Rita Ora', is it?"

We walk in silence for a couple of minutes, then Bass grabs my jacket sleeve and pulls me over to one side. Before I can mutter my dissatisfaction with this assault he whispers the one word (well, one of the few words) which is guaranteed to stop me in my tracks: "Katie"

Thoughts of Phil's unsurprising exit from the band disappear from my mind faster than if Snape had walked out from behind a bush, pointed his wand at me and muttered: "Obliviate!"

Instead, all I can think of, all I can visualise, are breasts. Very big breasts.

Sit down at the back, there. Get a hold of yourself. I know you think the three of us are despicable, immature, hormone-addled school boys who snigger at the mention of the word sexism because it begins with sex – and you're probably right – but let me tell you about Katie.

Alternatively, if you're easily offended, or just bored with my puerile meanderings, just speed-read the rest of the chapter. Whatever.

Katie lives with Pete. Not their real names. As far as I know. Pete's a rep, a travelling salesman of some sort, if his two-year-old Mondeo is anything to go by. They live in a detached mock-something house on a new development that we pass through as we walk to school.

They've no kids, that we've seen, so they must be using an excellent method of contraception. Every morning, about this time, Pete sets off for work. Katie walks to the car with him, unless it's raining, in which case she stands in the doorway and blows kisses at him. She kisses him and then he gets into his car. He lowers the window so she can kiss him again, then she stands there and watches him reverse out onto the road and drive away.

At least that's the way I'd describe the routine if I were writing an essay about it for school. Though why the hell I'd be doing that, I have no idea.

To better understand the situation, to appreciate why we've named this happy loving couple and why we're so interested in the little drama which plays out most weekday mornings, you have to understand a couple of things. Literally. A couple of things. Ya feel me?

Katie is well-endowed in the mammary gland department. And that is definitely an understatement – like saying Adele has earned a few bob, or Jimmy Saville had a dark side.

Warranting a mention at this juncture are The Childress Laws of Breast Nomenclature. You're either sighing irritably at this point or shaking your head, wondering when I was going to saunter up to the point of this chapter and embrace it warmly, like an old and very dear friend.

Developed and refined in association with Bass and Red, over the last couple of years, these laws are based on cup-size. Clearly. I'm not sure on what other basis you might want to classify breasts. Texture? Globularity?

A-cup breasts are *tees* or *Ts*. Smaller than this would be *tees squared* or *T²s* (*tee-tees*). Next size up, B-cup, would be *baubles.* And a little bigger again (C-Cup?) would be *Christmas baubles, or CBs.* I hope you're not getting confused. I know it's a little complicated, but it's important, so try to keep up. Next, and we're into impressive D-cup territory here, we're in the *fruit salad* section. This includes your common or garden spherical fruits – cantaloupes, melons, watermelons, pumpkins. And you can further qualify these according to size. Small, medium, large, family-size, catering pack, and so on. Finally, larger than anything else, we have the *KTs,* named after Katie. Unsurprisingly. And none of us have seen *KTs* in real life on anyone other than Katie. You'll find *KTs* on the internet, but you'll find miniature dachshunds dressed as Yoda and people sticking knitting needles through their cheeks on the internet so that doesn't count.

So, there you go. In ascending order: *T²s, Ts, baubles, CBs, fruit salad* and *KTs*. Don't forget. To ensure precision when communicating breast size, I promise that it's preferable to stick to the Childress Laws of Breast Nomenclature.

See that wasn't so difficult, was it? What's that? You've got your own laws? OK. About penis size? Not sure I want to hear this. In descending order? Cucumber, banana, hot dog, Twix, Atticus? Funny. You should write a book.

Katie has KTs. No doubt about it. Huge, massive, sun-eclipsing KTs.

And they must have some peculiar form of internal scaffolding as they just stick right out there, like two basketballs strapped to her chest. They are exceptionally prominent.

They could be fake, of course. Bass, Red and I have discussed this endlessly, which will come as no surprise. They have their theories and I have mine.

I will admit that, yes, Katie may have had a boob job. Internet evidence would support this hypothesis – and the internet is never wrong, is it? – but I'd rule this out for three reasons. One, I can't imagine that a plastic surgeon outside of Mexico would ever consent to performing such a procedure. Two, surely they don't make silicone implants as big as catering-size bags of oven chips, do they? And three, I can't believe any woman, no matter how eager to please herself or her partner she might be, would actually *choose* to have a pair of 3XL water-melons grafted onto her chest.

I might be wrong, I guess. Hey, let's be honest, I frequently am.

The other thing is, they just don't look like implants. OK, OK, I hear you. How can a spotty seventeen-year-old tell the difference between the real things and twin bags of silicone? Last summer, we went on holiday to Spain. I could write a couple of thick volumes on that particular experience, but suffice to say that I spent a lot of time on the beach and sitting around the hotel swimming pool. I whiled away hours watching the acres of exposed flesh on view and became something of an expert, even if I do say so myself, on the variations of the female anatomy, and crap tattoos (yet another book waiting to be written). A side-effect of this strict education was that I had to develop a number of methods of concealing my interest – the use of dark sunglasses, feigning sleep by holding my head at a certain angle, the correct semi-reclined posture, a rolled-up towel in my lap, that sort of thing.

Accordingly, I became proficient at distinguishing the appearance and behaviour of real breasts from those of augmented ones. I mention behaviour because, as most clichés are based on truth, appearances *can* be deceptive. If a woman was to stand still in front of me, clothed or unclothed (I should be so lucky), it could be tricky to ascertain whether or not her breasts were as God had intended them. However, if this hypothetical woman was to move, to stoop and pick up a coin, for example, I believe I could detect the presence of silicone within.

You see, unaugmented breasts move more naturally. Inertia. That's the key. During movement of the torso, normal breasts *follow* the chest, lagging slightly behind, moving with a natural rhythm. Swaying, if you must. Silicone breasts either don't move independently at all, as though they were set in cement and fastened securely to the chest, or their mass so far outstrips the capacity of the chest

62

to lug them around that, during a sudden twisting movement, you half expect them to complete their circular trajectory and whack their unfortunate host somewhere up near her armpit.

So, I think I can safely say that Katie's KTs are all her own. Bass usually agrees with me, but Red has a variety of alternative theories, with the details of which I will not bore you.

The other thing I must tell you about Katie is that she appears to be utterly unselfconscious. She just doesn't seem to care *who* sees her KTs. And, believe me, at times, there is a lot of her KTs on display.

Except on the coldest winter mornings she rarely wears anything more than a tee-shirt or a light jumper. Mind you, to conceal them you'd need a coat four sizes too big, or a two-man tent.

Not that *we* mind, of course. But I have considered, in the occasional moment of quiet contemplation, what other people might think about Katie's KTs. What about her father? What does he think when his daughter comes around for tea on a Sunday afternoon? I guess he doesn't even notice them. I mean, what if my sister had gigantic breasts? I probably wouldn't notice them. I suppose I'd have to put up with a constant barrage of lewd comments from my peers, but that would be it. Your sister's your sister, isn't she? Unless you're exceedingly warped.

On this fine summer morning, Katie has excelled herself. She's wearing a bikini top for goodness sake! Red will kill himself when he hears about this. I know the weather forecast was for the mid-twenties but this is ridiculous. It's only quarter past eight in the morning. The fabric of the top is stretched so tightly across the surface of her KTs that an embarrassing explosion is surely on the

63

cards. Bass is so enraptured by her progress towards Pete's car that he's forgotten to let go of my sleeve.

Most wives, if they even bother, would give their husbands a quick peck on the cheek to see them off to work. In fact, these days, most wives probably set off for work before their partners, if the poor sods have got a job to go to. But Katie seems intent on giving Pete an explicit reminder of why he's not going to forget to come home this evening. She allows him to open the rear door and toss his briefcase onto the back seat, but as soon as he's shut the door, she grabs him around the waist, presses her KTs up against him and, from the vigour with which she kisses him, tries to perform a tonsillectomy with her tongue. I'm trying hard to keep things just the right side of prurient (though in this endeavour I fear I have failed) but, honestly, I wouldn't be surprised if she stripped her husband right now, on the drive, and... well, I'm sure you can guess my train of thought. Pink train in the tummy tunnel, in case you weren't sure.

However, she manages to extract her tongue from his mouth and allows him to get into the car. The window slides down and she's in there again! This time she's bent over, for better access to her hubby's face, and her KTs are hanging down. I'm sorry, I am not exaggerating. I'm just telling you what I'm seeing. OK, look, they're not touching the ground or anything so dramatic, but, with Katie bent over, leaning in to snog hubby Pete, they look huge. The impression of their mass is overwhelming.

I'd better convince Bass not to even mention this to Red or he'll be in a foul mood all day.

When Katie eventually decides that Pete has, after all, like a good boy, flossed his teeth, she stands up and watches him reverse into the road. I watch her standing

64

there as she follows the car moving in our direction. She smiles and it's as though she's smiling at me. A cold feeling settles in the pit of my stomach and I tell myself that she couldn't possibly be smiling at me.

In all the times we've watched this ritual – and, believe me, we've watched it *a lot* – Katie has never given the impression that there is anybody else in the world apart from her beloved hubby. Then, as she starts to walk back to their house, she looks in our direction and waves.

Waves.

It's a simple movement of the hand and wrist, a pleasant *'Hello boys, nice day, isn't it?'* sort of gesture. The cold feeling in my stomach spreads outwards, as if I'd swallowed liquid nitrogen. Bass's grip on my sleeve becomes vice-like. Immediately, we turn and start walking quickly. I feel like running. Fifty metres up the road we pause to wait for Red.

"Oh my God," grunts Bass. "She saw us."

"I know."

I feel as though the vicar has just popped into the newsagent's and found me flicking through a copy of *Pornography Illustrated*. From the pallor of Bass's features, I suspect his sentiments are not dissimilar. We both jump when Red comes up behind us.

"Morning, fellow students." He looks back toward Katie and Pete's house, and the empty drive. "Did I miss the show?"

"Yeah," grunts Bass.

"But don't feel left out," I say, fixing Bass with my best *keep your trap shut* gaze, "I think Pete must have left early this morning."

"Damn, there was a documentary on hot air ballooning on the telly last night. Kind of put me in the mood."

"Always watching, Wazowski," says Bass.

[10] Five Get Overexcited

"What a hosepipe," says Red when Bass tells him about Phil's message.

Bass reminds Red that Phil was the best guitarist we've had. "Or will ever have," he adds.

I try not to take that personally. Instead I ask: "So, how are we going to phrase the advert?"

"'Guitarist wanted'," starts Red, "'to join trio of manic metal monsters. Attitude most important. No time-wasters.'"

He grins as though he could easily walk into a job with a top advertising agency.

Bass beats me to a laser-like rebuke. "You keratinised anal sphincter! Can you imagine what kind of idiots that's going to attract?"

"Well, what would you suggest then?"

"'Guitarist and keyboard player required. Previous experience mandatory. Enthusiasm and commitment essential. Metal/Hard Rock influences preferred.'"

Bass has obviously given this some thought.

"What's this *Hard Rock* malarkey? We're a *Metal* band, aren't we?"

"Yes, but metal and musical proficiency aren't mutually exclusive."

"Well, you can slice me open with a sharp sabre if I'm wrong, but I don't believe I suggested they were. *If* we're a metal band then we don't want anybody who's into coma-inducing solos. We want metal-heads. We want someone who's on the edge. We want someone who's walking the thin line between-"

"Red!" I interject. "Shut up, will you, and get a life."

And so it goes until we arrive at St. Mick's. It's just after half past eight. As we walk through the gates, we spy Sandun Wiratunga and Graeme Brennan, both in our year. They see us and immediately all five of us break into a run, heading toward the lower sixth common room.

Initially Bass is in the lead, but Sandun overtakes him as they bolt through the main doors. The stairs to the first floor double back on themselves and Bass and Sandun are racing up the second flight while Red, Graeme and I are still leaping up the first. Red shoves his hand through the metal railings and clips Sandun's ankle, causing him to cry out and lose his balance. Bass reaches the top of the stairs ahead of him and bolts for the common room, with Sandun, limping slightly, following.

By the time I enter the room, Bass is standing by the pool table with the solitary cue clutched triumphantly in his fist. Sandun turns to the door, his face dark.

Red slides past me, grinning. Sandun glares at him. "What the bloody hell did you do that for?"

"Do what?"

"You know bloody well what! I could have broken something, you muppet."

"All's fair in love and war."

"And this is neither, you dipstick."

"True," says Red, and I can see he's struggling to produce a more suitable aphorism. He can't.

"Doubles?" I suggest.

"There are five of us," says Bass.

"Three against two?"

It's wretched, really, this ritual. Sometimes, we get to the pool table first. Sometimes, Sandun and Graeme beat us. But, more often than not, it ends up in a foot-race which concludes with all five of us playing. If we were sensible, we'd either draw up some kind of rota or just accept that we should all play. I guess we enjoy the struggle.

"It's your parents' party tomorrow, isn't it?" asks Graeme after missing an easy pocket. He hands the cue to Red.

I look at Graeme, which isn't as easy as it sounds because he's got a squint and I always tend to look at the wrong eye, so I think he's looking away from me. It's rather unsettling.

"Don't tell me you're coming, too," says Red, lining up a shot.

Graeme watches the cue ball clip a red and thunk into a corner pocket. At least I think he does.

"Apparently your mother invited all of us," he says, to me, without moving his head, so maybe he was looking at me all the time. I don't know.

"Good shot, you differently-abled cream-puff," says Sandun, snatching the cue from Red before turning to me. "I hope you've had a couple of extensions built on your house. From what I can see, your parents have invited half the bloody town."

"Do you mean all of us, as in all of us here, in this room, or all of us, as in all your family?" asks Bass.

Talk about delayed reactions.

"Family," Graeme says then turns to me and raises his eyebrows in a *God, what an imbecile* sort of way. This, I might point out, in association with his squint, looks most bizarre.

"So that means your sister will be there?" asks Bass earnestly.

Graeme's twin sister, Beth, is also in our year. Obviously. It would be odd if his twin sister was in *another* year, wouldn't it? She's seventeen but looks twenty-five and has the most heavenly body in the whole school. Unfortunately, whoever invented the phrase *the lights are on but nobody's in* was definitely thinking of Beth Brennan.

I mean, in the desirable physique department Beth Brenna has everything. She's like a cartoon. Jessica Rabbit, or something. Long legs, firm arse, slim waist, primo Christmas baubles. Check. Full lips, huge brown doe-eyes, like pools of liquid milk chocolate. All the boxes ticked with black Sharpie then highlighted in fluorescent yellow.

Distressingly, her personality completely lets her down. Don't get me wrong – she's pleasant enough. But that's just it – she's *pleasant*. Period. She's *nice*. Yuk.

If I am allowed to fulfil only one ambition in this life then, apart from marrying Apollonia Wallace and walking arm in arm with her into the sunset, day after day, it would be to never have anyone describe me as *nice*. On my headstone it will say 'Here Lies Atticus Childress. He Wasn't Nice'.

OK, I accept I'm being a little cruel here. Look, Beth Brennan is agreeable, attractive, friendly, good, kind and tidy. Oops, I think that last adjective just gave the game away. It's a fair cop. I just looked up *nice* in the thesaurus. Maybe *tidy* isn't how I'd describe Beth, although I'm sure her bedroom is immaculate. The thing is this: she smiles if you tell her a joke, but you get the impression she really didn't understand it. When you see her with her group of friends, she's always the one nodding and smiling while someone else speaks – she never seems to have anything to say for herself.

Until I got to know her a little – she was in my German class at one point – I shared the views of my male peers. I too fantasised about lying between satin sheets with her, exploring all those dangerous curves, and so on – blah, blah, blah. But now I know (arrogant, moi?) that she'd just lie there, being pleasant and *nice*. Not that I'd refuse, mind you. I mean, let's face it, despite whatever protestations to the contrary my brain might make, if any woman between eighteen and fifty invited me into her boudoir I'd be in there like a shot, tumescence and all. As long as she wasn't, you know, riddled with a *social disease*. Ah, who am I kidding? I'd probably still take a chance.

The fact is, though, that I'm extremely unlikely to be invited into Beth's boudoir. Among other reasons, she's going out with Mansoor. Mansoor Khan. The fourth. Mansoor is nineteen or twenty with money coming out his ears. When he goes to the toilet, he probably pisses pound coins, and shits fifty quid notes. He drives a 911 with the registration number MK 4. *Daddy* is the CEO of some multi-national mega-corporation that sells things nobody needs but everybody wants: Bluetooth speakers and fizzy pop to the third world, that sort of thing.

Anyway, how Mansoor occupies his time is something of a mystery, if he does anything that might loosely be termed work. What he *does* do is turns up at the gates after school most days and waits for Beth. She gets into his penis extension and kisses him lightly on the cheek. He scans the area to ensure the presence of an audience and then burns off down the road at about three hundred miles an hour. Makes me sick.

"I think she's going out somewhere with Mansoor," says Graeme.

"Well, that's a shock," I say. "Are you sure the two of them wouldn't rather come over to our house?"

"What does she see in him?" asks Bass forlornly.

Bass has got a minor crush on Beth Brennan, and has done since her boobs were the size of cherries. Mind you, he's got a minor crush on every half-decent female he's ever met, or seen on the box, or on YouTube, or... you get the picture. During orchestra rehearsals he sits there at the back, in the brass section, scoping the girls. From time to time, his expression, somewhat dopey at the best of times, softens even further when his gaze alights upon the object of one of his infatuations.

"What do *you* think, you leaky faucet," says Red, wincing as Sandun pots a ball. "I'll give you a clue: it's not his sparkling wit or generosity of spirit."

Graeme pulls a handkerchief from his pocket and blows his nose, loudly. He's got a sinus problem. Chronic terminal fatigue sinusitis, or something. I don't know. I'm not a doctor. "I think you're being a bit hard on him, you know," says Graeme. "Mansoor's not so bad when you get to know him."

"I wouldn't mind my sister marrying into so much dosh," says Sandun, rubbing a tiny sliver of chalk across the tip of the cue.

Red's face creases. "You haven't got a bloody sister."

"No, but if I did, I wouldn't-"

"I didn't mean that," says Graeme, shoving the handkerchief back into his pocket. God knows what's secreted within its sticky folds. "I meant he's quite..."

"Nice?" I venture.

"Well... yeah."

"They make a lovely couple," I say, slapping him on the back in a pseudo-matey sort of way. "I'm sure the wedding will be absolutely *super*."

[11] Another Day in Paradise

The bell signifying the end of the last morning lesson rings. I am in the library. Supposedly, I have spent the last forty minutes revising biology. Exams are only a couple of weeks away. In reality, I have spent approximately half of that time helping Bass refine the advert for the band. The remaining time has been spent dressing various female members of the student body.

Sitting a couple of metres from me is Aysha Bhat, upper sixth, and she is looking especially elegant in a lovely khaki and black, colour block, bandage, bodycon dress I saw on the Topshop website last night. Crafted from a structured bandage fabric to the bodice, it flatters and contours the silhouette. Aysha's CBs are accentuated appealingly by the plunging V-neckline and cut-out detailing.

Anouk Johannes, Aysha's best friend, who, as I watch, is packing textbooks into her bag, is wearing a cupped rubber mistress dress. The mistress dress is a classic fetish image, with its high neck, long sleeves and figure-hugging lines erotically covering rather than revealing the body. Rubber dresses of this kind should be sculptured across the bust for a truly flattering fit – most are not, but the style I've selected for her has a cupped bust to make the most of her natural curves. The overall effect is enhanced by the use of a long back zip to keep the front view smooth, sensuous and uncluttered. To complete the outfit, I have selected a pair of red patent leather court shoes: no fetish outfit is complete without skyscraper stilettoes and these elevate her on five-inch heels with style and elegance.

74

Hazel Drury, hockey team captain, must be at least six feet tall. I want to dress her in a dominatrix-type outfit but I don't want to be too predictable so I'm going to mix and match a bit here. Her long auburn hair has been drawn up tightly to the vertex of her head, tied with a red ribbon and then allowed to cascade down onto her shoulders. She's wearing a skin-tight crop top with high neckline, long sleeves, and a bold geometric print. Her six-pack is mesmerising. A tight denim skirt, with holographic detail, making it look almost metallic, hugs her backside and thighs, with the hem just above her knees. I complete the outfit with knee-length, lace-up leather boots, seven-inch inch heels, two-inch platforms. The effect is startling. Ambulation in such footwear is not something the uninitiated should attempt. Hazel, though, with her Amazonian physique, makes it look easy. Even so, I can see her leg muscles working overtime. It is a truly amazing outfit and one which, if only Hazel knew what I was thinking, would probably give her justifiable cause to slam her fist into my face and knock me into next week.

"Are you absolutely certain we shouldn't mention the name of the band?"

Trust Bass to bring me down.

"What?"

"We could put 'The Handsome Cucumbers Require Guitarist and Keyboard Player' right at the top."

"For a start, I was under the impression we'd changed our name to Silicone Implants and secondly, I thought we'd decided just to put 'Wanted: Guitarist and Keyboard Player'."

"Silicone Implants was Red's suggestion, with which, if you cast your mind back, I never agreed."

"I don't remember, actually."

75

"Well, I didn't."

"So there," we say in unison.

"Let's have a look, then," I say, snatching the sheet of paper on which Bass has been scribbling.

THE HANDSOME CUCUMBERS require a
GUITARIST and a KEYBOARD PLAYER to
augment the three existing members who
play rythym guitar, bass and drums.
Our influences include metal and
hard rock. Previous experience is
extremely desirable, though not
mandatory. Enthusiasm and commitment are
essential.
Contact Atticus Childress or Oscar
Clarke.

"You've spelled rhythm wrong."

Bass gives me a dark look, grabs the paper and scrawls on it in that awkward fashion peculiar to left-handed people. He hands it back to me. "Happy?"

He's somehow managed another incorrect spelling, which is most distressing. In the interests of diplomacy, I decide not to pursue the matter, opting instead for a different tack.

"I mention this only so that you can have time to prepare your reply, but Red is going to want to know what other influences we have and, more to the point, why he's not mentioned as a contact."

"We have lots of influences."

"We do?"

"Lots."

"Such as?"

"Well, things like... er..." he says, floundering pathetically.

"You better think up a few before Red sees the ad."

"Melodic rock?"

"Procuring a life should really be your first priority. If you sincerely believe that Red's even going to admit the existence..."

Bass is ignoring me, his attention having been diverted elsewhere.

"Winter is coming..." he mumbles.

I follow his gaze and snort.

Suzana Comănici-Jenkins is making her way from the far end of the library. 'Weird' doesn't even begin to describe her. Eerie, mysterious, odd, queer, strange, uncanny. Can you can tell I've been at the thesaurus again?

Suzana likes black. At least, she likes the *colour* black. Whether she likes things black in a metaphysical sense I wouldn't know as I've never exchanged more than a couple of words with her. I can tell you that she likes to *wear* the colour black. Which is a slight problem at St. Mick's, as the school uniform for girls is based around the colours white and navy blue. Suzana appears to content herself by accessorising in her favourite colour. Thus she has black pens and pencils, black pencil-case, black bag, black everything possible, really. Her hair is black but, as far as I can remember, it wasn't always so. I'm sure it was dark brown a few years ago. And it really is a very black black, so I'm pretty sure she dyes it.

She passes us, her expression indicating a disturbingly profound degree of preoccupation. Bass and I watch her leave the room. As soon as the door swings shut behind her it opens again and Red appears. He pauses on the threshold, looking over his shoulder, presumably watching Suzana. After a moment, he walks over to us.

"To be sure," he says, hopelessly attempting an Irish accent, "that girl's a strange one." He leans over Bass's shoulder and reads the band advert. "What's this '*include* metal *and* hard rock' rubbish? And why's my name not down there?"

"Duty calls," I say, standing up. Red has grabbed the advert and is re-reading it. Bass is nearing the end of a long resigned sigh. Neither seems bothered by my impending departure. "So I'll leave you to it, then." I pick up my bag and exit.

As I walk from the library to the dining hall I am accosted by at least ten individuals, all making some form of reference to The Childress Annual Jamboree tomorrow night. It is becoming very tiresome. Thankfully, this will probably be the last one I'll have to attend for many years. Once I've left for University, or joined the Foreign Legion, such events will be but distant memories. This will be the first one Zach's attended for many years and, as far as I'm aware, he'll be coming entirely of his own volition. Unless, I suppose, my parents are exerting some kind of leverage of which I am unaware. Maybe he was arrested for cocaine smuggling, my parents bribed the feds with a five figure backhander and now Zach has to do what they tell him. That's probably what's going on.

The dining hall is slowly filling up as I wait in the queue. Billy Gibson, from my physics class, is in front of me. He turns to ascertain the identity of the person behind him, turns back, then looks around at me again, this time with a more convivial expression. Not surprisingly, I know exactly what's coming next.

"Hey, it's your party tomorrow, isn't it?"

78

I nod stoically.

"I remember it last year. Didn't Killington cough up his dinner right down the front of that woman in the black velvet dress?"

I nod again, smiling wanly. Mrs Goodfellow-Atkinson, the head of the St. Mick's parents' association, is not one of Red's biggest fans.

Thankfully, it is Billy's turn to be served so I am spared further reminiscences. I buy a cheese and ham sandwich, which looks as though Little Bennie might have made it, and a can of generic cola. As I make my way over to an empty table near the far wall, I spot Rosie sitting with Dawn, Mamta and a girl whose name escapes me. Unfortunately, avoiding passing their table would entail a route so circuitous I'm positive it would attract unwelcome attention, so I am forced to walk right past them, which I do, as purposefully as possible, keeping my gaze fixed on the scratched surface of my intended table, some two or three metres away. No sooner have I passed them than the hall starts ringing with the teeth-rattling cacophony of four sixteen-year-old girls giggling and screeching their heads off. The first thought that pops into my head is that the zit on the left side of my mouth has gone super nova. Rosie is going to die for this.

When I sit and calm myself sufficiently to steal a glance in their direction, I note that the abominable clamour, the echoes of which are only now beginning to subside, was made by only three of them. Dawn is staring at Mamta with such poorly-disguised malice that, if looks could kill, Mamta would be slumped in her chair, her blank eyes staring lifelessly at her still-beating heart lying on the table in front of her. Before I can assess this tableau more comprehensively, Sandun Wiratunga appears from nowhere and sits down opposite me.

"What's all that racket about?" he asks.

"How should I know?"

Sandun's eyes narrow as he inspects my sister and her friends. "It looks as though someone's put a hot poker up that Dawn Ferner's arse."

"Does it?"

"Either that or she's got the worst case of PMT I've seen in a long time."

I want to ask him how many cases of PMT he's seen in his extensive career as a gynaecological counsellor to young women but I remind myself that discretion is the better part of valour. Plus, I don't particularly want to start trading acerbic licks with him. Instead, I grunt quietly which he seems to take as an acknowledgement of his wit.

"Which is a shame," he continues, "as she's pretty easy on the eye, normally."

I hold up my cellophane-wrapped sandwich, attempting to obtain a reflection of the suspect zit. I am unsuccessful and resign to make a detour to the toilets immediately after lunch.

"Your sister's not so bad, either."

I look up to see him taking a large bite out of an apple. "Oh, please! She's barely out of puberty, for God's sake!"

Sandun is slightly taken aback. "Hey, sorry, I was just saying, you know. I didn't mean anything."

I would be more easily convinced of his sincerity if I wasn't being given an unappetising view of various apple fragments in his mouth. We eat in silence. I open my can of cola as Bass and Red make their way toward us.

"How's it hanging?" asks Red, sitting down.

"Down to my ankles," answers Sandun.

"Must be bloody uncomfortable on a cross-country run."

"I just wrap it around my waist two or three times."

"Two or three times, eh? Would that be before or after you've whacked off?"

The two of them continue in a similarly laudable vein. I watch Bass making repeated attempts to puncture a cardboard carton of fruit-flavoured drink with the wrong end of a straw-shaped implement. The urge to point out his error passes quickly. He'll work it out eventually. My thoughts return to Rosie's table. Resting my chin in my right hand I am able to adopt a posture suitable for inspecting the girls while at the same time looking as though I am paying attention to Sandun's and Red's conversation.

I've come to the conclusion that it's virtually impossible for me to assess Rosie objectively – certainly as far as her appeal to the opposite sex is concerned. There are just far too many other factors to take into consideration, half-remembered fights from childhood, and so on. But, increasingly, comments from friends are compelling me to look at her as impartially as I can.

[12] Rosie Siobhán Persephone Childress

That's right. Persephone. In Greek mythology, she was the wife of Hades, head honcho in the Underworld. Hardly a name any self-respecting parents would bestow on a sweet little newborn baby girl. I agree, entirely. Unfortunately, for Rosie, Dad was something of a Wishbone Ash fan in his younger days, and they'd written a song called Persephone on one of their albums. I've never been told of any other reason, so you'll just have to accept that one. Granny Childress says that, for as long as she can remember, Dad's liked the name. Mum, understandably, hated it but, over the years, he wore her down and when the opportunity eventually arose he got his way. Rosie was Mum's choice, and Siobhán comes from somewhere on her side of the family.

I spent many years referring to her as Pursy and, even now, if she makes me see red I'll call her that, enjoying her fury and the *Oh! You beast!* expression which clouds her face. In quiet moments, however, I admit that it's not her fault. In rarer instances of fleeting benevolence, I even foresee the possibility that a future suitor may even find it romantic. But enough, for now, of my parents' questionable talent for naming their offspring.

One of my earliest memories of Rosie is from the Christmas when I was six and she was four and a half. She had received a tricycle – a typical girlie affair in pink and lilac, with plastic streamers attached to the handle-bars – and was enraptured by it. Whether or not it had dawned on me at that stage that having a birthday on Christmas Day was not the most satisfying of coincidences I'm not sure. For one reason or another, I took it upon myself to push her off the tricycle and climb on myself. Peddling as fast as I could, leaving Rosie screaming in the lounge, I raced into the hall and slammed into the foot of the stairs, buckling the front wheel in the process. Looking back, I don't see how the tricycle could have been constructed to exceptionally high standards, but that certainly did not influence my parents' reaction to the incident. I can still see the enraged expression on my father's face and the tearful disappointment on my mother's. Now, years later, I can understand the dynamics of the situation but then, it was Rosie I blamed for my punishment. Being sent to your room for two hours on Christmas Day morning, without access to the enticing array of presents, is more than most six-year-olds can be expected to withstand.

I could relate dozens of similar incidents over the years. To do so would be soporific for you and embarrassing for me. Essentially, Rosie and I have not enjoyed what might be termed a *warm* relationship. This may be related to the difference in our ages: eighteen months is possibly too short an interval to allow the growth of tolerance which I believe forms the basis of a good inter-sibling relationship. I won't expound this argument further as I suspect it might disintegrate on close examination. For example, I get on reasonably well with Zach, who's seven years older, whereas the sight of Bennie, who's seven years younger, invokes debilitating nausea.

Probably, though, the quality of the relationship between two siblings is dependent on their respective personalities and these, as far as I can make out, are determined by pure chance. However, what really scares me is the possibility – which, over the years, is becoming more of a probability – that Rosie and I are more alike than either of us would care to admit.

Do you ever experience the unsettling phenomenon of proving the opposite when you've been attempting to justify something? I mean, here I am, trying to explain why Rosie and I don't get on very well. I start off by trying to demonstrate that we have incompatible personalities and end up concluding that we're very similar. And the logical extension of that argument is that we should get on better than we do. The fact that we don't, however, leads to the possibility that two people with similar personalities will not necessarily get on like a house on fire. I've given this thesis a fair amount of thought and have ended up asking myself how I think I'd relate to someone who was just like me. Initially, I thought it would be great – what would there be to argue about? We'd want to watch the same programmes on the box, like the same music, etc. But then I realised that after a while it would become extremely tiresome. In the end, there'd be no point spending any time with someone so similar. I'd be as content spending time by myself. So, maybe we need a certain amount of conflict to keep life interesting.

Have you ever come to the conclusion that I've got no idea what I'm talking about? I have.

Distilled to the essence, with no psycho-babble, my relationship with Rosie at this point in time can be described as thus: I feel guilty for the way I have behaved in the past and wish to change that pattern of behaviour in the future. Maybe this is what they call *growing up*. I don't know. What I do know is that this is the reason why I want to get her something special for her sixteenth birthday.

Don't get me wrong. I don't believe for a pico-second that even if I were to give her a *signed* copy of

4Tune8's latest disc of detritus (which is what she covets above all consumer durables) then our relationship would blossom into something special, warm and loving, as if that's what I want. As much as I've tried to analyse this urge that's been creeping over me for the last few weeks, all I know is that I must get Rosie something exceptional for her birthday. Something extraordinarily... extraordinary. But not a tattoo.

[13] The OSP

Red and Sandun are now discussing body piercing, a subject in which Red has taken an unnatural degree of interest of late. Thankfully, Bass has managed to hack his way into his fruit-flavoured drink carton, though not, I might add, by the method its manufacturer intended. I continue my covert surveillance of Rosie and her friends.

I recall the name of the fourth member of the group: Virginia Fleming, a slight girl whose only characteristic of note is a peculiarly irritating habit of continuously pushing her spectacles up the bridge of her nose, immediately after which they slide back down.

I observe Dawn Ferner's face slowly return to a normal hue – that artificial tint exclusive to those female teenaged acne sufferers for whom copious amounts of generic foundation is the chosen method of camouflage – and wonder what Mamta did or said to upset her. Not that I care, of course. I almost close my eyes and, squinting through my lashes, agree with Sandun that Dawn isn't really that bad looking. Mind you, using this technique, the school caretaker probably wouldn't appear that bad.

School uniform flatters no girl that I know of. Only Beth Brennan's physical attributes are undiluted by the standard, shapeless, navy blue and white checked dress. Nevertheless, Dawn does appear slightly more rounded than I've noticed previously. Her breasts are filling out the top of her dress a little more than they might have done a few months ago. Definitely moved on from T^2s to Ts, and, maybe, with the eye of faith, baubles. Her legs – what I can see of them – are possibly a tad shapelier. I try her in a jade, back-laced vest dress which combines a scoop neck and full-length front zip with a laced back, open to the waist. The back-lacing allows a very close fit to any figure. Except Dawn's. Try as I might, my mental image of her dressed in anything remotely sexy keeps reverting to one where she's in uniform and walking down one of the school's corridors with Mamta and Rosie. It's no good. However much I struggle to picture her otherwise, she's a larva.

I switch my gaze to Mamta who, to my surprise, is well into another OSP: over-stuffed sausage phase. This discovery causes a certain amount of bewilderment as Bass, Red and I can usually spot this phenomenon happening at the earliest possible stage. I must be losing the knack – a frightening thought. I suspect you would welcome elucidation.

Between the ages of eleven and sixteen the female of our species undergoes puberty. Many changes occur, but the one that concerns us here is growth. Breasts bud and blossom, hips expand, and so on and so forth. In general, there is an inexorable (and welcome – to males, at any rate) transition from the immature, twig-like physique to the mature, curvaceous form. Buxom and callipygous.

As we are frequently reminded, English, as a language, is constantly changing. New words appear. Some stay. Some disappear as quickly as they came. Some come back. Did you know that to 'twattle' was to gossip, or talk dirty? What a tremendous word! Shakespearean times, apparently. Look at those girls over there, twattling as if their lives depended on it. We need to bring that one back.

Callipygous means fair-buttocked. What an excellent word, and how appropriate these days, with so much media attention on the nether regions.

I am digressing, but before I do a three-point turn in the middle of this B-road and try to get back on the dual carriageway that is the point of this chapter, I'm going to pull over into this convenient lay-by. The sign at the entrance reads: 'LARVA: EXPLANATION'. Which is opportune.

I was explaining how puberty is a process, not something which happens overnight. They don't go to bed one night as girls, and wake the next morning as women. More's the pity. A larva (plural larvae) is a distinct juvenile form that many animals undergo before metamorphosis into adults. Now, obviously, *technically,* humans don't have a larval stage, but if you think about, they do.

A popular online encyclopaedia – let's call it Zikipedia – says something like this about larvae: the appearance of the larva is generally very different from that of the adult (e.g. caterpillars and butterflies). Larvae frequently have unique structures and organs that do not occur in the adult form. The diet of the larva may also be radically different.

QED

Girls like my sister and her cronies *look* different, they have different structures and organs, and they eat different stuff. Rosie does not look like she did when she 12, and she doesn't look like she will when she's 25. Dawn Ferner doesn't have a human brain inside her head, she has a 3D-printed contraption which looks vaguely like a human brain but functions much more like that belonging to a monkey with syphilis. Mamta Malhotra doesn't eat *normal* food – she exists on a diet of crisps, cereal bars and diet Coke, with the occasional caramel decaff skinny cappuccino thrown in for good measure.

Never one to ease up on an analogy when I can flog it to within an inch of its life, consider, before we move on, the caterpillar. The larval stage of butterflies and moths. Not the American corporation which designs, manufactures, markets and sells machinery, engines, financial products and insurance to customers via a worldwide dealer network.

Caterpillars have soft bodies that can grow rapidly between moults. Tell me that doesn't sound familiar. Only the head capsule is hardened. Hard head, soft body. Need I carry on? OK, if you insist. The mandibles are tough and sharp for chewing leaves. Or for constantly nagging male humans to put the toilet seat down, not leave bowls in the sink without washing them up and refrain for farting in mixed company. Behind the mandibles of the caterpillar are the spinnerets, for manipulating silk. "Manipulating silk"? Handling material, more like. Which means *shopping for clothes!* Antennae are present on either side of the labrum, but are small and relatively inconspicuous. OK, admittedly, I've not yet noticed any antennae behind the jawbones of any 15-year-old girls, but that doesn't mean they're not there. Think about it.

Right, someone rang 999 and the paramedics have arrived. They're working on that analogy. It's touch and go but it might pull through. Let's get back to puberty as it affects the female of the species.

The process (puberty – keep up at the back) is infinitely variable. Some girls can turn into women seemingly overnight: not a spare ounce of fat one day and adipose tissue deposited in all the right places the next. In others it happens slowly and evenly over years. It can occur in fits and starts: tremendous increase in height one year, breasts the next and hips after that. Sometimes, this

89

evolution goes awry. A girl who, at a tender age, develops breasts can be later overtaken by her initially envious peers and ultimately left somewhat lacking. The appealing appearance of a well-proportioned pair of breasts can be followed by a complimentary expansion around the hips which proceeds unchecked until the lass in question resembles a ripe pear. Nothing wrong with that, of course.

Whatever the pattern in the individual, the process is complicated by the necessity of the girl to wear clothes – in this instance, a St. Mick's dress. A girl's parents can't be expected to clothe their daughter in a dress exactly tailored to her measurements. These might well be changing on a weekly basis and, inevitably, there will be periods when the dress will fit either too loosely or – surprise, surprise – too tightly. When a girl's body has outgrown her dress, she is in an over-stuffed sausage phase (OSP).

There is an analogous phenomenon which affects pubertal boys. I haven't yet given it a name because, as you will have gathered, I tend to spend more time dwelling on the female form than that of the male. You notice it mainly among the boys in the second to fourth years of senior school. I've heard that lads can grow up to six inches in a year, and some lads do seem to shoot up. I grew fairly steadily, but Bass rocketed up nearly four inches one year. They grow so fast that it's tough for parents to keep up with appropriately sized trousers. Sometimes the trouser hems are nearly on the floor. After a growth spurt, they can be an inch or two clear of the top of the shoe. Frankly, I'd rather spend time looking at a girl in an OSP than a lad with his trousers flapping freely, but to each their own.

Now, obviously, there are degrees of OSP and, unsurprisingly, Red, Bass and I have divided OSPs into five classifications, based not particularly on the discrepancy in size between the garment and its wearer but more on the overall effect. Thus, other factors must be taken into consideration, such as the actual (rather than relative) dimensions of the girl's body, her age and general physical appearance. Grade one is noticeable only to the trained observer. Recognising grade two takes a little practice. Neither would draw comment under normal circumstances. Only when bored senseless would we mention a sighting. Grade three is something of a grey area and a reference to an example would very much depend on the other factors to which I have already alluded.

Spying a grade four would always result in a comment. If Red were to say 'Grade four ahoy' I would expect to see either a girl of a similar age to ourselves whose garment was showing obvious signs of distress, or perhaps a younger girl whose dress was ripping at the seams. Grade five not only requires qualification – 'Take cover! Spectacular grade five by the newsagent's' – but also necessitates the taking of whatever measures are practical to ensure a closer inspection.

Mamta Malhotra is in a grade four OSP. I can see the fabric of her dress stretched uncomfortably (I presume) tight across her breasts. Her hips and buttocks seem similarly constricted and the hem of her dress is undoubtedly two or three inches higher than school rules allow. The more I think about it, I'm certain I would have noticed this before. I assume the dress she's wearing is a size smaller than that she usually wears. Perhaps the washing-machine at home is misbehaving. Maybe she's wearing it on purpose, in order to attract the admiring glances of a possible suitor. And I might vomit up a gold doubloon after lunch.

For a few admittedly pleasant moments, I imagine what Mamta's going to look like in ten years. Then I pour her into a wet-look PVC vest dress and experiment with a variety of stiletto-heeled footwear. There are worse things.

I look back at Rosie, my darling sister, and, for possibly the first time, I look at her – *really* look at her – not as my sister but as a young woman.

Thankfully, there is no evidence of an OSP. Her dress, if anything, is perhaps half a size too large. The hem reaches her knees and there is practically no indication of the size or shape of her chest or hips. Thankfully. And this next bit *really* kills me. I am not exaggerating. My sister, irritating little harpy that she's been these last few years, actually has a pretty nice pair of legs. More than that, I will not say. I've sailed close to the coastline of *Dodgy-land* too many times in this story already.

Rosie's light brown hair turns much fairer in the summer. From early childhood it was straight and hung half way down her back. Mum used to go to town with a variety of accessories and there's hardly a photograph in our house where Rosie doesn't have ribbons or brightly-coloured clips in her hair. Sometime last year, to Mum's great disappointment, Rosie had her hair cut much shorter. In addition, she's forsaken all types of hair management accessories, preferring instead to adopt the habit of repeatedly running her hand back through her hair to keep it from falling in front of her face, something I would find exceedingly tiresome. As if on cue, she performs this affected manoeuvre and I am able to see her face more clearly. Studying it, I am mildly startled. Gone are the last vestiges of puppy fat, a term only adults could construct. Revealed are her cheekbones which, while not exactly sharp enough to cut paper, are fetchingly prominent.

Furthermore, unless I am mistaken, she is wearing lipstick – nothing garish but a subtle shade which, I have to admit, admirably compliments her skin tone.

Rosie is listening to something Dawn is saying and I watch her face. She laughs. Her mouth widens and her eyes narrow. Fine creases accentuate her features. She's not wearing any foundation. This pleases me, but I couldn't say why. She starts to speak, addressing Dawn primarily, turning occasionally to face the other two, and her features dance in time with the cadences of her speech. Her eyebrows rise and fall. The tip of her nose twitches intermittently. Occasionally, her head bobs up and down, presumably to help emphasise a point, and her hair gradually falls further forward, eventually obscuring her face from my view. I frown, vexed. After a moment, she pushes her hand back through her hair and her features are once again revealed. I smile and realise that this manoeuvre, though undoubtedly affected, is quite effective in the way it exposes that which has slowly, and somewhat tantalisingly, been concealed.

I begin to feel a little strange. I can sense the stirring of emotions deep within me – emotions that have never before risen to the uneven surface of my consciousness. I feel on the verge of something miraculous. Am I making this sufficiently dramatic? I feel as though I am about to experience a quasi-religious conversion.

And then I lift one buttock off my chair and trump loud and long.

I don't do that. Just trying to keep things in perspective.

The truth is, I really am sensing a change. It's something akin to the Doppler effect. You know, the way the tone of an ambulance siren alters as it passes you. You stay the same and the ambulance is the same vehicle it was before it passed you, but *something* changes. I am the same person I was five minutes ago, just as Rosie has not altered substantially. Yet, there *is* a difference. There's a difference in the way I perceive her, just as the siren tone is perceived to have altered.

It takes me a few moments to work out exactly what I'm feeling. When I do, it's difficult to describe. In a way, it's *pride*. I'm proud that Rosie's my sister, or I'm her brother, or both. But that's not all of it. It can't *just* be pride, because that suggests a job well done, and I've done *nothing* to influence Rosie's personality, not in a positive way. It's also a kind of gladness, or contentment.

Or something like that.

So, I'm glad that she's my sister, and proud of the young woman she's becoming.

Until the next time I discover she's been using my zit cream.

I am shaken from this bizarre reverie by the sound of Red pushing back his chair and standing. I look up to find him gazing at me quizzically.

"Earth to Johnny. Come in, Johnny."

"What?"

"Are you coming to look at the notice, or what?"

"What notice?"

"The bloody band advert! What do think we've been talking about for the last five minutes?"

"Uh, I wasn't paying attention."

"Well, you might find it easier to follow the conversation if you could concentrate on anything apart from the latest email from *Global Women's Fashion News* or whatever filth it is cluttering up your inbox these days."

"*Intimate piercings* dot com, actually. 'When you see where this woman has her secret piercing, it will BLOW YOUR MIND!!!'"

This fazes him temporarily.

"Really?"

"Yeah," I say as we fall in behind Sandun and Bass. "Don't tell me you haven't seen that one."

"You're joking, aren't you?"

"Maybe."

We approach Rosie and her friends. I hesitate for a second then stop and lean over the table and deliberately inspect Rosie's face.

"Oh dear, Pursy, looks like you forgot to squeeze that zit I mentioned to you this morning."

As I turn away, Red laughs loudly, making it difficult for me to hear Rosie's response although it would be reasonable to assume it's not pleasant. On the way to the main school notice board, Red regales me with a series of questions about *Intimate Piercings*. Eventually, I assure him that I've never even heard of such a site, never mind being on the mailing list, but that should I ever find a link then he will be the first to know. We join Bass and Sandun in front of the notice board. The advert is prominently displayed next to a faded green sheet of paper extolling the virtues of last year's Christmas Fayre.

```
SILICONE CUCUMBERS
    require a
    GUITARIST
    and a
KEYBOARD PLAYER
The existing nucleus comprises a
drummer, bass player & rhythym
       guitarist.
```

95

Our influences are principally Heavy
Metal & Hard Rock.
Prospective members should share these
influences although consideration will
be given to those with different –
though not TOO different – influences.
Previous experience is extremely
desirable – though not mandatory.
Enthusiasm, commitment and ATTITUDE are
essential.
Contact Atticus Childress or Oscar
Clarke.

"Rhythm's not spelled like that," comments Sandun.

"I told you, you pine-effect bedside cabinet," says Red, punching Bass's shoulder.

I consider asking Red to define *ATTITUDE* then I think about asking Bass how he managed to keep Red's name off the advert. Either option would undoubtedly result in a protracted, and probably heated, conversation. However, I feel compelled to raise one issue.

"Silicone Cucumbers?"

Bass and Red look at each other, then at me.

"Never mind," I concede.

[14] Hair Extensions & White Stilettos

After much prevarication, Bass has eventually decided to accompany Red and me tonight. He was torn between practising for some kind of recital – which is in three months' time, for God's sake! – or witnessing The Suppurating Sores. When I last saw him, at lunch-time, he had decided that his beloved trumpet deserved his undivided attention. However, I've just messaged him and he's changed his mind, again, hopefully for the last time. Red and I are waiting for him at my house. Dad has very kindly offered to give us a lift to *The Electricity Showroom*, where The Sores, as they are affectionately known by the metal cognoscenti, will be attempting to burst a few eardrums.

I stare into the mirror above the telephone table and scan my face for any hitherto undiscovered zits. I carefully pick off the small scab covering the one near the left angle of my mouth which I noticed two days ago (and which I popped that night). I wait a moment to ensure that no bleeding ensues before returning to the kitchen. Red is sitting at the table reading one of Rosie's magazines.

"There's an article here about safe sex which mentions condoms about three million times – every other word, almost – but which yet fails to instruct the reader how to put one on."

"How wondrous."

"Makes me laugh, is all," continues Red. He's off on one. "It's not like just having the rubbers in your handbag protects you from the clap, is it?"

"Have you got a job interview as a sex education worker coming up, or something?"

Red shakes his head, dismissing my attempt at humour. "I'm being serious."

I can see that, and it's making me uncomfortable.

"I can just imagine all these larvae", he says, "thinking that they'll be protected from every Jason that gives them the eye, just because they've got a packet of three in their handbag."

"Well," I suggest, "perhaps you should drop a line to the editor offering to write a more explicit article. You could call it 'What to Do with That Banana That's Been Lying in the Fruit Bowl for Five Weeks'."

Red tosses the magazine onto the table. "Yeah, and maybe once they'd mastered the art of slipping a rubber over a nice big banana they'd think up a few interesting things to do with it."

On the back cover of the magazine is a photograph of one of the members of 4Tune8. Luke, I think. Or *Lovely Luke* as he is more commonly known by his legions of admirers. I flip over the magazine, hoping that the vacuous warbler is involved in a *lovely* road traffic accident in the very near future.

"Just think," continues Red, "I could be responsible for hundreds, maybe thousands, of young girls discovering the joys of-"

"OK," I interrupt. "I get the picture. No need to turn it into a PowerPoint demonstration."

Normal service has been resumed. There's no one quite like Red for taking a simple notion and developing it into the Kama Sutra.

Looking at him staring into the middle distance, it's obvious that the ancient Hindu text in his head is the lavishly illustrated edition, perhaps even the interactive version. After half a minute he shakes his head and focuses on me. "That was Bass earlier, I take it?" he asks, nodding at my phone.

"He'll be here in a few minutes."

"Wonder what made him change his mind."

"He mentioned something about having important news."

"Maybe he's lost his virginity."

"Since lunch-time?"

"Stranger things have happened."

"More likely something to do with the band advert."

The only response we'd had to the first advert – the one we'd put up on the school noticeboard – had been from a couple of fourth form wannabe reality TV stars, so we wrote out another one took it down to The Zone. Mike, the owner, magnanimously agreed to stick it up on the wall. The chance is infinitesimal that it will attract the attention of anyone suitable. And even is someone suitable *did* see it, the likelihood of such a person *wanting* to join Silicone Cucumbers is even smaller. Still, hope, as they say, springs eternal in the human breast.

Red pulls out his own phone and reads his messages – well, one conversation in particular – for the tenth time since he arrived.

When he's not wasting his life on the pr0n sites – and I've already mentioned that that takes up a *lot* of his time – he's poring over a website called *MetalMatch*. It's a dating website for metal-heads. I could point out that other metal-related dating sites are available but they haven't sent me any brown envelopes of used twenties so let's just call it *MetalMatch*.

There's a section within the main site – *Missing Link* – where metal fans can attempt to contact other fans they met – or saw, or vomited on – at a gig (or pub, bus-stop, massage parlour etc) but failed to exchange contact details, in the hope that they could instead be exchanging bodily fluids.

A typical message might be: 'Venue: Biffy Clyro, Birmingham. Message: To the heavy guy with long dirty/fair hair, wearing a red/black shirt and blue/black jeans. I'm the girl with brown hair, wearing a black G n'R shirt who kept looking at you. I fancy you like crazy!'

Another: 'Venue: Market Square, Little Fartlet. Message: To the two fabulous girls waiting at the bus-stop. One of you was wearing a Ramones shirt and black jeans. The other was wearing a Maiden shirt and a red mini-skirt. I was the long-haired guy who asked if you had a light. I was wearing a green sweat-shirt and my friend was wearing a Bon Jovi top. Please get in touch.'

Indicating desperation would be something like: 'Venue: Muse, Wembley, ten miles from the stage. Message: To the long-haired guy with two arms and two legs who was wearing clothes. I was the cerebrally-challenged pre-pubescent girl who you threw up over. I was wearing a black Nirvana shirt (now sadly discoloured) and my friend (who soon afterwards was knocked unconscious by a flying two-litre bottle of urine) was wearing a lime-green 4Tune8 top. While the fluctuating levels of hormones surging through my veins make it difficult for me to be certain, I think I fancy you. Please contact me!'

On one level, it's all rather pathetic and disheartening. On another level, though, hey, we all want to love and be loved, so, you know, whatever, dude. If nothing else, it offers a fascinating insight into the protocols of dress and behaviour pertaining to the metal subculture.

Red does not view *MetalMatch* in quite the same way that I do. As far as he's concerned, it's far and away the most promising route to a sexual liaison with a member of the opposite sex. Every week he scours *MetalMatch: Missing Link* for suitable messages. His search parameters are extraordinarily narrow: the message must be from a female within fifty miles. Any other details are entirely immaterial. If the message read 'I was the fat girl drowning in my own vomit behind the mixing desk' I think he would still attempt to make contact.

Over the last year or so, Red has succeeded in persuading six girls that he was the *guy* they were seeking. He bottled out of the first tryst. On the next two occasions he made it to the chosen venue but couldn't locate the girl. Or, more likely, they saw him first and bolted. The next time, he spotted her but still couldn't bring himself to introduce himself. When he approached the next girl, she looked at him as if he was from another planet and told him where he could stick his offered alcoholic beverage. The last time, about three weeks ago, he was given similar advice.

Neither Bass nor I can fathom why he persists with a strategy so spectacularly destined for failure. Bass often asks him why, if he's so desperate, he doesn't just cut his losses, walk down one of a couple of notorious streets in town, fork out a few quid and get it over with? An extreme suggestion, perhaps, which usually receives explicit advice for Bass on the possible uses of an exceptionally sharp knife.

"Let me see that original message again," I say.

Red opens the browser and finds the page then hands me his phone.

"'Venue: Lamb of God, Astoria'," I read aloud. "'Message: To the guy standing at the entrance with short blond hair, holding a programme, who kept looking over at us. I had a Weezer shirt and denim shorts. My friend was wearing a white Killswitch shirt and black leggings. From: Chelsea and Georgia.'"

I look at Red and shake my head. "Which one did you speak to?"

"Chelsea. I think she's the one that fancies me."

"You mean she fancies the guy at the Astoria."

"OK," says Red, as though I was being irritatingly pedantic.

"So what about Georgia?"

"What about her?"

"Well, where does she fit into it?"

"Oh, I got the impression she was just coming along for, you know, moral support, something like that."

"I should think this Chelsea will need a bit more than 'moral support' when she finds out it's you and not Mr Astoria Hunk."

"You're so cruel, Johnny!" he moans, clutching his chest. "I don't think you realise how much you really hurt me when you say things like that."

"All I'm saying is that, maybe, just maybe, you ought to be a little better prepared than you've been in the past."

"Yeah, well, point taken, and I've been giving it some thought."

"Colour me impressed."

"I'm just going to be honest. I'm going tell her that I thought she sounded like a nice girl from her message, that

102

I didn't have the courage to tell her the truth on the phone, and that, if she'd just give me a chance, I'm sure we could be friends."

"Friends?"

"Hey, you've got to start somewhere," he says then continues before I can even begin to entertain the notion that aliens have transplanted his personality: "Plus, if I tap off with Chelsea, maybe I can put in a good word for you and you can get your tongue down Georgia's throat."

"You'll excuse my bad manners, I'm sure, but, bearing in mind your track record with the opposite sex, I think I'd like to try to survive without your help."

"Silly me," he says, slapping his forehead. "How could I have completely forgotten that 90% of the all the girls at school have got you on speed-dial?"

Burn.

"How are you going to recognise her?" I ask, adroitly steering the conversation away from me and back to the subject of Red's ardour.

Red stares at me for a few moments to ensure that I know he's spotted my strategy. "Chelsea says that I'll be able to recognise her easily."

"Because…?"

Red doesn't reply. He just stares at me, the start of a smile at one corner of his mouth.

"How are you going to recognise her? You've never seen her before."

He just sits there. I'm not sure what's making more noise, the ticking of the clock on the kitchen wall, or the cogs stiffly turning in my brain. I look down at the screen of Red's phone, still in my hand.

"Is she going to be wearing the same thing again? Denim shorts and a *Weezer* shirt?"

103

Red's grin widens. "Nope," he says, reaching out and grabbing his phone. He finds the right messages and starts reading.

"'Really looking forward to seeing you tonight. Hope me and George will be there on time. We're getting our hair done this afternoon. New extensions.' Then she's got five, no six big smiley faces. Then this bit: 'And I've bought some new shoes! Lovely white heels! You won't miss me! See ya!' Then a whole line of Xs."

I'm dumbfounded. "What the...?" is all I can manage.

"If you can't ride two horses at once then you should get out of the circus."

True that.

I scan his face for any sign of deceit. "What the...? I mean.... How the expletive deleted did you manage that?"

"Absolutely nothing to do with me. This is all Chelsea."

He stares at me, eyes wide, head slowly shaking. He can't believe his luck. I can't believe his luck.

"Hair extensions," says Red, "and white stilettos."

OK, everyone knows the *golden rule,* don't they? For *not* looking like a tart. I suppose if you were raised by wolves in the forests of Norway, then you might not know the golden rule, in which case I'll tell you. It's simple.

Cleavage or legs, but not both.

Easy, eh? You can show as much cleavage as you like, or as much leg, but not both. Déclassé, my dear. Arguably, Cheryl Fernandez-Tweedy *might* be able to get away with it – though I think not – but anyone else is going to look like a tart.

Informative flashback.

A couple of months ago, during the Easter holidays, I was sitting in the lounge, half snoozing, half looking at people failing *epically* on YouTube on my phone. Mum was there, reading a Jack Reacher novel. Rosie was watching some kind of reality show on the box. *Wives of Toxteth* or *Every Which Way But Wilmslow*. I can't keep up with all that. Anyhow, Mum glances up at the screen to see a fake-tanned vixen getting out of a taxi, flashing her crotch (or nearly), baubles bursting out of her top.

"Oh dear," sighed Mum. "That's not a good look."

Rosie sniggered. "Right, look at those shoes!"

Which made me look up at the telly. The lass was wearing a pair of Perspex stripper heels. Seven-inch heels, three inch platforms.

"Oh," said Mum, clocking the heels. "She'll snap her ankle if she tries to walk in those!"

This set Rosie off in a fit of giggles. Maybe she finds lower limb fractures particularly amusing.

"Far too obvious," said Mum. "Too much chest and far too much leg. She's leaving nothing to the imagination."

While I feigned half-sleeping interest in my phone, I listened to my mother and sister discuss just what made a woman look like a tart. They agreed on: the golden rule; stripper shoes; skirts that barely cover the buttocks; orange fake tan; lipstick lighter than the surrounding facial skin; and eyebrows that look – as Rosie suggested – 'more like the Nike *swoosh* than proper eyebrows'.

Rosie thought that white stilettos were slutty, but my Mum argued that, in the right circumstances they could be elegant. Mum said it was difficult to look classy in a tight, short, red dress. Rosie thought that jeans with rips which revealed your bum were a sure sign of being a tart.

"I just don't see why any woman would even *want* to dress like that," said Mum, shaking her head.

Rosie did not reply. I stole a glance at the TV. The cast of the show were now in a nightclub. The vixen from the taxi was laughing like a horse, revealing £30,000 worth of fake teeth. I looked quickly at Rosie to see that she was thinking about what Mum had said.

After a minute, Rosie said: "It's just for the attention. Me, me, me. I mean, it's not for those lads, is it? They look scared of her. Look at their eyes. Nah, she just wants everyone to look at her. Lads, girls, she doesn't care."

"Well," said Mum, "I think it's sad."

That conversation struck a chord with me and I've since discussed the subject several times with Bass and Red. You won't be interested in the details of those conversations, and I'm sure you don't want *The Childress Top Ten Signs That You're A Tart* or similar.

The only sign that the three of us added to the list compiled (expertly, in my humble opinion) by my mother and sister was hair extensions. Bad extensions. Extensions that are *obviously* extensions. Extensions that make it look as though you've got hair down past your arse. I mean, come on, what is that even about?

If you don't believe me, just Google 'Taylor Momsen hair extensions'. Tell her Johnny sent you.

So now, perhaps, you can understand my shock when I learned that Chelsea – the object of Red's desire – will not only be wearing white stilettos and showing off her new hair extensions but she's actively been boasting about them.

"Bloody hell," I murmur as Bass rings the front door bell.

106

[15] The Electricity Showroom

I lean back into the car. "Look, Dad, it's all right. We'll get the bus home. You *don't* have to pick us up." I slam the door and turn to find Bass and Red giving me that look that says: *Parents. Huh. What can you do?* I roll my eyes and turn again, this time to give Dad an exaggerated wave goodbye. We watch him pull out into the road and drive away. When his car disappears from view, we start walking. We've been dropped off a few hundred metres from the club. Few things are as detrimental to your reputation as being seen in town, on a Friday night, getting out of your parents' car.

Red adjusts the angle of his baseball cap and looks at Bass. "So, what do you think about that, then?"

He means the fact that Chelsea will be wearing white stilettos and showing off her new hair extensions – not the angle of his cap. Red spent the entire journey giving Bass chapter and verse about tonight's assignation. Would I be appearing overly cynical if I was to suggest that the whole thing might end in tears?

"Great, yeah," says Bass absently. My spider sense is telling me he may have other things on his mind.

"What made you change your mind about tonight?" I ask Bass.

"I got a couple of calls about the advert."

"Yeah?" asks Red. "Who? Are they metal-heads of the first degree, or what?"

"One was a bloke called Derek-"

"Derek!" shrieks Red. "What kind of name is that?"

Bass and I stare at him.

Red pulls a face. "It's not exactly *metal*, is it?"

"Fish," I say, "from Marillion."

"Whose real name," says Bass, "is Derek Dick."

We pause, giving silent thanks to Momus.

Red snorts.

"You can laugh," I say. "You should have a tenth of his talent. And Derek something used to play keyboards for Dream Theater. And then there's Derek and the Dominoes. And more, probably. Anyhow, you can talk. 'Dominic' doesn't exactly scream *metal*, does it?"

"You *know* my stage name's going to be 'The Dominator'."

"Right, I forgot, for some unknown reason." I give Red my most withering look. "Bass, what do you know about this Derek?"

"He's coming on Wednesday night, for an audition."

I wait a few moments, but no further information seems forthcoming. We walk past *New Look*. Red and I glance at the scantily clad mannequins. One is wearing a rather fetching pair of leopard-print hot-pants, black bra and a black net jacket. On its feet are a pair of espadrille wedges, two-and-a-half-inch flatform cork wedge soles, ankle tie-up laces. Move along, please. Nothing to see here. "OK, what else did you find out?"

"Like what?"

"Like, whether he plays guitar or keyboards, where he's from, how long he's been playing, whether or not he can sing, previous experience, influences, *attitude*," I say, glaring at Red.

"Oh, he plays guitar."

"And...?" I ask, exasperated. Extracting information from Bass is often like getting blood from a stone. In fact, that's not quite true, as getting blood from a stone is impossible, of course. No, it's more akin to squeezing a zit which isn't quite ready to be popped: a lot of pain and effort followed by one or two tiny beads of whatever that pale straw-coloured fluid is that seeps out. Let's call it 'zit nectar',

"That's it," he says matter-of-factly.

"Bass!" moans Red.

"You mean," I say, modulating the tone of sarcasm in my voice to blindingly obvious, "this character rings you up and says: 'Hi, I'm Derek. I play guitar.' And you say: 'That's interesting. Why don't you come to an audition next Wednesday?' And that's it?"

"More or less."

We walk in silence until the Showroom heaves into view. There are perhaps a dozen people queueing outside. I walk in front of Bass then turn to face him, forcing him to stop. I open my mouth to speak but Red interrupts me.

"We didn't put anything in the advert about singing."

"No, Red, you're quite right, we didn't," I say, "and thank you for pointing that out."

"Hey, hang on, there's no need-"

"Sorry, but I think we need to get this straightened out, don't you?"

I look from one to the other, awaiting acquiescence. Red shrugs and begins adjusting his cap again. Bass thrusts his hands in his pockets and meets my gaze.

"OK, so we know nothing more about this Derek apart from his name and the fact that he plays guitar."

Bass nods.

"I presume you gave him Red's address."

He nods again.

"Right, so the plan is to wait and see what he's like on Wednesday, but for all we know he could be a fourth form Munchkin who got *Dora The Explorer Learns To Play Guitar* for Christmas."

"In which case," says Red, "he'll be better than you."

Touché. Nobody died and made me Joe Satriani, did they?

"I don't think he goes to school," says Bass, his features contorted into an expression we have come to know represents concentration but which can be easily interpreted by others as acute pain. "He mentioned something about coming straight from work on Wednesday."

"Work?" asks Red, as though the concept is alien.

I sigh. "Anything else you forgot to tell us?"

Bass shakes his head.

"Fine, so what was the other call?"

He draws a deep breath and narrows his eyes. "A keyboard player called Suzz is also coming on Wednesday and, no, I didn't get any other details."

Red snorts. "What sort of a name-"

"Think, now," I suggest, interrupting Red, "whether or not he said anything else. Perhaps he has to finish his homework first, or maybe he has to be in bed by nine."

"She," says Bass flatly.

"*She* what?"

"He's a she."

"A girl!" exclaims Red, horrified. "A girl in our band? Forget it! No way!"

It takes me a few seconds to process this twist. A girl – a member of the opposite sex – who has presumably read the advert, has expressed the desire to audition for a position in Silicone Cucumbers. Most bizarre.

"No, wait," I say, addressing Red. "Think, for a minute, what kind of girl would read our notice, have a telephone conversation with Bass, the prince of erudition, and still want to come along for an audition."

He looks at me quizzically.

"Can you think of any girl we know, or know *of,* who would want to join our band?"

"No, of course not."

"Why?"

"'Because we're a metal band."

"That's crap. There are loads of girls into metal. Almost half the audience tonight is going to be female."

"Yeah, but girls are no good at *playing* metal."

Accusations of overt sexism hover on the tip of my tongue, stare uncertainly at Red, then flee back down into my lungs. Mention the words *girls* and *metal* in the same sentence and Red automatically thinks of nubile *babes* cavorting around wearing leather basques and high heels. I conclude that, as far as attempting to convince Red to maintain an open mind, I am barking up the wrong tree, on the wrong planet, in the wrong dimension.

"Never mind," I say, then turn to Bass. "I presume you've still got this girl's number on your phone?"

Bass squints as though I've just asked him to work out the cube root of 57, thinks for a minute then says: "Nah, unrecognised number. Can't ring her back."

"Why am I not surprised?"

I look at Red. "These two are going to turn up next Wednesday and it doesn't look as there's a great deal we can do about, does it? Unless they phone Bass again. And seeing as the response to our advert hasn't been exactly overwhelming, I suggest we give both of them a fair hearing, OK?"

Red glowers at me. "I'll bet she's as ugly as sin."

"Yeah, well, none of us is looking forward to a career as an underwear model."

Red grins, his eyes mischievously aglitter. The situation, which was, for a moment, threatening to become somewhat uncomfortable, seems defused – of which all three of us seem equally aware.

"You mean I sent off my CV for nought?" asks Red.

Bass and I laugh – in a hearty men-of-the-world sort of way, of course.

Outside the Showroom we join the end of the queue which during our conversation (for want of a more appropriate word) has become swollen by another dozen punters. I glance over my shoulder at the two rejects who fall in behind us.

My grandmother has two terms for males between the ages of fifteen and thirty-five: *nice boy* and *young man*, the latter being reserved for those she'd cross the street to avoid. One of the *young men* behind me has the glazed appearance indicative of the ingestion of more than few cans of Stella, an inference supported by the lager fumes he's pumping out with each stertorous breath. The two inches of ash attached to the cigarette hanging from the other's slack mouth looks ready to fall down his stained tee-shirt at any moment.

The couple in front of us are wearing hand-painted leather jackets. The bloke's jacket is embellished with a remarkably good facsimile of the cover of the latest Maiden album. He has a mass of curly brown hair, the type which usually prompts my grandmother to respond with something like: 'Hasn't that young man got a *lovely* head of hair?' He does have a lot of hair which, combined with his over-sized jacket, makes his arse and legs look positively wasted. I am once again provoked to wonder where men with such non-existent lower parts buy their jeans. I mean, do they even make jeans with nineteen-inch waists?

His partner's jacket has *Disturbed* scrawled across it, so that it's supposed to look as though it was painted with blood. Her back-combed, blonde hair gives the impression that she has recently stuck a finger in a wall-socket. She turns to say something to twig-legs and I see she has a large gold hoop through her nasal septum. I can't look at such piercings without (a) thinking about an angry bull charging at me and (b) wanting to reach out and give it a good tug. Also, if you're not really paying attention, and you catch site of someone with a fancy ring in their septal piercing, your first thought is that they really ought to wipe away all those blobs of snot hanging from their snout.

"Dezz," says Red, his eyes glued to nose-ring's arse.

"What?"

"Dezz. We could call Derek Dezz. Dezz and Suzz. Much more metal."

"I'm sure he'll love it," I say. At least he's trying.

"Hey! Childress! Clarke!"

Near the front of the queue, Harry Earnshaw, from school, chess club, future UKIP MEP, is hailing us. Uncertain about what sort of response he expects, I half raise my hand and nod. He seems satisfied, thankfully, as I've no wish to speak to a train spotter who has memorised the catalogue number of every Metallica release. Vinyl and CD.

"Dingleberry," murmurs Red.

A taxi pulls up outside the door of the club. There's a bit of a commotion at the front of the queue as one of the doormen, known as Big Jeff, for obvious reasons, pushes

114

through the punters and walks up to the taxi. Evidently, someone of import is about to alight. Bass and Red move nearer the kerb to get a better view.

"Who is it?" slurs fag-face behind me.

"Could be the band," suggests lager-breath. "No, it's just some girl."

When the identity of the taxi passenger becomes apparent, every drop of saliva in my mouth disappears and my heart begins to race. *Just some girl!* Lager-breath's words echo inside my head. If every muscle in my body wasn't frozen solid, I'd turn and punch his nicotine-stained teeth right down his throat, saying: 'That isn't *just some girl*, you great steaming pile of horse excrement! On your knees! You're in the presence of Apollonia Wallace!'

For it is she.

My gaze is fixed upon her bewitching face so I am only peripherally aware of her attire. Let's be frank, she could be wearing a pastel-coloured onesie from Primark and it would make no difference. As it happens, she's wearing the fairly standard black leather jacket, white tee, skinny jeans combo. On her feet are a pair of black ankle boots with, I'd guess, from this distance, five-inch heels. To paraphrase the mighty Tavares, heaven must, truly, be missing an angel.

I'm so enraptured that I fail to notice the other taxi passenger until he's standing next to Apollonia and she turns to smile at him. I blink, knowing that it would be impossible otherwise to tear my gaze away from Apollonia, and look at her consort. I want to recognise him quickly, the sooner to return my attention to Apollonia, but I cannot.

"Who is he?" asks Red.

"Don't know," answers Bass. "Johnny?"

I shake my head, still staring at the man, glaring at him, hating him. OK, so he's good-looking, in a ruggedly handsome, blue-eyed, square-jawed sort of way. OK, so he looks as though he's just stepped off the cover of one of those glossy male lifestyle magazines – Hunk, Man Health, Ripped Torso, whatever. OK, so he could probably make otherwise sane women drool with desire simply by glancing in their direction. But what right does he have to go out with Apollonia Wallace?

I recognise the futility of my anger and switch my gaze once more to Apollonia, in time to see her flash that smile again, the smile that could make any man's heart explode with joy. This time, it's directed at Big Jeff, who is ushering the couple past the plebeians at the front of the queue and into the club.

I look around and everything seems grey and dreary. The poster-plastered wall to one side. The oil-stained pavement underfoot. The cheerless people in the queue. Only seconds before, all were illuminated by Apollonia's beauty. Enriched for a few ecstatic moments, we all revert to our colourless existence.

Behind me, lager-breath belches loudly. The queue begins to move slowly. After a few minutes, a glum Harry Earnshaw walks past.

"Hey, Harry," says Bass who seems immune to Harry's predilection for Metalli-minutiae. "Change your mind?"

"Big Jeff wouldn't let me in. Said I wasn't eighteen."

"Oh dear," says Red, "what a shame."

Harry, as thick-skinned as any train-spotter I've met, smiles pitifully, accepting Red's counterfeit condolences, and crosses the street, heading for *Beryl's Café*.

"We could have got him in with us," says Bass.

116

Red rounds on him. "Shiver me timbers! Why didn't I think of that? Why don't you run after him?"

Bass frowns. "I don't see why you don't like him, Red. He's all right when you get to know him."

"That's a theory I'd rather not-"

"Shut up, you two," I say. "You sound like a couple of larvae, speaking of which, Red, you'd better keep your eyes peeled for Chelsea."

Big Jeff admits nose-ring and twig-legs. I don't think I've ever seen him grinning so widely, which isn't a particularly pleasant sight as he's only got four teeth and they're right at the back of his mouth somewhere.

"Hey, Johnny!" he says with the kind of lisp you'd expect from a twenty-five stone bouncer with very few teeth. "How ya doin'?"

I can only assume that the appearance of Apollonia has triggered his jolly mood. Not that he's been hostile toward me in the past, you understand. Being the son of a local GP does have certain advantages. Big Jeff's one of my father's patients and he has, on occasion, done a bit of work around our house: fence repairs, repointing, that sort of thing. He's allowed Red, Bass and me into the club for the last year or so, even though patrons are technically supposed to be eighteen or over. Apart from girls, who are allowed in as long as they at least look eighteen (and, these days, what fifteen-year-old doesn't?), the rule is usually pretty strictly enforced. However belligerent – or drunk – you might be, the one thing you wouldn't do is argue with Big Jeff. If you fancy keeping your arms and legs attached to your body, that is.

"Doin' good, Big Jeff," I say as Red and Bass squeeze past him. "Doin' good."

"That Apollonia Wallace," he says, leering and bending toward me, at least as far as his bulk will allow, "she's somethin', ain't she?"

I nod and return his leer, deeming this this most appropriate course of action. "Do you know that bloke she was with?"

He shrugs, several kilogrammes of muscle and fat rising up and down ominously. "Something to do with a record company. Someone rang earlier, said they were coming, told me to keep a look out and make sure they got in OK."

"Figures," I say and start to move past him. Then a thought occurs to me and I take a step backwards and stretch up to whisper in his ear. The stench of cheap aftershave – Lynx Urban Anal Gland or something – almost makes me pass out. "I think one of these geezers behind me is carrying."

I notice the glint appearing in his eyes as I move off to join Bass and Red. At the sound of raised, slurred voices we turn and watch Big Jeff move to block the doorway completely.

[16] A Tricky Tryst

These days The Electricity Showroom hosts mainly third division domestic bands. Occasionally, American and Continental bands will play here, either on their way up or on their way down, or, possibly, if their managers know no better.

In the 60s and early 70s the Showroom – then *The Palais* – was a bingo hall. Then, in its heyday, it was *Le Discothèque*. During the 80s, according to my brother, Zach, from whom this potted history originates, the name changed on a regular basis. The club would close for months or years, change hands, open up for a few weeks or months, then close again. Since the turn of the century, however, it's been open (mostly) and operating under its current (how very retro, darling) moniker as a live music venue.

Inside, remnants from each incarnation induce the overriding impression that you've walked into an indoor scrapyard, in the middle of which a space has been cleared. For instance, a glitter-ball (seventies disco) hangs from the ceiling which is painted matt black and dotted with Day-Glo psychedelic designs (late eighties rave). Rumour has it that at the back of a cupboard somewhere is the original bingo machine.

The foyer in which we are now loitering is a claustrophobic cavern with purple walls and tiny lights overhead which give off less illumination than the burning tip of a cigarette. Deducing the original colour of the distressingly squelchy carpet underfoot is impossible. Deep in the bowels of the club the DJ is playing something by Rage Against the Machine and the thunderous strains of their hip-hop/thrash hybrid reverberates along the gloomy corridor that leads from the foyer.

"Any sign of them?" I ask.

Red shakes his head. He's looking decidedly anxious – with good reason, bearing in mind his previous experiences. He looks at his phone for the millionth time.

"What time did you say they were supposed to be here?" asks Bass.

Red shoves his phone in his back pocket. "Fifteen minutes ago." He rubs both hands across his face.

"They may have already gone in," says Bass. "Why don't Johnny and I go and have a look. You can wait here, in case they're later than we are."

Leaving Red pacing up and down in the foyer, Bass and I walk down the dingy corridor then turn right and push open the double doors that lead into the main hall. Our ears are assaulted by the cacophonous roar of Asking Alexandria – a pastoral ditty from their last album but one.

The room is built on two levels. Before us, half a dozen steps lead down to the main floor area. Raised platforms, about three metres wide, stretch around each side. The main bar is to our left and the mixing desk to our right. Bass and I scan the crowd for Chelsea and Georgia.

Punters occupy the tables and chairs dotting the platforms. The club is about half full, which is a pretty good turnout. Twenty-five or thirty die-hards are pressed up against the stage, already jostling for position even though The Sores won't be on for at least another hour. Over in one corner, three metal-heads are thrashing away at their air-guitars. Not far from us, sitting at a table near the bar, are four girls who've obviously been watching *way* too many hair metal videos on *MTV Why Aren't They Dead Yet?* (or something). I could describe them but just put this book down and spend ten minutes looking at 1980s Whitesnake videos on YouTube then let me know if you're still unclear. The girls look as though they're expecting Jon Bon Jovi tonight – or Big Long Jobby, as Red calls him. If so, they're in for a bit of a shock.

I look for Apollonia, even though I could tell, the minute we walked through the doors, that she wasn't in the main hall. Firstly, everybody would be glancing in her direction, and secondly, I've got this sixth sense that can discern her presence within fifty metres. The latter is patently not true, otherwise I'd have known it was her in the taxi, but I often feel as though I'd know she was in the vicinity, just by picking up some sort of intense vibration. Or at least that's what it feels like. And I'm not going to get any more specific than that.

"See them?" shouts Bass in a slight lull between songs.

I suggest we separate, each taking one side of the chamber, and meeting back here in five minutes. I'm pretty certain that Chelsea and Georgia are not here – I've got a kind of built-in radar, or seventh sense (see above), for white stilettos – but it's not often I can justify scoping a crowd for girls wearing a particular variety of high-heeled footwear, except on purely aesthetic grounds, of course.

I pass the quartet of hair-metal-babes, one of whom is wearing white cowboy boots. I glance at her face to find her sucking hard on one of those e-cigs that looks more like a steam-punk electric toothbrush. She flicks her gaze in my direction, dismisses me in an instant, then blows out a plume of white vapour which billows above the painstakingly teased hair of one of her companions, disappearing within seconds. Under the pancake foundation, crimson lipstick and dark eye-shadow it's impossible to know *what* she looks like.

I walk over to the wrought iron balustrade which separates the platform from the main floor. The trio of metal-heads are still hard at it, arms windmilling at their non-existent guitars and heads... well, banging, I guess. It's a strange habit, that: headbanging. It looks pretty ridiculous at the best of times, even more so if the practitioner doesn't have hair half way down his back. I've tried it, on occasion, but it only made my head hurt – hence the term headbanging, I guess. I can see no sign of Chelsea and Georgia.

"Hey, Johnny!"

I turn to find Stan the Man hailing me from behind the bar. He's one of Zach's friends who's risen to the dizzy heights of working at the Showroom. His parents must be extremely proud of him. On second thought, these days, with graduate unemployment being what it is, I suspect that maybe they are. Not that Stan went to Uni. Or maybe he did. I can't remember. His real name's not even Stan. It's Ben or Adam or Brad. I don't know why he's called Stan. He's all right, though. In fact, Stan the Man is one of my brother's more agreeable friends. As far as I can remember, he played guitar in a band a couple of years ago and they almost made it. A&R men at a couple of gigs. I think they were just about to sign on the dotted line when their lead singer found God, or something like that. He went off to join some kind of cult in the States, that sort of thing. I didn't even know they still had cults but apparently they do. After that, the rest of the band – *Spirit Level*, I think they were ingeniously called – just couldn't get it together again.

"Stan The Man!" I say, grinning as I walk over to the bar. "How's it hangin'?"

"Tight, Johnny, damn tight. Tight as a crab's arse."

He always answers like that. Don't ask me what he means, though, as I haven't the foggiest. In fact, while you're not asking me things you can add your query about Stan the Man's name to the list because I've no idea.

"Bass and Red here?"

"Yeah, somewhere."

I glance across the room to find Bass hovering by the mixing desk, engrossed by its array of switches, sliders, knobs and dials. For all he knows, Chelsea and Georgia could be standing right behind him. They're not, of course. I describe Chelsea. He grins widely.

"Got a bit of totty lined up for tonight, have you?"

I judge elaboration of the situation to be extraneous and instead return his lascivious leer.

"Not seen them, but you could do worse than them over there," he says, indicating the hair-metal-babes. Working in such a murky environment has obviously damaged his eyesight. I bid him adieu and walk back to the main doors. Bass joins me, having torn himself away from the mixing desk.

Before I can ask him if he was under the impression that detailed scrutiny of the mixing desk was going to reveal a clue as to the whereabouts of Chelsea and Georgia, the door behind me is pushed open, clipping my ankle in the process. I turn to see who has entered and find none other than the objects of our quest, a blonde and a brunette, dressed as anticipated, although, perhaps, in total, not quite what I had imagined.

They're both wearing white shoes, denim shorts and baseball caps. They've both very obviously got hair extensions. There the similarities end, but it's not immediately obvious which one is Chelsea and which is Georgia. Not *immediately*. After half a minute I think I've worked it out.

The blonde is probably about five foot seven, but she's taller than me (five eleven if you're asking) in a fairly impressive pair of white platform sandals. The heels must be eight inches. They look expensive. No change from thirty quid at Primark, I'd wager. She has a decent pair of pins, no doubt, which look preternaturally long with those heels at one end and an eye-wateringly brief pair of cut-off denim shorts at the other. The back pockets of the shorts hang a good inch below the shorts themselves.

Blondie is wearing a baggy, black Nirvana top so she could have anything from T²s to CBs. She's wearing a black snapback baseball cap with 'YOLO' embroidered on the front in huge gold letters. Her iron-straight, platinum blonde hair – well, not all *her* hair, if you see what I mean, but she paid for it so I guess it's hers now – falls down to the waist-band of her shorts. Her lips are dark red and streaks of blusher highlight prominent cheekbones.

Up to this point, I'd have guessed she was about nineteen or twenty but there's a look in her eyes which me think she's a lot older or, you know, she's 'seen things'. Her gaze flicks across me and her eyes – dark grey or dark brown – make her look almost menacing. She's scanning the crowd and I find myself anxious to make sure our eyes do not lock.

The brunette looks completely different, almost meek by comparison. The blonde is like a drone looking for a target. The brunette is like a puppy looking for someone to play fetch. Her white courts are standard high-street fare with stout three-inch heels. She's around five foot three and looks anything from sixteen to early 20s. Her arse is maybe a size too big to be wearing denim shorts. She seems to know this and is wearing thick, red, ribbed tights.

She's wearing a plain black tee, probably the same size as that worn by her friend, but she's definitely filling it out a lot more. Her breasts are definitely CBs, maybe even fruit salad, though more pineapple chunks than melon medley. And she's got a bit of a belly. Her auburn hair, as straight and long as her friend's, medium chestnut with light golden highlights. She's wearing a New Era 9Forty NY Yankees baseball cap. She has a pretty, animated face, though she's gone a bit overboard on the slap. Nothing too crazy, though.

Chelsea – for I am positive it is her – looks around eagerly, eyes glistening.

After half a minute standing six feet from Bass and me, the two girls – Chelsea and Georgia – turn and walk toward the bar. It's tough to drag my gaze away from Georgia's backside, and I'm aware that most of the blokes around me, and not a few of the women, are experiencing similar difficulties.

I eventually look down at their shoes and am struck, though not by any means for the first time, by the way that high heels divide women into two distinct groups: wobblers and naturals. There are those who seem born to wear stiletto-heeled shoes, who move with a sensual grace while wearing them, whose hips sway gently in a natural rhythm and whose calf and thigh muscles contract and relax almost imperceptibly with each stride. The heel of each of their shoes is a simple extension of their Achilles tendons, remaining vertical at all times.

Then there are those women who would be better off accepting that the world of narrow-heeled footwear is one they should probably avoid at all costs. In heels any higher than a couple of inches, each step becomes an adventure doomed to failure. Their hips and buttocks swing from side to side, caricaturing normal gait. Each leg takes on the appearance of a stormy sea as, beneath the skin, a multitude of muscles contract spasmodically. Their ankles appear unstable, wobbling uncomfortably and threatening with each precarious step to snap at any moment.

Even to the untrained eye, differentiating these two classes of the fair sex should not prove too difficult. However, if any doubt remains then I recommend The Childress Stiletto Suitability Test. To perform this, one must observe a woman's feet while she is standing quite still with her ankles less than six inches apart and wearing shoes with heels at least four inches high. In the case of the natural stiletto wearer the heel of her shoe will be absolutely perpendicular to the ground and there will be not even the slightest movement. By comparison, the wobbler's shoes will be at an angle and her ankles will be oscillating, often virtually imperceptibly at first but eventually so wildly that she will be forced to adjust her stance.

Anyway, Chelsea (a wobbler) and Georgia (a natural) are at the bar. Stan the Man has spied them – well, Georgia, at any rate – and is grinning inanely as he takes their order. From this distance, Georgia's shorts, impossibly, look even briefer. Chelsea is holding her phone up close to her face and tapping on the screen.

"That must be them," says Bass.

"Yeah, but where the hell is Red?"

Bass looks at the double doors as if Red is now going to appear, having been given his cue.

"He couldn't have missed them," I say then notice Stan the Man trying to catch my eye. He jerks his head

126

toward Georgia and Chelsea, a manoeuvre which they must surely notice. Just as I start to draw my finger across my throat Georgia turns and looks across at us. I rapidly turn to stare at the mixing desk, stroking my chin with the hand that was hovering by my throat a split second earlier. I grab Bass's arm and pull him through the doors. "Come on, let's find the stupid hosepipe."

Red's waiting for us in the foyer, hopping from one foot to the other, sweat trickling down his brow.

"Did you see Chelsea?" he demands. "What a babe! What a fox! What a lay-me-down-and-have-your-wicked-way-with-me, prime piece of T'n'A!"

"Hey, calm down, Fido," says Bass. "Down, boy."

"Didn't you see her?"

"Yeah, we saw them," I say, "but there's no need to stroke out. You haven't even got life insurance. How would we get by without you? We'd have to, like, get jobs, or something."

"What do you mean, *no need*? Have you taken leave of your senses? Didn't you *look* at her? Don't you realise she's here to meet *me*?"

Bass and I exchange glances. I don't think either of us have seen Red in such an agitated state. To tell the truth, it's not a very pleasant experience.

"No she's not," says Bass.

Red's response is to cock his head to one side like a perplexed Labrador pup. I *saw* you throw the ball, so where is it?

"She doesn't know *you're* who she's supposed to be meeting, does she?"

"So?"

A-ha! Evidence of sentience.

127

"Look," I say, "all this is neither here nor there." I meet Red's wild-eyed gaze. "Chelsea's the brunette, not the blonde one with the legs."

Now both of them are looking at me like confused puppies. Slowly, mania returns to Red's eyes.

"No way!"

"Trust me."

Red opens his mouth to speak but says nothing. Uncertainty flits across his face then his eyes narrow and he looks at me with what appears to be anger and resentment. I sense disaster, like a pit-bull with a boil on its bum, lurking just around the corner. Red closes his mouth, glares at me then starts walking down the corridor. Bass reaches out and grasps his jacket sleeve but he shrugs him off.

"Let him go," I say.

"But he might do something really stupid."

"So what's new?"

"Johnny," he pleads.

"Look, if Red wants to embarrass himself, that's fine by me, but I don't want to be a part of it. That Georgia will probably just give him the brush-off."

"I still think we ought to go with him."

I frown, knowing he's right. "Oh, come on, then."

Bass pushes through the doors and into the club. The thunderous din of Motörhead's *Killed by Death* fills the air. Red has wasted no time and is standing between the bar and the two girls. Bass and I walk toward the three of them. Georgia looks as though she's just stepped in a freshly-deposited dog turd which, to be honest, is the usual female reaction to Red. Chelsea looks confused and disappointed, another common reaction. I grab Bass's shoulder when we're within earshot but still a third-party-ish distance from them.

128

"I know I don't look like guy from the Astoria," shouts Red, "but if you'll just let me explain."

In the cold white light of the fluorescent strips behind the bar Georgia's features are like stone, her eyes glinting with fury. "Piss off, you little shit," she says and, even though I am not the object of her wrath, I feel like running.

Bravely, foolishly, Red persists. "Just a couple of minutes and I can explain everything."

Georgia glances at Chelsea then back at Red. "Are you deaf, or what? I told you to piss off."

"Oh, come on," Red implores. "If you'll just give me a couple-"

Before he can finish, Georgia grabs him by his shoulders and it's his turn to look confused. But only for a second as, before any of us know what's happening, Georgia pushes him up against the bar and jerks her knee up into his groin with enough force to make her almost lose her balance. She releases Red from her grasp and lets him fall to the floor in a crumpled heap. Then, pulling Chelsea behind her, she turns and struts toward us.

"Enjoy the show?" she asks, glaring at Bass then me.

We quickly step to one side, allowing Georgia to pass. Trailing behind the harpy, Chelsea looks bewildered, and somewhat shell-shocked. I doubt, though, whether her sensibilities have suffered the extensive damage sustained by Red's genitalia.

[17] Aftermath

I don't want to get out of bed this morning. No, I really, *really* mean it. I *do not* want to get up. Not only is it the dreadful Childress Annual Bash tonight – which, of course, is reason enough not to leave my lair – but there is the Damoclean prospect of explaining last night's events to my parents.

I suspect, though, that you're wondering what happened after Red's ability to father children was seriously threatened. Forgive me if I don't go into too many details – don't worry, I promise it's only a temporary lapse in my normally florid narrative style – but the memories are still too embarrassing and painful.

I watched Georgia and Chelsea leave then joined Bass as he crouched beside Red who was whimpering and moaning – justifiably, I might add. Stan the Man had vaulted over the bar and was standing behind Bass. He caught my eye then looked toward the double doors.

"Jesus, Johnny," he said, "did you see that?"

I nodded. I could see Stan the Man was trying hard to find the words with which to articulate his disbelief at what had just transpired but all he could do was stare at the doors and slowly shake his head from side to side. I crouched down next to Bass and peered at Red's contorted features.

"Hey, Red," I said. "You OK?"

"Course he's not OK," said Bass. "You saw what she did to him."

"Do you think you can stand up?" I asked Red but all I got in response was a long groan.

Bass turned to me. "Look, I think he's hurt. Hadn't we better phone for an ambulance?"

"It can't be that bad, can it?"

"Well I don't bloody know, do I? How would you feel if you'd just had a knee jammed into your tackle?"

Stan the Man leaned over. "He's right, man. That bitch put everything she had into it, and you should have seen the look on her face. Evil, it was."

"Yeah," said Bass, nodding, "I think we've got to get an ambulance."

"No," grunted Red, grimacing, "I'll... be... OK... just... need... a minute."

I stood up and scanned the circle of people gathered around us. When I saw Dawn Ferner it was my turn to groan. From her expression of disgust and fascination I knew that she'd seen everything, and that meant that Rosie would know what had happened first thing in the morning, and my sister would wait approximately three milliseconds before blabbing to Mum and Dad. I knew then that there was practically no point whatsoever in attempting any form of damage limitation.

I looked down at Red and realised that even if he recovered sufficiently to stand, there was no way he was going to be able to get the bus home. I decided I'd have to call Dad and ask him to pick us up.

I pulled out my phone and was about to call when I saw Apollonia, standing just behind Dawn. She had been looking down at Red but then she looked right at me. I couldn't tell from her expression whether or not she'd also witnessed Red's assault. Before I could scrutinise her face for evidence of what she was thinking, Mr Music Business appeared from nowhere – although I suspect he'd been standing just beside her – put his arm around her shoulders and pulled her away, the same way a husband will gently pull his wife away from a beggar on the street. *Don't give him anything, honey, he'll just spend it on booze.*

I watched them walk to the top of the stairs leading down to the main floor where they stopped and turned to face one another. He leaned down and planted a kiss on her lips. Apollonia put her arms around his waist and drew him closer. As they kissed again, nausea swirled in the pit of my stomach and I had to look away.

I phoned Dad and gave him as few details as I could get away with. After a few minutes, Red managed to get to his feet. With Bass and me practically carrying him we struggled through to the foyer where we waited for Dad.

As we drove home, Dad quizzed me about Red's condition. He wouldn't accept my repeated reassurances that he'd experienced only a minor mishap and that I was sure he'd be all right. Eventually, I explained that a punter had inadvertently struck him in the groin during a particularly frenetic bout of moshing. I lied in the full knowledge that the truth would be known to half the town as soon as Dawn opened her big fat mouth the following morning, Don't ask me why. Force of habit, I guess.

When he discovered that Red's parents had gone on holiday for a week, Dad insisted on helping Bass and I take the wounded man up to his room. Even though I could fully understand Red's reluctance to allow my father to examine him, I wasn't one hundred percent happy to leave him alone in his quasi-mansion. However, Red was adamant that he would be fine and urged us to leave.

As we drove home, dropping off Bass *en route*, my mind filled with visions of local newspaper reports about a seventeen-year-old male, left alone by his friends and a local GP to die from massive internal injuries sustained during an altercation at a well-known club.

And that's about it, really. Quite a night, eh? Not, believe me, an experience I'd like to repeat in this lifetime, or any other, for that matter.

I lie in bed listening to the sounds of the house around me. I should probably put my headphones on and chill out to some ambient grindcore or whatever but I really can't be bothered.

I hear Bennie running down the stairs. I know it's him because he has this exceedingly irritating habit of tapping his hand on the bannister as he descends. When climbing the stairs, he has the equally infuriating routine of hunching over and slapping the steps two or three above the ones his feet are on. I have told you what a pain it is living in the same house as the little monster, haven't I?

Then I hear the ringtone of Rosie's phone – 4Tune8, of course – which lasts no more than two seconds. On the bedside cabinet, the Ben Ten alarm clock I've had since I was a foetus tells me it's ten to eight. I wonder who could be ringing Rosie this early. Yes, I wonder.

I can hear the sound of Rosie talking on the phone, but I can only make out the occasional word. At one point I'm sure she shrieks something like: "You've GOT to be joking!"

I think about last night, picturing Dawn standing there looking down at Red. Though I failed to register more than her presence and her expression last night, now I can see every clogged pore of her combination skin. This is due to the fact that, where girls are concerned, I have what amounts to a photographic memory. I can't say whether I was born with this handy faculty or whether it is something that has developed. Perhaps it is because I am infatuated with the appearance of the opposite sex. (You hadn't noticed?) Or maybe it's because I am so intrigued by the image a woman consciously or subconsciously presents that I have such accurate recall of their physique, hair, make-up, clothes, and so on. Sounds a bit chicken and egg to me.

Anyway, despite the fact that Apollonia is standing just behind her, I look at Dawn. Her shoulder-length blonde hair is gathered in a pony-tail which is perhaps a slight trichological error as her acne-covered face is now completely exposed. If you think I'm being mean-spirited then you may be right, but remember that I'm about to suffer as a result of her tittle-tattling ways. OK, OK, I give in. She's only got a couple of zits on her forehead, and she has done her best to cover them up. In fact, now that I look more closely, she's not done too bad a job with her make-up. She's applied foundation fairly evenly and the rouge on her cheeks is only just visible.

Wisely, she's eschewed eye-liner which, in my opinion, should only be used by girls with huge Disney Princess eyes. There's mascara on her lashes and grey eye shadow blended with a darker shade near her neat, moderately-thick eyebrows.

Here, I will admit to liking girls with fuller eyebrows – not bushy, you understand – and if there's one thing I certainly do not like, it's girls who've completely removed their eyebrows and paint a line instead which they think approximates to the shape and size of a natural eyebrow. This technique should be reserved for dolls and mannequins, not living breathing women. There's a woman who works at the local Spar who's shaved off her eyebrows and replaced them with two arcs drawn with a dark blue Sharpie. I will swear this to the deity of your choice. Blue

134

Sharpie. But back to Dawn who has also shown an impressive degree of restraint with the lipstick, choosing a subtle hue a shade darker than her lips' natural colour, then adding gloss for emphasis.

She's wearing a black leather jacket (of course) although it might be *faux* leather, leatherette, whatever. Under the jacket, a plain white tee which covers the waistband of a plain, dark green, cotton mini-skirt. Somewhat against my better judgement, I am forced to acknowledge the pleasing contours of her legs. Regarding accessories, these have been kept to a minimum and constitute a couple of medium-sized, gold-coloured hoops through each ear-lobe, a small silver crucifix on a slender chain around her neck, and a single silver ring on her right middle finger. So far, then, not too bad. Unfortunately, her choice of footwear proves to be her undoing – a pair of white Nike trainers, FFS! I will make no further comment. *You've said enough!* rings from the gallery.

All things considered, I'd give Dawn four out of ten for effort, having deducted two points for the trainers and another for having the temerity to stand so close to Apollonia. I think about this for a few seconds. I'd probably have given her an extra point (or maybe two) if she'd been wearing a decent pair of heels, which means that had I observed her in a different setting I might have awarded her eight (or nine) out of ten. Nine out of ten for Dawn Ferner, one of my sister's larval friends! Incredible! Either something very worrying has happened to me or Dawn has undergone a startling transformation.

I find either possibility somewhat unsettling. Previously, when considering Rosie's larval pals, I've had to try to envisage them five years older, at least. Now, though, worryingly, this no longer seems to be needed. Disturbing.

I shudder then roll over, reaching down under the bed where I stowed my laptop. Within a couple of minutes, I'm on one of my favourite websites – the imaginatively titled *Hide and Sleek*.

I flip through the pages until I find a photograph that steadies my nerves. A raven-haired maiden whose make-up might be most charitably be described as theatrical. On all fours, with her backside half-facing the camera, she's looking over her shoulder at the camera, her expression indecipherable. I imagine she's trying to appear distant but the over-riding impression given is a peculiar mixture of confusion, stupidity and semi-consciousness.

I can just hear the photographer: 'I said aloof, Trixie, *aloof*! Not asleep! For Christ's sake, Tristram, where did you get this one from? The local mortuary?'

That said, I have to admit that she's got pretty decent body, which, I suspect, may be how she got the assignment. She's wearing a black leather, silver-studded basque, with criss-cross lacing up the back. Coating her buttocks, thighs and legs with a patina of sheerest black latex are a pair of leggings. The effect, as always, is mesmerising. I know it's been Photoshopped but I like to pretend it hasn't. I can't find a single flaw. It is as though her lower limbs are not flesh and bones but shiny black rubber tubes moulded into anatomically perfect thighs and legs. On her feet are a handsome pair of platform ankle boots with six-inch heels.

Starting at the tiny metal disc on the tip of the stiletto heel of Trixie's right boot I let my gaze wander slowly upwards. *En route* to the lacing of her basque, it pauses at each gleaming swelling – calf, thigh and buttock.

136

I let it continue upwards, following each barely visible node of her vertebrae. When my gaze comes to rest not on Trixie's torpid face but Dawn's it takes every ounce of resolve I possess to resist the urge to fling the laptop across my bedroom. Instead, I switch it off, shove it back where I found it, then haul myself out of bed.

I thought I might have been able to forget the whole thing, what happened last night, but I realise I'm going to have to find out what, precisely, Dawn has told Rosie. Has she filled her in regarding every last tiny detail, or limited herself to those particulars likely to cause the most embarrassment?

I cross to my bedroom window and gingerly part the curtains, allowing bright sunlight to stream into the room. World of Bloody Warcraft! This is all I need. As if everything else wasn't enough, I'm now going to be forced to endure repeated comments from my parents about how fortunate we all are that the weather is so good. It's the same every single year. For two weeks before the party Mum and Dad prattle on about how they hope it'll be a fine evening because it's *so much more pleasant* if the guests are free to roam around the back lawn while they drink themselves stupid, babble about the appalling state of the economy, rabbit on about so-and-so's wife leaving him for that sculptor from Milton Keynes, blah, blah, blah, and blah.

I switch on my sound-system and find something tolerable on my phone. I'm terrible at playlists. Bass has about a million of them, each one with some specific purpose. I've tried but just lose interest. I need something comforting, something a bit retro. *Hell & High Water* by Black Stone Cherry. Acceptable. Do you like southern rock with a modern rock sensibility, Evan?

Humming along, I pull on a pair of jeans then pick up the tee-shirt I was wearing last night. It stinks of beer and sweat. I consider trying to smother Bennie with it but toss it back under the bed instead. Matters do not need complicating today. Standing in front of the mirror mounted on my wardrobe I stare at my reflection. Inconceivable as it sounds, I can find no new zits. Just as I begin to play host to the notion that things may not be as black as they seem, Bennie starts hammering on my door.

"What do you want, ADHD-boy?" I ask, holding open the door a few millimetres.

"Dad says 'hurry up.'"

"Fascinating."

"He says 'and don't spend half an hour in the bathroom.'"

"I'm lost for words," I say, staring at his idiotic grin. "Where's Rosie? She still on her phone?"

A glint appears in his eyes. My parents would describe it as impish. I, however, know it signifies unadulterated malevolence.

"That's for me to know and-"

I yank open the door and lunge toward him. The little creep ducks beneath my outstretched arm and sprints for the top of the stairs. I stand in the corridor, listening to him tapping on the bannister and praying he loses his footing.

"-you to find out!" he yells.

From her room I hear Rosie emit another excited screech. I sigh. If she's still on the phone, then Dawn (it has to be her) must be giving her a blow-by-blow account. Leading up to one very big blow. I walk into the bathroom feeling like a cartoon character with a dark grey rain-cloud hovering a few inches above my head.

Twenty minutes later, I'm sitting at the kitchen table, scrolling through messages on my phone, munching cereal, and half-listening to Dad. This morning, the plan is to buy the alcohol for the party and Dad's going through the shopping list, for the tenth time. He looks at me.

"Do you think two cases of dry white will be enough?"

I grimace slightly, as though imagining inserting my foot in a bowl of cold custard. How should I know how much white wine my parents' alcoholic buddies will want to neck?

From his unchanged expression, I gather that his inquiry was rhetorical.

"Should be," he says, "as long as we get a case of rosé, as well as two cases of red."

I know bugger all about wine but I'm pretty sure no one's drank rosé in the last 30 years.

He carries on like this while I finish my cereal. I think there will be enough ale tonight to keep Metallica on the road for, oh, a week. Having said that, there's usually very little left afterwards.

"Malibu," says Dad as though he's discovered the answer to a cryptic crossword clue he's been struggling with for days. "I wonder if we've still got that bottle in the cabinet."

As Dad leaves the kitchen on his reconnaissance mission Rosie walks in wearing a Day-Glo pink pair of leggings and an ancient pair of basketball boots which once belonged to Zach. As they are at least five sizes too big, the effect is most clown-like. Ignoring me, she pours a glass of orange juice from the jug on the counter. I expect a sarcastic comment at any moment, but none seems forthcoming as she leans over Dad's chair and studies his list.

"Who were you on the phone with?" I ask, ensuring my tone is as neutral as possible.

"Your business?"

"Just asking."

"Free world."

I am perplexed. She must be virtually salivating at the prospect of making some pointed comment about last night's events. Even though I'm squirming, I have to concede that she has more patience than I've previously acknowledged. I want to play her at her own game but I can't control my desire to know what Dawn said.

"It was Dawn, wasn't it?" I ask, disgusted with myself for voluntarily putting myself into a very weak position.

"You should have your own YouTube channel, with paranormal powers like that."

Rosie's playing this one as cool as liquid nitrogen. She's yet to look at me. I'm impressed, and very irritated.

"I've got my agent working on it."

Still no response. This is becoming farcical.

"What did she want?"

Finally, she looks at me and I study her face which is so utterly blank that I realise our relationship has moved on to a completely new level. The stakes have been raised beyond recognition. If Rosie can appear so totally indifferent, knowing what she must know, then I've certainly got my work cut out for me. I can see I'm going to have to retreat and regroup. I'm going to have to think this one through before getting all Leeroy Jenkins on her ass. I push back my chair.

"We discussed what we're going to wear tonight."

140

I stare at her, making a final attempt to discover a chink in her armour. None is apparent. "Oh."

"Happy now?"

"Much."

"Why the sudden interest in Dawn?"

"I have no interest whatsoever in any of your infantile acquaintances," I say, trying to nip her supposition in the bud.

"If you say so," she says, a hint of a smile appearing at the corner of her mouth.

I have many faults but not realising when I'm beaten isn't one of them. I begin to formulate a method of retreat that will entail as little further embarrassment as possible. The house phone rings. No one rings the house phone, except solar panel salesman and my grandparents. I don't even know why we still have a house phone. Dad says we need to keep it because of his job, or something.

"I'll get it," I say, rather too quickly.

Rosie waits until I've entered the hall. "Maybe it's Dawn."

I'm too late. Dad's already picked it up. I think someone is offering to tarmac the drive. My phone buzzes in my pocket. It's Red. I wander into the lounge.

"Hey," I say. "How are you feeling?"

"Couldn't be better."

"Doesn't it hurt?"

"Doesn't what hurt?"

"What do you think, you noob."

"Oh, that. A little. Listen, you won't believe who's just called me."

"Who?"

"Guess."

"I haven't got time for this, Red."

"Come on. Guess."
"Oh, bloody hell, I don't know. Tell me."
"Chelsea."

[18] Party

There are so many people in our house it takes ten minutes
to move from one room to the next, not that I've had much
chance to *circulate*. Sandun's forecast was correct: half the
town *is* here. The kitchen looks a bit like an off-licence:
there are cases of wine and crates of lager stacked waist-
high. As usual, Dad completely ignored his list when we
got to the supermarket and just wandered up and down the
aisles thinking up various reasons for buying what seemed
like half the stock. His car's suspension squealed in protest
all the way home.

My telephone conversation with Red was cut short
when Dad hauled me off to Waitrose so it wasn't until he
arrived at quarter to eight that I had a chance to question
him about Chelsea but, as the guests began to arrive soon
afterwards, all I learned was that she had apologised for
Georgia's attack.

During the last two hours, we've poured countless
glasses of wine. On the kitchen floor behind us is a skip-
load of empty wine, lager and soft drink bottles. The plan
had been to try to keep on top of things as we went along,
taking the empties out to the garage, but we've been too
busy.

Only now, nearly half ten, does the pace appear
seem to be slackening. Ten minutes ago, Bass wandered
off, supposedly to relieve himself (more than a couple of
bottles of lager have ended up down his neck) but I suspect
his true aim was to locate Beth Brennan who, so rumour
has it, and for reasons unknown, decided to bring Mansoor
to the party. You'd think they'd have better places to go
and better things to do. Perhaps we should be flattered.

Red is pouring a glass of Australian dry white sparkling wine for Mrs Wiratunga, Sandun's mother. She looks a bit like an ageing film starlet who's not come to terms with the fact that she never even got her fifteen minutes. She thanks Red and flutters her preposterously long false eyelashes at him. It's at least her tenth visit to the kitchen and there's a definite lilt in her walk as she totters through to the hall. She's wearing white and gold court shoes with gold rosettes on the toes and four and a half inch heels which, in addition to the bottle of wine (and the rest) inside her, probably aren't helping her gait. Red's eyes are glued to her arse. As she disappears from view he turns to me and winks conspiratorially. "Any port in a storm."

I punch his shoulder, harder than I meant to, but probably not as hard as I should.

"Your attacks feel as light as love taps, Character. Try again."

I smirk. "An ache has appeared somewhere in the region of my ribs."

He raises a bottle of plonk to his lips and swallows a mouthful. "Not bad."

"So what's the story with Chelsea?"

"Ah, I was wondering when you were going to get around to that."

"Unless I'm getting Alzheimer's, she wasn't the one you were interested in last night."

"No, but," he says slowly, "on reflection, she wasn't that bad looking, you know. I mean, we're not talking girl-of-the-month or anything but you have to admit-"

"No, you're right, she was quite sweet," I say, grinning.

"Hey, there's no need to insult her."

I hold up my hands. "Far be it from me to criticise your beloved's physical appearance. Anyway, she did actually look quite sweet, and I actually mean that. Actually."

"Look, do you want to prattle on or shall I tell you what she said?"

Brian Brennan, Beth and Graeme's father, walks in. He asks for a double whisky and soda and three gin and tonics.

"Atticus, isn't it?"

I nod and smile. Red starts to search for a new bottle of gin while I pour out the whisky. "Beautiful weather," I say.

"Circus," says Red as he pulls a bottle out from a case near the sink.

Mr Brennan looks at Red as though he was a clock inexplicably running backwards.

"Hot as a circus today," says Red.

Mr Brennan looks at me for explanation.

"Don't let the sun go down on me," I sing, somewhat tunelessly, as I hand over the whisky and soda.

"Atticus's favourite song," says Red, splashing gin into three glasses.

"Beth enjoying herself?" I ask Mr Brennan.

"I think so."

"Can I get you anything else?" asks Red as he tops up each glass with tonic water.

"No, that's fine."

Mr Brennan picks up the four glasses then, after giving the pair of us a look of utter bewilderment, walks slowly into the hall.

"Don't be a stranger," I call after him.

Red bursts out laughing.

Early on, we found ourselves rather stuck when it came to making conversation with the guests as we prepared their beverages. It was Bass who came up with the idea of speaking sentences which begin with successive letters of the alphabet, starting with the surname of the guest ordering the drinks. Hey, I never claimed we were members of Mensa, did I?

"So what did Chelsea say after she apologised for Georgia trying to interfere with your procreative abilities?"

"She asked me out."

"Whoa, hang on," I say, banging the heel of my hand on my forehead, "I think the metal plate in my skull is picking up radio waves again. I could swear you just said she asked you out."

"Read 'em and weep."

"*She* asked *you* out?"

"Yep."

"What happened next is going to blow my mind."

Bass saunters in. "What is?"

"Chelsea has asked Red out."

Bass gives the impression that, instead of a brain, there's a Heath Robinson steam-driven contraption inside his skull which, when he's digesting information, whirrs, clicks and pops spasmodically.

"Times infinity plus one," he concludes. "When?"

"This morning," answers Red.

"What, you've already been out with her?"

"No, you unicorn fart," says Red. "She phoned me this morning. I'm meeting her at seven next Friday."

Bass shakes his head incredulously.

"Hey, hang on," I say, "aren't we going to see Pickaxe at the Showroom next Friday?"

"*You* might be," says Red, raising his eyebrows.

146

At the outermost edges of my consciousness I sense a subtle but significant change. I can guess what it is but I realise I'm going to need time to evaluate it properly.

"Yeah, right," I say, smiling.

"Guess who I've just seen," says Bass.

"Would it by any chance," I say, "be the well-upholstered Miss Elizabeth Brennan whose father, by a strange quirk of fate, was standing in this very room not five minutes ago?"

"No."

"Oh," I say, a tad disappointed. "Who, then?"

"Katie and Pete."

No way. I had no idea my parents knew them. Maybe they don't. Maybe Pete and his buxom wife have crashed the party. They look just the sort.

Red's eyes light up "Really?"

"Yep. Just came through the front door."

"Five minutes after her KTs, I'll bet," says Red.

I look at him. "Hey, I thought you were spoken for."

"Oh, no, Chelsea and I have a very open relationship. Each of us is free to see other people. In fact, I think I'll just go and see Katie right now."

"No way," I say, moving quickly to the other side of the table. "It's my turn to patrol the perimeter. You stay here with Bass."

On my way out of the kitchen, I step to one side to let in Dawn's mother, Kathy Ferner, and Glen Atkinson, one of my father's partners.

"Keeping on the straight and narrow, Atticus?" asks Dr Atkinson.

"Doing my best."

"Don't try too hard," he says, winking laboriously. These doctors. Can't hold their ale. It's a shame. There should be some kind of support network.

I smile half-heartedly then exit. As I make my way down the hall I can hear him telling Mrs Ferner what a *serious young man* I am, the subtext of which is: *he doesn't laugh at my pathetic jokes.*

I stop and peer into the conservatory, which has evolved into the smoking room. In years past, this has driven my mother into fits of apoplexy. Frankly, I'm astounded that, in this day and age, so many people still smoke, never mind within the social circle of people like my parents. But they do, and large quantities of alcohol seems to bring out the 'social smokers' as well as their more committed brethren.

In the far corner stands my father's senior partner, Dr Gibbons. The mushroom of tobacco smoke hovering above his head looks as though it should be the result of an atom bomb and not the pipe hanging from his mouth. Sahana Malhotra, Mamta's mother, is holding court a few feet from me. She falls into the 'various' group of smokers, which means she has a style all her own. It won't surprise you to learn that I have a classification system for cigarette smokers: addicts, casuals, neurotics, poseurs, secretives and various.

Addicts never let go of their cigarette. They inhale deeply, hold the smoke in their lungs for as long as possible, and exhale slowly. They're the type who, when faced with an empty packet at three o'clock in the morning, will drive out to the nearest 24-hour petrol station.

If an ashtray is nearby, Casuals will leave their cigarette to burn away, only smoking it if they happen to see it lying there. If forced to smoke without the convenience of an ashtray, small grey cylinders of ash collect around their feet like bird droppings.

Neurotics smoke because they need something to do with their hands. They are constantly tapping the ash from their cigarette, holding it up to look at it, changing the way they hold it, rolling the tip in the ashtray to form a perfect cone then tapping it again, and generally fiddling with it in every way possible. If it wasn't painful to stick it in their ear they would. They stub it out when it's half smoked so that they can enjoy the additional activity of extracting another from the packet, rolling it between their fingers, messing about with their lighter or box of matches, and so on.

Poseurs can be divided into a number of sub-groups but I won't bore you with all the details. Basically, they like to be seen with a cigarette. They include those who hold it at face level, cupping their elbow in the opposite palm, holding the tip angled upwards, inhaling with it inserted in the corner of their mouth, and making a show of blowing the smoke vertically out through the same corner of their mouth. Some Poseurs hold their cigarette as if it was a dart pointing toward their mouth. They also include those who, while holding a cigarette, perform other tasks with the same hand such as smoothing out their trousers or skirt or picking up small objects. One particular variety of poseur is the female compact poseur who can withdraw a compact from her handbag, open it and inspect her reflection, all without releasing her cigarette.

Secretives attempt to conceal the fact that they are smoking which they do by holding it cupped in their palm at all times. This variant is very common among teenaged males although all ages are represented.

The various group self-evidently includes all other types of smokers. There are those for whom a cigarette is merely an extension of their lower lip and those whose faces contort with the effort of inhaling as though they were attempting to suck a very thick milkshake through a straw.

Mrs Malhotra's style is closest to that of a poseur. She smokes very long thin white cigarettes which she lights with a comparably long, slim, gold lighter. She holds her cigarette never more than six inches from her mouth between index and middle fingers. When she inhales she does so with great enthusiasm but then she appears to forget to exhale. Instead, because she hardly ever stops talking, wisps of smoke curl out from her mouth and nostrils for the following fifteen or twenty seconds. She looks not unlike a malfunctioning dry-ice machine.

"Hey, Atticus!"

I'm not entirely certain from which direction I have been hailed but I recognise Bennie's dulcet tones. I make the wrong decision and walk toward the foot of the stairs. Bennie is sitting half way up, his legs protruding between the balusters. Lionel Atkinson, who's Bennie's age, sits beside him, a couple of steps further up.

Bennie points at me. "That a new zit or have you got a cherry stuck on your chin?"

I laugh. "Hey, Lionel, did you know Bennie wets the bed every night?"

"Do not!" screams Bennie.

Declining the tempting opportunity to further embarrass my sibling in front of his friend, I enter the lounge, sliding past an older woman whose utterly blank, flawlessly smooth complexion suggests an expensive Botox habit. There are at least twice as many people in the room as there were during my last reconnaissance mission. It's going to take me at least five minutes to make my way to the French windows at the far side. I decide to take a detour and head off towards the table on which various snacks have been laid out. I take up a position standing behind Mrs Wiratunga who is speaking at William Wallace QC. She's holding forth on the 'absolutely shocking' state of the British judicial system. Mr Wallace is peering over his spectacles at her, no doubt wondering how he can get away from her without appearing discourteous. He catches my eye and raises one eyebrow a couple of millimetres, enough to say: *You, boy! There're a couple of guineas in it for you if you can get me out of this mess.*

I gaze down at Mrs Wiratunga's arse, impressively firm for a woman well into in her forties. She's wearing a tight-fitting beige pencil skirt with a rear split. I've always considered Mrs Wiratunga a natural when it comes to wearing heels but now her ankles are wobbling furiously even though she's got one hand on the table to steady herself. She lifts her glass to her lips, finds it empty, then gazes about the room with a glazed expression as if searching for a waiter. Her right ankle begins to oscillate even more violently and I watch the movement spread upwards. Her arse starts swinging from side to side and, when the resonant frequency of her torso is reached, I realise she's going to topple over any second. Thinking that you never know when you might need a good lawyer, I reach out to steady her. She turns to me with a lopsided grin and mumbles something I can't understand.

"Excuse me?" I ask, watching Mr Wallace beating a hasty retreat.

Mrs Wiratunga says something else but it's only by the way she holds up her empty glass that I conclude she'd like another. Keeping a firm hold on her upper arm, I guide her towards a vacant armchair, into which she falls backwards then starts giggling.

"Are you all right?" I ask.

"Yes, thank you, Atticus," she says. "I'm as pissed as a newt, of course. Off my face, if truth be told, but, basically, I'm fine. Thank you for your concern."

Naturally, she says nothing of the sort. In fact, she seems as oblivious to all external stimuli as the guests standing in the vicinity are to her. I quickly assess my options and determine that a speedy exit would be the most appropriate. A dozen mumbled apologies later I come across Sandun and Graeme flicking through my father's compact discs.

"What the hell's this?" asks Graeme, holding up *Bavarian Folk Music*.

I suppose that sometimes a squint might come in rather handy. At the moment, for example, Graeme appears to be regarding both the CD *and* me.

"Zach's idea of a joke last Christmas," I say then turn to Sandun. "Your mother's completely bladdered."

"You should see my father. He's so hammered he was trying to persuade Apollonia Wallace to go fishing with him tomorrow."

"Apollonia? She's here?"

"Unless she's got a twin."

"Impossible," says Graeme. "There *couldn't* be two of her."

"Where is she?" I ask, only slightly worried that saliva will be tricking down my chin any second.

"Out on the lawn, I think. At least she was, ten minutes ago."

152

"Better take that bottle of bubbly out of your pocket, Johnny," says Graeme, "because she's got someone with her."

"Who?"

"Some blond guy. Looks like a coke dealer."

"Oh," says Sandun, "you come across a few of them, do you?"

"Might do. Just the other-"

I leave them to it and make a bee-line for the French windows. I almost make it.

"Atticus!"

For a second, I wonder whether my mother has discovered that I left Mrs Wiratunga slumped in the armchair. During the next second I consider making a run for it. Then, of course, I look around for her.

"Over here!"

She's standing with a couple I haven't seen before. The man is wearing brown corduroy trousers and a blue sweat-shirt and the woman is wearing a red skirt and a purple blouse. Clearly, they are colour blind. As I draw nearer Mum slings her arm around my shoulders and pulls me close then plants a sticky kiss on my forehead. I have passed the stage of expressing my disgust by furiously rubbing off the lipstick from my face so I merely grin sheepishly then surreptitiously wipe away the offending traces while being introduced.

I learn that the woman, Dr Penny Popplestone, has recently started working at the infertility clinic. Her husband, Colin, is a biologist.

"Colin plays the violin," says Mum, looking at me as though I should share her excitement.

"Really," I say, smiling at him. I glance over my mother's shoulder and spot Katie. She's facing away, so I haven't got a view of her KTs, but I can tell it's her. She's wearing dark red low-heeled court shoes, a floral-patterned knee-length skirt and a white cotton halter-top. Although partially hidden by her hair, I can see her bra-straps digging deeply into her flesh. They've a difficult job to do.

"I've been trying to get him to join the orchestra for *Pirates*."

My mother spends a lot of time working for AFWA, the Assisted Fertility Welfare Association, a charity that gives financial support to couples who can't afford private infertility treatment. In a couple of months, they're putting on a charity performance of *The Pirates of Penzance*. Bass is playing trumpet and I've been roped in to help as an assistant, a glorified gopher.

"And I've been trying to tell your mother that I'm really not that good."

"Now, Colin, it's enthusiasm we're looking for. You don't have to be a virtuoso, do you, Atticus?"

I'm not entirely certain how I should interpret this question.

"I'm not entirely certain how I should interpret that question."

The three of them laugh, allowing me to continue my surveillance of Katie who turns to speak to a pot-bellied man on her right. Every drop of moisture in my mouth evaporates as her KTs heave into view like twin hot air balloons. It's a struggle to swallow. I lick my lips. They really are utterly mesmerising.

Look, I know it's sexist, chauvinistic and probably dehumanising, but I've got these hormones, you see, and they make me think certain things in response to certain stimuli. I really don't have any control over it. Every time I see Katie, my mind fills with thoughts of sweaty, athletic

154

encounters, usually featuring Katie in highly improbable situations, her KTs adopting even more implausible positions, as though they had lives of their own. Honestly, if I could prevent myself from thinking such things, I would. Well, maybe.

"I'm not going to take no for an answer, Colin."

"Really, I don't think I'm-"

"We really do need another violinist, don't we, Atticus?"

I'm staring at Katie's right nipple which is so clearly delineated by the thin fabric of her top that she might as well be stark naked. How pot-belly is managing to keep his eyes off her chest is completely beyond my comprehension. I'm only vaguely aware that I'm being addressed.

"Um... what?"

"Another violinist," says Mum. "We need one, don't we?"

I tear my gaze away from Katie's KTs and look at Mum. "Er... I'm not sure."

Mum looks back at Colin. "We really ought to speak to Lucinda Knight. She's the one that's sorting out the orchestra. She plays the cello, I think, and she's been absolutely marvellous. There's no way I could have organised things without her. She was here only a minute ago. I wonder where she's got to?"

"I'm sorry, Elaine," says Colin, looking quite worried, "but it's really not the sort-"

"Oh, come on, Colin," says Penny, "why don't you give it a go?"

He looks at her in the way only a husband can look at his wife – a brief twitch of the muscles between his eyes and an almost imperceptible nod of his head which says: *Shut up, will you? Can't you see I don't want to do it?* Mum is too busy looking for Lucinda (sounds like a song title, doesn't it?) to notice this excellent example of body language.

"There she is," says Mum. "Lucinda!"

Katie turns to look at Mum and my jaw drops.

Lucinda is Katie?

Katie – sorry, Lucinda – says something to pot-belly and starts walking toward us. Like a rabbit caught in the glare of headlights I am transfixed by her KTs. I've never been so close to them and my skin is tingling. My heart is beating triple time. Sweat breaks out on my brow. I feel slightly faint. The impression of their mass is overwhelming, as is the urge to reach out and fondle them. Maybe I shouldn't have had those three cans of lager.

Get a grip, Atticus.

Although I can hear the little voice in my head, I ignore it and continue to stare at Lucinda's magnificent breasts. My fingers are twitching. The desire to run my fingertips over her flesh engulfs me. I imagine lying next to her, slowly peeling the fabric of her top away from her glorious KTs, gradually exposing her velvet skin. I should definitely not have had that glass of single malt.

GET A BLOODY GRIP, ATTICUS, YOU SLOBBERING FOOL!

I screw up my eyes and concentrate on picturing my grandmother's face. It takes a moment or two, but eventually I succeed and my physiological parameters begin the long trek back to near normal. Despite my somewhat flamboyant description, all this has taken place in less than ten seconds. Such is the plight of the male adolescent.

"Lucinda, darling," says Mum in her best Women's Institute voice, "let me introduce you to Penny and Colin

156

Popplestone. Penny's the new doctor I was telling you about on the phone and Colin, here, plays the violin."

I open my eyes to see Lucinda smiling and nodding. "And this is my son, Atticus."

Lucinda's smile widens. "Hello again, Atticus."

When I hear her speak two burly men in white coats appear from nowhere. One grabs me from behind and pins my arms to my sides. The other pulls a bottle from his pocket. It has the word *SHAME* written on it in large letters. He prises open my mouth and pours the cold liquid down my throat. My stomach freezes and my heart turns into a solid block of ice. My soul becomes an arctic tundra where the only thing that grows is a single green shoot of humiliation.

If I hadn't seen Lucinda's lips move, I could have sworn a four-year-old girl had just spoken. Sweet, light and musical, the impression given is so far removed from my despicable fantasies I suddenly wish a mammoth weight (with *10 TONS* carved in its side) would come crashing down on my head, driving me through the floorboards and down into the dank cellar below, where I properly belong. If the men in white coats were to reappear, intent on castrating me, I would submit willingly.

"Hello," I try to say. A guttural squeak would be a more accurate description.

"Have you met before?" Mum asks Lucinda.

"Oh, not properly," Lucinda says – or sings. "Sometimes I see Atticus and his friends on their way to school."

"Oh," says Mum.

How can she dismiss the implications of this information so peremptorily? For how long has Lucinda been aware of Bass, Red and me watching her? Does she know of the dreadful fantasies we've woven? Where the bloody hell is that ten-ton weight? Where is the nearest corner to which I might repair and die?

Gradually, my thoughts of suicide abate as I listen to Lucinda talking to my mother and Colin. After a few minutes I begin to find her voice as mesmerising as I once found her breasts. She speaks with a sing-song lilt and sounds as if she might break out into a tinkling laugh at any moment. Instead of a compulsion to paw her breasts, I just want to sit and listen to her talk. I want to sit by her side on a Ferris wheel and listen to her giggle as we sway back and forth.

What's going on here? Is this the pedestal/gutter syndrome? Is it hormone-induced adolescent mood swings? Or is it caused by the not inconsiderable amount of alcohol swilling around my system? I don't bloody know. I abandon analysis and begin to walk toward the French windows. Lucinda takes a step sideways and lays her hand briefly on my arm. She touches me for less than a second.

"So nice to meet you properly, Atticus," she says. "Your Mum's always talking about you."

"Er, that's great," I say then hurry away, positive that the skin of my forearm is glowing.

That's great?

158

[19] Proposition

I walk through the French windows and then move to one side to allow the Clarkes – Bass's parents – to pass. I nod and smile as they greet me then I watch them join a knot of guests on the far side of the terrace. It must be fifteen minutes since I left the kitchen and I consider, briefly, returning to help Bass and Red. I imagine, though, that they're capable of holding the fort for a while longer and I could do with a few minutes by myself. I could go to my bedroom but that would entail another encounter with my half-goblin brother. Just thinking about his gargoyle-like face poking between the balusters makes me shudder. So, instead, I decide to head for the shed at the bottom of the garden where I've spent many an hour over the years pondering the meaning of life and other such trivial matters.

Though less densely packed than in the house, there are dozens of guests on the terrace, all jabbering at one another and guzzling gallons of wine and spirits. As I make my way toward the lawn I nearly bump into Lakshan Wiratunga, Sandun's father, who's carrying a tray of drinks. I wonder if he knows that his wife is slumped in an armchair, sliding in and out of consciousness. He looks at me with the vaguely curious expression of the intoxicated and I realise that even if he does know he probably, at this precise moment in time, doesn't give a fig.

This morning, after returning from the supermarket, Dad, Zach and I went to the local church hall to collect a dozen tables and four dozen chairs. Zach had borrowed a large van belonging to Forked Tongue's manager into which we humped the tables and chairs. This afternoon we

159

set them up, half on the terrace and half on the lawn. Aunt Frannie, my mother's younger sister, is sitting alone at a table near one edge of the terrace. She hails me and pats the seat of the chair next to her. Though I'm in no mood for a chat, she is my favourite relative so I oblige.

"Why so glum?"

"I'm not glum."

Her brow furrows, suggesting I'm not fooling her.

"It's nothing."

"Don't want to talk about it? That's OK."

Frannie reaches out for the cigarette packet lying on the table and flips open the top. I notice she's painted her fingernails bright red – probably *Double Decker* red, or *Really Red* or *As Red as the Blood That Would Gout from Your Chest if I Drove a Pitchfork Into It* red.

This observation is not as banal as it might at first seem as the condition of her fingernails is the most dependable sign of her mental state. When she's happy and content they are long, carefully manicured and painted in a bright colour. When she's depressed they're bitten to the quick and unvarnished.

Frannie has the most pronounced mood swings of anybody I know. I'm not saying she's bipolar or anything like that. I have a brain the size of Jupiter but I lack formal psychiatric qualifications. I'm just saying that her mood swings more wildly than a bisexual in a room full of open-minded people of both sexes.

I can only assume, therefore, from the garish colour of her well-manicured nails that she has been in good spirits recently. She pinches the filter of a cigarette between the nails of her thumb and index finger and slowly withdraws it from the packet.

"You mind?" she asks, picking up her lighter.

160

"It's a disgusting habit," I say, half-mimicking my mother, and half telling the truth. "You smell like an ashtray and you're going to lose ten years of your life."

Frannie shakes her head and chuckles. She sticks the fag in her face and lights up. I wonder if she'd even bother smoking if it didn't wind up my parents – especially my mother – so much. She's definitely a casual smoker, with distinct poseur tendencies. Although the frequency with which she inhales is low, she makes no attempt to conceal the fact that she's smoking.

She crosses her legs and leans forward slightly, resting her elbow on her knee and holding the cigarette up near her chin. Cigarette smoke twists upwards past her face as she scans the crowd on the terrace. If a few appropriate props were added to the scene I can almost imagine her in one of those black and white photographs from the 40s or 50s that can be purchased from any online poster emporium.

Frannie's attractive in a small-but-perfectly-formed sort of way. She's about five foot two, slim and graceful. Her face is well-balanced, open, likeable. She keeps her thick, dark brown hair in excellent condition and usually has it tied back in a short pony-tail. If she has a personal grooming fault it's her make-up. Normally, she wears none so she can look rather plain. On special occasions, she goes somewhat over the top: thick mascara and eye shadow, great streaks of blusher over an emulsion of foundation and lipstick that looks as though it was applied with a trowel.

Tonight, she's applied the war-paint a little more moderately although I notice that, after only two puffs, the cigarette filter is already heavily lipstick-smeared. She's wearing a baby blue and white polka dot wrap dress, cinched-waist with scooping v-neckline and softly ruffled

161

wrap to the waistline and neck. It suits her, emphasising her narrow waist and slender arms and shoulders. She's wearing matching baby blue ballerina pumps. Frannie rarely wears heels, even though, being on the short side, you'd think she'd favour them, and when she does wear them she tends to kick them off at the earliest opportunity.

I love Frannie. She doesn't take any shit from anyone.

She inhales deeply – the burning cigarette tip flares brightly – then blows out a thin stream of blue-grey smoke through pursed lips. Her gaze flips from the crowd to me.

"Sure you don't want to talk?"

"It's just some stuff. Nothing for you to worry about."

"OK. Whatever."

She daintily taps the ash from her cigarette. I could tell her about Lucinda/Katie, how one of my personal sexual icons has evaporated into thin air, that I am consumed by guilt and confusion, that I feel like shit.

"Where's Dick?" I ask.

"*Richard* is getting me a drink."

Richard is the boyfriend she's been living with for the last six months – or 'that bloody Trotskyist Frannie's shacking up with' as my mother so quaintly refers to him. In fact, he's a lecturer in politics and modern history at a local college and he's not so bad if you can see past the beard, the Lennon spectacles and the left-wing rhetoric. Mum detests him, mostly because of the tiny pony-tail that hangs like a rat's tail over his collar. I just like to wind him up. As if on cue, he staggers through the French windows. His unsteady gait is almost certainly due to his struggle through the packed lounge as I've only ever seen him drink mineral water.

162

"Got to go," I say to Frannie then stand up. "Hey, Dick, how's it hanging?"

"Hello, Atticus," he says, without a trace of humour, "or should I call you Johnny?"

"Richard!" says Frannie, obviously annoyed.

"Either's fine by me, Dick," I say, impressed by my grace under pressure, then walk off toward the lawn without giving either of them a second glance.

Two questions. How does Richard know about my nickname? Or, to put it another way, how does Dick know my nick? And does he know it's significance? Judging by Frannie's response, I can only conclude that the answer to the second question is that yes they do. Which is embarrassing and distressing in equal measure. But who told Frannie?

It was Red that came up with the (rubber) Johnny moniker in the first place and clearly Bass knows and understands. I'm known now to most of the kids in my year as 'Johnny' but very few of them know that it relates to my, er, passions for (certain) fashions.

Which leaves my family. I discount my parents as neither has ever asked why Bass and Red call me Johnny. I assume *they* assume it's one of those 'Kids today, eh?' matters. Bennie's a clever little sod but I don't think he's quite old enough to understand.

So, it has to be Rosie. The opportunity to communicate her knowledge must have arisen at some point as she and Frannie are as thick as thieves but how has Rosie discovered my fascination about flexible fashions? Just wait until I find the little witch.

I don't have to wait long. As I negotiate the horrendously overgrown rhododendron bush which juts out from one side of the garden I come across Zach holding

163

court. I take two steps backwards and peer at the group of larvae enraptured by one of my brother's monologues. Even I have to admit that Zach has a remarkable talent for telling stories. He can make the most commonplace event sound fascinating. He can describe a trip to the corner shop and have you believe that, in comparison, Scott's Antarctic trip was little more than a Sunday afternoon stroll.

Most of us spend our time noticing only what we want to see. We choose a route through life, ignoring the myriad side-roads available to the more intrepid traveller. Even though I'm not certain exactly what I want to do with my life in the long run, I have the next week or two fairly carefully mapped out. The upcoming end-of-year exams aren't going to pose significant problems (he says, hopefully) as I've always been good at planning in advance. If only everything in life was as simple as sticking to a revision timetable. I'm also involved in various clubs and societies so that takes up time. Then there are orchestra rehearsals – there's a big concert coming up in early July. There are the Silicone Cucumbers auditions on Wednesday, Pickaxe on Friday and Rosie's birthday party on Saturday. In between, there's eating, sleeping, defaecating and all the other small but significant aspects of my life.

Zach, on the other hand, has no real plans whatsoever. 'Go with the flow, Atticus,' he's always telling me, 'and ride the tide.' If Forked Tongue were to disband tomorrow, it wouldn't faze him. He'd just kick back and wait for a new window of opportunity through which he'd dive headlong. 'Something will come up,' he'd say. And the thing is, it would, and while he was waiting he'd be watching and listening and absorbing every detail of other people's lives as they trudge along their chosen paths.

Which saga is holding the larvae's attention so steadfastly I can only imagine as, due to the general hubbub behind me, Zach's words are inaudible. With his back toward me he's sitting on a table, facing a semicircle of perhaps half a dozen captivated larvae. Rosie, Mamta and Courtney Khan are seated, while Dawn and two girls whose faces look familiar but whose names I can't place are standing. Intermittently, their enchanted faces break out into wide grins and they turn to look at one another, giggling, their pert little breasts aquiver with delight.

After a minute or so, I realise that I am as beguiled as they are, though for a different reason. One of the girls whose name I can't remember is wearing a green and white checked dress. Sleeveless, with a high neck, it clings to her torso. The skirt is circular, the pleats draped casually over her hips, the hem falling just below her buttocks. Her long tanned legs are bare, her thighs flawless, her calves taut. She's wearing green flat shoes but I quickly pop her into a nice pair of Louboutin five-inch courts. Zach reaches another humorous juncture in his tale and as his audience start laughing again I watch the girl's Ts moving beneath the checked dress.

Guilt at my voyeurism gnaws slowly at me but not enough to prevent my gaze travelling to Dawn who, despite her lengthy conversation with my sister early this morning, appears to be wearing nothing out of the ordinary. A black long-sleeved blouse is tucked into the waist of a black mini-skirt. She's wearing sheer black tights which, judging from their translucence, are fifteen denier, or possibly even ten. All in black? Perhaps Suzana Comănici-Jenkins has a blog of which I'm unaware and is giving out style tips. Sadly, Dawn, like the lass in the checked dress, is wearing flats, but at least they look a sight more elegant than the bright pink wedge trainers Mamta's got stuck on her feet.

The larvae all start giggling again and I flick my gaze to Dawn's chest in order to observe the rhythmic movement of her breasts only to discover that I have seriously misjudged her. Unless it is a trick of the light or of my imagination, her blouse is as opaque as her tights and I can see she's wearing a black bra. When she turns to say something to Rosie I note that, barring a significant amount of padding, her breasts are one heck of a lot more pleasing to the eye than I remember them. Bloody hell! What am I thinking? I really do need help. Perhaps Opus Dei have opened up their membership and I could join up in time for the next class on mortification. My mood darkens one shade further. Here I am, skulking behind a garden bush, spying on my sister's girlfriends.

"Hey, Atticus!"

My brother's voice makes me lose my balance slightly and the resultant shaking of rhododendron leaves makes flight impossible.

"What are you doing hiding behind there?"

"I wasn't *hiding*," I say, strolling as casually as I can into full view of the larval gallery. "I was looking for someone."

Zach grins. "We were just talking about you."

I'm just starting to regain my composure, having been discovered lurking behind the rhododendron, when all six larvae break out into gales of hysterical laughter. I can feel my face flushing as I stare from one to the other.

Mamta is laughing so hard she begins choking and Courtney slaps her on the back. Rosie is doubled up with glee and the girl in the checked dress is wiping her eyes.

Dawn manages to control her delirium for a few moments and gazes at me with what appears to be pity.

This is the last straw and I turn to glare furiously at Zach. He grins again then spreads wide his arms in contrition. I struggle to find an appropriate response but I can't displace the vulgar crowd of expletives milling around on the tip of my tongue. Enraged though I am, I realise that to release them would only exacerbate the situation. Instead, I walk away, my head spinning.

My brain seems completely dissociated from the rest of my body. It feels swollen and sore, ready to explode into a trillion grisly fragments. Images swirl, kaleidoscope-like, in my mind. Katie's KTs, as swollen as my brain. Frannie and Dick, pointing at me and smirking. Zach grinning, mouthing the words: *Ride the tide, Atticus*. Rosie and her larval friends, their badly-painted faces contorted with laughter, their pitiful bodies convulsing.

I pass a table at which Beth Brennan and Mansoor Khan are sitting. To be more precise, Mansoor is sitting on a chair with Beth on his lap. Mansoor's got his tongue so far down Beth's throat, he looks like a dog trying to lick out a yoghurt pot. She's got her hands on the back of his neck and he's pawing her right breast. They are as aware of my presence as I am interested in watching them.

I walk further down the garden, toward the shed. Sanctuary. There is no one down here, for which I'm extremely grateful. You can't mope properly if there's anyone else around, can you? As I approach the shed I see the door handle move. Not wishing to be seen by anybody, least of all whoever's in the shed, I step quickly to one side just as the door is opened. I push myself up against the side wall of the shed and hold my breath as I listen to a male voice whispering. I'm getting good at this lurking and hiding lark, aren't I?

"Robert!" squeals a female voice which sounds familiar.

More whispering then giggling.

"We should be getting back," says the male voice. "Your parents will be wondering where we've got to."

"Not just yet."

I start to feel slightly faint then realise I'm still holding my breath. I exhale as quietly as I can. Having been discovered spying once already this evening I have no wish whatsoever to be branded a Peeping Tom. However, at this precise moment, I am caught between two hard rocky things and I have little choice but to listen. I thought Beth and Mansoor were making a lot of noise but they were amateurs compared to this pair. The wet, sucking sounds they're making are so loud as to be almost deafening. It sounds as if one of them is drowning, or maybe both of them. She's moaning and sighing, and he's grunting and gasping, and they're both breathing hard through their nostrils. I put up with the sounds of their determined snogging – at least I hope it's just snogging – for a couple of minutes, all the while wishing I was anywhere else, even sparring with Bennie, before my curiosity gets the better of me.

I peer around the corner of the shed.

Big mistake.

Very big mistake.

Apollonia is facing the house, standing on her toes to suck the lips right off Mr Music Business's face, although I know now his name's Robert. His shirt's completely unbuttoned and she's got one hand up behind his back and the other on his bare chest. He's facing the shed, with his head fortuitously angled away from me, one hand fondling Apollonia's left breast through the fabric of her partially unbuttoned blouse and the other up under her skirt massaging her left buttock. This is like something on the Discovery channel, FFS. They are really going at it, fingers clenching and relaxing, tongues slipping in and out, hips grinding.

I feel sick, and no, I don't mean metaphorically. I can feel my stomach contracting and vomit rising up my gullet. I take a couple of steps back into the shadows and crouch down. As if in some slow-motion horror film sequence, I envisage myself staggering out toward Apollonia and Robert and spewing all over them. But there is a limit to the depths to which even I can sink and I force myself to swallow repeatedly until the urge to honk passes.

When I feel well enough to stand and peer around the corner of the shed again, I see Apollonia and Robert have recovered from their bout of unrestrained passion and wandered a few metres up the garden. He's tucking his shirt into his trousers and she's pulling her skirt back down over her buttocks. I note she's wearing stockings and suspenders and that she's forgotten to reattach one of the suspender clips. Hand in hand they walk further up the garden and as they disappear from view my nausea returns, this time ten times stronger than before. I give in and toss my cookies.

Just when I think I've sunk as far as I can go I look up and see a sign.

Welcome to Rock Bottom.

Sigh.

After a few minutes, I wipe drops of acid vomit from my chin, feeling a little better. Not a lot, but better than before. That said, I can't really imagine feeling any worse. In the last twenty minutes, just about everything I hold dear has been snatched away from me. My perception of the woman with the most impressive breasts I've ever seen has been changed forever. I find out that the impression my favourite relative has of me has also been transformed. To my sister and her ghastly, larval cohorts I am an object of derision. And, to top it all, Apollonia, the woman I regard above all others, was practically having it off with Robert right in front of my eyes.

I walk slowly back to the shed and grasp the door handle. Then it hits me. Never mind almost having it off – Robert, the slimy toad, must have deflowered Apollonia right here in this shed. OK, not literally deflowered, as I doubt very much that it was the first time, for either of them. Pass that bottle of mind bleach when you've finished with it.

My shed. My sanctuary. If I open this door I'll smell them, the scent of her, the odour of him. I feel like holding out my arms and wailing at the moon. Why hast thou forsaken me?

Instead, I trudge over to the swing my father bought Rosie for her sixth birthday. The seat is a little too narrow for me now, but I manage to squeeze into it. Keeping my feet on the ground, I begin rocking slowly back and forth. I shake my head, thinking that surely this is the bottom now. Sub-basement level ten. Tonight is the nadir of my short life. There's no way things can get any worse. No way.

I try to clear my mind, to push away my thoughts and feelings. I have a lot of confidence in the power of denial. Needless to say, my attempts are unsuccessful. I move on to another defence mechanism and start blaming everyone else but me. I condemn Lucinda for not being Katie, for not being a wanton, pneumatic sex machine. I denounce Frannie for knowing about my plastic

170

preoccupation and for telling Dick about it. I charge Rosie and her giggling companions with the heinous crime of laughing at me and I blame Zach for drawing their attention to me and for being more popular than I am. Most of all, though, I hate Apollonia for not being the immaculate goddess I want her to be.

"Atticus?"

I do not know for how long Rosie has been standing there, watching me.

"What?" I bark.

"You all right?"

I scowl. "What do you care?"

Silence.

The full moon is behind her so I cannot see her face. Unfortunately, I am aware that she can see me quite clearly. I consider moving to a better position – tactically, I mean – but, to tell the truth, I really can't be bothered. It is as though Mrs Wiratunga stuck a knife in my back when I helped her into the armchair. It must have only just pierced my skin because I felt nothing at the time. Since then, practically every woman I've come across in the last half hour has grabbed hold of the knife and driven it further toward my heart – Lucinda, then Frannie, then Rosie and her friends. Finally, Apollonia used both hands and all the strength she could muster to thrust the blade home, slicing open my heart. I am bleeding, my life force ebbing away.

I think this is self-pity. Mind you, despite the cardiac trauma, there's still a fair bit of anger left in me.

"Come to gloat, have you?"

"Atticus, that's not-"

"Look, I think you'd better get back to Dawn and Mamta and your other stupid friends. Just leave me alone."

More silence.

Damn, I wish I could see her face. I am staring at what I judge to be her centre, a spot half way between her belly button and the lower edge of her breast-bone. As the seconds tick away my gaze travels around her silhouette. Her dress is not unlike the green and white checked one her friend is wearing although the hem is a little lower. Her feet are bare now but I know she had been wearing a pair of simple black courts she'd borrowed from Frannie. She's standing with her hands on her hips and her feet spread apart – a rather determined stance, to be honest. I can see that, whether I like it or not, she's going to have her say.

"What do you want?" I ask.

"Why do you have to be so... so... awful?"

"Hey, I've had enough abuse tonight, OK? And I don't need-"

"That's not what I meant."

"Oh, what did you mean, then?"

Rosie looks away from me and the moonlight illuminates her profile. I can see she's struggling to find the right words.

"Do you *like* me, Atticus?" she asks, still not looking at me.

"What kind of bloody question is that?"

She turns to face me again but makes no sign of answering. I am tempted to get up off the swing and return to the house but I decide to see this through.

"I don't *dislike* you."

"That's not what I asked."

"Perhaps not, but..."

I can't seem to finish the sentence. What does she want me to say? Actually, Rosie, I've recently come to the conclusion that you're not all that bad. In fact, physically, you're becoming a rather attractive young lady, and if you

172

weren't my sister... Right, that would really be impressive, wouldn't it?

"Right. You don't like me but you don't *dislike* me?"

"No..."

Oh, bugger it.

"OK, I like you. There. I said it. I like you. Happy?"

"And what about my friends?"

"What about them?"

I do not like the sound of this, at all.

"Do you *like* my friends?"

"What, all of them?"

"Well, no, not all of them, but let's start with Cheyenne. Do you like her?"

Cheyenne? First, what kind of name is that? Second, I've no idea who she's talking about.

"Who?"

"Cheyenne, my friend. I've known her since primary school."

Maybe she means green and white check dress girl. Maybe not. Am I supposed to keep track of *all* her larval friends? Maybe I am. Would be just like me to have missed that email. I shake my head.

"Sorry, Rosie, I'm just not sure which of your friends is Cheyenne."

I watch her shoulders rise and fall as she sighs dramatically. "Fine, then what about Dawn? You know her, I know you do. Do you *like* her?"

Objection, your honour. Miss Childress has not made it clear where she's going with this line of inquiry. She's confusing the witness. Sustained.

"I don't know what you mean."

"*Atticus*," she says impatiently.

The fact is, of course, that I actually *don't* know what she means. I've never even considered whether or not I *like* Dawn Ferner. Why should I? What possible point would it serve? She's a larva. Full stop. Whether I like her or not is completely immaterial.

"How could I like anybody who listens to that abhorrent bunch of eunuchs."

"What?"

"4Tune8"

"You see," she says, "that's exactly what I meant before. Why do you have to be so beastly? What possible difference does it make if Dawn happens to like them?"

"A lot."

"Oh, so you'd like her if she was into Killswitch *Bloody* Engage, Pierce The *Fucking* Veil or whatever other silly metal band you happen to like."

"Maybe," I mumble. Frankly, I'm more than a little unsettled by Rosie's obvious anger.

"You are pathetic, Atticus," she says, becoming even more animated. "Why can't you just admit that you can't say whether or not you like Dawn, or any of my friends, for that matter, because you don't *know* her, or them."

I have absolutely no idea how to reply to this. "Maybe," is all I can come up with. "Maybe I don't want to *know* her, as you put it."

"Yeah, well, maybe you don't. Maybe you'd prefer to spend the rest of your life hanging around with your dopey mates and looking at those websites that you think nobody else knows about. Maybe you'd be happy just making oh-so-clever remarks and making out that you're so much better than everyone else."

174

And maybe I could stand up and bop you on your stupid larval nose.

"It wouldn't occur to you, I suppose," she continues, "to try to find out a bit more about her, to get to know her a little, and then you could decide whether or not you like her."

"What, you mean ask her out?"

"Would it be so terrible?"

Before I can answer, I hear the crack of a twig snapping. It seemed to come from behind a bush just two or three metres away. I jump to my feet and stare in that direction and I'm pretty sure I can make out the silhouette of a crouching figure. I turn to Rosie.

OK, *now* I get it. This is all some kind of set-up. I can only see one person, but I'll bet every single one of Rosie's bloody larval pals is probably crouching just out of view, filming all of this on their phones, getting ready to upload it to bloody You-bloody-Tube. I'll have to change schools. Change my name. Maybe emigrate. I am equally angry and distraught.

"Hey, I wouldn't ask Dawn Ferner out if she was the last female on the planet! I wouldn't go within a hundred metres of her, even if she was wearing nothing but thigh boots!"

I'm so angry at this point, I can see, in the moonlight, tiny droplets of saliva spitting from my mouth. Something in my head ruptures and I growl: "I wouldn't touch that little skank if she was on her hands and knees, bloody begging for it."

I'm just getting started but I pause to inhale, only to hear the sound of the crouching figure getting to its feet. I turn to see Dawn running up the lawn, back to the house.

175

There are no signs of any other girls. When I look back at Rosie I see she's walked right up to me, her eyes blazing.

"You stupid, *stupid* fuck-face!" she hisses then slaps me hard across the cheek.

My face stinging, my pride stung, I watch Rosie run to catch up with her friend.

[20] Psychoanalysis Я Us

Early Sunday afternoon in the park provides an excellent opportunity for talent-spotting, especially on warm summer days. The three of us are sitting on a bench set a yard back from a path. The boys watch the girls while the girls watch the boys who watch the girls go by. Except, as you might imagine, most of the females passing this bench would probably prefer it if a yawning chasm to hell opened up beneath the three of us.

"An entire flute section," says Bass as a quartet of girls walks towards us.

Red scans the foursome. "Hen party. They're all dressed to the nines. Heels, legs, short skirts, Christmas baubles all round. Pre-loaded and ready for action. The door-bell rings. It's the taxi, come to take them out to a night-club. But the taxi-driver's a stud and the bride-to-be asks if he wants to wait inside for a few moments as they're not quite ready. She's half-cut, eyes lidded. While her friends watch, she reaches down and unzips the taxi-driver's jeans. He's clearly more than capable of going the extra mile. The future Mrs Assistant Credit Manager kneels down and-"

"Red! The line!" exclaim Bass and I.

A few seconds pass as the girls draw closer. One with short, tightly-permed, dark hair looks vaguely familiar.

"Johnny?" asks Red.

"Oh, skater dresses all round, I suppose. Various pastel hues."

Neither Bass nor Red comment on my lack of enthusiasm as the subject has already been raised and very quickly lowered again. They believe I had too much to drink last night and I've said nothing to suggest otherwise.

The girl I think I recognise turns to look at us as she walks by.

"Hello, Atticus," she says, smiling.

Her friends start giggling and I realise that she was in Zach's audience last night, standing next to Dawn. I look away, across the park to where a group of boys are kicking a football around. After last night, I don't think any kind of abuse, implied or real, can make me feel any worse so I don't see much point in getting worked up about four stupid girls who happen to find my mere existence so rib-tickling.

"What the hell was that about?" asks Red.

"What am I, psychic?"

"Who was she?"

"Some girl. I don't know," I mutter, becoming irritated.

"Well, she seemed to know you."

"What is this, the third degree?"

"No one expects the Spanish Inquisition," mutters Bass.

Red turns to me. "OK, no need to bite my head off just because you can't hold your ale. Only asking."

I stare down between my feet at a gob of discarded chewing gum. "Look, she was at the party last night. One of Rosie's cronies. Other than that I don't know anything about her. Satisfied?"

"I fancy an ice-cream," says Bass diplomatically. "Coming?"

"Yeah, sure," says Red, getting to his feet.

"I'm all right, thanks," I say, scrutinising the teeth marks in the chewing gum.

"Famous last words," murmurs Red as he walks off.

After a few seconds I look up and watch Bass and Red sauntering toward the ice-cream van parked a couple of hundred metres away. They pass two lasses wearing brief shorts, and both look over their shoulders to enjoy the rear view. Bass says something which elicits a sharp punch on the shoulder from Red. When they both start laughing I look away. Given the absence of any significant external stimuli, my brain fills with thoughts of last night's events, as it has done during every waking moment since Rosie assaulted me.

I suppose you think I'm a bit of a twat, don't you? Hey, I mean, you wouldn't be alone or anything. I'm pretty certain that Rosie and Dawn are busy setting up the Atticus Childress Depreciation Society and they'd be glad to hear from any interested parties. I think I might even consider joining myself if I wasn't sure that they'd shoot me on sight. It's not that I blame them. I did behave like a Neanderthal last night – or even a *stupid, stupid fuck-face*, as Rosie so eloquently put it. But when I saw someone crouching behind the bushes I honestly thought that Rosie was just winding me up, a continuation of whatever process Zach had begun earlier. I realise now, of course, that just the opposite was the case. Rosie was admirably trying to cut through the brother/sister bullshit that's complicated our relationship so far, which is a heck of a lot more than I've managed to do, whatever benevolent thoughts have been crossing my mind during the last week or so. The end result is that I've not merely burned any half-constructed bridge that may have existed between us but I've gone all *Independence Day* on its ass.

Take this morning, for instance. When I came down to the kitchen, Rosie was sitting at the table, flipping through one of her glossy fashion mags. As soon as I

179

entered, she just stood up and walked out, leaving a half-eaten bowl of cereal on the table and giving me such a look of utter malevolence that, given the choice, I'd choose a showdown with the testicle-smashing Georgia any day. Fifteen minutes later, I cornered her in the hall. As soon as the immortal words 'about last night...' had left my lips, she was out through the front door, the jamb juddering with the force with which she'd slammed the door behind her.

But I really can't criticise her. My hope of a reconciliation is pinned, no doubt unrealistically, on my plan to buy her something special for her birthday. I just can't work out exactly what to get her. Maybe I should reconsider Red's suggestion of a tattoo. What sixteen-year-old, after all, *doesn't* want a tattoo of some ivy creeping up her arm, from fingers to arm-pit?

Needless to say, Rosie is not my only problem at the moment. First of all, there's Dawn, then there's Frannie (and Dick), then Lucinda and, finally, Apollonia. Details of my ruminations would only cause severe boredom so I'll just relate my conclusions, and I do this only in an attempt to win a soupçon of sympathy and to convince you (and myself) that I'm not the self-centred chauvinist my tale so far may have led you to believe.

Right. Deep breath. Here we go.

Dawn Ferner is a fairly attractive young lady who, for reasons unknown, must have expressed to my sister an interest in me. I will have to give serious consideration as to whether or not I can reciprocate her feelings and, whatever I decide, apologise for my behaviour.

Frannie has always shown an interest in me, and never demonstrated any tendency to denigrate my habits or hobbies. I do not know for how long she has known about my raiment-related pastime so, supposing that it may have

180

been for a while, I should not treat her any differently. Dick, on the hand, no matter what he knows about me, is still a bit of a humourless houseplant, and I see no particular reason not to regard him as such.

My fantasies about Lucinda Knight were unfounded. She is a kind, generous woman and I shall endeavour to show her the respect she deserves. Furthermore, I will, in future, attempt to ignore her KTs – oops, sorry, I mean that I will pay no attention to her physical attributes.

Just thinking about Apollonia, though, still causes a great deal of discomfort. Look, OK, I know it's stupid of me to have built her up in my mind into a goddess of mythical proportions, tautologically speaking. And I know that I probably deserve to have had the senselessness of such a fantasy driven home so blatantly. But it hurts. It hurts so much I can hardly begin to describe the emotional trauma. So I won't. I can only hope that, in time, the pain will ease.

Finally – and this may be the most important realisation – I accept that my attitude towards women is in dire need of a thorough overhaul. I'm neither blind nor feeble-minded and it has not escaped my attention that all the aforementioned subjects of my angst are members of the opposite sex. Unfortunately, I remain incapable of sorting and assessing the various, and mostly contradictory, emotions buzzing around inside my head. So, while I acknowledge my deficiencies, doing something about them is, I believe, going to be a formidable task, and one which I think will be delayed for a while yet.

And that's about where I'm up to at the moment. If you still think I'm a twat you should at least realise that I'm not incapable of seeing the writing on the wall, even if it is through a fairly grimy pair of rose-tinted spectacles.

Hey, end of confession or whatever. It's back to the wild and whacky world of your average angst-ridden, teenaged fashion-fetishist!

I watch Bass and Red returning with their frozen powdered-milk products. Having embraced acceptance with open arms, if not with a song in my heart, I realise that sulking in front of my friends is going to achieve nothing. If I alienate them, I will truly have nothing. Besides, any more introspection and I'll have my head so far up my arse I'll never get it out again.

"Mega-Sharons, twelve o'clock high!" I call out, indicating with a jerk of my head two specimens coming up along the path to my right. Bass and Red are on the same path, ten metres to my left. When they spot the Sharons, a blonde and a redhead, they increase their pace so that they are in position on the bench.

We adopt the time-honoured posture of the undercover female surveillance experts that we've become. I incline my head, apparently inspecting the chewing gum. Red attacks his ice-cream with starved-dog fervour and Bass looks into the middle distance.

I couldn't possibly imagine what kind of night these two have had. Hell, I had a shitty night, didn't get to sleep until after three, and only got up just before noon, but I look, and probably feel, like an Olympic athlete compared to these two.

They're *staggering* more than they're walking, holding onto each other for support. If I was half the man I should be, I'd be paying for a taxi to take them home. But I've only got three pound coins in my pocket.

The blonde is at least two stone overweight. Dilapidated court shoes, blotchy legs, tight mini-skirt, tight blouse, too much jewellery, too much make-up and greasy hair that was once tied up to one side of her head but now hangs limp around her corpulent face.

The redhead is wearing knee-length black leather boots with two-inch stack heels, ground down to an inch with the effort of carrying their owner's bulk. She's stuffed her size 20 arse and thighs into a pair of size 16 jeans. Under her white blouse, a black bra struggles to contain her fruit salad. She's tied her hair into a knot at the top of her head so tightly, it gives the impression that she's attempted an amateur face-lift – an endeavour destined to fail, bearing in mind the too-many-chip-suppers puffiness of her features.

As they pass, the blonde stumbles, setting her excess body fat aquiver, and her friend, reflexes slowed by alcohol and/other psychoactive substances, struggles to hang on to her. A stream of expletives erupts from her mouth, quelled only by the reinsertion of a cigarette between her lips. Beside me, Red shudders.

"*Slags Monthly*," he mutters. "Readers' Wives section, featuring Helga and Olga."

"*Hags Monthly*," says Bass.

"*Hags and Slags Shag Monthly*," I say.

Bass and Red chuckle, quietly though, for it's not recommended to dwell too long on the subject of Sharons. As I've mentioned before, the images that can leap unbidden into your mind can be most unsettling.

"Hey, Red," I say, "heard from Chelsea this morning? Or does one refer to her as Chel?"

"Ho-ho-ho and, furthermore, ho."

"Look out, Johnny," says Bass, "young mum heading this way. Looks like Francesca to me."

"Good call, Bass-meister," says Red.

I would tend to agree with the opinions of my peers. Francesca does appear to be a cut or two above the run-of-the-mill, park-using young mothers. She's wearing Nike trainers, beige ribbed Lycra leggings and a brown sweat-shirt with no prominent logo. I love flesh-tone leggings, and the nervous tingle that swarms over my body when I first spot a woman wearing them and, for a split second, it appears as though she's wearing nothing. Her highlighted blonde hair has a lustrous sheen and has been expertly cut in an asymmetrical page-boy style. She's pushing an expensive-looking stroller whose occupant, a girl of about eighteen months, is fast asleep.

If Francesca's daughter is wearing clothes from Mothercare or Boots, then I'm a shrinking violet. Everything about Francesca screams money, and lots of it. There's a Range Rover and a Jaguar in the garage. She goes to aerobics classes two or three times a week. She tops up her tan in the Seychelles instead of on the sunbed. I'm surprised there isn't a personalised number plate on the stroller.

"French horn," says Bass.

Her nose wrinkles as she passes the Sharons. She glances over her shoulder and when she looks forward again there's a look of disgust and disbelief on her flawless features, as if she's saying to herself: *Black brassiere and white blouse! How terribly gauche!*

"Full evening dress," says Red. "Nothing showing, just an 'I need a *real* man, now!' look in her eyes."

This is very unusual for Red. If he doesn't have a woman stripped and enthusiastically soliciting sexual activity, then there's definitely something special about her.

When Francesca is a few metres away, I dress her in glossy black, wet-look PVC, cropped leggings, the better to show off her muscular calves, and a pair of Jimmy Choo courts. Just four-inch heels, though. Francesca needs to save her energy. I strive to complete the ensemble but can't decide between a short denim jacket over a black sports bra or a well-cut upmarket tee-shirt.

She walks past, glancing at us with the familiar expression of wariness and repugnance. Admiring her lower register, I decide to go with the sports bra and forget the jacket, the better to show off her well-developed shoulders, trim waist and firm buttocks.

"Good party last night, wasn't it?" asks Bass.

Why Francesca's arse should remind him of the party, I do not know.

"A sufficient level of talent was achieved," says Red, "larval component notwithstanding."

"Did you see Beth?" asks Bass.

Now I see.

"No," says Red.

"What about you, Johnny. Did you see her?"

"Yeah," I grunt. I'm torn now between letting Bass enjoy whatever sordid fantasy he's constructed or trying to expedite his long and arduous journey back into the real world. I think about it for a moment or two then decide he'll have to face the facts sooner or later. "She was with Mansoor on the lawn, acting like a bitch on heat. If he'd had his tongue any further down her throat it would've come out her backside."

"Oh," says Bass as if I'd just told him there was a small chance of rain today.

"Earth to Bass," says Red, holding his nose. "Earth to Bass. We've received a message that Beth Brennan doesn't know you exist. Your mission is cancelled. Please come home now."

I laugh, pleased that I do not have sole responsibility for divesting Bass of his pathetic delusion.

"Of course she knows I exist," says Bass, hurt. "We're both in the school orchestra, aren't we?"

"That A* in A-level pedantic studies is in the bag," says Red.

If I've got to face a few home truths, it's time Bass did as well.

"Look," I say, "I really think you'd be better off looking elsewhere, Bass, because Beth's completely besotted with Mansoor and even if he was to spontaneously combust, well, she's just not worth it."

Exasperated, Bass sighs loudly. "And how is it, Johnny, that you're so certain about that."

"Oh, come on! You know as well as I do what she's like. She's an utter air-head – a very pleasant air-head, with an exceptional body, I'll grant you – but you'd be bored to tears."

Red snorts. "After the first few years of exploring every square millimetre of her succulent flesh."

"You've got to move on, Bass," I continue. "Set your sights on another target."

"Oh, right, like I'm going to listen to someone with such extensive experience in matters of the heart?"

"Hey," says Red, "it's not my *heart* that gets excited by Beth Brennan."

We sit in silence while a man exercising his dog walks past. The dog, a mongrel with cataracts, pauses and sniffs Bass's left shoe. It's about to cock its leg when the man jerks it away.

Red removes his spectacles and holds them up for inspection. "I know you're going to think I've lost my mind-"

"I wondered what that lump of gristle was that I found at the back of our fridge," I say.

"Touché Turtle, but listen, I thought Dawn Ferner looked pretty damn fine last night."

"Yeah," says Bass slowly, "I noticed that as well."

"I mean," says Red, "I know she's a larva but, well, larvae have got to grow up some time and... well, *all* that lot looked pretty good, I thought. You know, Dawn and Mamta and Courtney and..."

Red lets the sentence hang in the air.

"Rosie looked pretty good, too," says Bass, then carries on, oblivious. "I mean, she'd done her hair pretty nice and that dress she was wearing was... well, I don't think I'd really noticed before how-"

"We get the picture," says Red, punching Bass's shoulder.

"Oh, yeah, sorry, I... I didn't mean..."

"Hey, it's OK," I say. "Red's right. They're all growing up, Rosie included. Anyway, what would you expect? My sister must have inherited some of the same genes as me. You know, the ones that have blessed me with such overpowering physical beauty and animal magnetism."

"You wish," says Red.

"Oh my God!" cries Bass. "Red! Quick, tie Johnny down!"

"What? Where?" splutters Red, nearly dropping his spectacles.

"Stiletto-heeled siren approaching fast," says Bass. "Batten down the hatches!"

Needless to say, I am already transfixed by the lascivious vision sashaying toward us on her towers of power. Fleur, for that seems to be the most appropriate name for her, looks as though she's travelled through time from some advertising executive's version of the fifties. She's wearing a broad-brimmed white hat, black Wayfarers, a floral print cotton bustier and white cropped Lycra leggings. I guess she'd stand five eight in her bare feet. She's got blonde hair with a matching blonde body. She looks more like an air-brushed painting than a real woman. On her feet are a pristine pair of truly mesmerising dusky pink court shoes with five-inch heels, maybe even five and a half inches. Their vamps are uncreased and cut low to show a little toe cleavage.

Fleur strides past, the rat-like terrier she's exercising trotting resolutely by her side. Click-click, click-click go her metal-tipped heels. Thump-thump, thump-thump goes my heart. If she's aware of our presence she makes no outward sign, her eyes hidden by her Ray-Bans. Slack-jawed, I stare at the muscles of her buttocks, thighs and calves contracting and relaxing as she walks away. If confirmation of my theories about elevated footwear was needed (which it isn't) then Fleur could be called Exhibit A.

It's a good two minutes before Fleur eventually disappears from view – the most enjoyable two minutes I've spent in the last twenty-four hours, I might add. Bass bites his lower lip and lets out a long sigh, a comment on the delightful Fleur to which neither Red nor I can add.

[21] The Childress Elevated Footwear Theories

Right, first of all, I want to get one thing straight: I do not have a high heel fetish, despite what I may have said earlier. A fetish is a pathological sexual attachment to an inanimate object. If so afflicted I would become excited at the sight of a pair of stiletto-heeled shoes lying at the bottom of a wardrobe – which I don't, OK? What does fascinate me is the effects induced by high heels, on both the wearer and the observer.

Elsewhere, I've rambled at some length on naturals and wobblers, the two groups into which high heels divide women, so I'll not labour that point again. There are, however, a number of theories about high heels, their wearers and their effects on me (and a large proportion of male *homo sapiens*) that I have formulated.

The key word when thinking about high heels – and clothing in general – is *control*. When we choose what we wear we are attempting to control two things: how we see ourselves and how others see us. Patently, this is untrue in certain contexts: if you're a police officer or on an arctic expedition, there's little margin for personal expression. You can pop down to your local bookshop and take your pick from dozens of heavy tomes on the psychological aspects of clothing but just consider one example.

Say you've got an appointment to see the bank manager – or, if you are a bank manager, imagine you've been called to head office, or something – and you walk into his office. In the interests of political correctness (ho-ho), I should point out that I'm aware of the fact that your bank manager might well be female, but I'll stick to the gender stereotype of a male bank manager for the time being. I'm not even sure they even have bank managers anymore. They barely have functioning high street banks now, do they? Everything's online, innit? They certainly have bank managers in the movies, and I guess that's more what I'm thinking.

Anyway, you walk into his office and see that he's wearing a dark three-piece suit, white shirt, conservative tie and dark brogues. He's clean-shaven with a short back and sides haircut. Got the picture? Right, typical senior management situation. Consider an alternative scenario. What if he's got scruffy hair hanging half way down his back, an earring, and... oh, a neck tat, for example? He's wearing a Grateful Dead tee-shirt under a brown leather bomber jacket, ripped jeans and engineer boots.

Now, I don't know about you personally, but I think you'd accept that the majority of bank customers are going to feel more comfortable with version number one. The suit says: 'I'm business-like, efficient and capable. You can trust me with your money.' In essence, he's *controlling* your response to him – or at least attempting to.

Similarly, a woman in high heels controls – or attempts to control – the reactions of others. And it's not just about sex. Sure, the American term for high heels – *fuck-me pumps* – highlights the fact that it's often, or even mainly, about sex, but not *just* about sex.

In some ways, certainly with *some* shoes, it's not just the wearer trying to control the reactions of others, it's about the shoe controlling the foot. Encased in a six-inch-heeled shoe or boot, the foot is forced into an unnatural posture, arched and trapped. The toes are pointed, the arches peaked, the legs pulled taut. Wearing high heels can be punishing. Walking with your feet distorted into unnatural positions entails a significant degree of discomfort and difficulty, bringing to mind the concept of feminine vulnerability. The ultimate example of the Discipline Theory of Elevated Footwear is the ballerina-style shoe or boot, a variety of 'posing' footwear with a heel higher than six inches where the foot is constrained, pointing almost vertically downwards. Walking is quite impossible. The wearer is rendered helpless.

The Domination Theory states that a woman's high heels are twin towers of power which she uses to distance herself from her admirers. Her footwear can then be appreciated for its many aesthetic properties: the lustrous sheen of the leather, the smooth, streamlined, almost aerodynamic qualities, the fantastically long, slender heels. Furthermore, there are the assertive qualities imparted to the woman in high heels: the taut calves, the swaggering strut, the majestic carriage of the upper body with bust thrust aggressively forwards, the overall impression of confidence and superiority.

The Mating-Call Theory alludes to the characteristic sound of a woman walking in high heels. The tap-tap, tap-tap sound says: 'Here I am, here I am, look at me, look at me'.

The Phallic Symbol Theory is pretty much as obvious as it sounds, considering the sharpened toe and stilt-like heel. Interestingly, the shape of the toe of a high-heeled shoe can emit different signals about its wearer. The pointed toe can indicate aggressive belligerence while the rounded toe might signal a more demure personality.

The Secondary Sexual Characteristics Accentuation Theory is based around the fact that when a woman is walking in high heels, male attention is drawn to her hips and breasts for reasons already explained. Bearing in mind that the desire to procreate is a deeply-rooted compulsion, it is an odd fact that, in our culture, at the present time, it is not considered acceptable for either men or women to draw attention to their genitalia. In other periods, this situation has been both more and less pronounced. Consider the practice of wearing brightly coloured cod-pieces. Later, in Victorian times, a bulge in the front of your tight trousers was considered to be in very bad taste and fashion-conscious men went to great lengths to tuck their genitals back between their legs. Then there were voluminous skirts for women which hid from view everything from waist to toes. So, when male interest is transferred from genitalia to breasts and hips, anything which draws attention to those parts of the anatomy becomes relevant.

Finally, we have the Contextual Theory of Elevated Footwear which can be roughly interpreted as: 'When a woman should wear high heels and how high the heels should be'. Definition of the term 'high' seems appropriate at this juncture. I'll dispense with 'sensible shoes' straightaway, as this means shoes with heels of three inches or less. After that there are high heels, higher heels, highest heels and the extreme bedroom-only heels (such as the ballerina-type already mentioned). The height of heel a woman chooses to wear depends on the occasion and the signals she wishes to send. Except in situations where a great deal of walking is likely, all women of child-bearing age should, in my humble opinion, wear high heels. Even a happily married woman who has no wish whatsoever to attract the attention of other men should wear shoes with heels at least four inches high. If she has thin legs they will look more curvaceous. If she has full legs they will appear elegantly streamlined. The alteration of her posture enforced by her elevated heels will make her look and feel more confident.

You see, what a woman wears is about creating an illusion. The illusion may be only a slight exaggeration of her underlying personality, or it may be something completely different. The nature of the power of the high-heeled shoe depends utterly on the inclination of the wearer or the role she wishes to play. Changing from everyday footwear to a pair of patent leather court shoes with skyscraper heels can be the final act of *dressing up*, a quasi-theatrical process which can often bring a change of personality with a change of clothes. Black patent leather court shoes with five-inch heels can transform a shy, retiring woman into a sexually-assertive dominatrix, if she so wishes.

(This chapter is an abridged version of an article I have submitted to The British Journal of Sexual Psychology – A.W.B.C.)

[22] Lair of the Indifferent Enchantress

I look up at the clock above the refrigerator – 6.15pm –
then steal a glance at Rosie. It's four days since the party
and our little argument, during which time she's said not
one single word to me. A simple grunt or two would have
made me feel a tad less wretched. As it is, whenever I see
her, I feel like an ugly bottom-feeding fish – you know, one
of those sad looking things, with white bodies and various
antennae protruding all over the show, that meander along
the sea bed, scooping up plankton (or whatever it is they
feed on) with their slack, big-lipped mouths. Every time
I've dropped my pride into the waste-disposal unit and tried
to communicate my regret she's either simply ignored me
or glared at me with undiluted hatred. Only the knowledge
that on Saturday night I was completely out of order
prevents me from throwing in the towel.

I have resolved one matter, though: Rosie's birthday
present. After much soul-searching, I've finally made up
my mind what I'm going to get her. I saw it in the Zone
yesterday, beckoning me, in the same way a zit speaks to
me when it needs squeezing. *Atticus*, it said, in a thin reedy
voice, *buy me. You know Rosie wants me*. I stared at it for a
minute or so, only vaguely concerned that any of my
friends might spy me paying so much attention to
something so heinous. I left The Zone in a major quandary.
Not only would its purchase reduce my savings to nothing
but I didn't know whether I had sufficient strength of
character to return with the cash and actually ask for it.
This morning, after being rebuffed by my sister once again,

I finally made up my mind. I would buy it, but not in person, if I can avoid it. Who I shall delegate as my agent in this most clandestine of operations is as yet unknown. Bass seems the most likely candidate but even he may baulk at the challenge.

OK, I hear you. Just what is it that I have decided to buy Rosie for her sixteenth birthday? Right, brace yourselves. I am going to buy her a box set of the three *proper* albums recorded by that most lovely of quartets, 4Tune8. On vinyl. Not only is this extremely desirable item imported from Japan, and therefore rarely found in this cream and pheasant land, but it includes two (count 'em) bonus discs of rare tracks and alternative mixes of their so-called hits. This veritable treasure trove – nay, this corpulent cornucopia of sweet sounds, vivacious voices and resonant rhythms – can be mine for only the equivalent of the average weekly wage. Truly, a bargain at half the price.

I can envisage the typical *Fortunette* walking into the Zone, eyes glittering expectantly, brow slick with sweat and hamster heart virtually vibrating with anticipation. Clutched in her sweaty palm is a wad of crisp notes, fresh from the cash dispenser. Or maybe she's got Daddy's plastic in her paw. I've got a fevered imagination but that doesn't mean I work out every last detail. She walks up to the counter, head pounding, stomach churning, and asks in a croaky voice, hoarse with excitement, for the box set. The salesperson frowns then stares at the cash in her hand and raises an eyebrow. The misguided larva's gaze is fixed on the box set as the salesperson reaches up and brings it down from the top shelf. Parted from her money, she cradles the box set in her arms as if it was a sleeping baby then trots out of the shop with an inane grin on her shining face.

Myself, I'd rather get down on my hands and knees and eat dog turds off the pavement than be seen buying such musical excrement, which is why I'm thinking of approaching Bass. I've seen it online but it's actually considerably more expensive so it rather looks as though that copy in The Zone has my name on it. I'm hoping to have a word with Bass tonight, see if he'll buy it for me, but if he can't or won't then I'll just have to gird my loins and buy it myself.

If I'm left with no alternative, I'll go down to The Zone tomorrow after school and sit on our bench. From there, I'll have a good view up and down the street. When there's no one in the shop and the street is clear of prospective patrons, I'll dash in. Once I've ascertained the coast is clear, made sure that Apollonia isn't serving behind the counter, and double-checked that that there's no one around who could pick me out in a line-up, then I'll point an accusatory finger at the damned thing and say:

"*That*, please."

"What, Abba: The Purgatory Years?"

"No, the one next to it."

"The St. Winifred's School Choir: A Retrospective?"

"No, you cream puff, the one on the other side."

"Oh, you mean the 4Tune8 box set."

"Yes, that one, you tube of spermicidal jelly, and be quick about it."

"It's quite expensive, you know. It's a Japanese import."

"Hey, I'm shaking with fascination here. Just give me the bloody thing, will you?"

"OK. That'll be seven thousand pounds, sir, and ninety-nine pence."

"Here, it's all there. You don't need to count it."

A year passes while the anencephalic toadstool holds up each note to the light.

"Thank you, sir. Would you like a receipt?"

"Just stick it in a brown paper bag, thank you."

"We're doing a 4Tune8 promotion this week: a free poster with any purchase of a 4Tune8 product over the value of five pence. Would you like one?"

"Only if I can ram it down your throat, you demented leprechaun."

Half a dozen friends enter the shop.

"Hey, Johnny, what's that you're buying?"

"Nothing."

"Hey, he's bought that 4Tune8 box set!"

They start laughing and pointing at me. I drop the box set and the discs spill out, one of which has a photograph of Luke on the cover. I stare at it and, as the volume of my friends' raucous laughter increases, I can see Lovely Luke winking at me. My bones disintegrate with shame and I collapse onto the floor in a gelatinous heap. Existence in this form proves impossible and I shuffle (gratefully) off this mortal coil. No one attends my funeral. On my headstone, it read: "Here Lies Atticus Childress: A Big Girl's Blouse".

As my malignant male sibling scoops the last of the ice-cream from his bowl I pray that Bass will consent to buy Rosie's present for me. When Bennie's removed all the ice-cream that he can with his spoon, he lifts the bowl up to his face and starts licking it.

"Benjamin!" hisses Mum. "Where are your manners?"

"Same place as his brain," I say. "He flushed them down the toilet years ago."

Bennie grimaces, his version of a sarcastic leer. "You're *so* funny, Atticus. You really ought to be on the telly."

"Yeah, right. On the news, for killing my baby brother."

"I am not a baby!" he screeches.

"Well, only babies wet their beds."

"I do not wet my bed!"

It's amazing how quickly the twisted Munchkin rises to the bait.

"Tell him, Mum," he says imploringly.

"Atticus," says Mum in her you-know-better-than-that voice.

"So," says Dad, addressing Rosie, "have you decided what you want to do on Saturday?"

A few months ago, it had been planned to amalgamate the Childress Summer Hog Roast and Rosie's party. Then, for a number of reasons, not least the fact that Rosie decided she didn't want a truck-load of our parents' alcoholic friends at her party, a separate event was scheduled. My parents offered to fork out for an elaborate *Sweet Sixteen*-type party – pink balloons, mobile disco, etc. – which Rosie understandably declined. The last I heard, Rosie was prevaricating between a smaller affair, to which only close friends and relatives would be invited, and Dad's offer to take us all out for a *slap up meal*, as he so delicately put it.

"I thought I'd just have a few friends around."

Dad looks confused. "Eh?"

"You know, Mamta, Dawn, a few others."

"To do what?"

Rosie begins to speak but Mum pre-empts her. "To sprawl on the furniture and stare at their phones while talking about boys. You know, the things sixteen-year-old girls do."

"I don't think we'll be talking about boys," says Rosie, looking at me.

"Oh," says Dad, "you mean you don't want to go out for a meal, then?"

Mum clucks. "You and your stomach."

Dad assumes an expression of profound distress. "And what's wrong with wanting to spend some time with my favourite daughter on her sixteenth birthday?"

"Dad!" says Bennie. "She's your *only* daughter."

He always falls for that one.

Mum turns to Rosie. "Well, what about we all go out for lunch?"

Rosie glances at me then Dad. "I don't know..."

"We'd like to spend *some* time with you on your birthday," says Mum.

"Yes, I know, it's just that..."

Rosie seems to have been struck by a curious inability to complete a sentence. I feel like standing up and putting her out of her misery. *Hey, everybody, the reason she doesn't want to go out for a meal is because she can't bear the sight of me.*

"She doesn't want Atticus there," says Bennie, smirking the smirk of the perpetually irritating little three-toed sloth that he is.

While Rosie glares at our diplomatically-challenged sibling, Mum and Dad exchange perplexed glances.

"What?" asks Mum.

Bennie continues to smirk alternately at Rosie and myself. If I could be absolutely certain that I could convince a jury it was justifiable homicide, I'd grab the paediatric Judas by his ankles and swing him like a baseball bat into the refrigerator. Repeatedly.

"What's he talking about?" asks Dad, looking around the table.

"No idea," I say.

"Rosie?"

"How should I know?"

I sense yet another shift in the general scheme of things. Until now, Rosie would have been only too ready to inform Mum and Dad of our altercation, but she realises, as do I, that this is between her and me. Unlike Bennie, who clearly relishes the possibility of a good old-fashioned family fight, with accusations flying like flying things, Rosie appears to prefer to keep this a strictly inter-sibling squabble. Strangely, I feel closer to her. Also, I perceive the opportunity to score a few Brownie points.

"Look, Mum, it's really nothing," I say. "I made a few disparaging remarks about Rosie's friends which I admit were completely out of order and for which I apologise one hundred per cent. There's nothing I'd like more than to celebrate Rosie's birthday *en famille* and I'm absolutely certain Rosie would love it as well."

Mum purses her lips then turns to my scowling sister. "Rosie?"

Dad is looking at me sceptically. His bullshit detector is a lot more sensitive than Mum's. I suppose it's more or less a prerequisite for being a GP. I give him my best lupine smile. *Hey, I know I'm bullshitting and I know* you *know I'm bullshitting, but let's just run with it and see what happens, OK?*

"Of course I'd like us all to go out," says Rosie.

"You see," I say, "Bennie just got the wrong end of the stick. He should keep his anteater nose out of other people's business, that's all."

"Good," says Dad, having sensibly decided to keep his reservations to himself. "In that case, I'll book a table tomorrow."

"Got to go," I say, rising to my feet. "Auditions tonight."

"I thought they were the week after next," says Mum, looking bewildered.

Now, I'm confused. "No, tonight."

"I'm sure Lucinda said they were the week after next."

The penny drops. "No, not *that*. We're auditioning a guitarist and a keyboard player for our band."

"The Liquid Pineapples?" asks Dad.

"Actually, it's Silicone Cucumbers now."

"*Silly* Cucumbers," says Bennie.

"Ow, my ribs," I say, deadpan.

"Silicone Cucumbers," says Mum. "That sounds a bit-"

"Silly," says Bennie, chortling.

"-suspect."

"Suspicious, more like," says Bennie.

"Well, I'd love to stay and chat with Mr Tautology here but, as I said, I've got to go."

On my way out of the kitchen I walk past Rosie who wrinkles her nose and glowers at me. I blow her a kiss, secure in the knowledge that, however she subsequently considers me, she's going to get one heck of a surprise when she opens her birthday present.

Normally, the walk to Red's takes me past Lucinda's house but I am reluctant to tempt fate this evening. Instead

I opt for a more circuitous route that allows me to purchase a packet of chewing gum from the *The Corner Shoppe*, where I can also ascertain what Sandra is wearing today.

That I am fascinated by Sandra – the twenty-year-old seductress who serves behind the counter – will not come as a big shock to you. However, what may surprise you is that my interest in her is of an utterly asexual nature. This is because Sandra is an *indifferent enchantress*, one of that group of peculiar women who apparently go to great lengths to appear sexually alluring yet who are so obviously unconcerned about the effect they might exert on members of the opposite sex that their lasciviousness is quite nullified. The aloofness of the indifferent enchantress goes far beyond the prostitute's clinical detachment, the overriding impression gained being a few light-years the other side of apathy. Overall, the effect is more than a little disconcerting.

This evening Sandra is wearing a denim outfit, an all-in-one affair, the top of which looks like a suit jacket with cut-off sleeves, the bottom part being very brief shorts. She's wearing black fishnet tights and a pair of black shoes that look like school-girl sandals with a kilogramme of thick rubber grafted onto their soles. It's as though The Spice Girls are alive and well and working in your local fishmonger's. Her top is unbuttoned an inch further than might generally be considered acceptable, revealing a lavish expanse of tanned cleavage, and her shorts are cut high enough to enable a tantalising glimpse of the swell of her buttocks. Long, straight, dark brown hair frames her pleasantly round face. Her make-up has been skilfully applied, highlighting rather than concealing her features.

So far, so good, you're probably thinking – or *What a tart!* depending on your sexual orientation – and I would agree with you, if only she would smile, or exchange meaningless pleasantries, or do or say something that might indicate an interest in anything. As it is, she merely stares blankly at an invisible object approximately twelve inches in front of her milk chocolate eyes. Fruit and nut, I think.

I thought at one point that Sandra might be myopic – short-sighted people who do not wear spectacles, whether through forgetfulness or vanity, often appear indifferent, as well as bloody silly. Then, I considered that it might just be me with whom she is so offhand. One day, I stood at the end of a long queue of people waiting to be served. Each patron, male and female, young and aged, she treated in the same manner. I can remember that day quite clearly because she was wearing a cropped top and I watched her carefully for five minutes as she served each customer – turning to pick a pack of cigarettes from the display behind her or bending to open a jar of confectionery – observing the pleasing sway of her Christmas baubles.

I suppose she has a boyfriend somewhere, although I've never seen him. I hope, for his sake, when with him she behaves more congenially. I suspect, though, that, if he exists, Sandra's partner is a male version of the indifferent enchantress – the soporific stud, perhaps. Together, arm in arm, on a Saturday afternoon, they probably go the local covered shopping mega-mall, her curves drawing admiring glances from passing men, his square jaw and prominent muscles attracting similar attention from young mums, both oblivious to each other and their environment, their minds awash with God knows what. In the evening, they drive in his car to a quiet spot where they have an extended session of mindless, pneumatic sexual intercourse, the air filling with her quiet moans, his muffled grunts and the unmistakable aroma of indifferent sexual secretions.

Actually, the more I think about it, the less specious the possibility becomes of Sandra being an alien sent to earth to observe the indigenous population.

"Tea. Earl Grey. Hot," I mutter under my breath as I drop a pound coin into her immaculately manicured hand. Her lack of response neither proves nor disproves my theory. If she is an alien, they must be a very stupid race. I saunter over to the magazine rack, glancing at the top shelf. The skin-mags are all wrapped so that only the titles are visible. Sigh.

I pop a stick of gum in my mouth then pick up an issue of a magazine dedicated to consumer tech. *Shite You Don't Really Need But Want Really Badly* it's called, or something like that. I turn to the spread about a third of the way in where there are several high-def photos of a shapely beauty cradling various models of TV remote control, or 3D printer, or something. I'm not looking at the tech. She's wearing a very fetching pair of gold stripper heels. Massive clear plastic platforms and, I'd wager, nine inch heels. Nearly impossible to walk in. But I wouldn't want her to be walking anywhere. If we met in real life, she'd no doubt be kicking them off as fast as possible and running in the opposite direction as quickly as her Pilates-toned legs could carry her. Chewing the gum, I spend a happy minute wondering what we could do if she *didn't* find me abhorrent.

I glance at Sandra who is staring blankly at the display of bread and rolls opposite her, reinforcing the impression that she's an android awaiting input. As an osteoporotic granny enters the shop(pe), I abandon further meditation on matters pornographic and make my way to Red's house.

204

[23] Prospective Cucumbers

Bass, Red and I have arranged to meet at twenty to seven, giving us the best part of an hour to warm up before the two prospective Silicone Cucumbers arrive. This was my idea, strongly supported by Bass – neither of us have any wish to embarrass ourselves. Red, typically, was in favour of purposely *not* rehearsing prior to the arrival of Derek and Suzz, in order that they might experience the full force of Silicone Cucumber music in its most 'raw, in-your-face magnificence', as he put it. Bass and I eventually persuaded him that they were unlikely to be impressed by the tuneless, unsynchronised clamour that would most probably result. Convincing him that drum solos would be equally ill-advised proved more difficult. Eventually, though, he relented which is why, presumably, it sounds as if a herd of elephants are stomping around the garage as I walk up the drive.

Bass hails me from behind and I wait for him to catch up.

"What an infernal racket," he says.

"At least he's getting it out of his system."

"One can but hope."

"These two still coming tonight, are they?"

"As far as I know."

"I mean, you've not forgotten to tell us that they can't make it, or anything?"

"No," he says curtly.

"Just checking."

As Bass opens the side door the cacophonous roar of Red's frenzied tub-thumping suddenly stops. The silence is almost as deafening.

"Oh, it's you," says Red as we walk in.

"Who were you expecting," I ask, "the noise pollution police?"

"I thought it might be Derek or this Suzz person."

"There not coming until half past," I say, looking at Bass for confirmation.

"No," he says slowly, "seven."

"What? You said half past."

"Did I? I'm sure I told them to come at seven, although it might have been half past."

"Bass, you bedpan! Which is it? Seven or half past? Message them now. Find out when *exactly* they're coming."

"What does it matter? Even if it's seven, we've still got twenty minutes to run through a few numbers."

"He's right," says Red, adjusting the high-hat screw. "It doesn't matter."

Further argument is pointless so I cross to the other side of the garage and open my guitar case. It takes Bass and me a few minutes to tune our instruments. Red knows better than to make a sound during this procedure so he sits on his stool and stares alternately at the two of us. Finally, the minuscule amount of patience at his disposal runs out.

"OK," he says, exasperated, "enough bloody noodling. It's good enough for metal."

"*Sanitar-?*" Bass starts to suggest before being drowned out by Red's explosive interpretation of the drum riff that comes in half way through the song.

After exchanging glances of resignation, Bass and I join in. We plod though it but with Red's over-amplified thundering and no one singing or playing the guitar solos we sound worse than third-rate.

"Brilliant!" whoops Red as we finish. "See? We didn't need to run through anything, did we? Derek and Suzz are going to be blown away."

"They might *run* away," I say.

"Let's go through it again," says Bass, "but you've got to bring it down, Red. The drums are just *way* too loud."

"Metal can never be too loud," all three of us say in unison.

Bass and I grin at Red's petulant expression.

"Fine," he says, turning around and flicking off his amplifiers, "if that's the way you want it."

We start again, this time with Red merely keeping the beat with his bass drum. After a few bars, Bass and I stop playing. The echo of my last chord bounces around the garage. Bass, looking decidedly pissed off, walks up to Red.

"What the bloody hell do you think you're playing at?"

"Hey, *you* asked me to bring it down."

"Ha-ha-ha-ha-ha. Very funny. Why is it that the drummer always has to be a bloody joker?"

Red looks away and I check the time. "Come on, you two, we've only got another ten minutes."

Bass walks back to his original position, muttering something under his breath. Red has discovered a minor imperfection in one of his sticks and is holding it six inches from his face.

"What about *Steel Through Flesh*?" I suggest, hoping this will cheer up Bass. "You can *handle the vocal chores*, can't you?"

"You know I can't sing."

"You can sing better than me."

"OK, OK," he says, holding up both hands.

"Red, why don't you switch a couple of amplifiers back on?"

He shrugs apathetically. A few seconds pass before he sighs then reaches out to flick on one switch.

"One, two, three, four..." I shout.

Bass's singing voice makes him sound a bit like one of Leonard Cohen's distant relatives, from a funereal branch of the family that *really* knows the meaning of despondency. Still, it rather suits the lyrics and as we get to the chorus for the last time I'm surprised to find that I'm impressed. Despite my disparaging remarks, and his own protestations, perhaps the best person to sing Bass's songs is Bass. He turns and sees me looking at him.

"That was the shizzle, mate," I say.

"Really?" asks Bass.

Red shrugs. "Could've been worse, I suppose."

I walk across to Bass. "Have you finished *Decaying Emotions*?"

"Yeah," he says, reaching down and pulling out a few sheets of paper from his guitar case. "Here're the chord changes and I've got the lyrics somewhere."

I watch Bass as he hums the first few bars of the melody and beats out the rhythm on the body of his guitar that he'd like Red to follow. A little encouragement from me and he seems transformed. I smile, watching him playing the main riff. It's funny, really, the different roles we adopt in different situations. Outside this garage, Bass and Red generally look to me for leadership. I'm too lazy to make up my own analogy, which is a shame because I could then dazzle you with my piercing insight, so I'll compare the three of us to chess pieces instead. Boring and predictable, perhaps, but pertinent just the same.

208

I'm the king; surveying the field, making decisions and plotting strategies. Bass is a bishop; thoughtful, introspective, approaching problems obliquely. Red is a knight; brave, foolhardy, charging around the place erratically. Of course, our ultimate aim is to capture the opposing queen, albeit in our own different ways.

When it comes to Silicone Cucumbers, though, things are different. Like all good leaders, I know when to delegate. Bass, the musician, is best placed to deal with the nuts and bolts of song structure, who should play what, when and how. I hesitate to use the word *arrangement* for obvious reasons. Red is, as Bass has already pointed out, the irrepressible joker, and he's the one whose character alters least. When it comes to my role in the band, I've always been pretty certain that, should we get anywhere, which is pretty unlikely, I'd stop playing and move into management. The history of rock 'n' roll is littered with men who used to play in the group they end up managing. Of course, a few years later, when the band reach near-stadium status they usually ditch their old friend (often acrimoniously) and sign up with a proper management company. Whether or not my ability to foresee such an event would help me prevent it happening is another matter entirely.

"Hey, Johnny, you following this?" asks Bass.

"Sure, looks easy enough," I say, squinting for the first time at his barely legible handwriting.

"OK, then."

Bass nods at Red who taps his sticks to lead us in then starts up a rolling drum pattern which sounds not unlike something off the first Joy Division album. Bass comes in with an insistent rumbling riff and I begin to cautiously strum a few chords. When we play through it for the fourth time, Bass adds some vocals. Without the benefit of the written lyrics, I'm unable to make them out although the words death and decay crop up fairly frequently. It's quite some time before I glance at my watch.

"Hey, it's almost eight!"

"Where are they?" asks Red, sweat streaming down his frowning face.

"You did tell them it was tonight, didn't you?"

Bass's expression is a dissertation on perplexity.

"Bass, you turbocharged twit," says Red, "don't tell me-"

Someone knocks on the door then opens it and enters. I recognise Derek immediately from behind the counter at The Zone. Though I never knew his name, I've spent many an hour discussing all things metal with him. And Derek, it seems, knows *my* name.

"Hey, Johnny," he says. "I didn't know you'd be here."

"And I didn't know you played guitar."

He laughs. "I'm the original bedroom superstar."

"In that case, you should fit right in."

"Hey, Red," he says. "You as well, eh? And Bass! I had no idea it was you lot that put up that notice."

While Derek opens his case and withdraws a battered Stratocaster, the three of us exchange a series of confused shrugs and grimaces.

"Have I got much competition tonight?"

"Uh, no," says Bass. "You're the only guitarist who phoned but we are expecting a keyboard player."

"Yeah? So I'm in with a chance, am I?" he asks, strapping on his guitar.

"That looks as though it's seen better days," says Red.

Derek holds up the Strat. "This baby's been around the world a few times. Used to belong to one of the blokes in Maiden or one of them in Leppard, you know."

"Wow," says Red, staring at Derek's guitar as though it were made of solid gold.

"Hang on," I say, "don't you know *which* one of them it belonged to?"

"No, but it *was* one of them."

"How do you know that?"

"Polly gave it to me last Christmas and she said she couldn't remember which one of them had given it to her although she was certain it was definitely someone from either Maiden or Leppard."

"You mean Apollonia Wallace gave it to you?"

"Yeah."

"Wow," says Red.

"Wow," says Bass.

"World of bloody Warcraft," I add, not wanting to be left out.

"Hellfire," says Derek, scoping the array of amplifiers and stacks behind Red. "There's enough power here to blow the bloody doors off."

"Damn straight," says Red, unable to contain his glee.

"Which one?" asks Derek, holding up his guitar lead.

While Red and Derek sort things out, I beckon Bass.

"What shall we start with?"

Bass shakes his head. "Why don't we ask him what he knows?"

"No, we want to play something *we* know, don't we?"

211

"I guess. What about *Sanitarium*, then?"

The air is split by the teeth-jarring howl of a power-chord. Red and Derek grin inanely at each other. Then Derek starts playing the main riff from Maiden's *Hallowed Be Thy Name*. Bass and I turn to watch him. When he gets to the solo, it's note perfect. Red, totally enraptured, turns to look at us, his eyes shining, then returns his attention to Derek's fingers which are skittering up and down the fretboard like a spider on crystal.

I nudge Bass, who's as mesmerised as Red, and nod toward the door. Smiling, I give Derek the thumbs-up sign as I lead Bass outside.

"He's bloody good," says Bass.

"Yeah. Maybe too good."

"Pearls Before Swine Part Two?"

I nod then turn as a huge black Mercedes estate with very dark windows sails up the drive. "Are Red's parents back from wherever it is they were?"

"I don't think so," he says as we both watch the purring car gently come to a halt. "I think he said they were arriving late Saturday night."

"Who's this, then? One of his Dad's business friends?"

The car's engine is switched off, the driver's door opens and Suzana Comănici-Jenkins climbs out. She closes the door then walks around to the front of the car. Her jet black hair is tied back in a pony-tail. She's wearing a black singlet, black mini-skirt over black tights and black Doc Marten's. She is strikingly tall and slim. The virtual translucence of her pale skin is arresting. Hanging on a chain around her neck is a large silver crucifix. Each of her fingers is crammed with silver rings, as are her wrists with silver bangles. Through each ear-lobe passes a large silver hoop. It definitely looks as if she's plumped for the good old black and silver look tonight. What remains unfathomable is what she's doing here.

I stoop to pick up my jaw from the ground then say: "Hello." In reality, my mouth is so dry, what comes out is more of a croaked *ay-oh*. I cough noisily.

Seeming to understand, Suzana nods. I really don't remember her skin seeming so pale when I've seen her around school. Maybe she donated blood this afternoon and they left the tubing in her vein for too long.

"Lost?" I inquire.

After a few seconds silence, during which Red has presumably turned the volume knob up another notch, Derek starts chopping out a Megadeth riff.

"I don't think so," says Suzana, glancing at the garage door then back at us.

I look at Bass to see whether he's as stumped as me. His face, initially blank, lights up.

"You're Suzz," he says, pointing at her, supposedly in case she didn't realise she was the focus of his accusation.

"Bingo," she says, deadpan.

A few hundred questions make a dash for the tip of my tongue but I decide to keep my mouth shut for the time being and see how things pan out. Unfortunately, things seem unable to pan out just yet, the three of us are frozen in a tableau which might be called: 'Three Confused Teenagers Wondering What Happened to Their Tongues'. Finally, Bass clears his throat.

"I spoke to you on the phone," he says, eschewing situation development in favour of recapitulation.

"Right," she says, extending her left hand to lean on the bonnet, "Oscar, isn't it?"

213

"They call me Bass."

"Do they?"

"And this is Johnny... I mean, Atticus, but we call him Johnny."

Suzana looks directly at me, nodding her head slowly. "Do we indeed?"

The dozen words Suzana Comănici-Jenkins has spoken so far more or less doubles the number I've *ever* heard pass her lips – or Suzz's lips, I should say. Earlier, I've mentioned that the overriding impression one gets of her is that she's not quite of this earth, but I realise now that I've never really been the target of her attention, as I am now.

Her dark stare roots me to the spot and I feel as though I am being scanned – probed, even. The sensation is really quite uncomfortable and I can only meet her gaze for a few seconds before I am forced to look down at her chest. She has no breasts to speak of although I can clearly see the outline of her nipples. I realise that she must know I'm looking at her chest so I quickly return my gaze to her face. Thankfully, she has turned her attention back to Bass, though a nagging concern about what she must now think of me lingers like a bad aftertaste.

"I didn't realise it was you," says Bass. "I mean, when I spoke to you on the phone, I didn't realise that you were... you know, that you-"

"No?" she says calmly.

"Did you know who we were? You know, that I was... well, you know... that I... that is, that we..."

I watch Suzz while Bass manages to make a dog's dinner out of a simple question. I'm now almost certain that I've seriously misjudged her in the past. From her keen, appraising expression, I think that there's one hell of a lot

214

more going on inside her head than I've ever given her credit for – by at least a couple of orders of magnitude. I had classified her as a kind of gothic bimbo whereas I now get the impression that it's more a case that she chooses very carefully those people with whom she wishes to interact on a meaningful level, which is why, presumably, she's just staring at Bass as though he was an upended tortoise struggling to right itself. I have to agree with her because, to utilise another simile and a few more commas, Bass is, for some reason, behaving like a flustered child trying to explain that it was 'Mr. Nobody' that broke that expensive vase.

"Yes," she says finally, putting him out of his misery.

"Oh," he murmurs.

"Nice car," I say, immediately wishing I hadn't.

Suzz smiles sweetly. "Daddy gave it to me for my birthday."

"Really?" asks Bass, obviously impressed, and just as obviously immune to her sarcasm.

"No," she says, shaking her head sadly, "I just borrowed it."

The pause button is pressed again as Bass licks his lips and stares at the car. Suzz stares at him, presumably trying to work out if he's as stupid as he seems and I stare at her, wondering just what the evening has in store for us all. After half a minute, Suzz walks toward us then turns and heads to the rear of the car.

"I'm going to need some help," she says.

I start to follow her but Bass grabs my shoulder and turns me around. I can't be certain but I think his expression means: *Leave this to me.* You *go back into the garage, OK?*

I could be wrong but, nevertheless, I stand to one side, allowing him to trot after Suzz like an exuberant puppy.

Red and Derek are jamming – *Voodoo Chile*, I think – and take no notice of me as I enter the garage and walk across to the far side where I slump down into a battered armchair. I am unable to assimilate everything that's happened in the last ten minutes, never mind compute significance.

Go with the flow, Atticus.

I heed my elder sibling's words of wisdom and attempt to clear my mind, which isn't easy with the racket Red and Derek are making. The door opens again and Bass backs in, carrying one end of a black (surprise, surprise) case. Suzz follows and I turn to watch Red, waiting for him to identify her. He's so absorbed, however, that it isn't until she walks right in front of his kit that he sees her. He freezes, mouth gaping, sticks held in mid-air. Derek squeezes out a flurry of notes before realising that his accompaniment has disappeared. The last note ricochets around the garage, bouncing off the walls and finally striking Red right between the eyes. His jaw snaps shut in surprise and he looks over at me for explanation. All I can do is shrug.

"Hey, Suzz!" cries Derek.

Red silently mouths her name at me and raises his eyebrows.

Suzz and Bass set down the case then she walks over to Derek, with Bass following obediently behind.

Derek slots his plectrum between strings and fretboard. "They didn't tell me it was you that was coming tonight."

Suzz's face is transformed by a wide grin. This is the first time I have ever seen her smile. "I don't think they knew it was me, either."

I'm not certain I like being referred to as 'they'.

"That sounded good," she says, looking at Derek then turning to Red.

"You know Red, don't you?" asks Bass. "Well, his name's Dom – Dominic – really, but we call him Red."

"Hey," says Suzz.

Red nods, emotions whizzing across his face like one of those time-lapse films of clouds scudding across the sky. I can't see Suzz's face but I watch her head slowly swivelling from one side to the other as she studies the stacks behind Red. Her singlet is cut very low at the back, almost to the waistband of her skirt, revealing an expanse of white flesh, bisected by the long, ridged profile of her vertebrae. Within a few years this blank canvas will probably be covered by a detailed tattoo of Cthulhu rising up from his watery domain.

Ph'nglui mglw'nafh Cthulhu R'lyeh wgah'nagl fhtagn.

Couldn't have put it better myself.

"Quite some setup you've got here," she says, which invokes an uncertain grin from Red.

"Thanks," he mutters.

"Makes a bloody good noise," says Derek.

"So I heard."

"Do you want me to help you set up your keyboard?" asks Bass.

"Sure, why not?"

Suzz walks over to her case and squats down to unfasten a series of clips. Bass follows her and kneels down to help. Derek strolls across to watch.

217

"Hey, that bootleg CD you loaned me was pretty OK," he says to Suzz.

"Glad you liked it."

As Derek and Suzz begin to discuss the merits of some obscure South American death metal band, Red takes the opportunity to scurry out from behind his kit and over to me.

"That's Suzana Comănici-Jenkins," he whispers.

"What was your first clue?"

"Jesus! Suzana Comănici-Jenkins is in my garage. My mind is *way* past blown. Brain fragments are spattered on the ceiling."

Bass helps Suzz to lift the keyboard out of its case. They angle it forwards to extend its legs and I can see that it's a top-of-the-range Roland.

"God, look at that!" hisses Red.

Leaving Bass and Suzz to get on with it, Derek wanders across to where Bass usually stands. After scrutinising the music sheet on Bass's stand for a few moments he withdraws his plectrum and plays the first few chords of *Decaying Emotions*.

"You write this?" he says.

"Um, yeah," answers Bass as he plugs in the keyboard lead.

"Not bad. Got any more copies?"

Reluctantly leaving Suzz flicking switches and nudging sliders on the Roland, Bass walks across to his case, bends over and picks up a sheaf of photocopies. Despite his many faults, Bass takes his music very seriously and has obviously come well prepared tonight. He sorts through the sheaf, occasionally picking out a sheet and handing it to Derek.

"You write all these?"

218

Bass nods, pleased that Derek is impressed.

"What's that one?" asks Derek, pointing at a music sheet in Bass's hand. "*Stiletto Stamina*?"

"Oh," says Bass, looking over at me, "that's one Johnny wrote."

His dismissive tone irks me slightly – well, quite a bit, actually – but I'm determined to ride the tide. Suzz plays a long jazz-tinged run on the Roland, using the digital piano voice, then a sequence of staccato chords which initially sound random before I realise she's improvising on the final section of *Stairway to Heaven*. During her mini-recital, Bass and Derek wander across and stand behind her, grinning appreciatively. Suzz finishes off with the piano refrain from *Epic* by Faith No More. Bass is practically quivering with excitement. *Epic* is his number one favourite song. I could not even begin to tell you how many times I've argued with him about this, but he won't budge.

"God, that's brilliant!" he exclaims and I can see it's all he can do to stop himself from clapping. Or wetting himself.

"She's pretty good," whispers Red.

"Yeah," I say hoarsely. Anybody with a brain bigger than a walnut would realise that Suzz can play – and, luckily, Red just about meets this criterion.

"Just a little thing I picked up at the academy," says Suzz, leaning to one side to check some switches.

"The *Royal* Academy of Music?" asks Bass, astonished.

Suzz twists around to look at him. "Just joking."

Derek sniggers. "Hey, Bass, are we going to stand here all night all are we going to play something?"

Bass bites his lower lip, as if he *would* rather stand there listening to Suzz playing. "OK, what do you want to start with?"

Before Derek can answer, I leap up and walk swiftly over to them. "How about *Sanitarium*? Do you know that one?"

"I can play it in my sleep, Johnny, my son."

"Right," I say, trying not to let my disappointment show. "What about you, er... Suzz?"

Try as I might, I am having a great deal of difficulty becoming accustomed to calling Suzana Comănici-Jenkins *Suzz*.

"Sure, whatever."

"Hey, hang on," says Red as he comes over to join us, "you can't have keyboards on a Metallica song."

Silence.

I stare at Red, uncertain whether he is purposely being a major hosepipe or whether he really is that insensitive. Derek is scowling, presumably with similar thoughts to mine running through his head. Bass, on the other hand, looks ready to explode. His eyes are practically bulging out of their sockets. His face is turning dusky red. And the visible pulse in his neck veins ticks like a time-bomb.

"Red!" he splutters, as though the name was like dog shit in his mouth. "If *we* want to have keyboards on a Metallica song, or any other bloody song for that matter, we can, because it's *our* band and we can do whatever we want, and if you're not happy with that, you can bloody well piss off, OK?"

Red seems somewhat taken aback by the force of Bass's tirade, as am I. He looks at me then Derek but can find no evidence that we support his viewpoint. He does not look at Suzz.

"Fine," he says, walking around his kit to sit on his stool.

"Hey, I can always sit this one out," says Suzz.

"No!" shouts Bass with way too much urgency. "You'll do no such thing."

Red is sitting very still, staring blankly at his high-hat.

"Johnny," says Bass, "start with the intro, will you?"

I walk over to my guitar, pick it up, and sling the strap around my neck. I strum a chord then adjust the volume. When I look up, all four of them are looking at me expectantly and my pulse quickens a little. It's not that I'm nervous or anything, it's just that I'm... well, OK, so what if I feel slightly anxious? Who wouldn't? Suzz is obviously something of a virtuoso, and Derek's even better than Phil. It crosses my mind to ask Derek if he wants to play the intro but I know exactly how that would make me look.

Ride the tide.

I grit my teeth – it always helps to tense yourself up, doesn't it? – and start playing. The first few bars are mostly harmonics and it's difficult to go too far wrong. Thirty seconds into it, I realise that Red should have started playing as well – striking a few cymbals in an aesthetically pleasing way. When I glance over at him, he's still sulking, glaring at his high-hat as though waiting for it to agree with him that keyboards have no place in a Metallica song. I look at Bass who's staring at Red, infuriated by his childish behaviour. I stop playing.

"One moment," I say to Bass as I walk over to Red.

I crouch down next to him and lower my voice so that no one else can hear. "Listen, you puerile hedge-trimmer, you're acting like a spoiled child. *I* know you've set yourself up as the defender of all things metallic but, look, for *my* sake and for *Bass's* sake, just try and pull yourself together."

"You can't have keyboards," he hisses and, if I didn't know him better, I'd say he was close to tears.

"Look, I'll tell you what. Just play along, exactly as you always do, and let Suzz play whatever she wants, and if it sounds crap I promise you I'll be the first to say so."

"Come on," says Bass. "What's going on?"

I look over my shoulder at him. "We're just discussing how Red should play during the intro."

"Exactly as he always-"

The anger in my eyes silences him. I'll bet you never guessed the interpersonal dynamics of a Silicone Cucumbers rehearsal were so complicated, did you? I turn back to Red.

"In case you hadn't noticed, Bass has got a big-time thing for Suzz."

Red's eyebrows shoot upwards.

"That's right, although God knows why. And, if you bugger this up, I'm not going to be responsible for what he'll do to you. OK?"

"OK."

"Sure?"

He nods.

"Right," I say loudly as I stand up, "we've got it sorted out now, haven't we, Red?"

"Yeah, right," he says to Bass. "Sorry, I thought Johnny was going to play the intro on his own."

I walk back to my original position. "Off we go, then."

Red glances at Suzz who's staring at him suspiciously. "Sorry," he says.

I start playing once again and this time Red comes in at the right moment, followed soon afterwards by Derek, pulling a few comical grimaces as he plays the lead. I'm reassured to see Bass smiling at Derek's antics. After a couple of minutes, Bass leans over to the microphone and starts singing. His eyes are closed and I can see he's putting as much emotion as he can muster into the words. Whether or not this has anything to do with Suzz's presence, I can only guess, although I'd stake a few million quid on it. He really has fallen for her in a big way.

Four minutes in and we hit the main riff for the first time. It always sends a few shivers down my spine. I meet Derek's gaze as we chop away gleefully. Bass sings another chorus and then Derek's off with a staggering solo. I glance at Suzz for the first time. Her head is bobbing up and down, eyes closed, and I have to concentrate to hear the quiet string-voice accompaniment she's playing. Red is hunched over his kit, solidly keeping the beat, smiling as Derek lets rip. We enter the final section in a major groove. We're all into it and, even if I do say so myself, we sound as tight as rat's tight thing. Derek's really flying and Bass has an exceptionally stupid grin plastered right across his face. We reach the last few chords, each one more ponderous than the last, and Red does his manic metal drummer routine, hitting every item of his kit as hard as he can. The last chord reverberates around the garage and we all look at each other, nodding and smiling.

"Bloody amazing!" gasps Derek, and I have to agree with him. "I can't believe that's the first time we've played together."

Bass's eyes are glazed with ecstasy. "Again," he mumbles.

"Yeah!" shouts Red, adding a quick drum roll for emphasis.

Derek is nodding in agreement. I look at Suzz whose shrug I interpret as consent. We play the song once more and this time, unbelievably, it's sounds even better. As we're all hammering away at the main riff I realise that this is not only because Suzz is playing louder but because she's also playing a kind of counterpoint. Now, I'd be the first to admit that Metallica songs are not renowned for their intricacy of arrangement, so I am more than a tad astonished to discover how much Suzz's keyboards augment – nay, improve almost beyond recognition – this standard.

We reach the final chord again and all of us are sweating buckets, except Suzz who looks as though she's just sat down after a leisurely stroll. She gazes around the garage at each of us while we catch our breath. Red's face is buried in a towel while Derek and Bass are just standing there, grinning at each other. After a minute, during which my heart rate gradually returns to normal, Red looks up and shakes his head, his face bright red with exertion.

"That was absolutely incredible," Red says to no one in particular then turns to Suzz. "That was brilliant, what you were doing."

"Thank you," she says matter-of-factly.

"No, really," says Bass, "I thought you were fantastic. You made it sound thicker – fuller, even. The keyboards added a whole new layer to the sound."

Suzz smiles, as though uncertain about the presence of another agenda hiding behind such lavish praise. I could put her mind at rest.

224

"What shall we do next?" asks Red.

"What about one of Bass's songs?" suggests Derek.

"Oh, I don't know," says Bass. "I don't think any of them are much good, really."

"Rubbish!" I say. "Let's do *Decaying Emotions*. You'll like that one, Suzz. It could do with a *whole new layer*."

"Which one's that?" asks Derek as he flicks through the sheets on Bass's stand. "Oh, here it is. Yeah, this looks OK."

"I'm not so sure," mutters Bass.

Derek frowns. "Oh, shut up, Bass, there's no need for modesty here. We're all friends, aren't we?"

Bass look uncertainly over at Suzz, whose expression is as indecipherable as it has been since she arrived, more or less. "Well, OK, then."

Derek shuffles the music sheets. "Got a copy, Johnny?"

I nod.

"What about one for Suzz?"

"It's all right," she says. "Just start playing and I'll pick it up as we go along."

"You don't need the sheet music?" Bass asks Suzz, looking at her appraisingly. "You got perfect pitch or something?"

Suzz meets Bass's gaze, saying nothing.

"Right, OK," says Bass, eyes like wide round things. "Perfect pitch. No worries."

"Come on, then," I say. "Let's get going. Keiran, dim the lights."

Red starts the Joy Division-ish drum pattern then Bass comes in. Derek's marking time with his fingers on the body of his strat, his head and neck writhing like a spaced-out tortoise. Having recognised the key, Suzz begins to play, weaving a tapestry of synthesised strings. I join in and Derek follows my lead. When Bass starts to sing, I am startled by the increased strength of his voice. I can hear the lyrics more clearly this time, although they're not really worth reproducing here. If you can imagine an angst-ridden teenager's suicide note set to music, you'll have a rough idea. Still, his performance is nothing short of impressive. When we finish, Derek immediately looks at Red and commands him to start again, which he does, gladly. Once we've played it through another three times, Red stands up.

"Hey, I'd love to do it one more once," he says, walking past Derek and Bass, "but if I don't get some fluid in me, I'm going to faint. I'll get some stuff from the house. Back in a sec."

Bass unhooks his guitar and props it up against a speaker cabinet. "You want to sit out on the lawn? It'll be cooler."

Five minutes later, Red sits down on the grass beside us and begins to hand out cans of Diet Coke. "So then," he says to Bass, "have you asked these two if they want to be Silicone Cucumbers?"

"Yes, and no," says Bass, opening a can.
"Eh?"
"Yes, we'd love to be in the band," says Derek.
"Great!"
"But Suzz isn't too happy with the name."
"Oh."
"Bit too phallic for her liking, you see?"
"Uh-huh," says Red, looking at Suzz. "Well, that shouldn't be too much of a problem seeing as we change the name every other day."

"That's what Johnny was saying."

"And have you come up with an alternative?"

"Suzz fancies something with the word 'black' in the title," says Bass.

I can see Red's mind whirring as he tries to come up with a suitable comment. Sensibly, he resists the temptation. "Does she?"

"With an umlaut," says Suzz.

"What?"

Suzz sighs. "Two dots over the 'a'."

"I know what an umlaut is, thank you," says Red. "But wouldn't that mean it'd be pronounced *bleck* or *block*?"

"Not necessarily."

"So," says Bass, "we thought we could make the rest of the name something contrasting. You know, something that wouldn't normally make you think of black."

"Like a flower, or something," says Derek.

"Hey," says Red, "we're not calling the band after a flower."

"What's wrong with Bläck Petunia?" I ask, sniggering.

"Bläck Steel?" suggests Derek.

"Too obvious," says Bass. "Bläck... oh, I don't know. We need something pure. Something innocent."

"Baby," says Red. "Bläck Baby."

"I don't think so," says Suzz, rolling her eyes.

"No, no, wait," urges Red, grinning. "That would work, especially if you add another umlaut. Bläck Bäby. *The* Bläck Bäbies. What do you think?"

"No," all four of us say.

"I like the double umlaut idea, though," says Derek. "Bläck Räg. Bläck Bäg. Bläck Fläg. No, that's been done already."

Bass is staring at the Mercedes. "Bläck Cär. Bläck Jäg."

Derek laughs. "No, wait. What about Bläck Jäck?"

"Yeah," says Red. "That's pretty good."

"Not very contrasting," I say.

Bass continues to look around. "Bläck House. Bläck Tree. Bläck Shoe. Bläck Grass. Hey! What about that? Bläck Gräss?"

Suzz nods her head. "Could be a possibility."

Red holds his can up to his mouth as if it was a microphone. "'Joe Twit here, from Metal Insanity dot com, interviewing 'The Dominator', drummer with Bläck Gräss, currently topping metal charts around the world with their eponymous début album. So tell me, Dom, how did the band get its name?' 'Well, Joe, we like to think the name accurately reflects our scorched earth, post-apocalyptic terms of reference.'"

"And," says Derek in a slurred voice, "there's the inherent ambiguity of a thinly-veiled drug reference."

"Bläck Gräss," mutters Bass. "I'm not so sure."

"Wait a minute," I say, "I've got it. Bläck Gläss. That's perfect. Black: dark, absorbs light, supernatural. Glass: clear, reflects light, shiny."

The others look at me uncertainly. Bass is the first to start nodding.

"Possibly," he says. "What do you think, Suzz?"

"I quite like it."

Bass's eyes light up. "Yeah, it kind of grows on you. Bläck Gläss it is."

"Until we come up with something else," says Red.

228

As Derek, Bass and Red discuss the relative merits of tuning up the G-string on a bass guitar by one hundredth of a tone – or some other aspect of train-spotter-like musical minutiae – I kick back, cola can in hand, and mull over the proceedings so far. Red seems to have overcome his initial reticence about adding a keyboard player to the band. Just as well, really, as he'd be off his trolley otherwise. I knew Derek relatively well before tonight and I can't foresee any real problems, notwithstanding the possibility that he'll soon realise he could do much better elsewhere. There must be a hundred semi-pro metal bands that would kill to have a lead guitarist of his calibre. The same goes for Suzz, really. Just what she thinks she's doing here is completely beyond my ken – as is practically everything about her.

While attempting to appear as if I'm staring, preoccupied, into the middle distance, I covertly inspect her. She's leaning back on her elbows, crossed legs stretched out towards Bass. With her long, slender legs and slim torso, she's crying out to be dressed in glossy black latex – sorry, I mean bläck lätex. A high-necked, long-sleeved mistress dress would do the trick nicely, thank you very much. Her head is tilted up to the sky, allowing the setting sun to lend some colour to her pale skin and glint off her silver earrings. Her profile is not unappealing and, all in all, she is not exactly unattractive. It's not that I'm being particularly grudging with my praise here – OK, I am – but I continue to find it difficult to accept that Suzz is the same Suzana Comănici-Jenkins that I've seen practically every day at school for the last few years. Suzana Comănici-Jenkins is a seventeen-year-old quasi-Goth who, when addressed, gives the initial impression that you're speaking a different language. She reeks of profound introspection and pretentious mysticism.

The girl semi-reclined on the grass here, who wishes to be referred to as Suzz, gives off the powerful, and somewhat unsettling, aroma of supreme self-confidence. She has no doubts whatsoever about her musical skills, nor any qualms about what others might think of them. Not that she has any reason to be reserved, you understand, it's just that my own personal reaction is to treat self-assurance with liberal doses of caution. Of course this may be a character flaw on my part, and in some way related to feelings of low self-esteem but hey, you are what you are. If I don't watch out here, I shall be crawling up my arse again.

I glance at Bass who has left Red and Derek to argue about whether or not Metallica would still be in their current position of metal world domination if they'd maintained their original line-up. Instead, he's gazing at Suzz, gently biting his lower lip. If a picture paints a thousand words, then a portrait of his face would be a comprehensive definition of the word *smitten*. I fail to see what it is, exactly, that's caused him to fall head over heels for this girl. As he's never shown any interest in her before I can only assume that it's her recently uncovered musical prowess that has so impressed him. On the other hand, I've already admitted that Suzz bears little resemblance to the Suzana Comănici-Jenkins we knew, so maybe his interest isn't quite so unfathomable.

Sadly, Bass's sentiments appear to be one-sided. A comparison with his infatuation with Beth Brennan springs to mind. The problem is, though, that I feel I know enough about Beth to know that she wouldn't touch Bass with a long stick, whereas I can only assume the same about Suzz.

I feel that, for Bass's sake, I ought to find out a little more about the enigmatic Suzz. I consider asking how she would feel about a physical relationship with the passionate, if slightly obsessed, Bläck Gläss bass guitarist. Instead, I opt for a more oblique approach.

"Hey, Suzz."

She angles her head to face me. "How curious," she says. "That boy's speaking to me."

Well, she doesn't say that – not with words, anyway.

"What did you think about *Decaying Emotions*?"

She stares hard at me for a good ten seconds then looks across at Bass, who appears as anxious as a gladiator awaiting the Emperor's decision. Finally, a wry smile curls her lips.

"I only wish I could write something as good as that."

I scrutinise her face for evidence of irony but can find none. I glance at Bass whose expression could not be easier to read. If Bass's idol, Billy Sheehan, had complimented him, his grin couldn't be broader. I look back at Suzz to find her grinning also. Spooky.

"Really?" asks Bass. "You thought it was OK?"

"Hey, I just said, I wish I could write something like that."

"But you must have done, surely?"

"Why do you say that?"

"Well, you can play so brilliantly."

"Ah, but the world's full of technically accomplished musicians who couldn't write *Happy Birthday to You* if you stuck them in a room for a year. Completely different skills are needed to write a good song. You don't even have to play an instrument to write."

"No, but-"

"I'll bet even the grand master of the metal supremacists here," she says, nodding at Red who's still jabbering at Derek, "could write something better than I could."

She obviously hasn't heard *Satanic Sluts*.

Bass digests her opinion. "I suppose."

"Listen, I've got perfect pitch and I can sight-read almost anything apart from Liszt but the only stuff I can compose sounds like grade A shit."

"Surely not."

"Hey, I'm not about to embarrass myself with a practical demonstration so you'll just have to take my word for it, OK?"

"If you say so," mumbles Bass.

"I do."

"But you really liked *Decaying Emotions*?"

"Do you want it chiselled in stone or something?"

No, but I'll bet he wouldn't mind some gratuitous horizontal jogging as a token of her appreciation.

Bass laughs. "I've written a few others, you know."

"So I gather. I'm looking forward to hearing them."

"Yeah?"

"Sugar on a stick!" says Derek. "I nearly forgot!"

We look at him expectantly. I half expect him to tell us that he's about to emigrate, which would be par for the course.

"You know Lenny, the manager of the Showroom?"

"Not personally," I say.

"He pops into the Zone from time to time. He's a major Zep freak."

"Figures," says Red. "I've always wondered why the DJs are always playing *Stairway To Heaven*."

"Yeah, well, you know Pickaxe are playing there this Friday."

"Uh-huh, we're going," I say, looking at Red.

"The thing is, Blood Money, the support band, have pulled out and he was asking me if I knew anyone who could fill in at short notice. I said I didn't but that I was auditioning for a band tonight. He said he'd never heard of Silicone Cucumbers."

What a shock.

"But he did say that if they... you... we were any good, I was to let him know."

Red's eyes are bulging so dramatically they're almost touching the lenses of his spectacles. "You're joking? Our first gig?"

"Hey, we'd have to rehearse every minute between now and Friday."

"No, no, this can't be right," says Bass.

"Straight up."

Bass looks at me as if I'm the one that's going to say: 'Wake up, Bass. You've been dreaming. It's time to go home now. The auditions are over. Derek was a no-hoper and Suzz turned out to be a talentless larva.'

All I can do is shrug. Red leaps to his feet.

"Come on then, you lot. What are you waiting for? It's only just gone nine. We've got another three hours tonight and if we start right after school tomorrow, we'll have another seven or eight hours then."

"Is this Lenny character going to pay us?" asks Suzz.

"Who cares?" replies Red, hopping from one foot to the other. "*I'll* pay *him*, for God's sake."

I've had a considerable number of sharp pointy things thrown at me in the last few days but I get the feeling that maybe, just maybe, if I can only summon up the strength, I could snatch this one mid-air and hold it above my head in triumph. Not that my recent track record fills me with confidence, you understand, but somewhere deep inside me, a little voice, barely audible, is whispering: *Climb ashore, Atticus. You've gone with the flow and ridden that tide, now climb ashore and find that buried treasure.*

On the other hand, this particular sharp pointy thing might just hit me square between the eyes.

[24] Stagefright

It's half past six and I'm sitting with Bass and Derek in Beryl's Café. We finished the sound check half an hour ago, after which Suzz left for home saying that she wanted a bit of peace and quiet before the show. Red is busy plastering yellow Day-Glo strips of paper across the official posters announcing tonight's gig. *Special Guests: Bläck Gläss*. I gaze through the streaked café window and see him industriously applying glue over the poster by the front door of the Showroom. The Electricity Showroom. The Electric Chair, more like, because that's sort of how I feel – like a condemned prisoner 'enjoying' his last meal in a greasy spoon before an enforced appointment with his maker.

It's not that rehearsals haven't gone well. *Au contraire*, they've gone far better than I could possibly have imagined. What's worrying me – well, what's scaring me senseless, what's turning my blood to ice-water – is performing for an audience. In about two and a half hours, Bläck Gläss will make their first, and possibly only, appearance in front of the great unwashed. It's not really the prospect of an audience, per se, but rather the fact that almost everyone from our year is coming tonight, as well as significant numbers of fifth and upper sixth formers. Since yesterday lunch-time, when the word began to spread, hardly a moment has passed when somebody hasn't come up to me and informed me that they're looking forward to the gig, or words to that effect. Honestly, it's been ten times worse than last week, when the Childress Summer Shindig was the major topic of conversation.

I don't know why I'm so nervous. It's not that I haven't performed in public before, although I'm not certain that playing the percussion in the school orchestra really counts. I suppose it might be that, over the last couple of days, my suspicion that this could be a turning-point in my life has grown in intensity. Rightly or wrongly, I have built up in my mind the importance of tonight's gig. One of the guiding principles in my life is: if you expect the worst, you can't be disappointed, only pleasantly surprised. However, with regard to Bläck Gläss's début, I have not managed to adhere to this maxim. I desperately want tonight to be a spectacular success and I know that if it isn't then I'm going to be utterly devastated.

I only wish I could share Red's unequivocal optimism. As far as he's concerned we're going to *go down an absolute storm*. The fact that Chelsea is going to witness this downpour of musical excellence only heightens his sense of anticipation and certainty that Bläck Gläss's début performance is going to shake the world of heavy metal to its very foundations. The thing is, even if we sound worse than five dogs farting in unison, Red will still think that we were brilliant.

Although Derek seems to share Red's unshakable confidence, Bass appears to have at least acknowledged the possibility that A&R persons may not be waving chequebooks in our faces immediately we walk off stage. Whereas I am prepared to just sit here with my bowels loosening and my sphincters threatening imminent relaxation, Bass is channelling his nervous energy into planning the evening down to last minute detail. Having said that, he's changed his mind about practically every aspect of our thirty-minute set at least ten times – from the order in which we walk on stage to how many spare plectrums he should have taped to his microphone stand. As far as the set order goes, this has changed more often than Whitesnake's line-up.

"Right," he says, apparently to the scrap of paper on which he's been scribbling for five minutes, "we start with *Sanitarium*, then *Number of the Beast*. That'll be two familiar ones to get them going. Then it's *Steel Through Flesh*, *Jeremy*, *Decaying Emotions* and we finish with *Teen Spirit*."

"It's as though the last 20 years didn't even exist, isn't it?" I ask, automatically, not with any hope of a sensible answer. This subject has been discussed ad infinitum in the last forty-eight hours. "Apart from your songs," I add, pre-empting Bass's equally automatic response.

Bass recognises my rote baiting for what it is and ignores me.

"What about an encore?" asks Derek, changing the subject.

I snigger.

"No," says Derek, looking hurt, "it's possible."

"Yeah," agrees Bass, "we ought to have something planned."

"What, in case we haven't been laughed off stage after the first number?"

Derek swallows the last mouthful of one of Beryl's special extra-high-fat-content burgers. "Hey, Johnny, you're not getting cold feet, are you?"

"Just trying to be realistic."

"Supposing," says Bass, "that we're still intact, and not covered with rotting vegetables, we should decide in advance what to play for an encore, should the final applause last more than a few seconds."

"*All Right Now* or *Smoke on the Water*," says Derek.

"Too clichéd," argues Bass.

"That cover we've been working on," I suggest, "of last year's Eurovision Song Contest winner?"

Bass frowns, again ignoring me. "We're already going to play all our best ones in the set proper, so that doesn't leave much else."

"Why don't we just let Red play a drum solo?" I suggest.

Both Bass and Derek curl their lips.

"OK, then, I'll tell you what. Why don't we just see which number gets the best response, or the least unfavourable response, during the set then, if an encore seems appropriate, we'll just do that one again?"

"Seems fair enough," says Derek, nodding. "Bass?"

"I suppose, although it would be nice to do something they haven't heard."

"I spy a beggars and choosers situation," I say as Derek picks up and scrutinises the set list.

Bass is staring at a point approximately six inches above my head, his mind presumably whirring with thoughts of a leader-of-the-group persuasion. Having said that, I suspect there's an equal chance that he thinking about Suzz. I have been keenly observing their developing relationship. Hang on, don't jump to any conclusions. Suzz remains as aloof as ever, her demeanour rising above reticence only after a particularly well executed song. It's really Bass's response to Suzz that I have been watching.

Two nights ago he was captivated by her. I suspect he still is, although outwardly he has begun to show signs of bitterness. This sounds rather strange but it does provide further evidence for The Childress Infatuation/Resentment

Theory – I'll bet you were wondering when the next one was coming along. I can't claim that this is entirely original as it is really only the poor relation of the love/hate endless loop, and is a cousin (twice removed) of morbid jealousy. The basis for these conditions is that strong emotions are more closely associated than weaker ones, however polarised they are. Thus, intense devotion and uncontrollable rage are linked more strongly than mild affection and simple disdain. My theory states that an amorous fixation or a passionate obsession can, if bottled up, eventually develop or resolve into antipathy or even loathing. Put simply, infatuation, if unexpressed, can mutate into resentment. Yes, I've watched *Misery*.

You see, Bass is infatuated with Suzz – you could say he's her number one fan – but, because of her indifference, he's become more than a little discontented. On Wednesday night, whenever he looked in her direction, it was with an expression of undisguised ecstasy. However, by yesterday evening, he generally looked confused. During the sound check earlier, when events afforded him the opportunity to turn and look toward her, he did so with a definite scowl wrinkling his normally placid features.

Due to our rigorous practice schedule, I have not had the opportunity to discuss these matters with him, although I suspect, because of the depth of his feelings, he would not welcome a conference on the subject. After all, there are some things which you wouldn't want to talk about, even with one of your best friends. It's like the bro-hug, innit? Maximum of two pats, no eye contact, man-bits never to touch. The most searching question I could put to Bass on the subject of his emotions would be: "All right, mate?"

I turn to watch Red crossing the road, the big grin plastered across his face as bright as the Bläck Gläss notices he's been putting up. When he sits down next to me, Beryl comes over to take his order. I've never seen anyone with fingers more nicotine stained. It's disconcerting.

"What's today's special?" asks Red.

"Sausage and chips," rasps Beryl, ignoring Red's cheeky grin.

"Sounds good to me," he says, then turns to face me as Beryl shuffles away. "I'm going to need all those saturated fats tonight, eh?"

I recoil as he elbows me in the ribs. "Is that because of the gig or because you're meeting Chelsea?"

"Both," he says, wiggling his eyebrows up and down.

If he does that at Chelsea later on, he's going to end up with another knee in the groin. I tell him so.

"Ah, no, I'm going to be the soul of discretion tonight."

This shakes Bass from his reverie. "Which I'll believe when I see it."

"O ye of little faith."

"With good reason," says Bass.

"Speaking of which," I say, "you're sure the good and useful Georgia's not planning on making an appearance tonight?"

The silly grin slides slowly off Red's face. "I bloody well hope not. If she does, Bläck Gläss are going to be looking for another drummer."

"She sounds like an interesting lady, this Georgia," says Derek.

Red frowns. "Can we change the topic please? There's an uncomfortable ache developing down near the master of ceremonies."

Derek, who's looking out the window, emits a low whistle. "Hey, check it out. It's the delightful Dahlia."

Walking up the alley at the side of the Showroom are Dave and Dahlia, the Pickaxe guitarist and his consort. All four of us stare at them – well, at Dahlia – as they emerge from the alley and walk off in the direction of the nearest pub.

Before I carry on, and especially before I give you one of my particularly lurid descriptions of Dahlia, it would seem appropriate to fill you in on one or two significant developments since our rehearsal on Wednesday night.

When we finally decided to call it quits, it was almost half past midnight and my parents were less than chuffed to hear me trying to sneak into the house fifteen minutes later. I'd already sent them five texts saying I'd be home "in ten". It was over breakfast that I told them about the possibility that Bläck Gläss might well be performing in public for the first time. Bennie was full of abuse, as you can imagine, but I think he was secretly impressed. Rosie's opinion was harder to judge, seeing as she simply stared into her cereal bowl most of the time. However, I could tell that she was listening, and I knew that by ten o'clock that morning, most of the fifth form would know about the gig.

At lunch-time, Red and I went to The Zone where Derek told us that Lenny had agreed, on Derek's assurances that we would not let him down, to have Bläck Gläss support Pickaxe for the princely sum of £100 – a spine-tingling £20 each. These days, frankly, when support bands

241

can have to *pay* for the opportunity to play, such a sum shouldn't be sniffed at.

I also took the opportunity, while at The Zone during a weekday lunch-hour, to buy Rosie's present. Derek could barely stop himself from laughing out loud as he processed the transaction. Red, as you might imagine, excelled himself with quips and barbs all the way back to school.

Between lessons, that afternoon, Thursday, I telephoned Zach to give him the news. My misgivings about his behaviour on the night of the party were forgotten in my modulated excitement. After much light-hearted and superficially caustic banter he expressed his congratulations and offered his services as roadie/mixing desk operator. Bläck Gläss convened in Red's garage at five o'clock and rehearsed until eleven.

Immediately after school today, Friday, Bass, Red and I went back to Red's house, where Zach was waiting with the same van he'd borrowed last Saturday for the party. Red wanted to take a few of his amps and stacks to the Showroom, even though Derek had assured us that Pickaxe's PA would be adequate. Furthermore, as the support act, we would have no choice in the matter. The four of us arrived at the Showroom at half past four. Derek and Suzz were waiting for us in the main hall, sitting at a table near the bar. Tonight's *headliners*, for want of a better word, were on stage, running through *Symphony of Sin*, the best song off their latest album.

Pickaxe comprise Dave Reed (vocals, guitar and main songsmith), Steve Bullock (bass) and Alan Shackleton (drums). They are a non-league thrash metal act who made it into the third division a couple of years back with their début album, *Axe to Grind*. Their second album,

Axe to the Wall, unfortunately highlighted their one-dimensional capabilities and the backlash started. At the moment, they're touring dives like the Showroom to promote their third album, *Axe of Violence*, which Red bought a few weeks ago. As in actually exchanged money for a physical copy of the album on CD. Don't ask. I've listened to it on Spotify and suffice to say that their inability to mature or diversify is reflected by their persistent use of wretched puns for album titles.

Despite Pickaxe's lowly standing in the great metallic scheme of things, I couldn't suppress the shiver of excitement that coursed through my body as I crossed the empty floor to join our guitarist and keyboard player. While Zach walked over to the mixing desk Bass and Red sat down with Derek and Suzz. I stood at the railing and watched Pickaxe for a few minutes. Not having witnessed anything to cause revision of my lukewarm assessment of their ability, I pulled up another chair and joined the others.

In the extended lulls between songs, Derek explained the plan for the sound check and the gig later on. Essentially, as support, we were entitled to our own sound check only if time allowed. The doors would open at seven thirty and if the stage wasn't clear by that time, then it would be just our hard luck. We would have to set up our equipment in front of Pickaxe's. Basically, this would give us a space the size of your average shower cubicle in which to cram all five of us plus our equipment. Bass wasn't over the moon with the arrangements but Derek politely pointed out that this *was* our first gig, and we were supporting Pickaxe, after all, and not Iron bloody Maiden. Red, typically, could not have appeared happier if we were topping the bill at Donnington. Needless to say, Suzz looked bored throughout, resplendent, as she was, in black from neck to toe.

Bass's worst fears proved unfounded as Pickaxe finished their sound check soon after five o'clock. Red leaped up from his chair and trotted toward the stage, having informed us that he wanted to 'talk sticks with Alan'. Zach followed him and hailed Dave Reed who gazed at him uncertainly for a second before recognising him as one of the roadies from their previous tour. After a few minutes Zach brought him across to introduce us. I don't think Bass was overly impressed to be introduced as the bass player in 'my little brother's band'. Nevertheless, I got the impression that Dave was a decent sort of chap.

While Zach, Derek and Dave were discussing the joys of touring this fair land in a clapped-out Transit, Suzz was thinking whatever it is she thinks when she's staring vacantly at the rings on her fingers and I was absently watching a couple of Pickaxe's roadies doing whatever it is they do when they walk back and forth across the stage.

Thus, it was I who first clapped eyes on Dahlia as she walked through the backstage door and into the main hall. I'd say she was in her mid to late twenties but she could be anywhere from twenty to forty (just). She stood about five ten in her monstrous knee-length New Rock metallic boots, all studs, buckles and straps, and those thick platform soles. Densely patterned lace tights, very brief black cut-off shorts. A wide, silver and black belt covered most of her shorts at the front, almost like a boxer's championship belt. A loose Motörhead vest, strategically ripped at the front to show off even more of her chest. And we're definitely talking fruit salad. Her long black hair falls to the small of her back, not quite dreads, but not far off. Pale skin, panda eyes, full blood-red lips. Multiple facial and ear piercings. Both forearms covered in an assortment of silver bracelets and bangles. Almost every inch of skin, apart from her face, covered in multi-coloured tats. She's not classically beautiful or pretty. Frankly, it's rather difficult to tell exactly what she looks like under all the slap, tats and metalwork.

As she climbed the steps up to the mixing desk, it became more apparent that Dahlia is maybe half a stone overweight. She's definitely not rocking the anorexic junkie look. But she's got *something.* In spades. And she knows it. Here is a woman who's absolutely certain that every heterosexual male – and possibly every lesbian, for all I know – within 20 metres is captivated by her.

Dave grinned at her as she approached then wrapped his arm around her shoulders and introduced her. Dahlia barely acknowledged the presence of anyone but Dave. She just stood there with her boyfriend, looking vaguely bored, if truth be told. She said nothing. She met no one's gaze. She didn't seem to be listening to anything that was being said. And yet it was as though she was the most fascinating person in the room.

When I could summon up the strength to do so, I dragged my gaze away from her and looked around. Everyone was besotted with her, staring at her, some actually with open mouths. Suzz seemed immune to her charms but she was the only one. Zach's eyes were positively bulging and Derek's tongue kept running around his lips. Pheromone City.

Dahlia certainly wasn't my *type.* Ink and piercings do very little for me. And the bored, I'm-above-all-this-shit attitude would normally be a big turn-off. But there was something so primal, so sensual, so elemental about her it was impossible not to respond. Not quite *Zing went the strings of my heart.* My reaction was slightly more primitive. And, as noted, I wasn't the only one so affected.

I mention this only to further lower myself in your estimation, to offer one more example of how I am obsessed with the superficial, how I see only the lipstick and short skirt, not the personality and heart of the woman underneath.

Of course that's not why I mention it! I've prattled on (again) so that you understand why, when we see Dahlia later, on the arm of her boyfriend, as we're sitting in Beryl's café, we respond as we do. Got it? Super.

"Whoa, whoa, whoa," murmurs Red, gazed fixed on Dahlia.

"Be still my beating heart," says Bass.

Derek emits another low whistle. "Boy, I'd like to-"

"Sausage and chips," interrupts Beryl, plonking the plate down on the table.

I twist around in my seat to watch Dave somehow slip his hand into the tiny back pocket of Dahlia's ultra-brief shorts, a manoeuvre I find more than a little irritating. With at least four pairs of hormone-addled eyes on her, Dahlia disappears from view.

Red devours his meal in two minutes flat. The rest of us watch him. Not that it's an extremely pleasant sight, you understand. It's just that any conversation would be drowned out by the cacophony of slurping and chomping noises emanating from the direction of Bläck Gläss's madcap drummer.

"So," says Bass after Red has belched loudly, "what time are you meeting Chelsea?"

246

Red's face lights up, as it always does when Chelsea's name is mentioned. I should be happy for him, but I'm finding it just a little bit annoying.

"Half eight."

"I thought we'd agreed to all meet backstage at half eight."

"Yeah, well, I thought maybe she could come backstage with us."

Bass couldn't look more shocked, even if Red had just told him Lenny was insisting that we include a 4Tune8 cover in the set. "No way!"

"And why not?"

Bass does an admirable impression of a goldfish. If he could find the words, he'd want to explain that he'd like Bläck Gläss to spend half an hour *bonding* before we walk out to the tumultuous applause of the legions of our loyal fans. If Bass had his way, he'd have us all standing in a circle, holding hands, and *getting focused.* After ten seconds, he manages to control the fish-like movements of his mouth.

"It's just that I think it would be better... I mean, more productive if we were free of all er... distractions before we go on. That's all."

Red turns to look at me and I give him my *Hey, it's going to make him happy* expression.

"Fine, if that's what you want. I'll meet her at the door, make sure she's got a good spot to watch, then come backstage for a distraction-free session with my fellow band-members. All right?"

[25] The Bottom Line

It's twenty to nine and I'm sitting on a battered wooden chair in a broom cupboard somewhere deep in the bowels of the Showroom. Well, OK, it's not a broom cupboard exactly, but the room Bläck Gläss have been allocated doesn't feel much bigger, especially with Bass pacing back and forth like an expectant father. Derek is sitting astride a packing crate, calmly inspecting his fingernails. Bass checks the time on his phone for the fifth time in the last minute.

"Where are they?" he asks a rusty bucket in the corner.

Derek and I have long since abandoned attempts to placate him.

"Where the bloody hell are they?"

Derek checks that his shirt is correctly buttoned.

"If Red's not here in the next two minutes, I'm going to kill him."

I bend over to pull tight the laces of my Hi-Tec squash shoes.

"I'll kill him anyway. And where's Suzz?"

Having noticed a grey smudge on the toe of my left shoe, I lick my thumb and try to clean it off. Needless to say, this only makes it worse.

"And where's Zach? I thought he said he'd come back here to let us know everything was OK."

Derek picks up his guitar and begins tuning it, as though there was a distinct possibility that it had mysteriously gone out of tune in the five minutes since he last performed this routine. Bass has walked over to the door and is standing there with his hand hovering by the handle. If anybody opens it, he stands a reasonable chance of sustaining a severe head injury. At least it would shut him up. He turns and resumes pacing up and down.

"I'm not sure about the name, now. Bläck Gläss. I think it's too pretentious. Is it too late to change it? Maybe I should have a word with Lenny. He's introducing us, isn't he? Christ! Look at the time. We're supposed to be on in eighteen minutes. Where the bleeding hell are Suzz and Red? If he's with that nubcake, Chelsea, I'll kill him. I swear it. I'll find the nearest long sharp thing and drive it right up his-"

"Bass," says Derek quietly but firmly, "shut up."

Bass stares at Derek, frowning as though he'd never seen him before. Still frowning, he walks over to the corner where he's deposited his rucksack and pulls out a yellow tee-shirt, at which he stares for a few moments. He stuffs it back into the rucksack then withdraws a green one. He's been through this routine seven million times already, each time deciding not to exchange either for the black sleeveless shirt on his back.

If I've given you the impression that, while Bass is quite obviously a bundle of twitching nerves, Derek and I are as cool as cool things, then I've misled you. Derek's continuous fiddling about with his guitar hints at significant levels of anxiety while I couldn't be more apprehensive if Georgia was standing in front of me, taping drawing pins to her knee. For a few seconds, black spots float in front of my eyes as I convince myself that I've forgotten the *Sanitarium* intro. If I could move my legs, I'd make a run for it. As it is, I close my eyes and take a few deep breaths, trying as best I can to think of something pleasant. I imagine a clear blue sky and a hillside covered in purple heather. Just as I start to feel a little calmer, a horde of larvae comes running over a ridge, jeering and pointing at me. Leading the angry mob are Rosie and Dawn, both carrying placards. Rosie's reads: *4Tune8 4ever*. Dawn's says: *Atticus Is A Bastard*.

"Johnny?"

I open my eyes to find Bass's perspiring white face two inches from mine. "What?"

"Do you think we should open with *Number of the Beast* instead of *Sanitarium* or not?"

"Sure, why not?"

"What?" he gasps, looking at me like a frightened rabbit.

"No, you hobbit! As I've told you a hundred times already, I think we should stick to the order that we've discussed."

"Yeah?"

"Yeah."

"Oh, all right then, but what about-"

Zach opens the door and walks in. "Hey, how are you guys doing?"

"Have you seen Red and Suzz?" demands Bass.

"Hey, calm down, Bass," says Zach, taking a step backwards away from our psychotic bass player. "Don't blow a gasket."

"Don't tell me to calm down!"

Zach looks over at me. "How did he get into such a state?"

I shrug, unwilling to speak as I know the only sound I would make would be a hoarse croak.

Bass is definitely about to blow something. "Where the bloody hell are Red and Suzz?"

"I don't know about Suzz but Red's out by the bar with some girl."

"I knew it!" roars Bass. "I'll kill him. I'll rip his bloody arms off and beat him to death with the wet ends. He knows we're supposed to be on stage in fifteen freaking minutes."

"Ah," says Zach hesitantly, "there's a bit of a problem there."

Bass freezes, staring wild-eyed at Zach. The only visible signs of life are a throbbing blood vessel on his temple and the fact that he's still standing.

"What's up?" asks Derek as he sets down his guitar and climbs off the packing crate.

"You're not on until half nine."

It feels as though a black hole has just appeared in the pit of my stomach, sucking into it all my vital organs. The prospect of another forty-five minutes watching Bass turn into a gibbering wreck is just way too much to bear.

"I've just been speaking to Lenny. Apparently there's been a spot of bother with the police."

"The police?" asks Derek, looking more concerned than might be expected. I wonder if there's something he's not telling us.

"There's a queue of about two hundred people stretching down the street outside. Two policemen drove past and spotted that most of them were schoolkids. Anyway, one thing led to another, and, seeing as one of the policemen knew Lenny, they agreed that the kids could be admitted if Lenny didn't serve any alcohol at the bar. Lenny reckons that, with all the extra tickets he's going to sell, plus all the soft drinks he'll shift, he'll more than make up for what he loses in alcohol sales."

Derek takes a few seconds to digest this information. "How many people are there going to be?"

Zach grins. "Lenny reckons about six hundred."

251

"Six... six... hundred?" hisses Bass, emerging briefly from catatonia.

"I didn't think Pickaxe were that popular," says Derek.

Zach grins. "They're not coming to see Pickaxe."

Bass looks as though he's going to keel over. I'm just glad I'm sitting down.

"Anyway, that's why everything's been moved back half an hour. You're on from half nine to ten and then Pickaxe are on at half ten."

I'd known that there would be a fair number of friends and acquaintances in the audience. Even so, it takes a short while for all the implications of Zach's news to sink in. If he's to be believed, and I can't imagine why he would purposely torture us, then most of the fifth and sixth forms are streaming into the Showroom at this very moment. Whether or not suicide is actually pain-free, I begin to seriously contemplate such an ignominious end to it all.

Further thoughts of a morbid nature are prevented by Suzz appearing in the doorway.

"Hey, sorry I'm late. The car wouldn't start."

All four of us stare at her, although I suspect Bass may possibly still be in shock because of Zach's intelligence report rather than Suzz's startling transformation. She's wearing black ankle boots decorated with an assortment of straps and silver buckles. They've got five-inch stiletto heels and toes sharp enough to pick locks. I've seen similar on several websites but, in the flesh, as it were, they are stunning. As if the boots alone aren't enough to make my tongue run circles around my cracked lips, things only get more astonishing as my gaze travels slowly upwards over her skin-tight black PVC jeans. Even in the dim light cast by the sixty-watt bulb overhead, her calves and thighs are positively gleaming. Not a single crease is visible, so perfectly is her pelvis encased in the glossy material. The effect is utterly mesmerising. I realise that although I have scrutinised countless images of similarly clad women on websites too numerous to mention, I have never actually seen the real thing being worn by a living, breathing woman. I am overcome by the sudden urge to crawl across the room and kneel before her but I know that even if I managed to slump to the floor, I'd just lie there in a crumpled heap like a helpless infant.

Reluctantly, I peel my gaze away from her sleek pelvis. A wide, black leather belt, decorated with silver buckles and rings, encircles her waist. Beneath a black leather jacket, she's wearing a black fishnet cropped top, and around her neck hangs the familiar silver crucifix. However, the crucifix is the only familiar thing about Suzz. Above her neck is where the most sensational transformation has occurred, one that must have entailed at least two hours in front of the mirror. Over lightly applied foundation, well-blended rouge makes her cheeks look almost rosy – certainly an improvement on their previously somewhat consumptive appearance. Under several coats of gloss, her lips are painted dark red. Her eye make-up consists of black eye-liner, black mascara and dark grey eye-shadow skilfully blended up to her eyebrows. She's swept her black hair away from the right side of her face, revealing a long silver chain dangling from her ear-lobe.

I've already commented on the fact that Suzz, keyboard player with Bläck Gläss, bears virtually no resemblance to Suzana Comănici-Jenkins , decidedly odd pseudo-Goth. But neither of those two women look anything like this thrilling vision of PVC-clad loveliness standing before me. As silent seconds tick away, I can only assume that the others are experiencing the same combination of shock and stimulation as I.

"Hey, I said I was sorry."

"You... you.. look..." splutters Bass.

I would imagine that he's completely forgotten about Zach's news.

"...different."

"Yeah, well, I thought I'd better make an effort."

"Very nice," says Zach, the only one of us to recover his composure.

"Thank you," she says indifferently. "Hadn't we better be getting ready?"

Bass and Derek gawp at Suzz as though she had two heads – or three arms, or something – while Zach explains the new schedule to her. I would also be gaping in astonishment were I not suffering from an extreme case of sensory overload. I close my eyes and channel every joule of energy at my disposal into the flaccid appendages that are masquerading as my legs. Once on my feet, I open my eyes only to find the room whirling around me. I blink a few times and gradually the vertigo subsides to a tolerable level. Even so, as I walk slowly toward the door, I feel as though I'm on a small boat being tossed about on a very stormy sea. Standing as still as statue, Bass ignores me as I brush past him.

"Is it me," I ask feebly to no one in particular, "or is hot in here?"

Zach calls after me: "Better be back here by quarter past."

I think I nod or otherwise acknowledge comprehension – I can't be certain which. As I pass Suzz, the heady scent of her perfume snakes up my nostrils and my dizziness returns. I negotiate the doorway on autopilot and stumble into the dingy corridor, from one end of which comes the dull thud of something by Nickelback. Whatever.

Completely disorientated, I slump against a wall and wait until the musky aroma of Suzz's perfume, and my vertigo, fades. I push myself away from the wall and begin to shuffle down the corridor, at the end of which I find a large door marked 'Emergency Exit'. In my befuddled state, this seems more like a suggestion that a statement of fact. On the other side of this door lies freedom – from my commitments and responsibilities, from Bläck Gläss, from my family and from the incomprehensible Suzz (3.0). If I could only find the courage to cross the threshold, I could hitchhike across the country, to mainland Europe and beyond. I could lead the simple life of a traveller, unhindered by the crushing weight of my obligations.

Of course, I don't make an emergency exit, if only because I'd probably change my mind as soon as the door slammed shut behind me. Concluding that it's probably wired up to some sort of security system, I don't even open the door. But I do need some air and I decide to find a window. At the end of another corridor, I climb a flight of stairs, at the top of which I find a closed door. I turn the handle and pull open the door an inch or two. The claustrophobic roar of Soundgarden is released, underneath which lies the insect-like buzz of hundreds of people chattering excitedly. I open the door a little more and find myself looking down at the stage. An array of lights stretches out before me at waist level. I crouch down and gaze beneath the lights at the crowd.

Following a brief lull, the DJ plays some horrendous pop/punk 'tune', the perpetrators of which, in my quasi-fugue state, I cannot recall. In front of the stage are about twenty 15-year-old lads who, having obviously spent an hour on metalforbeginners.com, are jumping up and down, slamming into one another. The other members of the audience, packed onto the main floor area, have backed away from the epileptic fifth-formers, leaving a circular arc of space. Off to one side, I spot Rosie, Dawn and Mamta, huddled together. They are taking turns pointing at various people and laughing. Even though my head feels as though it's trapped in a vice, it's still gratifying to see my sister having a good time. It seems as though she hasn't smiled in weeks. And I'm to blame.

Red and Chelsea are standing by the bar. Chelsea's back is to the wall, against which Red is leaning on an outstretched hand. *What's a nice girl like you doing in a place like this?* I suspect I'm incorrectly interpreting his body language, though, because Chelsea is smiling and laughing as though she's having the time of her life.

Though Red and Chelsea have been messaging each other furiously all week, this is the first time they've met – to my knowledge – since Georgia tried to shatter Red's pelvis with her knee. I watch them for a minute or so. They seem to be getting on like a house on fire. Red's arms are waving about as he tells her some story. Chelsea's hanging on his every word. I watch her cover her mouth with her hand, upper body shaking in a fit of giggling. Even as I smile, happy that they're happy, other feelings, much more negative, hover at the periphery of my mind. I force my gaze away from Red and Chelsea.

Sandun, Graeme and half a dozen other lads from the lower sixth come through the double doors from the foyer. They pause at the top of the steps leading down to the main floor, their faces registering surprise at the number of people crammed into the club. Sandun looks at the stage and, for a few seconds, I feel certain he can see me but then he signals an empty table near the backstage door and leads his friends in that direction.

Next through the doors are Apollonia and Robert. She's wearing white basketball boots, tiger-print leggings and a simple white tee-shirt. He's wearing an exceptionally baggy designer suit. Arm in Armani, they pause long enough for everyone in the immediate vicinity to register their entrance then move off to their right, behind the mixing desk. Robert leans over to speak to Billy Gibson, who's sitting at a table with two other boys. Almost immediately, Billy jumps up, followed by the other two, allowing Apollonia and Robert to sit down.

That Apollonia is going to witness the full horror of Bläck Gläss's début performance fazes me less than it might once have done. I have given a great deal of thought to the garden shed incident six days ago and I have now accepted that, even though I still consider her to be the most magnificent woman on the face of the earth, I had no right to place her on a pedestal so high. As a human being, she has desires and physical needs and if she's chosen Mr Music Business to satisfy those cravings then so be it. Apparently, though, Robert is a little too keen to slake his thirst for all things carnal. He slings his arm around her shoulder and begins to nuzzle the side of her slender, perfectly-proportioned neck. For reasons unknown, Apollonia pushes him away. I only wish I could hear what she says to him. Something along the lines of *Get away from me, you conceited gigolo* would seem appropriate.

I would like nothing more than to surreptitiously observe the development of this fascinating scenario but, unbidden, nausea swells once more in the pit of my stomach. Whether this is due to the noise, the heat or unadulterated fear, I cannot say. However, unless I am to draw attention to myself by spewing a fountain of Beryl's half-digested chips down onto the stage, I had better beat a hasty retreat.

I stagger back down the stairs and retrace my steps to the emergency exit. I decide to risk the chance that it is alarmed and push open the door then step out into the alley. After propping open the door with a brick, I close my eyes and start taking long deep breaths. Gradually my nausea settles, though sadly not my intense trepidation. I can envisage six hundred people, including almost everyone whose opinions I value, jeering us off the stage. I can see Bass's black tee-shirt splattered with the remains of rotting vegetables, and Suzz's lustrous PVC jeans running with saliva gobbed up by the epileptic front row.

I open my eyes and tell myself to get a grip. Things might not necessarily go that badly. We might actually play as well as we have done in rehearsal. Perhaps Robert will be so impressed that he'll sign us on the spot. Yeah, right, and maybe I'm not an introspective, angst-saturated chauvinist with a propensity for developing debilitating nausea at the slightest provocation. I can just picture it. We walk off stage, the air ringing with the excited cries of six hundred people clamouring for an encore. Robert steps out of the shadows and approaches Bass. 'Absolutely brilliant, boys. I want to offer you a six album deal and a three-million pound advance,' he says, 'as long as you ditch that crap rhythm guitarist.'

I check the time – ten past nine – then walk back into the corridor and close the door behind me. The clang with which it shuts has a worrying tone of finality. And therefore never send to know for whom the bell tolls; it tolls for thee. Despite the likelihood of disaster, I tell myself, I know I'd never live it down if I bottled out. After all, it's better to have played in front of six hundred people and died a death than never to have played at all.

    Yeah, right.

[26] Welcome Back, My Friends

The scene which greets me as I enter the broom cupboard reminds me of a dentist's waiting room. Derek's face is so contorted that I can only imagine he has a gum abscess or some other cause of acute physical pain. Bass is sitting by himself in one corner, staring at the opposite wall as if expecting an ancestral spirit to appear at any moment and explain to him the meaning of life.

Having seemingly torn himself free of Chelsea, Red is now sitting in another corner, on the rusty bucket, on the sides of which he's quietly tapping his drumsticks. Even though he'd told us he was going to do it, I'm still surprised he's gone ahead with his plan to wear nothing but a pair of dark blue shorts and a pair of battered tennis shoes. His pale skinny torso glistens with a thin sheen of sweat. Like everyone, he's subdued – his normal (usually misplaced) bravura forgotten. Perhaps he has only now, with five minutes to go, been struck by the enormity of the situation.

Suzz, normally reserved, seems almost comatose. Eyes closed, face upturned, back to the wall, she's standing with her palms pressed against the wall, her long legs slick in black PVC. She's so still, she doesn't seem to be breathing but, as I watch, she takes a deep breath and lets it out slowly through pursed lips.

I walk across to pick up my guitar.

"Hey," says Red. "There's an awful lot of punters out there."

He glances up at me then looks quickly down again at his drumsticks.

"Yeah, I know," I say quietly.

Derek loudly cracks a knuckle. "I've never played in front of six hundred people."

"I've never played in front of anybody," says Red.

What we need is somebody to say: 'We're gonna knock 'em dead tonight. We're gonna play a blinder. So, let's go out there, show 'em why Bläck Gläss are gonna be The Next Big Thing, and blow the suckers away!'

Then, with guitars held aloft like machine guns and hollered war-cries we could stride purposefully onto the stage. There, we could gaze out across the sea of expectant faces for a few seconds while knobs are twisted, switches are flicked and connections checked for the last time before we let loose the barrage of thunderous metal noise that *is* Bläck Gläss.

"I'm so nervous, I think I'm going to piss myself," says Derek.

Not quite the rebel yell I had in mind.

"Yeah, well," I say, "do it before we go on, will you? I don't particularly want to get electrocuted from standing in a puddle of your urine, thank you very much."

Red laughs, albeit uneasily. "Better than choking on your own vomit in a drug-induced stupor."

"Or overdosing on Beryl's greasy chips," says Derek, smiling.

"I can just see the headlines," says Red. "'Atticus Childress, 17, rhythm guitarist with Bläck Gläss, was found dead late yesterday evening in Beryl's Café, lying face down in a plate of chips.'"

Nausea is gathering forces, preparing for a renewed assault on my stomach.

"Why is it you always have to be so fucking puerile?" demands Suzz.

Startled, I turn to see her glaring at Red. I had, perhaps, overestimated her state of relaxation.

Red groans sarcastically. "And lo, the ice-maiden speaks."

Suzz tenses, eyes blazing. Neither Derek nor Bass, who's still staring blankly at the wall, seem at all interested in the very real possibility of another knee-in-groin incident. It therefore looks as though it's up to me to deal with this warm root vegetable.

"Just shut up, Red. We're on in a few minutes and we don't need this, OK?"

Red scowls petulantly then resumes tapping the bucket. I check to see Suzz still glaring at Red, though with a little less vehemence. Situation defused. For now.

"Fifteen," says Derek.

Now it's my turn to glare. "What?"

"Fifteen minutes. We're not on until quarter to ten."

"Says who?"

"Does it matter? We're on at quarter to, OK?"

I look at our catatonic bass player and our capricious drummer and am forced to take their silence as confirmation. At the sound of rustling I turn to see Suzz unwrapping a packet of cigarettes. She stares directly at me as she places one in her mouth and lights it then shoves the packet and lighter into an inside pocket of her jacket.

"I didn't know you smoked."

"I don't," she says.

I watch her inhale deeply then blow out a thin stream of blue-grey smoke through pursed, glossed lips. It crosses my mind that there might be a smoke alarm in here. Then I snort quietly. As if.

"Is that a problem?" she demands, her head cocked challengingly.

I shake my head and turn away. In my head, in super-slo-mo, Georgia's knee drives once more into Red's family jewels. I squat down between Red and Bass and lean back against the wall. After a couple of minutes, the fire in Suzz's eyes fades. She drops the half-smoked cigarette to the floor and grinds it out with the toe of her right boot. Once extinguished, she looks over at me.

"Sorry."

"Forget it."

"All this hanging about is getting on my nerves."

"Yeah, I know what you mean."

Silence.

Except for Red's erratic tapping, which is beginning to grate, like a fly buzzing near your ear. I want to tell him to give it a rest but I know he'd only find something more annoying to do. I stare at Suzz's right boot and follow the line of the sole from the tip as it sweeps upwards past the vamp and shank, curving back down at the heel breast and down to the heel tip. I gaze at the straps and buckles and envisage her constricted foot within. I wonder if she's aware of any discomfort. I wonder what she'd think of me if I asked her. I wonder whether I'm going insane. A knock on the door throws the wrong kind of snow on the lines of madness along which my brain-train is hurtling. Suzz steps forwards and pulls open the door, allowing Dave and Dahlia to walk in.

"Bloody hell!" says Dave. "What a lovely room of death!"

I stand up and manage a thin smile. "First gig jitters, I guess."

Dave laughs. "Yeah, I just thought I'd come by and wish you luck."

"We're going to need some."

"No, you won't. I heard your sound check earlier. You sounded pretty tight to me."

"Yeah, well, thanks but, you know, that was then..."

"Anyway, from what I hear, most of the punters are here to see you."

I'm not quite sure how to respond. I nod and smile nervously then check the others to see if any of them feel like helping me out here. Suzz is just standing there, staring disdainfully at Dahlia. Derek is also looking at Dahlia, though not with disdain. Red remains hunched on the floor, sticks hovering either side of the bucket, looking like an emaciated street urchin with his pale back gleaming dully. His gaze, though, is also transfixed by Miss Animal Magnetism. Bass, on the other hand, is *still* staring vacantly at the opposite wall. This has gone far enough.

"Hey! Bass! Wake up!" I shout.

No response.

Exceedingly annoyed, I stamp over to where he sits, motionless. As I reach out to grab his arm, a gruesome thought flits across my mind. What if when I touch his flesh it's stone cold? Or worse, what if I prod him and he slowly keels over, his limbs frozen with rigor mortis? Or worst of all, what if I've been watching too many trashy horror movies on Netflix? I punch his shoulder. Hard.

Bass grunts then looks around, blinking. "What did you do that for?"

"Bass, you soporific sleepy thing, Dave's come to wish us luck."

"Uh... thanks," he murmurs, squinting at Dave.

Cue one heavily pregnant pause.

"Hey, well," says Dave, after a protracted labour, "I'm sure you'll walk it."

With Dahlia hanging onto his arm, Dave turns and walks through the door. Just before she disappears from view, Dahlia looks back into the broom cupboard and smiles. Fairy lights sparkle around her head. A bright white light grows between her teeth then explodes towards me. The light smashes into my head, forcing me to take a step backwards. I am suddenly filled with the certainty that nothing will make Dahlia happier than to watch Bläck Gläss absolutely slaughter the room. The light fades as quickly as it appeared. Dahlia is gone.

None of that happened, of course. Well, Dahlia smiled, but the rest of it was just in my head. What? You knew that? Don't let me keep you. That Mensa application form isn't going to submit itself. I glance around at Red, Bass and Derek. They're smiling. Maybe it wasn't just in my head. Suzz, it would seem, saw and felt nothing.

"It's twenty to ten, boys and ice-maiden." says Red excitedly. "There is only one god, and his name is Death. And there is only one thing we say to Death: 'Not today'."

"Yeah, right," says Derek, shaking his head as he picks up his guitar.

"Let's kick some ass!" whoops Bass, immediately looking abashed.

Suzz groans. "Bloody hell, are we playing a gig or is this the boys changing room?

Both, I think as I make sure I've not left my fly unzipped. I sling my guitar around my neck. The other three lads have left. Only Suzz and I are left in the broom cupboard.

"After you," I say, allowing her to precede me through the door.

When I reach the bottom of the few steps leading up to the stage I discover that, to my amazement, I am not feeling quite as nervous as before. This may have something to do with the fact that, all the way from the broom cupboard, I was able to watch Suzz's black PVC-encased bum. This is not to say that I still wouldn't toss my cookies at the slightest provocation, you understand, but I am feeling better.

AC/DC's *Heatseeker* stops mid-riff. The house lights go down and the crowd, hidden from our view, begins cheering enthusiastically. I'm standing between Derek and Suzz. The smell of his sweat and her perfume fills my nostrils. Standing on the stage, Lenny leans over toward us.

"You guys OK?"

Red, perched on the top step, nods. Lenny crosses to the microphone centre-stage, illuminated by a single white spotlight.

"Ladies and gentlemen! Headbangers, one and all!"

Out of the corner of my eye I can see, beside me, Suzz shaking her head.

"Welcome to The Electricity Showroom!"

This is followed by a barrage of heckles and catcalls.

"Tonight, it is my great privilege to present to you, making their début performance, your very own... **BLÄCK GLÄSS!!!**"

The spotlight snaps off, as do my fingers. Well, no they don't, but I wouldn't be surprised. It's pitch black and I can't see a thing. *Also Sprach Zarathustra* starts playing over the PA.

"What the bloody hell's that?" shouts Bass.

"The theme from *2001*," says Derek.

"I bloody well know *what* it is," he bellows, "but what are they *playing* it for?"

"It was Zach's idea."

Good one, Zach.

"Jesus Christ!" Bass screams. "They'll think it's the *Elvis Presley 'Back from the Grave' Revue*!"

"What are you waiting for?" shouts an invisible Lenny.

Everyone has a plan, until they get punched in the mouth. And my gut tells me I'm about to be on the receiving end of several painful body blows.

I feel Suzz's hand on my shoulder then I start to climb the steps up to the stage. Although the stage lights remain extinguished, the club is illuminated by an array of dim bare bulbs in the ceiling – fire safety regulations, I suppose. Even though I *know* there are six hundred people in the audience, there appear to be six thousand, or six million, and each one of them is staring at me, or seems to be. Suzz's keyboard is set up on the left side of the stage, near the top of the steps. When she releases my shoulder and sits down, I feel as if I have been set adrift – as if she was my anchor and I am now free to float away in the shark-infested waters of profound anxiety. My legs turn into stiff cylinders of a lead-like substance, and it is only with great determination that I force them to carry me onwards.

Also Sprach Zarathustra is still blasting from the PA, ponderously nearing a climax. I glance around nervously. On the far side of the stage, Derek is standing stock-still, staring out at the audience. Centre-stage, Bass stands, back to the audience, head bowed. Behind his kit, Red is adjusting the height of his stool. I am standing between Bass and Suzz, a position I realise now is way too close to the front of the stage. I consider asking Bass if it wouldn't be a good idea if I were to move back a bit – say, back to the broom cupboard, perhaps.

Suddenly, the introductory music stops. Following a heartbeat of silence, the crowd erupts into frenzied cheering and whistling. Unless my ears are deceiving me, which is a distinct possibility, there are more than a few girls screaming their larval heads off. I wipe sweat from my clammy forehead with the back of my hand. The sensation is not unlike wiping condensation from a window in midwinter.

"Come on, Johnny," hisses Bass.

I move my fingers into position and start playing the *Sanitarium* intro. There are a few hoarse cries of recognition from the front row and a spotlight above me comes on with a thud, illuminating a metre-wide circle of the stage just to my right. It's just as well that we've rehearsed the song a thousand times because there's no way I would be able to play it on anything but a brain-stem level. Behind me, Suzz says something. If the sound of my pulse pounding in my ears wasn't as loud as a pneumatic drill, I might have been able to hear what it was she said. My gaze is fixed on the fluorescent glow of the bar lights on the opposite side of the club. I dare not look down at the faces of the front row. Again, Suzz says something. Again, I cannot hear her words.

"Move over!" she bellows, though I can barely hear her. I see her lips move and I stare dumbly at her hand as she shoos me away.

It takes a few moments for my stunned neurones to process this advice. I take a step sideways, into the cone of white light.

This is greeted by more whistling. Thankfully, before my fingers freeze with embarrassment, Red starts to play. Another spotlight illuminates his kit and the audience's attention is diverted from me. When the light above Suzz comes on the air fills with the noise of a couple of hundred wolf-whistles and, somehow, I find the energy to smile. To my horror, this tiny lapse of concentration is followed by my playing a wrong note. I stare even more attentively toward the bar. As my legs would not support my brain's command to run away, this is my only option. Derek starts to play and then Bass begins to sing.

The next thing I know, we've reached the end of the song and we're all bashing out the riff in unison. I feel like I'm driving along a motorway. I can see my exit up in front of me. I can remember a sign a couple of miles back. But, try as I might, I can't remember a single thing between. And our version of the song is nearly seven minutes long. Who knows where the time goes? We hit the last chord and the crowd explodes. The noise is deafening. For the first time, I look down at the front row. Twenty lads are squashed up against the front of the stage, hollering and cheering, their arms aloft.

We speed through Maiden's *The Number of the Beast* and Bass's *Steel Through Flesh*. It isn't until Pearl Jam's more sedate *Jeremy* that I feel confident enough to scan the crowd in earnest. As I've previously noted, most of the front two rows are from the fifth form and I am relieved to see that the majority of them are watching Bass, even the handful directly in front of me. A couple are staring at Suzz and I can see from their expressions that they are wrestling with the unlikely possibility that they are actually looking at Suzana Comănici-Jenkins. I can sympathise.

About half way back, I spot Rosie, Dawn and Mamta. It comes as something of a shock to see Rosie singing along with Bass. And here was me thinking that she existed on a steady diet of 4Tune8 drivel. What I find even more unsettling, however, is the smile that lights up her face as she sings the line wherein the eponymous Jeremy is described as an innocuous, diminutive 'fuck'. Still, perhaps I should take this as evidence that her attitude toward me is softening slightly.

Unfortunately, I cannot say the same for Dawn as, while I can't be certain, I think she's looking directly at me. Imagining the hatred in her eyes makes me speedily look over to my left, where Apollonia and Robert are sitting. Obviously, I don't actually know what's been going on between the two of them in the last six days but, judging from Robert's fervent attempts to suck Apollonia's brains out through her ear, I'd say that Saturday night in the garden shed was the last time he refreshed his knowledge of her. In addition, I'd say that Apollonia's expression of irritation might indicate that abstinence was her idea. Further scrutiny is thwarted by the final refrain of the song. *Decaying Emotions* is next and, seeing as we only played it for the first time forty-eight hours ago, I need to concentrate.

Once the applause for *Jeremy* dies away, Red starts the insistent drum pattern. As the rest of us join in at the appropriate junctures, I note that the audience is quieter, presumably waiting to see whether we are about to segue into something recognisable. During the second verse I turn to watch Bass singing. It amazes me that his voice gets stronger each time we play this song and this time his vocals are crystal clear. This could be due to the professional PA or even Zach's mixing (unlikely), but I suspect it's actually because he's singing with incredible intensity. I suddenly realise that he's changed the words. What was a morbid song about teenage suicide is now a gothic profession of unrequited love. Furthermore, you don't need to be Stephen Hawking to work out the object of his desire.

"...my shattered soul, tossed like a vase on a block of ice," he sings.

I turn around to look at Suzz, to see whether or not she realises what's going on. If she has, she's giving nothing away. Eyes closed, her hands move slowly over the keys. The sound she's making gives the impression that there's a whole string section hidden somewhere.

"Your cigarette smoulders, a bright red eye, immune to my anguish as I testify."

OK, I knew he was infatuated, but *anguish*? Of course, I now realise that, during the pre-game show, when he was apparently oblivious to all stimuli, Bass was in fact a good deal more sentient than he was letting on. Plus, it's patently obvious that he's either composed the words in the last fifteen minutes or he's making them up on the spot.

"Without your lips on mine, I am lost. Without your hand in mine, I am dead."

Goodness me, he *is* serious.

Even though the relevance of the lyrics must be a mystery, their sentiments appear to have struck a chord with the crowd. Six hundred pairs of eyes are fixed on Bass as he repeats the last couplet over and over, staring in 'anguish' up at the ceiling, the veins on the side of neck bulging. I glance over at Derek who's staring at our tormented songsmith with something akin to trepidation. It could be he believes there's a chance Bass may finish off his display of emotional distress with a public suicide – ritual disembowelment, perhaps. When I turn around, I can't believe that Suzz is as oblivious as she appears.

Finally, Bass reaches a climax. The last word, *dead*, mutates into a long howl of desolation which reverberates around the club like a wretched pilgrim looking for sanctuary. Derek starts playing the mournful solo of the final segment. We build up to a crescendo and end the song, leaving Red's final cymbal crash ringing in the air like a funeral bell.

The audience seems stunned. Were it not for the electric hum of the PA, one might very well be able to hear a pin drop. After what seems like an eternity, someone starts clapping. I quickly scan the crowd for the lone aficionado and discover, to my astonishment, that it is none other than my sister. It looks as though tears are streaming down her face, although this could easily be a trick of the light, or my fevered imagination. One by one, then more quickly, other members of the audience start to clap, until the noise is almost deafening.

I feel drained, so God alone knows how Bass must feel. He's giving nothing away, however, as he's just standing there, staring down at his feet. Once more I turn to look at Suzz and find her also looking down, her hands by her sides. I get the feeling I'm missing something, a vital piece of information which could explain everything. Perhaps the two of them have had a discussion without me knowing. Not that there's any particular reason why Bass should have told me that he has professed his undying devotion to Suzz and then been categorically rebuffed. But, knowing Bass as I do, I just can't entertain the possibility that he would have chosen such a direct approach.

The audience is still applauding, a full two minutes after Rosie kicked things off. I see Bass turn to Derek, then Red, then me. His expression is indecipherable. He nods, indicating I should start the intro of Nirvana's *Smells Like*

Teen Spirit. What I want to do is pull him off to one side and ask him exactly what's going on but I understand this is definitely neither the place nor the time. As I play the ten second intro I see Bass's gaze flick from me to Suzz and the bitterness in his eyes, though not unexpected, is still rather unsettling and more than a little sad.

Red knocks out the brief drum fill that brings in the rest of us. Bass, energised by the aggression of the arrangement, plucks at the strings of his guitar with a vengeance. Facing Red, he bobs his head up and down, losing himself in the rhythm. When the pace slows, he wheels about to face the crowd and begins to sing. Compared with *Decaying Emotions* where his voice was plaintive and despairing, now it is strident, full of unrepressed anger. The audience, enervated, join in with the rousing chorus. The lads in the front row are going potty, leaping around like madmen. Red is making such a racket, I have to check that he is not breaking something. We reach the end of the song with Bass's and Derek's right arms windmilling frantically.

With Derek wringing out the last chord, Bass unhooks his guitar, leans forward to grunt a hoarse 'thank you' to the apoplectic audience, then turns and walks quickly toward the steps behind Suzz and I, glancing at neither of us.

I look out over the sea of cheering punters, trying to work out what happens now. Rosie, Dawn and Mamta are going bananas, jumping up and down and screaming. Near the bar, Chelsea is whooping, clapping her hands above her head, looking as though she's just watched Queen after Freddie Mercury came back from the dead and joined the band on stage to sing *Bohemian Rhapsody*.

273

Apollonia and Robert are clapping politely. When Robert leans toward her and says something, Apollonia's face twitches with annoyance as she recoils from him. I'd give my right eye to know what was going on over there. Well, not quite, but I'd dearly love to know, anyway.

I turn to see Derek grinning widely at the audience. Behind his kit, Red is standing, sweat running in rivers down his chest and abdomen, his sticks held aloft. He spies me watching him then throws his sticks out into the crowd, smiling idiotically. I grin, knowing for how long he's dreamed about doing that. Even more, he's wanted to join his fellow band-members at the front of the stage where we would hold hands and bask in the adulation of an audience whipped up into a frenzy of excitement.

Unfortunately, one of our members is missing.

I twist the other way and look at Suzz who's sitting calmly behind the Roland, gazing indifferently at the crowd. I think Red hit the nail on the head earlier. If anyone deserves the term 'ice-maiden', it's her. I am somewhat irrationally filled with some of the resentment I know Bass feels towards her. Irrational, because, after all, she's really done nothing to offend me. Apart from driving one of my best friends to near suicidal desperation, that is. I am struck by the urge to reach forward, grab and shake her shoulders, and ask her if she has any idea what she's doing to him.

I turn once more to face the audience and unhook my guitar. With a quick wave, which I'd like to think conveys reserved appreciation of their applause, I make my way past Suzz and down the steps where I find Lenny.

"That was great, kid."

"Yeah, thanks. Did Bass go back to the dressing room?"

274

Not waiting for a response, I trot along the corridor, back to the broom cupboard, in the middle of which I find Bass standing with his back to the door. His guitar, obviously thrown with some force, protrudes from a pile of cardboard boxes in one corner.

"Hey, mate, you all right?"

"Bugger off."

I'm not sure quite how I should handle this. Kid gloves spring to mind. On the other hand, Derek, Red and you-know-who will be along any second. I'd better get straight to the point.

"Look, I know you're feeling... I mean, I know this is difficult-"

"Just bugger the fuck off, will you?"

"Hey, Bass, come on," I say, talking to his back.

I hear Red shouting excitedly and walk swiftly up to Bass. I grab his shoulder and pull him around. I wouldn't go so far as to say that he looks as though he's been crying, or even that he's about to, but his eyes do look exceptionally moist.

"Hey, just don't make a fool of yourself," I hiss. "She isn't worth it."

As Red and Derek spill into the room, Bass turns away.

"I cannot fucking believe what just fucking happened," shrieks Red, staring wild-eyed at me. He holds his open hands either side of his head. "Mind equals blown!"

"Yeah, it went pretty well," I agree.

"What do you mean, *pretty well*? That was bloody incredible! We killed them! We slaughtered them! We eviscerated them and dragged their entrails around the fucking room! Pickaxe don't stand a chance of beating that!"

I smile and shake my head.

"You've got to admit, Johnny," says Derek, "that went a hell of a lot better than we could've expected."

"And what about *Decaying Emotions*?" asks Red. "I just can*not* believe how brilliant that was. Hey, Bass! When did you learn to sing like that? Holy fucking shit! Intense? If you Google 'intense' you'll find a video clip of you singing that bloody song!"

"Thanks," mutters Bass without turning to face his friends.

"I've got to hand it to you, Bass," says Derek. "You were phenomenal tonight. Abso-fucking-lutely phenomenal. No doubt."

I am unable to prevent myself from frowning as Suzz appears in the doorway. Derek spots my expression and turns to see who I'm looking at.

"Suuuuuzzzzzz!" he exclaims, drawing out her name as if he was a South American football commentator. "Here she is, the metal sex-goddess every right-minded head-banger dreams about! What a star! So, what did you think of that, then? Were we brilliant, or what?"

Suzz gives him a half-smile then looks over at Bass. It's clear to me now that I'm not, after all, the only one who's noticed that our bass player is not feeling on top of the world.

"Yeah, it was OK."

"What do you-?"

"Listen!" hisses Red, silencing Derek. "Can you hear that?"

"What?"

"The sound of six hundred people demanding an encore!"

True enough, the crowd is clapping as one and cheering loudly.

"Yeah!" says Derek, eyes wide. "Hey, what shall we play?"

"No question," says Red. "We've got to do *Teen Spirit* again."

Derek nods enthusiastically. "Right, that was easily the best one. What do you say, Johnny?"

"Sure, why not?"

"Bass?"

"No," says Bass curtly, as though he was reprimanding a disobedient dog.

Red and Derek look at each other, shrug, then look at me. I, however, am keeping a careful eye on Suzz.

"What, you mean you want to play something else?" asks Red.

Zach runs into the room, slightly out of breath, a huge grin plastered across his face.

"Guys! What a show. They *love* you! You've got to get back out there!"

When he gets no reply, he scans the others then looks at me.

"Two minutes," I say then jerk my head, indicating that his return to the mixing desk would be an appropriate course of action.

Unsurprisingly, he declines my advice. "What's going on?"

Surprisingly, it's Suzz that speaks.

"Bass doesn't want to play an encore."

"What?" whine Zach, Derek and Red in unison.

"Do you, Bass?"

277

I'm not sure I like her tone and, quite suddenly, I realise that, should things get to such a stage, I am prepared to support Bass's decision. He turns around and meets Suzz's steely gaze.

"No, I don't."

"Bloody hell!" squeals Red. "Why not?"

"I know why not," says Suzz, taking four long strides toward Bass.

She stops in front of him, having crossed that invisible line most of us draw around ourselves which demarcates our personal space. Because of my relative position, I am able to see only Bass's face, not hers. He looks frightened but defiant, an underdog set on confrontation whatever the consequences.

Suzz adjusts her feet so that they are set about eighteen inches apart. Her boot heels are absolutely vertical and the black PVC of her jeans is pulled taut from waistband to ankles. While Bass is unable to observe this phenomenon, he has apparently noticed something equally alluring from his vantage point. Perhaps it's something about Suzz's face, or her perfume. Whatever it is, his expression has softened and his pupils have dilated. Like a perplexed puppy, he lets his head fall a little to one side. Suzz lifts both hands and gently places them behind his neck. For a fleeting moment, I fear for his groin.

"Those," says Suzz, her voice husky, "were the most beautiful words I've *ever* heard."

A few moments pass, during which confusion and desire jostle for pole position on Bass's face. He opens his mouth to speak but, before he can utter a word, Suzz quickly moves up her hands a couple of inches and pulls his head towards hers. She plants her lips over his.

This catches me completely off guard, so much so that all I can do is stand and stare. I should feel guilty, standing and staring, but I don't. I can't even check to see if the others have turned away out of a sense of propriety or whether they are as transfixed as I. It's utterly mesmerising.

Bass's hands swing out from his sides then slowly drop back again. His eyes flutter as Suzz passionately pulls his lips even harder against hers. Again Bass's hands move outwards, this time more tentatively. They move forwards and hover either side of Suzz's hips, on which they eventually gently settle. Suzz thrusts her pelvis forwards. Bass's hands slip down over her glossy black buttocks. His fingertips indent the taut PVC. Suzz releases Bass's lips. I finally avert my gaze. I listen to them both inhaling deeply. I look back to see Bass's eyelids flickering open, revealing a patina of hungry lust. A copious amount of Suzz's lipstick is smeared across his lips and chin.

"You lot coming back, or what? They're not going to wait all night."

I turn to see Lenny standing behind Zach.

Suzz clears her throat. "You want to do an encore now?"

"Yeah," grunts Bass, although I would imagine he has other things on his mind. Well, maybe *one* particular thing.

Suzz releases Bass's neck and turns to face the rest of us, letting her left arm slide down Bass's back and come to rest around his waist. With his right hand still on her lustrous bum, the pair of them undeniably look like a *couple*. Part of me – a part of me I *really* don't like – starts to feel jealous. Hey, it's not like I want to rain on their parade or anything, but (oh, yes, there had to be a 'but') there are perhaps two neurones somewhere deep inside my brain that are furiously texting envious messages to one another.

"What are *you* looking at?" asks Suzz.

"Nothing," says Red, as I realise Suzz wasn't talking to me. I swallow.

"Are you up for an encore of *Teen Spirit*, then?" Suzz asks, looking around at everyone. "Or are you too knackered?"

Oddly, instead of the sarcastic half-smile I would've expected, she's grinning. Red seems to understand that the rules of the game have been changed and, unlike me, appears to have accepted the alteration without question.

"What are we waiting for?" he asks. "Let's go. Our fanatical public awaits!"

While Bass retrieves his guitar from its ignominious resting place among the cardboard boxes, Zach steps to one side to allow Derek, Red and me to file past him. I wait in the corridor as Suzz and Bass walk toward the door.

"Bass," says Zach.

Bass watches Zach rubbing his mouth for a few seconds before realising that he's going to look pretty silly if he goes on stage looking as though he's been bobbing for apples in a bucket of tomato sauce. Displaying that she has quickly mastered what was once a rarely practised gesture, Suzz smiles, this time in a maternal, *Oh, you silly thing* sort of way, then pulls out a paper tissue from an inside pocket and begins wiping Bass's mouth. Once the majority of lipstick traces have been removed, she tucks the tissue up her sleeve and steps across to a grimy mirror mounted on the wall. I note Bass's enraptured expression as Suzz begins to reapply her lipstick. I sigh and set off down the corridor.

Lenny, Derek and Red are waiting at the foot of the steps. When Lenny spots me, he sprints up onto the stage.

His appearance prompts a loud cheer from the audience, who's patience and persistence, while undeniably gratifying, are probably unwarranted. After all, we couldn't have been *that* good, could we?

"Ladies and germs," shouts Lenny, "would you please put your hands together and welcome back on stage... Bläck Gläss!"

To the immensely agreeable sound of six hundred people cheering and clapping, I follow Derek and Red up the steps.

Derek pauses at Bass's microphone and raises his fist in triumph. "Thank you, Wembley!" he bellows.

Red emphasises the sentiment with a machine gun drum roll. Being the reserved chap that I am, I merely smile benevolently. I check the controls on my guitar then play a chord to ensure everything's working. Derek does the same. I twist around to watch Bass and Suzz climbing the steps. While still concealed from the audience's view, Suzz gives Bass a light peck on the cheek. Bass's silly grin should warm the cockles of my heart but, instead, those two obstreperous neurones persuade a few neighbours to join their dissenting campaign.

The hysterical crowd raise the volume of their cheering by a few hundred decibels as Bass and Suzz stride into view. Suzz sits down at the Roland and Bass walks over to me.

"Just start with the *Teen Spirit* intro on my signal, OK?"

The crowd quieten as Bass walks over to his position and adjusts the microphone stand.

"We'd like to do something special for you now," he says, grinning. "This is a little number, currently riding high in the charts, as they say, by the country's favourite sons of metal, 4Tune8!"

He chuckles to himself and looks over at Suzz as he plays the refrain from one of their so-called hits.

"No, just joking," he says then waves a finger at me.

Needless to say (or is it?) the audience goes berserk as we gallop through the song and their applause at the end is louder than ever. We all look at each other and the unspoken question of a further song bounces between us. Bass, now the undoubted leader, answers by unhooking his guitar then holding it by the neck as he beckons each of us to join him. I stand at one end of the line, next to Suzz, staring in disbelief at the crowd.

"Thank you," shouts Bass. "You've been absolutely fantastic!"

I see Rosie and her friends, their faces beaming with excitement. At the back, Chelsea is jumping around like a small child on one of those giant inflatable castles.

Derek grabs the microphone. "Thank you and goodnight!"

I look to my left and see Apollonia getting up from the table. Robert's attempt to follow suit is thwarted by Apollonia slapping him on the cheek with sufficient force to turn his head. Ignoring the nearby punters who are gaping in astonishment, Apollonia moves swiftly toward the exit. Before I can properly assimilate this development, Suzz tugs my elbow. Looking over my shoulder as I walk off the stage, I watch Apollonia disappear through the double doors. Red turns and trots across to the microphone.

"Born to be wild!" he yells, then runs back to follow me down the steps.

"*Born to be wild*? What's that supposed to mean?" I ask.

He grins maniacally. "Hey, who cares?"
Indeed.

[27] Confession

"That was fantastic!" says Red as we walk along the corridor.

"Yeah, it was."

"Could you see Chelsea?"

"Sure, she was at the back."

"Was she having a good time?"

"Um, yeah, sure, I think so, from what I could see."

"Great. As soon as I've changed, I'm going to find her."

Derek ambushes us as we walk into the broom cupboard. He's so pumped he's practically gibbering.

"Jesus, that was brilliant! I can't believe it! We were *so... frickin'... tight!* And they absolutely *loved* us! Did you see the way they went berserk for the encore? Christ! I thought there was going to be a bloody stage invasion!"

He pauses for breath then extends his arms and grins at Red and I as if we were long lost relatives. "Red, what can I say? You were magnificent! And Johnny, you were sensational!"

For a moment, it looks as though he's about to hug us, but then he turns away. "Bass! My man! You were positively astounding! Why on earth didn't you let us know you could sing like that? And you were *so* intense during *Decaying Emotions* I was almost bloody crying. Hey, and I'm not joking either. I was honestly on the verge of dropping to my knees and crying my bloody eyes out! And that 4Tune8 bit! You had the bloody audience eating out of the palm of your hand! That was totally *inspired*!"

Is this man *on* something, or what?

"Suzz!" he bellows. "What a star! What a bloody *incandescent*, metallic, sex-babe, *super*-star! Did you see all those punters staring at you? Jesus! Their tongues were hanging so far out of their mouths they were licking the bloody floor! And the way you played during *Decaying Emotions*! God, it was *so* beautiful!"

Sex-babe?

"I've just got to say, you were *all* totally, one-hundred per cent excellent! *We* were all totally, one-hundred per cent excellent! How the hell are Pickaxe going to follow that? I'll tell you how. By packing up their kit, getting back into their van, and getting the hell out of Dodge! No band could follow that! No one. Bloody brilliant!"

At last, he seems to have run out of steam.

"I thought you were all right, too," says Red, straight-faced.

Derek's brow starts twerking or something, which looks as comical as it sounds, at least to Red, who bursts out laughing.

"You were stupendous, of course! They were hanging on to each and every one of your patented speed-of-light runs as if they were messages from Hendrix himself!"

This is exactly what Derek wanted to hear and he launches another barrage of extravagant congratulations. Red joins in and soon the pair of them are competing to see who can concoct the most ridiculous superlative.

"Metal-tastic!"

"Metal-abulous!"

"Metal-ificent!"

"Metal-mungous!"

And so on.

I lean down, withdraw a towel from my bag and begin to dry my hair. I glance at Bass and Suzz. They're holding hands, watching Derek and Red. I know I should find this sweet, or cute, and I know I should be happy for them, and I hate myself for feeling otherwise, but I'm starting to feel a little resentful.

Sigh. I know, I know.

I *should* be trying to quash such negative feelings. Hell, I *am* trying to quash such negative feelings. But it's hard, bloody hard. It's like trying to put a screen protector on your phone. No matter how hard you try, those pesky air bubbles persist. And, in my mind, the little air bubbles of resentment won't be massaged away. And I hate myself for it. This must rank as one of the best nights of Bass's life and here I am begrudging his happiness. Screw it. This *has* to be one of the best nights of my life too. I walk over to them.

"Hey," I say to Bass, "you *were* pretty spectacular tonight."

"Thanks, man."

I turn to Suzz. "You, too. The keyboards made all the difference. Took things to a whole new level. Honestly. No shit."

She nods. I look back at Bass. My phone buzzes and I glance at the screen. It's a text from someone called Mr Awkward. "Enjoying this moment, Johnny? There're more where this came from…" Well, no that doesn't happen but I can feel a rather odd dynamic developing, and I don't like it. Then Zach walks in.

"Just a little present from me, guys," he says, humping a case of Stella into the room "Just make sure Lenny doesn't see this, OK?"

Red and Derek each grab a can. Zach tosses one over to me, grinning.

"Hey," he says to me. "I'd never have thought my kid brother could've been part of such a great show. Respect due, Atticus, my man!"

I smile, pulling the tab on the can. "Gee, thanks." I consider adding something witty and self-deprecating but, to be honest, I can't be bothered.

Zach picks up three cans and walks over to Bass and Suzz. He gives them one each and opens another for himself. "So, I didn't know you two were... you know, an *item.*"

If Bass wasn't still glowing from his recent exertions he'd be blushing. "Er... we weren't."

Zach laughs and looks more pointedly at Suzz then back at Bass. "But you are now?"

Bass is flustered. "Um... er... ah...."

"Yes," says Suzz, smiling, "we are."

Zach lifts up his can. "Well, here's to both of you, then."

"Hey, Zach," says Derek, "what did it sound like from where you were?"

I cross to a chair and sit down as Zach moves over to Derek. Red drains his can in one long draught then towels himself and changes into a black tee-shirt and jeans.

"Got to go find the woman of my dreams," he says to me then trots out through the doorway.

I lean back then close my eyes for a few minutes, just trying to relax. Even now, my heart rate has not yet returned to normal. I can feel an odd sort of buzzing in my breastbone, like a vibrating tuning fork. Presumably an after-effect of being on stage. My limbs are dead weights. I open my eyes and sip lager. Bass and Suzz are facing each

287

other, their hands resting on the others hips, communicating only with their eyes. I can imagine what they're saying and wish I couldn't. The door opens again.

"Come and meet the band," says Red leading Chelsea into the room.

She looks flushed, excited, and rather sweet. Trouble is, I'm getting a little sick of *sweet* just at the moment. Anything else *sweet* and there's a risk of blowing chunks. Chelsea's wearing a loose Killswitch Engage tee, denim mini-skirt, black leggings and a pair of Converse Harley Quinn trainers (of which I, slightly grudgingly, approve). She's grinning uncertainly, like a five-year-old being led into Santa's grotto.

"Hey, everybody, this is Chelsea."

Red brings her over to me first. "Johnny, Chelsea."

I smile. "Hello, again."

"Hi," she says then giggles.

"Enjoy the show?"

Her eyes light up. "Oh, it was great!"

"Especially the drummer, eh?"

"That's enough of that," says Red, laughing. "Now then, you've got to watch Johnny. He's a dirty old man of the highest order and, whatever you do, don't go near him wearing six-inch heels. Eh, Johnny?"

"Er... no, that wouldn't be a good idea."

Well, that makes me feel just fucking peachy.

Chelsea allows herself to be led across to Bass and Suzz then to Derek and Zach. I drain my can then fetch another. Dirty old men need refreshment too, don't they? By the time I've finished the second can, Red and Chelsea have taken up a position sitting side by side on two chairs next to the pile of boxes. They're speaking quietly and Red is gently stroking Chelsea's bare arm. Gazing at him with pure adoration, she leans forwards and parts her lips. I feel like something inside me is on the verge of snapping and I look away, only to be greeted by the sight of Bass and Suzz engaged in an energetic bout of face-sucking. The thing inside me snaps and I jump to my feet. But I don't know what to do now. I stare helplessly at Zach.

"You want another one?" he asks, reaching down to the crate of lager.

"No," I say, perhaps a little too loudly, although not, I note, loud enough to attract the attention of either of the amorous couples.

"Hey, suit yourself," he says then turns to resume his conversation with Derek.

I can see that a swift exit would be wise – discretion being the better part of Valerie, and so on. Anyway, I just want to get the hell out of here, but before I move a muscle, Rosie's head appears in the doorway. Let me rephrase that, lest you get the impression that her disembodied head hangs, wraith-like, in mid-air. Rosie pokes her head around the door jamb. That still doesn't sound very elegant, does it? Still, I'll assume you get the general idea.

"Can we come in?" she asks Zach.

What's this? Has she married into royalty or what?

"Sure," says Zach. "The more the merrier."

Rosie walks in, followed by Dawn and Mamta. The sight of frantic snogging appears to faze them not one iota. Nor, apart from a quick scowl from Dawn, do they pay any attention to me. Instead they make a bee-line for Derek and Zach, which suits me just fine.

"You were brilliant!" squeals Mamta as I march out of the room.

Play your cards right, Derek, and you could be well away there, if you can stomach a gaggle of giggling larvae, that is. I clump along the corridor, thrust open the emergency exit, stamp out into the alley then turn and, with an explosive grunt, slam shut the door. With my toys tossed emphatically out of the pram, I feel a whole lot better.

Right, sure I do.

There's an upturned plastic crate close to the wall. I sit down, lean back, close my eyes and take a couple of deep breaths. My mind is a maelstrom of contradictory emotions. The Stella is not helping. I try to sort through them. First of all…

Hey, hang on a minute. You don't *really* want to hear me whining, *again,* about all my problems, do you? Well, I know I wouldn't if I were you. So what if I'm ticked off by my two best friends finding female company more pleasurable than mine? And who cares if I'm so self-absorbed that I can write off Chelsea as a well-intentioned but essentially half-witted, giggling child when I patently don't know the first thing about her? Yeah, well, let me tell you something: I can't be bothered to find out anything else about her. And I can't be bothered talking to you lot either, so you may as well piss off.

That's right. You heard me. Just bugger off and leave me alone. If I want to wallow in my very own, personalised, monogrammed, high definition slough of despond then I jolly well will.

Well, what are you waiting for? I told you to piss off.

What? You're wondering about the rest of this book, are you? Yeah, well, I'd just forget about it if I were you. Cut your losses. Candy Crush Saga doesn't play itself. You never finished that Breaking Bad box set, did you? Do what you like but just leave me alone, OK?

Look, I'm only going to say this one more time. Piss. Off.

Lorem ipsum dolor sit amet, consectetur adipiscing elit. Duis dignissim dui a gravida tristique. Nulla pretium non odio nec maximus. Vivamus in eleifend purus. Nulla quis purus libero. Praesent ac dictum massa. In lacinia nisi id faucibus auctor. Mauris ultrices sed nisi at laoreet. Quisque gravida lacus in turpis dapibus, vel porttitor risus varius. Praesent nec turpis tortor. Maecenas in metus rutrum, interdum massa in, malesuada nisl. Aliquam ex eros, accumsan sed finibus at, viverra sit amet eros. Etiam eget neque rutrum, consectetur odio et, ultrices sem. Curabitur vestibulum sem eget mauris bibendum, eu fermentum risus efficitur. Pellentesque egestas, metus sed cursus faucibus, urna sem faucibus leo, non eleifend nulla ex in sapien.

Fusce efficitur risus a purus mollis eleifend. Ut consequat nisi nisl, ut dignissim est elementum at. In nec scelerisque erat. Aenean condimentum eget odio non tristique. Phasellus bibendum porttitor erat, id egestas eros auctor ac. Etiam interdum finibus justo in viverra. Nunc auctor dui justo. Vestibulum vitae sapien pulvinar, consectetur risus ac, imperdiet elit. Cras interdum ultrices mauris at vehicula. Lorem ipsum dolor sit amet, consectetur adipiscing elit. Fusce maximus neque erat, sit amet euismod mauris ullamcorper a. Cras et elit eget ligula imperdiet vulputate. Vestibulum laoreet, leo sit amet dignissim blandit, ex dui volutpat libero, id sodales ligula libero non massa.

Integer gravida libero eget elit interdum, at posuere risus dignissim. Donec ut convallis ante, vitae molestie tortor. Sed fermentum tellus enim, et viverra elit vestibulum imperdiet. Nullam placerat eu elit a blandit. Lorem ipsum dolor sit amet, consectetur adipiscing elit. Sed porta ex tincidunt aliquet placerat. Fusce viverra suscipit bibendum. Vivamus luctus tellus condimentum, commodo turpis eget, venenatis leo. Phasellus at justo mi. Maecenas lobortis justo sapien, vitae aliquam lorem malesuada et. Morbi id quam scelerisque risus ullamcorper mattis quis et eros. Vivamus eget tellus eu orci bibendum accumsan eget non sapien. Ut commodo consequat lobortis. Etiam eu sagittis lacus, eget ornare leo. Nunc ullamcorper purus at libero rhoncus, vitae sagittis enim ultrices.

Praesent in dapibus dolor. Integer tempus id neque et consequat. Curabitur imperdiet felis sed velit mattis, id congue lacus eleifend. Nulla sed gravida magna, et semper sapien. Praesent efficitur lacus nulla, eu convallis risus porta a. Phasellus sed orci quis risus lacinia volutpat non euismod risus. Mauris scelerisque bibendum fringilla. In ultricies rutrum lacus, id tempor nibh pretium viverra.

Mauris a accumsan leo. Proin et urna dapibus, scelerisque enim non, blandit nisl. Sed et ex augue. Suspendisse tristique ante et ex placerat tempor. Nulla fermentum diam sed dolor viverra eleifend. Nam eget vulputate orci. Donec quis luctus augue. Vivamus at ultricies tellus, in porta lorem. Nulla vitae urna at ante suscipit posuere nec pharetra nunc. Curabitur posuere lacus vel ornare tincidunt. Aenean nunc nibh, porta in lacus iaculis, lacinia placerat lectus. Vestibulum tempus sem lorem, consectetur iaculis libero efficitur a.

Sed elementum, nisi quis fermentum suscipit, mauris lorem lacinia leo, rutrum euismod quam enim vel ex. Aliquam varius aliquam laoreet. Vivamus feugiat nibh ac efficitur gravida. Ut quis ante id mauris aliquet fringilla quis a justo. Vestibulum non tincidunt neque, eget sodales sapien. Cras vulputate tempor leo sed pharetra. Nulla vel efficitur lectus, vitae scelerisque sem. Integer lacinia velit nec vestibulum auctor. Proin lacus sapien, accumsan a dui lobortis, eleifend lobortis urna. In hendrerit urna lacus, sed elementum nisl interdum sit amet. Integer sed lorem fringilla, venenatis erat sodales, imperdiet ex. Pellentesque id efficitur dolor. Nam eget maximus nibh, a vehicula velit. Integer turpis nisi, viverra a nunc ut, feugiat vestibulum tortor.

Sed iaculis ornare ultricies. Morbi tempor ipsum ultrices pellentesque maximus. Suspendisse bibendum, leo eget congue interdum, purus nisi tincidunt nisi, euismod fringilla sapien tellus non diam. Integer at euismod est. In ullamcorper urna eu ligula blandit pulvinar. Sed sit amet metus eget leo malesuada scelerisque eu quis nisi. In quis velit dolor. Suspendisse potenti. Class aptent taciti sociosqu ad litora torquent per conubia nostra, per inceptos himenaeos. Fusce tincidunt aliquet malesuada.

Praesent at suscipit turpis, sed rhoncus orci. Curabitur sit amet ex ultrices, molestie dolor at, bibendum enim. Quisque lacinia tempor nisl non semper. Donec vestibulum et magna et congue. Nam odio felis, iaculis eget ligula quis, tempus auctor odio. Nullam ut efficitur erat, sit amet sollicitudin urna. Maecenas nunc ante, faucibus ut ligula et, aliquet efficitur augue. Praesent commodo arcu a diam rhoncus gravida. Maecenas dignissim lacus id porta gravida.

Donec elementum condimentum diam, vitae fermentum sapien cursus in. Curabitur interdum diam ac est mattis lobortis sit amet quis magna. Duis id dictum felis. Vivamus iaculis dignissim luctus. Maecenas et aliquet neque, bibendum vestibulum tortor. Fusce sodales commodo consectetur. Aliquam ac mattis dolor. Praesent efficitur ex in pellentesque feugiat. In sagittis aliquet felis sit amet convallis. Nam placerat commodo pharetra. Praesent dictum vehicula enim, non tincidunt tellus maximus sit amet. Quisque id erat massa. Pellentesque finibus leo a augue rutrum auctor. Duis malesuada blandit sem nec placerat. Etiam ac volutpat arcu. Phasellus fringilla tellus id orci lacinia, vel gravida massa pretium.

Suspendisse sollicitudin, tortor nec tincidunt mattis, nibh urna vulputate elit, quis vehicula massa lorem et nulla. Mauris pellentesque sapien ut dui aliquam dictum. Fusce condimentum efficitur purus, eu venenatis orci eleifend vitae. Quisque pharetra iaculis scelerisque. Maecenas ultricies justo in justo dignissim volutpat. Suspendisse in est enim. Aliquam ligula eros, vehicula vitae libero posuere, tempus rhoncus quam. Duis iaculis accumsan consequat. Cras eu congue justo. Nulla quis arcu vitae leo facilisis placerat vitae vitae elit. Aliquam eget elementum est, nec commodo velit. Nam condimentum quam lorem, eget feugiat urna ullamcorper ut. Mauris hendrerit purus eget leo interdum venenatis. Vestibulum elementum efficitur nisi, id molestie nisl cursus nec. Curabitur malesuada neque eget mauris fringilla, eu bibendum dolor rutrum. Phasellus felis est, venenatis eu fermentum porta, elementum a nisi.

Vivamus vestibulum a urna tempor dapibus. Vestibulum vel convallis dolor. Nam dignissim eros vitae lacus imperdiet molestie. Donec finibus convallis iaculis. Duis malesuada ultrices arcu in pulvinar. Donec turpis libero, malesuada in feugiat in, auctor sed neque. Pellentesque sollicitudin id metus et semper. Maecenas et euismod dolor, rutrum ultricies lectus. Vestibulum accumsan neque eget arcu gravida, eu consectetur ante pharetra. Cras sed auctor velit, sit amet vulputate urna. Cras vel velit vitae urna consectetur mattis ac at dui. Praesent tincidunt, elit vel porta aliquet, mi nunc egestas leo, eu tempus tellus dolor posuere tortor. Aenean fringilla non nibh nec lobortis. Sed urna tortor, tincidunt quis ullamcorper sit amet, luctus sed diam.

Suspendisse potenti. Proin eu venenatis elit. Duis sed lorem vel tortor ultricies varius eget in eros. Cras vitae mi metus. Donec sem justo, fermentum gravida commodo ut, elementum nec est. In ipsum mauris, placerat vel laoreet sed, pharetra vel sem. Praesent bibendum tincidunt volutpat. Proin id urna sed mauris accumsan auctor ac et est. Integer molestie sed quam sed interdum. Vivamus egestas finibus metus, nec luctus mauris venenatis et. Ut at nulla ultrices, molestie magna eget, iaculis tortor. Vestibulum ante ipsum primis in faucibus orci luctus et ultrices posuere cubilia Curae;

Fusce consectetur ante at lorem eleifend, et fermentum diam bibendum. Nunc mollis dui nunc, nec varius turpis placerat sit amet. Duis eleifend purus id ligula pellentesque, ac facilisis dolor viverra. Sed ut metus metus. Vestibulum ante ipsum primis in faucibus orci luctus et ultrices posuere cubilia Curae; Suspendisse nisl mauris, porta a egestas a, semper quis orci. Fusce vulputate lorem ante. Nunc et ullamcorper turpis, in aliquet nisi. Cras pulvinar diam efficitur, sollicitudin ex nec, lacinia est. Pellentesque venenatis, massa vitae dapibus vehicula, erat ante dictum ante, et aliquam enim tellus vitae dolor. Cras tincidunt blandit tortor accumsan sollicitudin. Aliquam condimentum malesuada metus non ultricies. Nunc pharetra mauris id lacus varius, ut sollicitudin magna tempor. Cras ut est sit amet tellus aliquet semper a a sem. Fusce nec nisi in nisi pharetra accumsan. Vivamus velit massa, blandit a suscipit quis, molestie eget turpis.

Etiam id massa suscipit, rutrum est in, pharetra nisl. Fusce porttitor scelerisque lorem vestibulum tempor. Class aptent taciti sociosqu ad litora torquent per conubia nostra, per inceptos himenaeos. In accumsan risus in ante rutrum cursus. Aliquam varius scelerisque ligula, eu egestas diam vulputate at. Integer sem mauris, congue id risus vitae, dictum ultricies quam. Donec mollis nisi nec sagittis rutrum. Mauris gravida est nisi, ac viverra massa suscipit sit amet. Aenean condimentum vel mauris elementum facilisis.

Donec hendrerit lectus neque, id laoreet enim sagittis non. Etiam lorem tellus, euismod nec lacinia sed, commodo at nisl. Etiam at dapibus dolor, quis fermentum neque. Quisque aliquam non erat sit amet commodo. Duis ac sem sem. Sed id vulputate erat. Donec lectus eros, pharetra eget quam ut, laoreet cursus orci. Aenean suscipit, leo quis rutrum laoreet, libero lacus tincidunt elit, vitae venenatis nisl dui nec dolor. Phasellus semper ut dolor non posuere. Cum sociis natoque penatibus et magnis dis parturient montes, nascetur ridiculus mus. Proin vel maximus nibh. Integer porta sodales mauris vel pulvinar. Maecenas congue arcu sit amet mi imperdiet, et congue leo eleifend. In maximus lacus vitae tortor ultricies volutpat. Fusce commodo iaculis lorem, sit amet tempus orci molestie eu.

Phasellus sollicitudin tincidunt ipsum sed facilisis. Pellentesque id pellentesque quam. Nulla laoreet tempor justo, at luctus massa maximus in. Sed tempor congue facilisis. Morbi laoreet nunc id metus eleifend, ac dapibus leo condimentum. Vivamus luctus in eros ut viverra. Duis scelerisque tristique porta. In pretium suscipit erat, sit amet vulputate justo suscipit eu. Etiam tincidunt urna eget nisl lobortis egestas. Mauris est lorem, malesuada non neque et, cursus lobortis dolor.

Nam nec lorem augue. Pellentesque habitant morbi tristique senectus et netus et malesuada fames ac turpis egestas. Integer mattis hendrerit felis ut ultrices. Nunc id rutrum magna. Pellentesque quis dictum dolor. Donec cursus sem ac massa fringilla, a accumsan metus egestas. Suspendisse imperdiet sit amet augue id viverra. Proin vel elementum velit. Interdum et malesuada fames ac ante ipsum primis in faucibus. Curabitur dapibus risus vitae est ultricies sollicitudin.

Mauris elementum, enim ac sollicitudin malesuada, enim enim mattis velit, sit amet sodales mauris lacus nec lacus. Curabitur maximus nibh in odio volutpat, a ullamcorper magna dignissim. Integer magna dolor, pellentesque non ultrices at, varius sit amet ante. Pellentesque nec tempus tortor. Sed quis aliquet nisl. Maecenas ipsum nunc, sodales ac neque in, condimentum consequat massa. Quisque mollis nunc maximus, blandit lectus in, fringilla nisi. Vivamus et dui eget risus scelerisque egestas. Integer mi est, lobortis nec pharetra vel, rutrum non purus. Nulla auctor lorem sed tempus aliquet. Nulla nec velit quis tortor aliquet luctus nec a ante. Sed id risus dapibus, varius nibh vitae, pretium lacus. Maecenas interdum congue ligula et rhoncus. Quisque tortor urna, condimentum non porttitor sit amet, malesuada in felis. Suspendisse dignissim tincidunt velit, vel tincidunt eros. Suspendisse aliquet pharetra finibus.

Morbi suscipit ex purus, quis venenatis metus mattis eget. Vivamus eu erat lacinia enim volutpat vestibulum. Maecenas egestas a orci sit amet tempor. Donec interdum hendrerit augue in fermentum. In mollis eu orci in ultrices. Integer rutrum ac urna id pellentesque. Curabitur cursus, augue quis facilisis mattis, nisl diam finibus mauris, et consectetur nisi eros in diam. Nullam at metus pellentesque, vulputate enim quis, feugiat lacus. Aliquam commodo eleifend libero a vulputate. Praesent interdum tempus purus eget consectetur. Integer eros quam, pretium in mi quis, vulputate tincidunt turpis. Nullam ac lectus maximus, pellentesque nibh id, consequat velit. Nulla dignissim eros purus, feugiat faucibus leo lobortis vel. Suspendisse velit erat, iaculis quis velit nec, sollicitudin pretium risus.

Nulla facilisi. Phasellus viverra lacus eu lacus bibendum, ut posuere tortor scelerisque. Mauris semper faucibus accumsan. In hac habitasse platea dictumst. Aenean dapibus scelerisque purus eu elementum. Morbi id magna laoreet, pretium ligula non, mattis mauris. Quisque tempor odio vel nisi interdum, eu fringilla urna laoreet. Curabitur luctus ex augue.

Suspendisse ante nunc, ultrices vitae lacinia ut, bibendum at mauris. Aenean commodo pharetra augue, a ornare ipsum auctor at. Cras tempor sit amet justo ut vestibulum. Vestibulum fermentum scelerisque laoreet. Sed nulla nisl, fermentum quis quam ut, cursus placerat arcu. Etiam laoreet est pretium aliquet finibus. Aenean sagittis magna nec velit tempus, sit amet rutrum lorem ultricies. Lorem ipsum dolor sit amet, consectetur adipiscing elit.

Sed posuere bibendum nibh, nec elementum quam pellentesque nec. Nullam iaculis vestibulum vulputate. Aliquam nec arcu pulvinar, fringilla magna nec, pulvinar nunc. Aenean sed ligula et tortor finibus posuere ac id mauris. Nam vehicula nibh mauris, eget condimentum erat interdum eget. Aenean blandit nisi massa, sit amet facilisis sem fringilla sit amet. Donec aliquet ante vel massa vehicula pretium. Ut ante augue, rutrum eget arcu et, sollicitudin molestie nisi. Fusce congue lectus nec quam suscipit imperdiet. Pellentesque habitant morbi tristique senectus et netus et malesuada fames ac turpis egestas. Suspendisse consequat mattis vestibulum.

Cras suscipit convallis condimentum. Cras tincidunt augue ullamcorper, suscipit sem a, malesuada nisl. Ut ultrices felis non lectus gravida, ut laoreet elit fermentum. Morbi id tempus eros. Integer vulputate scelerisque lorem et scelerisque. Vivamus dui turpis, volutpat ut consectetur eu, dignissim at urna. Etiam sit amet eros et leo feugiat ullamcorper pulvinar vel nibh. Maecenas vitae neque vitae urna bibendum iaculis sit amet ac nunc. Nulla sit amet tortor vel libero aliquet accumsan. Sed vitae nisl et nunc mollis faucibus. Fusce ut elit id purus molestie semper auctor nec orci. Suspendisse potenti. Proin urna nunc, condimentum et nunc ut, tempor lacinia mi. Cras vehicula vulputate nisi, sit amet pulvinar urna mollis vitae.

Cras bibendum bibendum nisi, nec finibus metus elementum ac. Mauris ut ipsum non nisi convallis facilisis. Phasellus id ligula commodo ligula dapibus ultrices. Fusce ullamcorper libero nec lorem sollicitudin porttitor. Sed nulla libero, egestas nec laoreet non, consequat sed enim. Donec ullamcorper urna at ex lacinia blandit. Donec nibh dolor, eleifend nec massa in, tincidunt convallis justo. Integer interdum non odio ut finibus. Duis sollicitudin sit amet arcu eu varius. Donec dignissim orci odio, id cursus mi sollicitudin vel. Sed in nibh posuere, mollis est et, vulputate lacus. Suspendisse sed eros non arcu semper aliquet. Nunc sit amet velit at ligula sagittis fermentum. Vivamus consectetur velit ipsum, in ultrices dolor vehicula in. Sed auctor velit at arcu porttitor rhoncus. Nulla laoreet odio vitae ultricies placerat.

Integer id iaculis neque, vitae consequat magna. Nunc scelerisque turpis enim, sodales iaculis diam blandit et. Pellentesque feugiat nisl et nibh auctor vestibulum. Sed quis sollicitudin neque. Proin augue augue, accumsan eget varius sit amet, finibus in erat. Proin eget ultricies urna.

Nam gravida magna eget augue aliquam suscipit. Vivamus id elementum ex, sed volutpat leo. Proin dignissim augue leo, at sollicitudin quam sollicitudin a. Ut eget augue metus. Etiam blandit hendrerit orci ut molestie. Proin varius convallis felis. Vivamus vehicula, urna sit amet consequat facilisis, tortor nunc porta est, porttitor posuere ex tellus sit amet metus. Mauris sollicitudin dolor nec metus placerat ultricies. Donec sit amet nisl a diam fringilla scelerisque.

Heus pendere minutis. Non tamen ploras audire me rursus quaestiones de mea, nonne? Bene, si novi te nolo. Ita quod, si Im ticked off per duos optimos amicos inveniunt societatem magis delectabiles quam femina mea? Et si ego ita sui cura occupatis possum Juventus scribo sed ut ipsa voluntate fuisse excordem, giggling inepta nescio qua primum pueri eius? Yeah, bene ostendam vobis quid ego de illa non aliud offendit invenire. Et non multum molesti estis loquentes, ita etiam ut tam longe defricatus urina.

Quod iustum est. Audistis me. Pedicabo sicut et me solum relinquatis. Si vis ad adlidet in ipsum, quis, monogrammed, princeps definition of novus exuviis igitur deficiant LONGE bene.

Quid exspectas? De quo locutus sum tibi defricatus urina.

Quid est? Reliqua huius miraris es? Yeah, bene vellem, si iustus fueris, eras. Concidite damna. Candy Cóntere Saga non ludere ipsum. Numquam Big Bang Box conplerentur quae fecit tibi? Sed dimitte me quod vis, OK?

Ecce ego dicere unum tempus tantum. Defricatus urina. Off.

OK, I'm sorry. No, I mean it, I shouldn't have been so abusive. And I really am sorry. Honest. You've stuck with me this far, for which I really am very grateful, and I guess you probably want to see how things turn out, as I do, even though I'm not exactly feeling very optimistic.

But look, I'm not going to prattle on, summarising the story so far, trying to explain why I feel so down, because, if for no other reason, in my experience, dwelling on these sorts of things only makes the whole situation a damn sight worse. However, seeing as you have been brave, or foolish, enough to get this far, I suppose I do owe you something, so it's probably time that I let you in on a little secret. My name's not Atticus and I'm not seventeen and I'm not even a real person.

Ha-ha-ha. Just joking. Gallows humour, it's called.

No, what I've got to tell you is a confession of sorts and it kind of explains why seeing Red and Bass so happily occupied with members of the opposite sex depresses and irritates me so much.

You see, the thing is, what I mean is... oh, verbosity be damned! I am a virgin.

I hope, after all that preamble, you didn't miss that, tacked as it was at the end of a poorly constructed sentence. Well, here it is again: I am a virgin. And just in case you missed it: I AM A VIRGIN! There, got it now?

I feel like I should be at an Alcoholics Anonymous meeting, or Virgins Anonymous. "Hello, my name's Atticus and I'm a virgin."

Well, it certainly doesn't make me feel any better but, then again, I didn't really think it would.

Sure, I know, I chatter on about big breasts and high heels, schoolgirls bursting out of their uniforms, the allure of latex, the eroticism of lipstick application, blah, blah,

blah. But I know diddly squat. About anything, really. Sure, I put on this oh-so-clever front, pretending I'm a man of the world with my pet theories and my razor-sharp insight, but I'm the Wizard of Oz, me. The Great Pretender. I'm lonely but no one can tell.

What was that? You'd already guessed I'd never 'been with a woman'? Oh, right, well you are clever then, aren't you? Well, listen to this: I've never even kissed a female, not counting immediate family or relatives. But wait! Before you sneer, just try to put yourself in my shoes for a minute. Just try to imagine what it's like being seventeen (and a half) and never having kissed a girl. Crap, isn't it? Perhaps – just perhaps – you can see where I'm coming from. Maybe, I can even squeeze a bit of sympathy from you – not that that's what all this is about, you understand. Just possibly though, you might be able to understand why I got so irate back there – with you, I mean, *and* with Bass and Red.

However, as I said, there's not much point in dwelling on these things. I am what I am, and if I'm yet to even feel the touch of a woman's lips on my own, then so be it.

Beautiful things happen when you distance yourself from the negative.

Nothing worth having comes easy.

You have to fight through the bad days in order to earn the best days.

Stop whining. Start doing.

Work until your idols become your rivals.

If you're sick in your mouth, spit it out.

Anyway, at least I've got that off my chest and I can now get on with things. Strangely, despite what I said earlier, I *do* feel a little better. Not a lot. Certainly not enough to return to the broom cupboard of iniquity. But sufficient to get off this plastic crate and go for a stroll perhaps. The only slight problem with that plan, though, is that I remain more than a little queasy. I might be about to prove that Stella tastes nowhere near as nice coming back up again as it did going down.

Yeah, that would be right. The perfect end to a perfect day. Rolling around a darkened alley, calling out for Uncle Ralph. Or maybe I could lie down on my back, the best position for choking on vomit. Then, in years to come, when some industrious rock journalist sits down to write a biography of Bläck Gläss, the globe-trotting super-group, I can be immortalised as Atticus 'Johnny' Childress, the original rhythm guitarist who sadly died in bizarre circumstances just when the group were on the cusp of stardom.

Eschewing the possibility of posthumous fame, I struggle to my feet and stagger down the alley. Realising that there's no reason I should be staggering – I'm feeling sick, I'm not out of my gourd – I adopt a normal gait. Then I realise I'm not actually feeling sick, I'm absolutely famished. It's nearly six hours since I ate and, despite everything, the exertion of performance has given me a terrific appetite. With my troubles temporarily forgotten, I decide to head for Beryl's Café. Like any *real* man, when faced with problems of an emotional or psychological nature, I choose the denial option and elect to feed my face.

I stop at the entrance to the alley and look around. There is a surprising amount of traffic and I have to wait before I can safely cross the road. I'm about to turn and walk the fifty metres to Beryl's when a figure sitting on a bench the same distance away in the opposite direction catches my attention.

Apollonia Wallace.

A week ago, I would have had no hesitation whatsoever in quickly stepping into the nearest doorway, where I could observe her for as long as possible. Yesterday, I would have stopped for a few seconds then moved on. Tonight, though, because I couldn't really care less what happens now, I start walking slowly towards her. Part of me hasn't forgotten what was going on between Apollonia and Robert during our set and I wouldn't mind finding out what *that* was all about. Most of all though, there's something about her posture that draws me closer.

Forty metres away, I can see her shoulders shaking. Unless she's quietly chuckling to herself – possible but unlikely – she's crying. Thirty metres from her, my eyes run up the curves of her legs, to her white tee, to her goddess-like visage.

Twenty metres away, I watch her pull out a paper tissue from the tiny purse she's clutching in her lap. She blows her nose, hardly making a sound. No elephants-frolicking-in-the-river sounds for someone like Apollonia. Ten metres away, I spot the tear-tracks on her cheeks and the goose-bumps on her arms.

Five metres from her, I stop, now uncertain. Apollonia begins to sob more forcefully, forcing me to act. I walk closer.

"Are you OK?"

Yeah, I know. Dumb question, but I can't think of anything more appropriate. My head's a mess but I'm still nervous as I address Apollonia Wallace directly for the first time in my life. All our transactions in the Zone having been conducted in silence. She sniffs away some tears, dabs her eyes and looks at me.

"Yeah, thanks."

She looks at me with damp, shining eyes. My pulse quickens. I know it shouldn't. I know I'm supposed to have lowered her from her pedestal. I know I'm not supposed to have any respect for her anymore. I know I've vowed to become a reformed man. But... well, there are just some things I can't change, I guess. Hey, the most indescribably beautiful woman in the entire universe is looking at me, and talking to me. How do you expect me to react?

Especially when she looks like an injured baby animal from a Disney film – big moist eyes and lower lip all aquiver. I know how I *want* to react. I want to put my arm reassuringly around her shoulders, then take her home and nurse her wounds. Except I wouldn't want to take her back to my actual house, my parents' house. I want to take her back to my cosy cottage, deep in the woods, where we could lead a simple but happy life, enjoying each other's company, and living out our days in blissful contentment. Makes sense. It could happen.

Apollonia appears to be on the verge of saying something then, with a convulsive shake of her shoulders, she begins to cry again. Even though outwardly I'm just standing here like a spare part, inside I'm racing back to my secret hideout, changing into battle-garb, arming myself to the teeth with a variety of implausible weaponry and plotting Robert's imminent demise. Beware, Robert! Beware Atticus the Avenger, righter of wrongs, defender of the downtrodden! For I have your heinous scent in my nostrils, and I'm out for blood!

"You don't look OK," I point out once she's regained some composure.

Yeah, that's me all right. Ever ready with the *bon mot*. She glances at the tattered paper tissue, balls it up then opens her miniature purse to look for another, even though

I doubt whether it could hold more than a couple of pound coins. Untroubled as I am by chronic sinus problems, I know for a fact that there are no tissues lurking in the pockets of my jeans, so I wrack my brains, considering my options. I could pull the tee-shirt off my back and offer it as sweat-soiled tissue substitute. That would be sure to impress. I could wait for the next pedestrian or run down to Beryl's. Or I could just stand here like a witless lump. Did you guess correctly? Ten house points for Gryffindor.

Apollonia snaps shut her purse then tips her head backwards, sniffs and looks at me again. Even though, in this position, I know that if I glance down I will see the fabric of her tee stretched taut across her breasts, I resist the temptation, surely a first for me. Instead, I meet her gaze for a femto-second, which is all I can manage, then look behind her at a darkened shop entrance as if expecting to find instructions there about what to do next.

Ride the tide.

Moving quickly, before I can reconsider, I sit down next to her.

"Look, I know you don't know me but if I can..."

"Anthony, isn't it?"

"Atticus, actually. You came to my parents' party last weekend. The Childress Summer Social."

As she once again bursts into tears, I realise that reminding her of the party was not particularly inspired. I also realise, with the woman of my dreams at my side, tears flowing down her perfect face, just sitting here is not very helpful. Neither, of course, is constantly analysing everything. Enough shoe-gazing. It's time for action. I'm just going to have to forget who she is, and what she means to me, and treat her as an emotionally distressed fellow traveller. What she wants is some comfort, and what I want

307

to do is comfort her. Right then, here goes. Goodbye caution. Hello flow. Mind if I go with you?

I lift up my arm and slowly extend it along the back of the bench. At the same time, I lean forward slightly, trying to make eye contact. God, this is difficult. Talk about emotionally retarded. I'm a walking, talking definition, me.

"Hey, come on," I say gently. "It'll be all right. Everything will be fine."

Acutely aware of each millimetre of movement, I let my arm softly fall across her shuddering shoulders. She jumps up, gasping, as though she's been hit by lightning. "What the fuck do you think you're doing, you little creep?" Her eyes are blazing and she shrugs convulsively, as though trying to dislodge any contaminants I may have deposited on her shoulders. She doesn't do any of that. In fact, she actually seems to relax a little. I can feel the warmth of her skin under the tee-shirt fabric.

I press on. "It can't be that bad. Come on. There, there."

There, there? I can't believe I actually said that. Still, she hasn't turned and given me a 'don't be so bloody patronising' look, so maybe I'm on the right track. I reach out with my other hand and gingerly grasp hers, then gently massage her fingers. I'm not sure I'm achieving the right tone here. I'm making it sound as if I'm coming on to her, which I can assure you I'm not.

You'll just have to take my word for it. What do you mean I've got *previous*?

"There, there," I say, becoming a little less self-conscious. I repeat this simple phrase a few more times, stroking the back of her hand with my thumb and gently massaging her shoulder. Slowly her sobbing subsides. I look around. There's still a lot of traffic, and people walking up and down either side of the road, a few people I recognise, but no one I know well. No one takes any interest in Apollonia and me.

"If there's anything I can do to help..." I say, unsure of what specific services I could or should offer. Enter Atticus the Avenger, the 'A' on his cape only a little frayed. "If that Robert did or said something to you then I-"

Apollonia nearly makes me jump out of my skin as she emits an anguished wail of despair then starts crying even more vigorously than before. Then, before I can begin to curse my insensitivity, she twists in her seat, throws her arms around my shoulders and buries her face in the side of my neck. Without thinking – which is highly unusual for me – I return her embrace and pull her closer.

Now, I know I'm labouring the point, but I feel compelled to ensure that you understand that, as unlikely as it seems, there is not a single sexual thought inside my head. The poor girl's crying, for goodness sake! What do you take me for? OK, OK, I'll admit that maybe, just maybe, there's a tiny degenerate neurone somewhere in my brain that's firing off excited impulses, but it's neighbours are ignoring it completely, I assure you – except maybe for those two jealous ones, who are still sulking about Bass and Red.

I'll also admit that I feel pretty good at this precise moment, even though Apollonia obviously doesn't. I had hoped that the first time I embraced a girl, it would be under slightly different circumstances but, hell, this is Apollonia Wallace in my arms! Who am I to challenge whatever forces are controlling my destiny? The warmth of her body, mirrored by that spreading within my chest, feels incredible. It just kind of feels very *nice* to have my offer of solace accepted. And I know I don't like the word 'nice' but there you go. Maybe I've discovered an appropriate use for it.

Her body is juddering with the force of her sobbing, and the heat generated by her breaths bathes my neck, down which her tears are trickling. We remain in this position for hours, days, centuries. The zombie apocalypse occurs yet we are curiously unscathed. A new ice age comes. Glaciers form and move past us. Aeons pass yet Apollonia and I remain, wrapped in each other's arms.

After what I suppose must be a couple of minutes, she releases me and pulls away. After wiping away her tears with the back of her hand, she sniffs a few times then looks at me and smiles.

"Sorry, I don't know what came over me."

"Hey, that's OK. That's why they call me rent-a-shoulder. Feel free to use me any time."

She laughs – a throaty, gruff noise. In my chest, my heart, now a spinning top, whirls madly.

Apollonia chuckles wryly. "Lord, I must look a sight," she says, drawing a finger beneath her eye, blending mascara into a black smudge.

I want to tell her I've never seen her looking so utterly beautiful, that I'd do anything for her, that I'd sail the seven seas for her, that I'd listen to the complete works of 4Tune8 for her. Well, not quite – I do have *some* self-respect.

"You look fine."

"I do not!" she says with mock-indignation. "Oh, if only I had a tissue."

"I'd give you this," I say, holding up the bottom edge of my tee-shirt, "but I think it's a bit sweaty."

She laughs again. I wish we could sit here forever. I wish I could make her laugh forever.

"How about a coffee?" I ask. "Mind you, I'm not sure what Beryl serves is technically coffee but at least it's drinkable. More or less. If you hold your nose at the same time."

"Sure, why not?" she asks, chuckling again. I become aware of a high-pitched whining sound. My heart is now spinning faster than a millisecond pulsar.

I stand up and offer her my hand which she accepts. As Apollonia gets to her feet our eyes meet and she smiles, and I feel good, better than I have done for a very long time. And, despite all my character flaws, I think I deserve to feel good, if only for a little while. As we move off, she releases my hand then, before disappointment can get a proper grip, she takes my arm.

I've never been quite sure what do with my hand when someone takes my arm. Needless to say, no one of Apollonia's stature has done this before – only elderly relatives and sometimes my mother. I never know whether to hold my forearm awkwardly across my stomach or thrust my hand into my pocket, which I worry makes me look ill-mannered.

However, with Apollonia's elbow hooked around mine, I realise that holding my arm across my stomach is not awkward at all. Instead, the formality of the position only helps to draw one's attention to the fact that I am in the company of an exceptional woman.

"I thought you were great tonight," she says.

"Thank you."

"Your singer's got a lot of talent."

"Yeah, well, it's been under a bushel for such a long time, I guess it had to come out sooner or later."

"I don't think I've ever heard that love song you played. Is it an original?"

311

It takes me a few seconds to work out she's talking about *Decaying Emotions*. "Yeah, Bass wrote it."

"For your keyboard player."

"Uh, yeah," I mutter, surprised but not really surprised. "How did you know that?"

"Men!" she says, laughing. "So transparent."

"I guess so," I say lamely. I sincerely hope I'm not *that* transparent. I wouldn't want Apollonia to know what I'm thinking. Or maybe I would. Except I'm not thinking anything like that. Or am I? Shut up, Atticus, you blethering houseplant.

"Are they going out?"

She means Bass and Suzz. But you knew that. It took me a moment to work it out.

"They are now."

"You mean it was that song that got them together?"

"No... well, yeah, I guess it was."

"Very romantic."

"I guess."

She turns to look at me, smiling. "You're not a cynic, are you, Atticus?"

Understatement of the millennium.

"No... it's just that... well..."

"You mean you don't believe in true love?"

"No... I mean, I suppose... well, yes, I guess that under certain-"

"Oh, don't be so serious. I'm pulling your leg."

We arrive at the entrance to Beryl's Café. It's about half full. Sitting at a table next to the window is Billy Gibson with a couple of other lower sixth formers. Unfortunately, they haven't yet noticed Apollonia and me. I say unfortunately because, unless someone sees me with her, neither Bass nor Red will believe me when I tell them about tonight. Before I can jump in front of her and chivalrously open it for her, Apollonia pushes open the door herself and walks in. I hurry after her, in case it should appear to anyone who might be watching – Billy and his cronies – that it's only by coincidence that Apollonia and I are entering together.

"I'm just going to tidy up my face," she says. "I won't be a minute."

"Sure," I say automatically.

I'm feeling distinctly light-headed again, although I know it's because I'm with Apollonia. I consider pinching myself but if this is a dream then I most certainly do not want to wake up.

"White, no sugar."

"Eh?"

She laughs at my vacant expression. "I thought you offered to buy me a coffee."

"Yes... I mean, no... I mean, of course..."

She laughs again, shaking her head with good-humoured disbelief. "Why on earth are you so nervous?"

"I'm not... I mean, it's just..."

What does she want me to say? That being within ten metres of her makes my heart beat like a gerbil's? That the mere fact that she's talking to me makes me sweat like a marathon runner? That every time she laughs my throat goes as dry as a dry thing? A white lie seems like the most sensible option.

"...it's just the gig, I guess. You know, nagging worries about whether we played OK, I suppose. That sort of thing."

"Oh, don't be so silly!" she says, scolding me like an anxious schoolboy, which I am. "You were great."

313

I smile uncertainly. She reaches out and gently touches my forearm, igniting a spark of joy which zooms up my arm, leaving an ecstatic track of fire, to my chest where it then explodes with happiness, sending burning shards of pure bliss to every part of my body. In other words, when Apollonia touches me, it feels nice. Bloody nice.

"Really, you were very good. You've got nothing to be nervous about, honestly. Now, you get us some coffee and I'll be back in a tick."

I watch her walk toward the toilets, hypnotised. She disappears from view and a huge black hole opens inside me. The café dims, all the colours fading away to grainy muted hues. Without Apollonia lighting up the room, everything fades to sepia. I'm still staring at the spot where she passed from view and am unaware of the other patrons. I can imagine, though, that they're doing the same as I – Apollonia just has that effect on people.

I turn to ask Beryl for two coffees. Unfortunately, this is not what passes my lips. In fact, hardly anything passes my lips.

"T-t-t-t-two c-c-c-coff..." is all I can manage. I've never stuttered in my life. It's as if Apollonia took my power of speech with her into the toilet.

He bangs his fists against the posts and still insists he sees the ghosts.

"T-t-t-t-t-t...."

Crikey, it's getting worse. I pray she brings it back with her. Knowing my luck, she's probably flushed it away.

"Two coffees?" asks Beryl, utterly indifferent to my predicament.

I smile pathetically and nod my head. My stomach rumbles. I grab two KitKats and drop them on the counter

314

then watch Beryl pouring liquid mud from a battered pot into two mugs which she sets down on the counter. I hand over the cash and wait for my change. I pick up a milk jug and splash a few drops into each mug.

"Th-th-thanks," I say, accepting my change. I shove the chocolate bars in my pocket, pick up the mugs and start walking over to an empty table in the corner near the window.

"Hey, Johnny!"

Billy Gibson hails me. I pause at his table and raise my eyebrows. Attempting speech seems foolhardy.

"Thought you were pretty good tonight," he says.

His two partners are nodding in agreement. I convey my gratitude with a mute twitch of my head.

"That Pickaxe are a load of shite, though."

I manage acknowledgement with more eyebrow elevation.

"What's with you and Apollonia Wallace?"

Ah, I was wondering when he'd get around to that. Seeing as I've more or less exhausted my eyebrows' repertoire I merely smile enigmatically then walk off toward the empty corner table. I set down the mugs then slide into the chair facing the wall. Immediately, I get up again and move around to sit in the other chair. From this vantage point I can keep an eye on the door in case anyone else I know comes in. I'll also be able to see Apollonia the instant she comes out of the toilet.

Famished, I wolf down the KitKats. My stomach burps a 'Thanks, pal' and I start to feel my blood sugar level rise. I sip coffee – as vile as usual – and think about Billy's question. What, exactly, *is* with me and Apollonia? Perhaps I shouldn't contemplate this conundrum – after all, where has over-analysis got me in the past? I mean, why

315

look the proverbial gift horse in the mouth? But I just can't help myself from wondering why Apollonia is here with me, in Beryl's Café. I can't believe she hasn't got better things to do. She must have more friends than she can shake a stick at. There must be hundreds of people she could summon within minutes with a phone call or text message. Perhaps she just wants to forget Mr Music Business for a while – that seems plausible. Maybe she's got a thing for spotty adolescents. Ha-ha-ha. Hey, it's my party and I'll delude myself if I want to, OK?

But seriously, though, I suspect her tiff with Robert is the real reason why she's here with me tonight – well, it's the only reason that makes sense, anyway. Except, she's not here with me, is she? She's in the toilet, 'tidying up her face' – or is she? What if she's suddenly realised she's stuck in a grotty café with a grotty teenager at half past eleven on a grotty Friday night? I'll bet that, even as her coffee grows cold right here on this table, she's climbing through a window in the toilet. In a minute she'll be running down the alley and then she'll leap into a waiting limousine, and inside ten minutes she'll be back in the loving arms of Robert, the music industry mogul from hell. 'Oh, Robert,' she'll say, 'it was *horrible*! I'm so sorry I didn't listen to you. Please forgive me! I'll do anything you want but please take me back!' Yeah, that sounds about right. Silly me! How could I possibly think that she'd be here of her own volition? Then, as I've just about convinced myself that she's half way across town, she emerges from the toilet. The ambient light level increases. Colour saturation improves.

I really hate to resort to clichés, especially of the cinematic reference sort, but I can't come up with an original way to describe the effect Apollonia's entrance has on me, and on Billy and his cronies. Imagine you're watching a movie in which the protagonist, a likeable youth, well-meaning but somewhat lacking in social skills when it comes to the opposite sex (*ie* nothing like me), beholds the woman of his dreams. Blonde hair, body and face – you know the score. Suddenly, everything shifts into slow-motion. She's bathed in golden light. Her ultra-white teeth sparkle. And so on. Well, as with most clichés, this one's grounded in reality. When you see the object of your infatuation, it really does feel like that. And as I watch Apollonia cross the café, *I* feel like that. Even though she probably simply walks toward me, I feel as though she's gliding, or floating, even.

However, I would imagine that you've more or less got a reasonable idea of what I think about Apollonia, so I'll skip all the pulse-quickening, beads of sweat on forehead stuff for the time being. She slides into her chair with all the grace of a graceful woman and smiles at me.

"Do I look a bit better now?" she asks, reaching for her mug of sludge, white, no sugar.

I can't stop myself from chuckling. What on earth does she want me to say? That the words don't exist to properly describe her beauty? Of course, I'd like to tell her exactly that.

"Fine," I say, as though my mother had asked me how she looked in a new tweed skirt.

God, I hate myself. Which is one of titles I was considering for this book. Funny, that.

She sips her coffee and turns to look out the window. I inspect her profile, marvelling at the exquisite line of the bridge of her nose, the slight flare of her nostrils and the ridges of her philtrum. I gaze at the fine hairs of her eyebrows, the two tiny creases at the corner of her eye, her long lashes, the reflection of a streetlamp in the white of her eye. She pulls the mug an inch away from her lips to swallow and I inspect the faint lipstick traces on the rim. Everything about her is perfect and if I died right now, gazing at flecks of dusky pink lipstick adhering to a chipped coffee mug, I'd die happy. Very happy.

She inhales deeply as she takes another sip, her chest expanding, her breasts rising, and then lets out a long sigh. She turns to me and smiles again, one of those uber-wry Hermione Grainger smiles. But more so.

Kill. Me. Now. My life is *never* going to get better than this.

"So, then," she says.

I gently bite my lower lip and meet her gaze.

"How long have you been together?"

How long have *who* been together? What does she mean? Does she think I've got a girlfriend, or something? I frown, wishing I hadn't.

"Your band," she says, cocking her head slightly, as though considering she may have underestimated my intelligence. Could I blame her?

"Oh," I say, grinning at my stupidity. "A couple of years, I guess."

I proceed to relate the history of Bläck Gläss. Throughout, she facilitates expertly, nodding and smiling appropriately, prompting me when I seem uncertain of the relevance of assorted items of information and maintaining an expression of intense interest at all times. I tell her about the various name changes, our early attempts at song-writing, Red's equipment, our inability to hang on to a lead guitarist, the auditions two nights ago and all the incidents leading up to tonight's gig. Of course, I omit anything that might put me in a bad light. Well, what do you expect? I'm hardly going to finish my tale by telling her that, in a fit of jealousy and self-pity, I stormed out of the broom cupboard, deciding that my life was at an all-time low, and that's how I came across her, am I?

"So, isn't there an after-show party or something like that?"

She's sharp, all right – I'll give her that.

"Uh, no, I don't think so."

"Oh, that's a shame."

Why, would you come with me if there was? I mean, just say the word and I'm certain I could whip up some sort of celebration. I'd try not to let it descend into one of those dreaded teenage snog-a-thons – you know, where you walk into the lounge of some poor parent's house and, peering into the gloom, you can just about make out a dozen couples lying around on the furniture and floor, motionless apart from their probing tongues.

"I don't see why," I say a little irritably.

She frowns and I feel guilty.

"You don't want to be with the guys in the band? After a great gig like that?"

"Bass and Red have got better things to do," I say. I wish I hadn't.

Apollonia's eyes narrow. I can't bear to meet her gaze and look down at my half-empty coffee mug. Talk about letting the cat out of the bag. Good God, I may as well have tattooed on my forehead: 'I haven't got a girlfriend and I'm pissed off because my friends do'. Except it wouldn't fit. Unless the font size was really small. 'Bitter and twisted' would fit.

I steal a glance at her. My worst fears are confirmed. She's seen right through me. I *am* transparent. What's even worse is the way she's smiling at me – a half-smile, really, a pitying half-smile. 'Never mind, Atticus,' that smile says, 'one day you'll get a girlfriend. One day, you'll find someone of sufficiently limited intelligence to enjoy your company.'

A million emotions rush into my head all at once, where they have a massive scrap. Anger takes on Irritation and wins hands down. Then Desperation enters the fray but Anger smashes him into a bloody pulp. Next comes Bitterness, biceps bulging. Anger, bloodied but unbowed, stands tall, eyes blazing. A protracted fist-fight ensues and more than once Anger looks beaten, but eventually, through sheer persistence, Anger wins. He drops to his knees, cheeks bruised, blood trickling from his mouth, his mashed fingers like split sausages. Then, Shame appears on the crest of a nearby hill, riding his trusty steed Pathos. Anger struggles up onto one knee, his breaths quick and shallow. With his one good eye, he watches his adversary draw nearer. Shame climbs down off Pathos and, eyes downcast, walks up to Anger. He extends a hand, as if to help Anger to his feet. Then, when Anger's attention is diverted for a second, Shame jerks his knee up into Anger's chin. His head snaps backwards with a crack. His neck broken, his spinal cord severed, his body slumps down onto the muddy battlefield. Shame gazes down at his opponent with watering eyes then drops to his knees and begins to sob gently.

I check I've not misinterpreted Apollonia's smile then get to my feet. "Got to go," I say quietly as I step away from my chair. "'Bye."

"Where are you going?"

"Home," I mutter. I can't look at her but neither can I move my feet.

"It's early yet."

320

"Well, yeah, but... parents, you know."

"They won't mind if you stay out another half hour, will they?"

I know damn well what she's doing.

"Maybe. I don't know," I mumble, staring at the door.

"Come on, then. Why don't we have another coffee?"

Blast! She must know I can't refuse her. Why doesn't she just let me go? I'm sure I could find a rock somewhere, one big enough for me to hide under. I pluck up the necessary courage and look at her. She's still smiling although now with encouragement rather than pity.

"One more coffee?"

"Sure, I guess so."

I realise that she would be quite entitled to tell me that I don't have to do her any favours. Hey, I'm the one with the problems, not her. Gee, yet something else to feel guilty about. Aren't I lucky? If she knows as much about me as I think she does then there's no way anything I do now can lower her opinion of me so, once again, I find myself in what's swiftly becoming an extremely familiar position – that of having absolutely nothing to lose.

"Do you want anything else?" I ask. "Chips and gravy? Deep fried Mars bar?"

She laughs, apparently genuinely, and I feel a little better. Never mind being on an emotional roller-coaster, I feel like I'm an emotional cliff-diver, slowly climbing up the rock-face, my feet occasionally slipping, sending showers of gravel tumbling downwards, then standing on a ledge, feeling both anxious and exhilarated, before pushing off and diving headlong into the abyss, not knowing whether I'll land safely or end up smashed on the rocks.

"Another coffee would be fine."

As I watch Beryl pour hot mud, I decide that I'm well and truly fed up with all these stupid emotional twists and turns, and I resolve – not for the first time, I might add – to attempt to put an end to them. OK, so I haven't got a girlfriend. So what? Yes, it annoys me that Bass and Red appear to have abandoned me, but – if I'm honest – I have to admit that if I were in their position then I dare say I would not behave any differently. And yes, I'm sitting in Beryl's Café with Apollonia Wallace and I can't understand why she would want to be here, but, hey, let's locate that flow and go with it.

I add milk to mud, thinking how pathetic I really am. It seems like every five minutes I make up my mind to ride the tide and then, before I know what's happening, I'm swimming against it, arms flailing, with my emotions in a turmoil again. Still, maybe *this* time I can do it.

With quizzical expressions, Billy and his pals watch me walk back to Apollonia. As I sit down, and after ascertaining that Apollonia won't see me, I wink at them. Don't ask me why – I just felt like it and, hey, I'm just going with the flow.

"So, what's with you and Robert?" I ask.

Except I don't. Ha-ha. Just showing you how relaxed and cool I am now. But I'm not that stupid.

"So, you enjoyed the Bläck Gläss experience, did you?"

She nods her head. "Yeah, pretty good."

"Unfortunately, the dressing room wasn't awash with chequebook-waving A&R men, though. Although I suppose they might have turned up after I left."

Looking somewhat pensive, she smiles. Maybe I *am* that stupid.

"Hey, I didn't mean..." I say quickly, hoping she didn't think I was referring to Robert.

"Didn't mean what?"

Well, I didn't want to remind you of Robert in case you start crying again.

"I didn't want you to think that I really think the band is that great. I mean tonight was great, for us, but we're not fooling ourselves. We know where we stand in the grand scheme of things. Really, we do," I say, feeling as awkward as my words sound.

She sips her coffee and turns to look out the window again. I follow her gaze and watch the steady stream of punters leaving the Showroom. I realise she must be thinking about Robert, but I can't be sure whether or not my little *faux pas* had anything to do with it. Probably not. Anyway, my resolve to accompany the flow is still intact and I decide to get the conversation going again. Above all, I want to avoid the subject of Robert.

"My sister was there tonight," I say.

God knows what made me say that. I wasn't even thinking about her and, really, I don't particularly want to think about her, or her larval mates.

"Yeah? Older or younger?"

"Younger," I say. "She's sixteen soon. Seemed to be enjoying herself."

"She's a fan, is she?"

"Well, no, I don't think she'd ever heard us play before."

"Oh."

"She's not exactly into metal."

"I though you said she was enjoying herself."

"Yeah, I did, but..."

323

Apollonia raises her eyebrows and looks at me in a QED sort of way.

"It's just that she's more of a 4Tune8 fan, really," I say, grimacing. "I mean, I guess she might like some of the old classic rock stuff. Who doesn't? Nothing very metal gets anywhere near the charts these days, does it? And Rosie, my sister, always makes it *very* clear that she *loathes* the kind of music that I like."

"That might be more to do with the fact that you like it, rather than that she doesn't like the music itself."

I swallow a mouthful of coffee and mull over this. It never crossed my mind that Rosie might like metal. I say so.

"Ah, well, we women are a lot more complex than you men would like to think we are."

I snigger ruefully. "You said it."

"Anyway, what's wrong with 4Tune8?"

A sarcastic quip shoots up from my lungs but I have to clamp shut my mouth when I see that Apollonia's not joking.

"Well?"

Crikey, what does she want? A two-hundred-page dissertation on why 4Tune8 are total crap? Why it is that manufactured male-model groups are one of the principle reasons for this country's socio-economic decline? Why they are an affront to any sane person's sensibilities?

"They're just not my cup of tea, that's all."

"Oh," she says, with an expression that seems to say: 'Are you quite sure you don't want to dig a nice deep hole for yourself?'

I switch to the offensive. "Why, do *you* like them?"

She inclines her head laconically. Talk about a hidden agenda. She's hiding something – presumably a sneaking regard for the reedy delights of 4Tune8. If so, I think I've finally seen a side of Apollonia Wallace I can't admire – not counting last Saturday's events, that is. Seemingly as aware of the impasse as I, she changes the subject.

"I can't remember seeing her at your party."

"Who?" I ask, still wondering how to incorporate this apparent partiality to 4Tune8 into the encyclopaedic entry on Apollonia Wallace that I carry around in my head.

"Your sister, of course. Rosie."

"Oh, she was there, hanging around with all her larv- ... friends."

She nods. "What was she wearing?"

"Oh... a dress, I think, and some shoes."

"That narrows it down, then, doesn't it," she says, laughing, thankfully.

"Well, you can't expect me to remember what my sister was wearing six days ago, can you?"

Needless to say, I can remember precisely what Rosie was wearing at the party, but I'm not falling into that trap.

"I suppose not," says Apollonia. Then, after a pause: "Do you get on with her?"

Lordy me, has she got psychic powers, or what?

"OK, I guess," I say, looking into her eyes. "Well, not really."

Then, before I can stop myself, and without any prompting, I launch into a long monologue about my sister. I tell Apollonia about how my feelings toward Rosie have changed recently, and about how much I wanted to give her something special for her birthday. I tell her about the 4Tune8 vinyl box set. I even give her a blow-by-blow account of last Saturday's *contretemps*. I tell her how I desperately want to make her think better of me, even though I don't really know *why*. Eventually, with all my cards on the table, as it were, I inhale deeply, sigh, and look at her, expecting a few words of encouragement at the very least. Instead, indifferently, she looks at her watch.

"Well, it's time I was getting off home."

I'm too stunned to speak.

"You coming?"

My jaw drops open.

"Catching flies?" she asks, chuckling. "That's what my mother always says."

I snap my jaw shut. Never mind being complex, women are completely beyond my comprehension, and this woman, Apollonia Wallace, is turning out to be the most unfathomable of them all.

She smiles. "You're not going to let me go home alone, are you?"

"Just what the bloody hell are you going on about?" I scream. "Look, am I going completely round the bend, or are you asking me to go home with you? Are you just toying with me, or what? Are you playing with me like a cat plays with a mouse before it kills it? For God's sake, put me out of my misery and tell me just what the bleeding hell is going on here!"

Except, I say nothing of the sort. I'd like to think my silence was connected with my resolve to walk hand in hand with Mr Flow, but I know it's really because I'm just too gob-smacked to say, or think, anything at all.

"Come on," she says, standing up and extending her hand.

Feeling more baffled than ever before in my pathetic life, I struggle to my feet. She waits for me to shuffle out from behind the table then takes my arm. Together we walk toward the door. We pass Billy's table.

"Hello, boys," says Apollonia.

If I wasn't feeling so light-headed, Billy's gormless expression would almost make me laugh. Apollonia pulls open the door and we step outside. The temperature has dropped since we entered more than an hour earlier. The cool breeze feels wonderful.

Apollonia shivers. "A bit chilly. I think we'll get a taxi."

As if by magic – how the hell does she do this? – a black cab emerges from a side-street and pulls up in front of us. Apollonia opens the rear door and climbs in, dragging me after her.

"Hi, Polly," says the driver, twisting around in his seat. "You all right?"

"Just great, Roy. And yourself?"

"Mustn't grumble," he says, looking suspiciously at me. "Anyway, who'd listen?"

Apollonia laughs. "And how are Mrs Johnson and the kids?"

"Just fine, thanks, Polly. Where to?"

"Home, thanks."

Roy slips the car into gear and we pull away. Whoever the hell Roy is.

[28] Fortunate Developments

I spend the short journey in silence, partly through choice, as Apollonia and Roy seem happy to discuss the appalling number of potholes in the roads these days, the difficulty finding a hair conditioner which doesn't leave your hair looking greasy, and other such fascinating topics, but mostly because my tongue is gummed to the roof of my mouth. I'm so stunned by what's happening that I may as well be handcuffed to Mr Joseph 'Go With Me' Flow.

The taxi moves up the drive to the Wallace mansion, tyres crunching on gravel. I've never been to Apollonia's house before, so this is all new to me. Even at what I suppose must be half-past midnight – I can't summon the strength to fish out my phone – light shines from nearly every window in the imposing house. Roy pulls up outside the front door.

"Here we are then. Is this going on your father's account?"

"That would be great, thanks, Roy," she says then turns to me. "You coming, then?"

I attempt a smile, which I suspect looks more like a leer, then follow her out of the taxi. I stand by her side as she watches Roy drive away, waving as he toots his horn. Grabbing my hand, she pulls me toward the door then opens it. I consider asking her what I'm doing here, having received no sensible response from myself, but speech is impossible. I follow her across the threshold and into the oak-panelled entrance hall. A broad staircase sweeps up the right side, leading to a balustraded gallery. Apollonia's bedroom must be up there somewhere. My heart rate climbs another notch.

"I must go and change," she says, releasing my hand.

"Uh... OK," I mumble hoarsely.

"The kitchen's down that way," she says, pointing down a corridor. "Why don't you go through and wait there and I'll be back down in a few minutes?"

I nod then watch her nimbly trot up the stairs. As she passes along the gallery, she looks down at me and waves then disappears. Again the ambient light level drops several notches. I am no longer in the presence of Apollonia Wallace. My heart rate slows and my adrenaline level subsides.

I stand and look about and, even though I've been invited, I can't help feeling like an interloper. I half expect Mr Wallace to appear and ask me, eyes blazing, just what the bloody hell I think I'm doing in his house. Excellent question, Mr Wallace. However, apart from the ponderous ticking of an impressive grandfather clock guarding the front door, I can hear nothing to suggest I am about to be questioned regarding my presence.

I walk down the corridor, feeling a little less numb, the effects of the Apollonia drug wearing off. Still nagging at me, like flies around a fresh dog turd, are questions about my presence in the Wallace mansion but, irritably, I wave them away.

The oaken theme, introduced in the hall, persists in the kitchen. I've seen pictures of rooms like this on the web, but never in real life. Everything's dark wood, or granite, or tile, with recessed lighting, and massive appliances. The fridge has four doors, FFS! My parents have been thinking about having a new fitted kitchen, and I've heard them talking about the costs involved. I look around the Wallace's kitchen, certain that most people's houses are worth less than this one room.

Suddenly thirsty, I cross to the sink and fill a glass with water then drink it in one long gulp. Gasping, I fill the glass again.

"Hi," says someone behind me.

I turn to see a young man, dressed only in boxer shorts. He looks vaguely familiar.

Not that I see a lot of young men dressed only in boxers.

(He says quickly)

I'm sure this isn't one of Apollonia's brothers – Greg or William Jr – unless they've undergone plastic surgery.

I nod in greeting.

"You one of Polly's friends?" he asks.

"Yeah, I guess... I mean, yes I am."

"So she's back, then?"

"Gone upstairs to change."

He turns and walks over to the refrigerator and opens one of the doors. He seemed to know which one to open. He pulls out a can of beer. "Want one?" he asks.

"Sure. Why not?"

He grabs a second can then walks back to me. "Have you known her long?" he asks, handing me a can.

"A while."

He opens his can then lifts it to his lips but doesn't drink. "You're not an old...?" he asks, letting the question hang in the air.

Boyfriend? Flame? Homeless person she found in the street and brought home for a nourishing meal?

Even though he's not explained his interest in the matter and I'm under no obligation to clarify the situation I

330

don't see any point in concealing anything. Not, of course, that there's anything to conceal.

"No, we're just er... friends."

This seems to make him much happier, whoever he is. "I see."

I open my can and watch him as I drink. I'm absolutely sure I know him from somewhere but I just can't think where. He seems to sense my thoughts.

"Rick," he says, holding out his hand.

"Atticus," I say, shaking his hand, "though some call me Johnny."

Why *do* I say these things?

"Oh, why's that?"

"Long story."

He shrugs, accepting my damage-limiting statement. "So, were you at the gig tonight, then?"

I nod, taking another gulp of beer.

"Were they any good?"

"Pickaxe?"

"Yeah."

"Don't know. I didn't hang around to find out."

Rick raises his eyebrows.

"We were the support."

"Yeah? How did it go?"

"A lot better than expected, to be honest. It was our first gig."

Rick considers this for a few moments. "You want to come out to the pool? That's where everybody else is."

"I don't know. Apollonia said I was to wait here."

He smiles, understanding my reluctance. "Don't worry, she'll find us. Come on."

"Sure, I guess so."

I follow him to a doorway at the other side of the kitchen.

"Oops," he says then trots back to the refrigerator, returning with half a dozen cans. "Nearly forgot why I came back here."

We walk into a small utility room then out through another door into a cavernous conservatory. In the daytime, I would imagine it looks magnificent, with the sunlight filtering through the greenery. Now, with hardly any visible light, and Rick only a shadowy figure, the overall effect is rather disquieting. We weave in and out, past large tubs of even larger plants, then through another door.

"Bit like a rabbit warren, this," says Rick as we walk down what seems to be a tunnel of some sort. Wide leaved plants line either side of the path and it's only after ten metres that I realise we're in an extension of the conservatory. My over-riding impression, apart from mild claustrophobia, is of the enormous cost of such a structure. We follow the path as it bends to the right and then I nearly walk into Rick as he stops to open a door. The sounds of water splashing and male voices shouting excitedly increase in volume as we walk down a short pine-clad corridor. A door with a small glass window is on our right, presumably a sauna, and two doors marked with male and female symbols are on our left. The smell of chlorine fills the air. I follow Rick as he turns another corner and then stop and gape at the sight that greets me.

To describe it as a covered swimming pool would be like calling Buckingham Palace a house. For a start, the pool itself has to be thirty metres long. Huge wooden beams arch up from either side. White tables and chairs, enough to seat about a hundred people, sit on the green carpet which surrounds the pool. I've seen this kind of thing in movies but never in real life. Mr and Dr Wallace must be absolutely raking it in. Or some relative must have died and left them a fortune. A good half minute passes before I finish staring at the architecture and scrutinise the raucous revellers.

Three young men are cavorting in the middle of the pool, splashing water at each other, protesting when on the receiving end, whooping gleefully, whirling their arms across the surface of the pool, sending up fountains of water over the other two.

"Hey!" shouts Rick, walking over to deposit the cans on a table. "I'm back!"

Getting no response from the three in the pool, he sits down then beckons me to join him. As I walk slowly to the table I watch the lads in the pool. I'm getting the same feeling that I felt when I met Rick: while I can't be certain, I'm sure I recognise them. I suppose I must have seen them in town, or maybe they were at St. Mick's two or three years ago. I turn to smile at Rick as I sit down and notice someone else lying, apparently asleep, on a lounger on the other side of the pool. Unless my eyes are deceiving me, which can never be discounted when I've had a couple of drinks, it is Robert. Titan of the UK music business.

"What's he doing here?"

"Who?" asks Rick.

I hadn't realised I'd spoken aloud. I point at Robert. "Bob?"

I nod.

"He's with our management," says Rick, opening another can. "He's supposed to be making sure we don't get up to any trouble."

Something inside my head clicks. I turn to see one of the swimmers making his way to our end of the pool, the

333

shallow end. He stands up and pushes his hair away from his face.

"Here, chuck as one of those," he says to Rick, who tosses him a can.

Whatever it is that's inside my head starts chattering like a Geiger counter at ground zero as I realise I am looking at 'Lovely' Luke, which means I'm sitting next to 'Ravishing' Rick, which means I'm in the presence of none other than 4Tune8.

Which explains Apollonia's rather odd demeanour earlier.

I am tempted to leap to my feet and hurl abuse at all and sundry. Well, no, I'm not, really. I take a couple of sips of beer, determined to analyse this development as calmly as possible.

"4Tune8," I mutter to myself.

"That's us," says Rick, "flavour of the month."

"What are you doing here?" I ask, seeing as it just happens to be the first of a million questions lining up inside my head.

"Didn't Polly tell you we were staying here?"

I shake my head.

"We *were* booked into a hotel in London but... well, the word got out," he says, shrugging as if I should understand. He sees my vacant expression. "You know, if the fans find out where we're staying, one thing leads to another – mobs of teenaged girls running amok in the hotel corridors, banging on doors, 'creating a disturbance.'"

"I see."

"So, Polly said it would be OK if we stayed here for a couple of nights, as long as nobody found out about it."

I watch Luke and the other two, whose names escape me for the moment although I think one of the might be 'Gorgeous' George, sharing the can of beer.

"My sister's a big fan."

"Yeah? Well, if you remind me later, I'll give you some stuff for her."

"Thanks."

"Sure, no sweat. There's a ton of shit up in my room. Photos, posters, CDs, all that crap."

Rick is clearly more cynical than I'd have thought, and I'm about to mention this, when Apollonia appears and my eyes literally pop out of their sockets. Literally. Mmmmm... plop! I can see only the floor, as my eyeballs, still attached by their optic nerves, hang wetly on my cheeks.

She's wearing a white bikini and... nothing else, just that. She's tied back her hair and tidied up her make-up. Waterproof, I assume, but what the hell do I know? I'm dimly aware of flip-flops on her feet but she could be wearing ski-boots and the SAS could be swarming all over the building because all I can look at, all I can think about, all I can drool over, is Apollonia Wallace's glorious body. Bizarrely, like some kind of drone strike, my gaze homes in, with laser precision, on her belly button. The most perfect belly-button in the entire world. I could stare at it forever. Really, I could.

"Hi, Rick," she says then puts her hand on my shoulder.

I slowly look up, my gaze travelling slowly up her tummy, stumbling over the valley between her breasts, to her heavenly face, and see her smiling at me.

"Here you are," she says. "I thought you might have found your way down here."

I lick my suddenly parched lips then swallow. "Uh, yeah," I croak, "I met Rick in the kitchen."

She's still smiling at me, in a *Well, what do you think of 4Tune8 now?* sort of way. I try to return this with a *Hey, you were right, I was wrong. It serves me right for having such preconceived ideas* sort of smile which I'm sure just makes me look one disc short of a box set, to use an appropriate analogy.

"Well, I'm dying for a swim. What about you?"

I shrug, no doubt enforcing the impression of sub-normality.

"There are swimming costumes in the changing rooms. I'm sure you could find one to fit."

"I don't know."

"Oh, come on. You're not going to leave me at the mercy-"

I realise she's spotted Robert and turn to find him sitting on the side of the lounger, watching Apollonia.

"Excuse me," she says, moving off around one end of the pool, toward Robert.

"This should be interesting," hisses Rick.

I grunt assent, watching Apollonia's swaying hips. As she draws nearer, Robert gets to his feet and holds out his arms in contrition. Apollonia stops about a metre from him and puts her hands on those divine hips. Because she's facing away from Rick and me, her face is hidden, although I suspect she's not exactly grinning from ear to ear. I watch Robert's mouth moving but his words are inaudible. He continues talking, pausing occasionally to wait for a response.

"She's making him work for this," whispers Rick.

"I know she was pretty upset," I murmur back at him, "but she didn't tell me what happened."

"Bob wouldn't tell us but earlier they were arguing about going to the gig tonight."

"Didn't she want to go?"

"No, it was Bob that didn't want to go. Said Pickaxe were third division bollocks and he couldn't understand why she'd want to go."

"Maybe she wanted to see us."

Rick glances at me, to make sure I'm joking. "Yeah, in your dreams."

I snigger quietly as I watch Robert reach out to gently touch Apollonia's bare shoulder. She shrugs him away. I glance at the three in the pool although I'd already guessed from their silence that they were watching the proceedings with as much interest as Rick and I.

"I thought maybe he'd been... you know, *playing away*, or something."

"Hey, if you were going out with Polly, would you so much as look at another woman?" he asks without turning to see my reaction. Not that any man with more than two neurones would answer in the affirmative.

Robert is still talking and I can tell by Apollonia's slightly more relaxed posture that she's hearing what she wants to hear, or her defences are weakening, or both. After a couple of minutes, Robert holds out his arms again. *What more can I say? Please forgive me.* A few seconds pass then Apollonia slowly shakes her head from side to side. *Oh, you silly man! Of course I'll forgive you.* She allows him to move closer and place a hand on each shoulder. As their lips meet, the three in the pool start whooping and clapping, which isn't quite what I feel like doing.

Rick turns to me. "Well, that seems to be that sorted out."

337

"Yeah," I murmur, watching the lovebirds getting increasingly worked up. Robert has let his hands fall down around Apollonia's waist and I can see his fingers rhythmically massaging the tops of her buttocks. Her hands are up behind his neck, forcing his mouth harder against her own. I start to work out how many limbs I'd be prepared to lose if only I could be in Robert's position and I'm soon debating whether or not I'd miss one arm and one leg more than both legs. As I reach the conclusion that such morbid considerations are purely academic, Luke and the other two are climbing stealthily out of the pool a few metres away from Robert and Apollonia, or Bob and Polly, as I should perhaps now refer to them. Or maybe I shouldn't. Anyway, so engrossed are they by the taste of each other's tongues that they fail to notice the three members of 4Tune8 sneaking up on them.

"Now!" yells Luke and the three of them run up behind Apollonia and Robert, grab them and push them into the pool, then leap in after them. All five start splashing water at each other and generally horsing around.

I lean back in my chair and watch all the excitement. Well, to be honest, I watch Apollonia – which is, of course, very exciting in itself. It's probably just the alcohol in my system but, every so often everything seems to decelerate to a kind of real life slow-motion, usually when Apollonia's jumping up out of the water. I can see, with hi-def clarity, every single water drop beading on her flesh, and in each drop the reflections of the overhead lights. And every time she whoops ecstatically, I can see – or I think I can see – every one of her perfectly white teeth, the matt finish of her waterproof lipstick, the single drop of water hanging from the tip of her nose.

Beside me, Rick shouts encouragement as Bob and the other two gang up on Luke and push him under the water, to the accompaniment of Apollonia's delighted squeals. She looks over at Rick then at me and, for a split second, our eyes meet before she returns her attention to Luke. And as I watch him lift her above his head then drop her back into the water with a loud splash I realised that, despite everything, I remain infatuated with Apollonia Wallace.

I've reconciled myself to her relationship with Robert. I know she'll *never* be mine, but I also know I can't expect her to never be anyone's. Even though she's still up there on that pedestal, my perspective *has* changed. After tonight, I see her much more as a real person, not some quasi-mythical object of desire. I know I can't really call her a *friend,* yet she's more than an acquaintance. Hey, until tonight, she wasn't even an acquaintance. I'm not complaining. If I sound confused, that's because I am.

"Another?" asks Rick, nodding at the cans on the table

I nod then catch the can he tosses me. "Don't you want to join in the fun?"

"I think they're doing all right without me."

I snap open the can. "Is everything all right. With the band, I mean, with the group?"

"In what way?" he asks, only slightly suspicious.

"Well, you're not going to break up or anything, are you? I mean, my sister's world would collapse like a bloody black hole, or something."

He stares hard at me for a few seconds – his gaze softened slightly by the beer he's had – and I do my best to look earnest.

"Why do you ask?"

"Well, it's just that I rather got the impression that you weren't... well, one hundred percent happy with things."

He snorts then leans back. "Tell your sister she's nothing to worry about. 4Tune8 will be around for a long time yet – at least until the middle of next year. Anyway, we can always reform in ten years and play the arenas all over again."

I can take a hint. It would seem, while he's aware of the ephemeral nature of groups like his, he doesn't really want to discuss it. I watch Apollonia and the others climb out of the pool and dry themselves.

"How long are you staying here for?" I ask.

"Until Sunday morning. Then it's Wembley in the evening."

"Oh yeah, I think Rosie, my sister, and her mates tried to get tickets. Sold out in four milliseconds, or something."

"You want a couple of freebies?"

"Hey, I wasn't trying to... you know..."

"Yeah, I know. You don't exactly look like a 4Tune8 fan."

"Well, no, but I can..."

I'm not quite sure how to finish the sentence. Luckily, the others are making their way around the pool towards us, Apollonia and Robert arm in arm and the others laughing and flicking wet towels at each other.

"Look," says Rick, sitting forwards, "I know our *target audience* is 11 to 15-year-old girls – Bob, and everyone else in *management,* never stops reminding us of that fact – who are just trying to make sense of their hormones, and I know that everyone else, apart from the odd grandmother or two, thinks we're a load of shite but-"

340

"Bloody hell," says Luke, grabbing the last can from the table, "not only has Rick finished off the booze but he's off on one of his bloody tirades again."

Apollonia laughs and looks at me. "I think Atticus must have got him going."

I try to look sheepish. Hell, I *am* sheepish.

Rick drains the last few drops from his can. "I was just saying-"

"Hey, we *know* what you were saying," says Luke, grinning. "We've all heard it a million times."

Apollonia sits down, facing me. I look at her face but it's as though her body is a massively powerful electro-magnet and my eyes are made of iron. Fortunately, she's looking at Robert as he and Luke discuss who should go back to the kitchen for more alcohol. There's a poolside bar but, apparently, the lads cleaned it out much earlier in the evening.

"Well, I think Rick should go," says Luke, "as he was the one that drank most of the last lot."

Everyone looks at Rick. "Oh, OK, for God's sake," he says, getting to his feet. "I wouldn't like to think of any of you lot having to make such a perilous journey."

Luke and one of the others laugh at Rick's apparent resentment.

"Why don't you go with him?" asks Apollonia, looking at me.

Almost an hour later, I'm standing in the entrance hall, weighed down with two carrier bags full of 4Tune8 paraphernalia. I've had way too much to drink and my head feels ready to slip its moorings and float off.

Apollonia looks at me with maternal concern. "Are you sure you don't want me to get you a taxi? I can call Roy."

"No, thanks. My name's Atticus, though some call me Johnny," I say, trying not to giggle.

"I think I will," she says, starting to walk across to a telephone table.

"No," I say, definitely too loudly, "I'll be fine. It's only a ten-minute walk."

More like half an hour but let's not quibble over minor details.

"Are you absolutely sure?"

"Yeah, yeah, really."

"Well, OK, then," she says, moving toward the front door.

She's wearing a pink and white striped dressing gown over her bikini. Her hair hasn't yet dried properly and hangs down around her face. Looking more beautiful than ever, she opens the door. Willing my feet to move, I walk past her and through the doorway then turn around.

"Thanks for tonight," she says.

"Eh? I didn't do anything, did I?"

"You know, just being there, really."

"Hey, no, thank *you*. I had a great time." My words are a lot more slurred than I'm making out here.

She looks at me for a few moments then leans forwards and kisses me on the cheek. "See you, then."

"Yeah," I grunt. "'Bye."

[29] Conversations

It's eleven o'clock when I become dimly aware of my phone buzzing. I grab it, drop it, pick it up, fumble to press the screen in the right place. My head is pounding. My bedroom door is open. I don't know why. I guess I never closed it last night when I got home.

It's Red. I grunt.

"Where've you been?" he asks. "I've rung you about fifty times."

I pull the phone away from me ear and squint at the screen. I've missed twenty-seven calls, there're are sixteen text messages, and innumerable other messages and alerts across all the usual social media platforms.

"Sorry. Not feeling so clever. Head feels like shit. Body feels like shit. All in all, it would be fair to say I feel like... rubbish," I say, as my mother appears in the doorway, carrying a basket of dirty clothes.

"Atticus, you look like shit," she says then turns and walks off.

She didn't say that. Not in so many words.

"What happened to you last night?" asks Red.

"When?"

"After the gig, of course."

"You missed me, did you?"

"Yeah, sure, what do *you* think?"

I want to tell him I think that, if they thought of me at all, it was probably along the lines of: 'Thank goodness Johnny Gooseberry has pissed off somewhere and left us to snog our wenches in peace.'

"Yeah? So, what did you get up to then?"

"We all went back to Derek's."

"Who's *we*?"

"Well, Chelsea and me, Bass and Suzz, Derek, Zach, Rosie, Dawn and Mamta."

The hammering in my head increases in intensity to such an extent that collapse seems imminent. Were I not still technically lying in bed, I very well might collapse. I screw up my eyes. A wave of vertigo slams into me then gradually subsides. Red's tinny voice squawks in the phone.

"Johnny! You still there?"

"Yeah," I croak. "I'm here."

"What's going on? Is someone else there?"

"No, I... I just don't feel too good."

"Right, so you said. How come-"

"What were *they* doing there?"

"Who?"

"Rosie, you bloody hosepipe, and the other two. Who did you think I meant?"

"Hey, it wasn't my idea."

"Well, who's was it then?"

"Derek. He asked them."

"*Why*, for God's sake?"

Red sniggers. "I think he's got the hots for your sister."

"What?" I whine.

"He was all over her."

"What?" I whine, even louder.

"Wait, you haven't heard the rest. You should have seen Zach and Mamta."

I pause for a few seconds, allowing this information to percolate. "You're winding me up, aren't you?"

"Aching men's feet."

"Derek and my sister?"

"Hole in one."

"What?"

"You got it."

"I got *what*?"

"Derek and Rosie."

"Derek and Rosie *what*?"

"What are you on about?"

"What are *you* on about?"

"Derek and Rosie."

"Look, we're going around in bloody circles here. Tell me exactly what went on between the two of them."

"Nothing."

"Nothing? But I thought you said..."

"I said I think Derek's got the hots for Rosie."

"And?"

"And what?"

"So what happened?"

"When?"

"Oh, for God's sake, Red! Are you deliberately trying to be obtuse or what?"

"What does 'obtuse' mean?"

"You know bloody well what it means, you infernal garden implement. Look, are you going to tell me what went on, or what?"

"Maybe."

"I give up. Why don't you ring me back when you're willing to talk sense?"

"OK, OK, don't blow a gasket. I'm just joking."

"Good. So nothing happened between Rosie and Derek, then?"

"No, but he *was* trying to tap off with her, though."

"But nothing happened?"

"No, she slapped him off. It was quite funny, really."

"Hilarious, I'll bet."

"Yeah, then he tried it on with Dawn."

"And?"

"And she was even less interested than Rosie."

"What, you mean Rosie was interested?"

"I just told you she gave him the cold shoulder, didn't I? Crikey, what are you, her guardian angel? Big brother Johnny watching out for his little sister," he says then starts sniggering.

"Yeah, well, something like that, I guess."

"So, do you want to hear about Zach and Mamta, then?"

"Only if I have to."

"Well, excuse me. I wouldn't want to force you or anything."

"Oh, go on, then."

"Do you want the blow-by-blow or just the headlines?"

"Headlines."

"Let me see, then. How about: 'Zach And Mamta: Wedding Bells?'"

"Wait! What?" I cry. This is not right. Mamta's only sixteen years old. OK, so I think she's seventeen in September, but my brother is a lot older than her. This is so, so wrong, on so many levels. "You *are* winding me up, aren't you? I mean, this is just so not funny."

"Well, it wasn't 'clothes off, utensils out' but it was touch and go for a while. They'd both had a lot to drink. I'm pretty sure nothing happened – you know, like underpants remained in the upright position – so I don't think Zach's going to need a solicitor or anything, but it was actually bloody hilarious."

"And how is it that you had so much time to observe all this."

"Ah," he says then pauses, "Chelsea had to go home soon after midnight."

"'Treat 'em mean to keep 'em keen', eh?"

"What?"

"Never mind," I mutter, still thinking about my brother and Mamta. He must be feeling even worse than I am now. "So, are you seeing Chelsea again?"

"Tonight."

"Blimey, are you putting an announcement in the paper? Hatches, matches and dispatches?"

"Ho-ho. Actually, that's why I rang."

"What, you're asking me to be Best Man?"

"You know my parents were supposed to be coming back this evening?"

"Uh, no, but if you say so."

"Well, Mum emailed me yesterday to say that they're staying for another few days. My Gran isn't getting over her hip operation as fast as they'd hoped. So they won't be home until Wednesday night."

"Sorry to hear that but I've got a bastard of a hangover. I need paracetamol and I've got to get my head down for another couple of hours. What's any of this got to do with me?"

"I've decided to have a party. Tonight."

"Tonight? What?"

"Just a small number of carefully selected friends. You know, a couple of hundred or so."

"Right, so it's beer and a take-out for six, is it?"

"Ouch! Your tungsten-edged wit has once again cut me to the quick."

"Well, honestly, why are you having a bloody party? I'm knackered. You must be knackered. I just want to sleep."

"I don't know. To celebrate the stunning début of Bläck Gläss?"

"So you can bloody well sneak off to your bedroom and tap off with Chelsea, more like."

"Yeah, well, that too."

At least he's being honest.

"I don't know, mate. It's Rosie's birthday today and she's having a few friends around later on. And I really do need to get some more kip."

"No sweat. They're all coming around here afterwards."

"I don't care how much this is blowing my mind. I don't believe it. Rosie and her mates said they would come to a party at *your* house? Tonight?"

"Sure. She wasn't too keen initially but Suzz persuaded her."

"What?"

"Yeah, they hit it off like a dwelling in flames."

"They did?" This does not compute. At all. My sister, Rosie Childress, and Suzana Comănici-Jenkins *hit it off?* The archetypal larval 4Tune8 fan and the Goth Queen from north of the wall? I say as much to Red. Then I think about all those unanswered calls on my phone, all those texts and messages. A lot of serious shit has been going down. "I just can't see that, mate."

"Yeah, well, just goes to show how much you know about women."

"Oh, right, thus speaks an expert on the subject, I suppose."

"Touché Turtle. So, you coming, then, or what?"

"Depends on whether or not my head's still in one piece by then."

"So, where *did* you get to last night, then?"

"Well, actually, I was with Apollonia."

Red laughs. "Yeah, right."

"I was."

"What, before or after someone gave you a funny little paper square and said: 'Here, just pop this in your mouth'?"

"I might be wrong, Red, but I'm detecting just a smidge of disbelief."

"I'm sorry, but Apollonia Wallace has got far better things to do than hang around with you."

"True."

"So, are you going to tell me what you *were* doing last night, or not?"

"I met up with Billy Gibson and some others, had a few beers, a few laughs, then came home."

"That sounds a bit more likely," he says, "but I still don't understand why you left us."

"I just needed a bit of air, that's all, and when I went back to find you, you'd gone."

"Oh, right."

"Satisfied?"

"Sure."

"So I can go and get a few paracetamols down my neck, then, can I?"

"I'll see you tonight, then?"

"What time?"

"Any time after nine, I guess."

"It's a date."

I toss my phone on the carpet, swing my legs out of the bed and sit on the edge. I can see my reflection in the dresser mirror. My pale complexion, dotted with smouldering zits, looks like currant bun mixture. Dark shadows lurk under my eyes. Greasy hair sticks out every which way. 'Look at Shock-Headed Peter,' my mother would say. I look like a junkie, strung out, desperate for another fix.

Strangely, though, I feel much better than my pounding head would suggest. I'm not *contented* or *happy*, you understand, but vaguely excited. I'm looking forward to this evening, when I'll be giving Rosie her present – or presents. Not just the box set, which cost me an arm and a leg, but also all the stuff Rick gave me last night.

I can't wait to see Rosie's face.

However, right at the moment, priority must be assigned to my parlous physical state. I stagger out into the hall then into the bathroom. After three glasses of water, each accompanied by a paracetamol, I take a long, hot shower. Which feels good. I bow my head and let the water fall on the back of my neck. I still can't quite believe what happened last night. By now, you'll be getting sick to the stomach with my penchant for rumination. I'll spare you every detail but I do want to mention a couple of things, so bear with me please.

Even though, at the time, I made a major effort to convince myself that there was no way Apollonia could ever... er, *have an interest* in me, I couldn't help but consider the possibility that she might. That is, just maybe, in a fleeting moment of complete insanity, she might have desired physical contact. This isn't going well, is it? I mean, I'm not expressing myself very articulately. Hey, I can prattle on about zit-cream theories and high heels until the bovine mammals return to their abode but when it comes to matters of the heart or, more pertinently, matters of a sexual nature, I'm completely unable to stick to the point, or even find the point.

What I'm trying to say about Apollonia is that, last night, it crossed my mind, more than once, that she might *seduce* me, or that she might let me seduce her. I know now that such flights of fancy were just that and, to be honest, I knew it last night but, well, I'm a 17½-year-old virgin and I can't stop myself from entertaining any possibility, however far-fetched it might be.

So it was, when Apollonia and Robert patched things up, that I felt more than a little pissed off, even though I knew it was what she wanted and that I was never in with a chance in the first place. But the funny thing is that my experience last night – being with Apollonia, talking to her, seeing what she's really like – has, if anything, made me think even more highly of her. I mean, what other woman, irrespective of her emotional state, would go out of her way to be so hospitable to me? The crux of all this is that, as far as I'm concerned, Apollonia Wallace is still the most wonderful human being on the planet. Bar none.

As far as 4Tune8 are concerned, I have to admit that my opinion has changed somewhat. I still think their 'music' is a load of canine waste product but, seeing as they concur with this assessment, or at least Rick does, then I can forgive them for it, magnanimous creature that I am. Hey, if someone offered me a crate-load of dosh to flex my pecs and mime to inane lyrics for a couple of years, I'd probably jump at the chance. Anyway, they seemed like *very nice boys*, as my perceptive grandmother would say.

OK, so I might need a few weeks (months) in the gym to get my pecs up to a standard where I could flex them for promotional purposes, but my point stands.

351

So, feeling a little more at peace with the world than usual, I step out of the shower, dry off, comb back my hair and move over to the mirror. There's a tad more colour in my cheeks and the half dozen zits blossoming over my face don't look quite as prominent. In fact, not one looks ripe for popping. Normally, I go out of my way to stamp on the toe of superstition but I can't help feeling that the absence of a volcanic zit on my face might be a good omen – perhaps, today might work out all right. Then again, one will probably sneak up on me at some point during the day so that when I hand over Rosie's present her friends will cover their faces, sniggering quietly, and Rosie will say: 'Gee thanks, brother dear, but pray tell, is that a bubo on the side of your neck or just the biggest zit in Christendom?'

After I've dressed, I make my way downstairs and into the kitchen. Rosie is helping Mum unload the dishwasher. Neither of them chooses to address me as I pour generic corn flakes into a bowl then sit down. I watch Mum putting crockery in cupboards for a minute or so.

"Where's Bennie?" I ask, hoping the social workers have been and taken him into custody, for causing his family undue pain and misery.

Mum turns to look at Rosie. "It speaks, does it?"

OK, I'm not blind.

"If it's about last night..."

"Three o'clock *in the morning*," says Mum, still to Rosie. "That's when he chooses to come home."

"Yeah, look, I'm really sorry about that. I kind of lost track of the time, that's all."

"Never crosses his mind to give us a ring, does it? Perhaps he's forgotten how to text? Oh no, why should *he* give a second thought as to what his mother might be thinking? Doesn't give two hoots that I might be worrying he's lying in a gutter somewhere."

"Look, I said I'm sorry. I really am. What more can I say?"

Mum turns to look at me and I can see she's not really *that* annoyed.

With my index fingers I pull down the corners of my mouth. "Look, this is remorse, see?"

Mum's features soften as she shakes her head. "Three o'clock," she says. "Do you mind telling me just what you were doing until that time of the morning?"

Luckily, I've prepared for this eventuality but before I can open my mouth Mum holds up an accusing finger.

"And don't try telling me you were with Dominic and Oscar because I know you weren't."

I glance at Rosie who has found something fascinating about a yellowing slip of paper attached to the side of the refrigerator by a strawberry shaped magnet. "I met up with some other friends and we just... hung out, that's all."

"Hung out? Until three in the morning?"

"Yeah."

Mum stares hard at me for a few seconds then seems to reach the sensible conclusion that, even though I'm obviously not telling the whole truth, I *am* back in one piece.

"He's out in the garden. Why?"

Is it just my mother that's capable of such knight's move thinking or is it a universal phenomenon? After a second or two I realise she's answering my question about Bennie's whereabouts.

"Just wondering," I say and resume eating my cereal. Mum is still staring at me. "What?"

"Haven't you forgotten something?"

God, I hate these games. Why doesn't she just say: 'Haven't you forgotten to do... whatever?' Instead, I'm expected to guess what it is I've forgotten. I've got a theory about this type of behaviour, called the Childress Guess What I'm Thinking Theory. School teachers are the worst perpetrators, irrespective of the subject being taught. Miss Teacher will ask a question, say: 'What's is the principle cause of the breakdown of the nuclear family?' Now, you can sit there and reel off two dozen causes, all of which could be considered quite plausible, but it's not until you finally hit upon the one she's thinking about that she says: 'That's right! Well done!' I think it's a sign of hardening of the arteries, myself – something to do with reduced blood flow to the brain inducing a kind of tunnel vision of the mind.

"I've forgotten many things," I say.

Mum's lip curls into a quarter-smile, mock-acknowledgement of my wit. Rosie is watching this enchanting scene with a slight frown.

"Oh, just tell me, then."

"What day is it today?"

"Saturday."

"And?"

"And..." I say, thinking hard, "it's... a fine sunny morning in June?"

Mum glances at Rosie then back at me.

I sigh. "Rosie's birthday."

"Well, aren't you going to wish her a happy birthday, then?"

I can only assume that this is her way of punishing me for coming home so late.

"Happy Birthday, Rosie," I say, like the child I am being treated as.

Rosie's only acknowledgement is a slight deepening of her frown.

"Now, then," says Mum, "what about a kiss for the birthday girl from her big brother?"

Both Rosie and I stare at Mum as if she'd just asked me to strip off and sit on top of the cooker. She waits a few seconds then starts chuckling. Never mind Bennie being carted away, I reckon they ought to be coming for Mum. I mean, this has to be mental cruelty, doesn't it?

"I'm off to find your father," she says, still chuckling, "and don't forget the table's booked for half past one."

How could I possibly forget that? The prospect of a family meal in a restaurant, where retreat to bedrooms is impossible, thrills me so comprehensively I could almost hurl. Judging from Rosie's pained expression as she watches Mum leave the kitchen I would guess that her feelings are not dissimilar to my own. Instead of making a swift exit, as I would have expected, Rosie continues to stand next to the refrigerator, leaning against the counter. It crosses my mind that she might wish to say something to me. They don't call me Mr Perception for nothing, you know. Despite being acutely aware that we have not exchanged a civil word for almost a week, I decide to play it cool. Rosie's apparent reluctance to make eye contact provides an opportunity to scrutinise her while finishing off my cereal.

She's in the trad larval outfit. Baggy, non-denominational sweatshirt, black leggings, white trainers. She does that thing with her hair, sweeping it away from her face, and I can see she's wearing red lipstick, nothing

355

garish, actually fairly subtle, but obvious enough for *me* to detect. Probably something called *Rose Blush.*

She attempts to steal a glance at me but finds me looking directly at her. Realising that I've forced her hand, she frowns and takes a deep breath then opens her mouth to speak. However, it would seem that she can't quite bring herself to formally open a dialogue. Instead, she pushes herself away from the counter and begins walking toward the door. It occurs to me to ask her if she's sure she doesn't want the birthday kiss that Mum suggested but I realise facetiousness would almost certainly be counter-productive, assuming, of course, that there is something to produce.

"Enjoy yourself last night?" I ask.

This stops her in her tracks. She turns to look at me. "What do you mean?"

Whoops. I don't think that came out quite right. Presumably, she thinks I'm referring to the events at Derek's place.

"The gig? Our set? Did you enjoy it?"

"Oh," she says, looking to one side then back at me. "It was all right, I guess."

"You certainly seemed to be enjoying yourself."

"Yeah, it was OK. I said."

Well, I didn't expect lavish praise or anything.

"What about Mamta and Dawn?"

"What about them?"

"Did they have a good time?"

Rosie raises her eyebrows indifferently. This is beginning to feel like a conversation with Bass when he's in one of his more intractable moods. I feel like saying: 'Look, it's obvious you want to say something so why don't you just spit it out?' Alternatively, it could be that she's expecting me to say something. Unfortunately, I haven't got the foggiest what it is. I opt for random pot-shots.

"Red tells me you got on well with Suzz."

She frowns as she realises I know something about what went on at Derek's. "Yeah, she's all right."

I try again. "Looking forward to lunch with the family?"

"Very funny."

"I wasn't trying to be funny."

Once again, she runs a hand through her hair. I note a diamond stud in her right ear.

"New earrings?"

She smiles briefly and fingers one of the them. "From Mum and Dad."

"Very nice," I say, as sincerely as possible.

As she absently scratches the side of her neck I determine not to give up. I'm going to find out what's bugging her one way or the other. Just at the moment, though, I'm struggling a bit.

"Is Zach coming?" I ask.

She nods. "And Frannie."

Crikey! This is a breakthrough. Volunteered information. What a shock.

"Really? Well, that'll be nice."

Yet again, there's another pause. I'm definitely running out of ideas.

"How many of your friends are coming this evening?"

"Six," she mutters. "Seven, maybe."

"So not a massive rave, then?"

She scowls at me, which I deserve, seeing as I was rather stating the obvious.

"What time are they due to get here?"

"Six-ish."

"Oh."

I can see a change of tactics is in order. I wave goodbye to the closed questions.

"What have you got planned? You know, charades, pass the parcel, truth or dare, strip poker?"

"Nothing, really."

It's my turn to frown. "OK, so just generally hanging out?" I fight the urge to make sarcastic comments about everyone staring at the phones.

"Maybe. I don't know."

This is getting more than a little ridiculous.

"So, sixteen, eh? Feel any different?" I ask

Despite receiving another scowl, I persevere.

"Sixteen," I murmur. "Well, not long ago you'd have been legally able to buy tobacco products, but not now, so that's a bit of a shame. You could have run down to the corner shop for twenty Benson & Hedges."

This isn't impressing my darling sister but I've grown tired of her recalcitrance so I press on. "If you can get Mum and Dad to agree, you can get married, or join the Army. That would be fun, eh? You can drive a moped, join a trade union and buy a lottery ticket. At sixteen, of course, and I hope you won't consider this too vulgar, but you can, of course, consent to sexual, er, *activity* with someone else. As long as they're 16 or older, *obviously*."

Rosie's glaring at me now, but at least it's something. Some kind of reaction.

"Apart from that, though, there's not much else to shout about. You can't drive or vote. Still, a milestone of sorts, I guess."

Suddenly, it dawns on me that perhaps she does want me mention what went on after the gig at Derek's flat.

Maybe my comments about the age of consent weren't so very wide of the mark. I mean, to my knowledge, Rosie has never received any advances from a member of the opposite sex – or from a member of the same sex, for that matter. Now, there's an interesting possibility. On the other hand, though, I can't for the life of me think why she'd want to discuss anything like that with me. Quite the opposite. Let's face it, when – and it must happen at some point – Rosie pops her cherry, big brother Atticus will be the last to know. And, let's face this, too: that's entirely as it should be. Still, nothing ventured...

"Red also said something about Derek taking a shine to you. That must have been an interesting experience."

She assumes a pained expression. Obviously, I have not managed to discover whatever it is that's on her mind. I sigh and shake my head.

"Look, if there's something bothering you then you're just going to have to come out and tell me because I don't know what it is."

She doesn't say anything but there's something about the way she looks at me that strikes a familiar chord. All of a sudden, I realise what this is all about. I could kick myself for not working it out right at the start. After all, it's been bugging me for the last week, to put it mildly. Maybe she feels guilty for slapping me. Right, and maybe Aerosmith's next tour is going to be sponsored by *The Priory*.

"This is all about last Saturday, yeah?"

Rosie bites her lower lip and stares at me, waiting for me to proceed.

"Look, I said I was sorry and I meant it. You were right. I was a dick, a complete cockwomble. No argument.

At all. I shouldn't have said any of that stuff about Dawn. Bang out of order. I didn't mean any of it. Honest. And you were also right about me not *knowing* any of your friends. I shouldn't judge them. I shouldn't have any opinions about them. I'm an utterly useless human being. Waste of space. Shouldn't even be breathing the same air as the rest of my species. Look, what if I text Dawn now and tell her that she can come round and throw stones at me? She could even get that axe from the garage and-"

"See?" barks Rosie. "That's exactly what I mean!"
"What?"
"Why can't you just be *nice*?"
We stare at each other for a few seconds. I think I've seen this film before, and I didn't enjoy it much the first time. I didn't think the characterisation was realistic and there was far too much exposition.
"OK, maybe I went a bit over the top just now, but-"

"But you *always* go over top," snaps Rosie, scowling. "You always have to be so *clever*, don't you? Always with the smart comments. Why can't you just be…. *pleasant?* Would it be anathematic to be *nice?* Just *once* in your life?"
Whoa, whoa, whoa! Let's just pause here for a few seconds.
Anathematic?
What. The. Fuck?
Where does she get off using a word like that to me?
I can't help myself from grinning, even though I know I shouldn't. Bearing in mind what we're talking about. But come on! *Anathematic?* It's clear to see that

Miss Childress has been studying *very hard* for her English Literature GCSE exam.

Rosie glares at me. "Oh, go to hell, Atticus," she says then turns and walks out of the kitchen.

"Good one," I mutter to myself.

I could chase after her, but I know it would be pointless.

I carry my bowl and spoon to the sink. Rinsing them, I curse myself for being such an idiot – for being so *clever*. Would it have killed me to have just smiled inwardly at her pretentiousness? I don't think so. 'Why can't you just be *nice*?' she'd asked. Point taken.

The thing is, of course, I don't particularly want to be *nice*, do I? Nice is naff. I want to be *interesting*. I want to be... well... clever, I suppose. Which poses a problem. If I want to be clever, erudite, witty, then I need to acknowledge *who* I'm trying to impress.

No one likes a smug bastard. And that's exactly what Rosie's calling me. Can I disagree?

My problem, arguably, is that I can't judge when to be clever and when to be nice. When to be erudite and when to hold my tongue. Except even that's not true, as I *do* know when a droll comment is appropriate and when it isn't. Just not, sometimes, until afterwards, which helps no one, least of all me.

I stow the bowl and spoon on the drying rack then return to my chair. This is a sad state of affairs. How many times can I cock things up? How many times in the last week have I done or said something stupid then vowed to change my ways, only to do the same bloody thing all over again, with only slight variations? It really is utterly pathetic. I am utterly pathetic.

I can't really see a way out, other than suicide. OK, too dramatic, I know. All I can hope for, really, is that if I keep telling myself to straighten up and fly right then one day I might actually manage it. After all, I honestly believe my intentions are good – I just can't seem to execute them properly. I'm sure you're getting sick of my emotional vicious circle. Imagine being me. Oh Lord, please don't let me be misunderstood.

Still, I have got a new angle from which to approach things. From now on, for today at least, I am going to try to be as *nice* as possible. Ha-ha-ha. Who would have thought it? Atticus William Blake Childress: Mr Nice-Guy.

My phone buzzes. Bass.

"Be nice," I mutter, accepting the call. Today, this is my mantra. "Hello. Childress residence," I say in a sing-song voice.

"Johnny?" asks Bass uncertainly.

"Speaking."

"Eh?"

"It's me speaking."

"I know that but what... oh, never mind. Where did you get to last night?"

We repeat much of the conversation I had with Red. Though I don't mention Apollonia. Bass asks if I'm going to Red's party.

"Of course. Wouldn't miss it. I can usually be found at all the *swingingest* joints in town. Will the delightful Suzz be coming?"

"I think so."

"Uh-huh."

"Did Red tell you he'd invited your sister and her friends."

"He did."

I listen to Bass breathing. My muted response is patently not what he was expecting.

"You don't mind?" he asks eventually.

"Should I?"

"Well, I don't know. I kind of figured you'd... you know... not be too chuffed, or something."

"No, it's fine by me."

There's another long silence.

"Are you feeling OK?"

"Fine."

"Oh."

Another silence.

"Are you sure you're not ticked off about something?"

"No, I couldn't be better. Why?"

"Oh, nothing, I guess," he says.

"See you tonight, then!"

"Uh... yeah."

"Have a nice day."

"Eh?"

"Missing you already," I say then hang up.

[30] Sweet Sixteen

I'm in the back of Dad's car with Bennie, returning home after an eventful birthday luncheon at *The Plump Partridge*. We'd had an outside table, on the terrace. The food was, if you don't mind me gloating, glorious. My steak was *to die for, darling*, and I finished off what Mum left on her plate, which was a fair bit, for reasons about to be explained. I am stuffed. I lean back in the seat, only really half listening to my parents. Rosie and Zach are in Frannie's car behind us, with Zach driving. Frannie was too upset to drive.

"He's really not as bad as you make out," says Dad to Mum.

He's talking about Richard, Frannie's partner, who was not present at Rosie's birthday lunch. I don't know where he was. Protesting against something, somewhere. Vegan Homoeopaths Against Starbucks, maybe.

Somehow – I'm not quite sure exactly how it happened – Frannie and Mum had a small disagreement about Richard's suitability, in the long run, as husband *material.* The thrust of Mum's argument seemed to be that someone so bound up in high ideals was ill-equipped to deal with the *real world* and therefore a poor choice.

I could see her point, to a degree, although, being very *nice*, I said nothing.

Frannie, however, justifiably – it's her life – made it crystal clear that she was free to choose whoever she wanted to live with and that she didn't appreciate Mum constantly denigrating Richard. Interestingly, she didn't argue with Mum's assessment of him as a *head-in-the-clouds socialist*. Zach's comment, that, in his opinion, *Red*

Dick was one of the most likeable Marxists he'd ever met did, not help matters.

It got to the stage where Mum and Frannie were glaring at each other over their deserts. *Death by Profiteroles* seemed like a real possibility. Dad, Zach and I were watching them, waiting to see where this was all going to go next. Bennie was attacking his brownie and ice-cream. Rosie was glancing around, smiling nervously at the other diners out on the terrace, as if to say: 'It's a trick of the light, you know. I'm not *really* sitting with them.'

Then Mum's conscience got the better of her and she informed Frannie that, as she didn't want to spoil Rosie's birthday, she would say no more about it.

Frannie's response – which was, frankly, unhelpful at best, and childish at worst – was to fish her cigarettes from her handbag and light up, knowing that this would infuriate Mum. She didn't go as far as to blow smoke into Mum's face – as that would surely have resulted in a cat-fight – but instead proceeded to puff away with petulant deliberation.

Mum's reaction caught me completely off guard. 'Be a dear,' she said, turning to me, 'and fetch the ashtray from that empty table over there. Frannie's decided to indulge her filthy habit again.'

As I plonked the ashtray down in front of her, Frannie smiled at me, smoke curling from her nostrils, as if to say: *Sorry about all this, but you know what your mother's like.* I returned to my seat then, as I munched my way through a monstrous slab of Black Forest gâteau, watched Mum politely picking at her apple pie.

Frannie smoked, right elbow cupped in left palm, and glowered at her sister.

I think Zach was sharing my perverse sense of enjoyment about the situation. Dad, on the other hand, was feeling much more uncomfortable, hence his repeated attempts to initiate a conversation on a neutral topic.

But Frannie wouldn't even look at him and all he received from Mum was a series of non-committal grunts. He'd just about got a conversation with Zach off the ground – about how it was about time the Health Secretary had his testicles removed and hung from a lamp-post outside the Department of Health – when Frannie forcefully ground out her cigarette, leaving a stream of smoke to waft up into my mother's face. She cleared her throat and smiled. 'So then, Rosie,' she said, 'how does it feel to be sweet sixteen?'

Presumably, a nicotine fix had helped Frannie to put her differences with Mum to one side. Even so, I wanted to suggest another conversation topic *might* be more fruitful.

Gradually, though, the embarrassing pall that had settled over the table dissipated. Fifteen minutes after their spat, the atmosphere was a lot less charged. By this time, though, Frannie had knocked back three large brandies, and Mum had had two enormous glasses of Pinot Grigio. Thus it wasn't that either of them had made a determined effort to play nice.

Alcohol: maybe not the answer to anything, but it can certainly be a solution.

By the time the bill arrived, things were more or less back to normal – or at least back to what passes for normal in our family.

"He's not good enough for her," says Mum. "That's all I'm saying."

"She *is* almost twenty-four, dear, and, as she says, old enough to make her own decisions."

366

"And just whose side are you on?"

"It's not a question of taking sides."

"Is it not? Well, I think the least you could do is back me up."

Dad decides not to reply to this. He glances at the rear-view mirror and, seeing me looking at him, raises his eyebrows a couple of millimetres. We drive in silence. Dad pulls up at a set of lights, with a handful of cars in front.

A woman is walking along the other side of the road, on Dad's side. She's in her early twenties. Black knee-length boots with chunky heels and a medium platform. Tight dark denim mini-skirt and a tight, black, sleeveless, scoop neck top. Her bleached hair is scraped away from her face and up into a bun. Her face has a hard look. Doesn't look like she takes many prisoners. Nice legs and decent breasts. Baubles, no more. Nothing especially notable but not to be sniffed at.

I'm half-watching her, stomach still too distended to pay full attention. Then I realise that Dad's clocked her.

Don't get me wrong. He's not staring and drooling. His head barely turns at all, but enough for me to realise that he's looking at her, checking her out, which I find disturbing.

I always find this unsettling, which isn't to say that my father's always ogling the ladies. Well, not that I'm aware of, anyway. It's as if I don't think he should look at other women at all, an opinion which doesn't withstand even superficial scrutiny. I mean, he's a living, breathing, heterosexual male, isn't he? Why shouldn't he appreciate a comely lass if he spots one?

Just because a man's in his mid-fifties, it doesn't mean his testosterone levels have dropped to pre-pubescent levels. You see, I know all this but... well, damn it all, he's

367

my flipping father! My father shouldn't be acknowledging the existence of any woman apart from Mum. Not in that way, anyway.

The thing is, I'm back once again to knowing that my gut instincts are questionable, yet being spectacularly unable to do anything about it. Anyway, how do I know what my father is thinking as he looks at this woman? Maybe he's spotted a suspicious mole on her arm and he's thinking that it might need to be looked at.

Pushing these confused thoughts out of my mind, I turn to look at Bennie and find him diligently exploring a nostril with his right index finger which he then withdraws and inspects.

"Do you have to?" I inquire, scowling.

He looks at me and smirks. "Want some?" he asks, thrusting his snotty finger at me.

"Stupid little twa… twit," I hiss, slapping his hand away.

He shrieks then glares at me.

"Cut it out, you two," says Dad.

"It was Atticus who started it," whines Bennie.

"I said cut it out."

I give Bennie my most withering look then stare at the back of Mum's head, wondering what horrendous acts of destruction I must have committed in previous lives to have deserved such an abominable sibling. I twist around to look back at Frannie's car. She's sitting in the front passenger seat, smoking. As I watch she flicks ash out the window. I smile, knowing how much that winds up my mother.

When we pull into the drive, it's almost five o'clock. Like any other close-knit family, we immediately disperse to different parts of the house. Having said that, Zach doesn't even manage to cross the threshold. Instead, he saunters off to the garage, mumbling something about changing an oil filter, or topping up the radiator.

Unlike many of my peers, I have very little knowledge of the workings of the internal combustion engine and furthermore, I have zero inclination to correct this deficiency. A car, or motorcycle, exists to get me from one place to another – the actual mechanics of the process are inconsequential. I dare say the next time I'm stranded in some Godforsaken backwater with a car that won't start, I'll change my mind, but I think I'll just take my chances.

Dad shuffles off to the lounge, no doubt to nod off, belly full, in front of the TV. Bennie trails behind him. Mum disappears into the kitchen to make herself a cup of tea, leaving Rosie, Frannie and I standing in the hall.

They're both staring at me, their expressions so similar that I know they've been talking about me. Rosie must have told Frannie about our conversation in the kitchen this morning. Frannie probably knows about last Saturday's little *tête-à-tête* as well.

I am, to say the least, at something of a disadvantage. Perhaps surrender is the best option. I could ask: 'Do you want to castrate me now or shall we wait until Rosie's chums arrive? Then we could make it a bit more of an event.' On the other hand, I could run away. I'm seventeen. The Marines wouldn't turn down a prime physical specimen like me. I say nothing and dash upstairs, not looking back, not wanting to see their faces, afraid that their eyes would be burning with malevolent green fire.

Once safely in my room, I lock the door then switch on my sound system. I fiddle with my phone and press play, not caring what comes on. Queens of The Stone Age. Could be worse.

I open my closet and pull down the 4Tune8 box set from the top shelf, then pick up the two carrier bags of boy-band paraphernalia. I set down the box set on my bedside cabinet and empty the contents of the carrier bags onto my bed. Then I sit down and begin to sort through it all. I won't bore you with all the sordid details but, essentially, it takes me a good ten minutes to divide the junk into four piles: CDs, tee-shirts, posters and assorted photographs. Everything signed by one or more members of the band. Looking at their scrawled signatures, I realise that the two members whose names I couldn't remember last night are Geoff (not George, as I'd thought) and Alan. Rick, Luke, Geoff, Alan.

I not sure what to do with it all. I'd bought some gold paper to wrap the box set. But I'm not wrapping all the rest of this crap. Not individually, anyway. Equally, I can't just dump on Rosie two bulging carrier bags, even if they are stuffed with extraordinarily desirable 4Tune8 clutter. Not quite the effect I'm hoping to achieve.

I rummage through the photos, then realise there are several duplicates. Once I've weeded these out – not much fun, entailing repeated careful scrutiny of *Lovely Luke's* chiselled features – I'm left with a much less unwieldy pile. I repeat the process with everything else then start wrapping. I end up with five parcels. Considerably more manageable.

As I apply the last strip of sticky tape I hear the front door-bell. Rosie's friends are starting to arrive. It's a larval party. Who knows? Perhaps it'll be a butterfly ball.

[31] Let The Games Begin

I stack the presents on my chest of drawers then stretch out on my bed, resting my head on interlocked fingers. I work out my battle plan.

Proper Planning and Practice Prevents Piss Poor Performance.

Well, to be honest, I've had my plan worked out for a few hours. I go over it again, taking into account as many eventualities as I can foresee.

Have I mentioned already how desperately I want everything to go well? More than once. I know. The spooky thing is, I actually think it might. Call me an unflinching optimist, if you must. Seriously, folks, I *do* believe everything might just work out. Let's just say I feel it in my water – whatever *that* means. If you build it, they will come.

I can picture it now. I'll walk into the lounge, struggling under the immense weight of all the 4Tune8 goodies. Rosie and the other larvae will be sitting in a semi-circle around a blazing log fire. They'll have been chatting in hushed voices about this and that – this square-jawed boy and that ripped McTasty with bacon – occasionally emitting a squeal of nervous excitement. When I enter, though, an eerie silence will fall over the room. Even though none of them utters a word, their expressions speak volumes.

'What's *he* doing here?' Mamta will be thinking, her lips so puckered one could easily confuse them with some other part of her anatomy. I *do* know how to paint an appealing picture.

'Where's the nearest blunt instrument?' Dawn will be asking herself, her bulging eyeballs reflecting the dancing flames.

Rosie will be glaring at me, her eyes flashing obscenities: 'You bastard, Atticus. How *dare* you come in here?'

Leaning against the hearth, Frannie will be looking at me, head slightly cocked, at the same angle as the cigarette between her fingers. 'Well, well, well,' she'll be thinking. 'If it isn't my nephew the plastic fan. I wonder what's drawn him into our little coven.'

Dawn will pull out a switchblade, press the release, and the blade will spring out with a loud click. She'll lock her gaze with mine then smile malignantly.

'Happy Birthday, Rosie,' I'll say, striving to keep my nerve. 'I've got a couple of presents for you.' Then I'll shuffle meekly towards her, holding out one of the parcels, the one containing half a dozen tee-shirts, maybe. Rosie will slowly get to her feet, keeping her eyes fixed on my face, searching for any sign that this might be an elaborate trick, one designed to humiliate her, perhaps.

Gingerly, she'll take the parcel from me then slowly begin to unwrap it. I'll be holding my breath as she sets down the parcel on the back of the sofa and lifts out the first tee-shirt. Gradually, a smile will appear on her face and I'll judge it safe to exhale. Rosie will hold the tee-shirt against her chest and turn to let her friends see it, then she'll turn to face me. I'll be looking at the tee-shirt, but when my gaze travels up to her face, I'll see not a delighted smile but her mouth twisted into a cruel grin.

Then she'll start laughing, a coarse cackle at first, rising in volume to a series of equine guffaws. Her friends, seeing my face drooping with confusion and disappointment, will join in, until the room is reverberating with their brutal roars.

When she finally gets her breath, Rosie will wipe tears of mirth from her eyes and look at me. '4Tune8,' she'll grunt. 'What a hoot! They're old hat, now, Atticus, you poor misguided sod. Yesterday's news. I'd rather be seen wearing a pair of Bennie's soiled underpants on my head than this.'

I'll feel as small as a small thing as, one after the other, Rosie opens my other presents, laughing louder and louder as she passes each 4Tune8 souvenir to her friends. Eventually, she'll get to the box set. Letting the gold paper fall to the floor, she'll hold it up to her face, inspecting it, scrutinising the Japanese writing. Her eyebrows will slowly creep upwards, possibly as she realises the financial sacrifice I've made, then she'll look at me again.

'Atticus, you sad excuse for a human being,' she'll say calmly, 'if you think this piece of crap is going to make up for you being such a cruel, sadistic twat to me and my friends, then you've got another think coming.'

With that, she'll turn and toss the box set onto the fire.

I'll glance from one larva to the other – then at Frannie – and the malevolence in their eyes will turn my blood to ice water. One by one, they'll get to their feet and move slowly forwards to join Rosie, until they're forming a menacing arc, each of them glaring at me with undiluted hatred. On the fire, the box set crackles and pops. The vinyl within begins to melt and the air fills with a sulphurous reek.

'I think you'd better leave,' Rosie will say, motioning with a slight wave of her hand for Dawn to put away her switchblade. 'Perhaps you might like to go back to your room. Why not check out the John Lewis website. I think there's a lingerie sale this weekend. Knock yourself out. And if you ever show your face around here again...'

She'll let the sentence hang in the air, allowing me to draw my own conclusions. Dawn, however, will not feel satisfied with such subtlety. I'll watch, sweat running down my spine, as she slowly draws a finger across her throat. Step by cautious step, I'll walk backwards toward the door, not for a second taking my eyes off the group of larval thugs.

I realise that I am actually sweating. Profusely. I sit up on the edge of the bed, starting to think I should reconsider. But, I've started so, as they say, I may as well finish.

Still, if I go downstairs and find Dawn toying with a knife, or Mamta twirling a chain whip, then I am out of here. You can eat my dust.

I glance at my phone. Ten past six. Only another forty minutes to go, which I spend in a rather uncomfortable state of increasing nervous excitement – not quite as bad as last night, before the gig, but pretty close.

I flip through songs on my phone, listening to each for an increasing short period of time. I can't concentrate. Nothing is steadying my nerves. I can't cope with the agitated aggression of metalcore. I fall back on the classics – Metallica, Sabbath, Purple, AC/DC, Van Halen, etc. Finally, I settle for *A Map of All Our Failures,* an album by Prince Harry's favourite doom metal gloomsters, My Dying Bride. Its ponderous, melancholic strains – tonic-like – calm me down. A bit.

I grab my laptop and open the browser. I start off with Facebook but tire quickly of my ten million 'friends' posting either photos of cute kittens or bogus news stories about men having sex with alligators. I check out a couple of metal sites but it seems more likely that Gene Simmons will undergo gender reassignment surgery before Metallica release an album of new material. Meh.

Inevitably, I drift, as always, to the old favourites. The usual succession of lovelies waits for me, either scantily-clad or sheathed in latex. This time, though, instead of feeling more calm, I find myself growing increasingly irritated. Why am I obsessed with this stuff? It's not healthy. I should be reading articles like 'How to Meet a Normal Girl' or 'How Not to Make Normal Girls Run Away as Fast They Can', not looking at eBay listings of wet-look leggings.

Am I doomed to wander the planet, searching for the latex-encased woman of my dreams – a shiny fantasy woman – never being satisfied with even the thought of a relationship with a woman who likes wearing jeans and a tee-shirt?

I definitely have too much time on my hands. They should bring back National Service, or something. I glance at the time and realise that I am nearly out of it.

Do or die.

'There is nothing impossible to him who will try,' said Alexander the Great, apparently. Mind you, he also said: 'Sex and sleep alone make me conscious that I am mortal.' At least I have one of those covered. Which might explain why, at the moment, I feel like only half a man.

I switch off the laptop and the sound system. I'm still wearing the shirt and tie I put on for lunch. I smooth back my hair, fasten the top shirt button and straighten my tie.

I keep telling myself that I don't have a true clothing fetish. It's not the thought or the sight of a shiny skirt or a pair of Louboutin courts that gets my pulse racing *per se*. It's the thought or the sight of a lovely lady *wearing* a glossy pair of wet-look jeans or a pair of Gianvito Rossi pumps that gets my blood flowing.

Is there *really* a difference? I think so. But if, in fact, I do have some kind of clothing fetish then I'm just going to have to live with it, however sad it might be to have to acknowledge this at such a young age.

Fetishes are for fat, balding, red-faced civil servants, aren't they? Not for seventeen-year-old school boys, surely?

An image suddenly pole-vaults into my brain, of me aged fifty, sitting behind a desk in a grey government building, rubbing my red face with my pudgy hands then running them across my pale, hairless pate, my bloated belly pressed up against a desk drawer. Each working day is torture. I live only to spend hours every night downloading highly questionable material from the dark web.

I shudder, shaking away such distasteful thoughts because, as I said, the time has come. Now is the time for action. Once more unto the breech, dear fellow travellers. I spy a river up ahead. It looks like the Rubicon although, knowing my luck, it's probably the Styx. I grab Rosie's presents and make my way downstairs.

Alea iacta est.

Squinting between the jamb and the hinged side of the lounge door I see that Rosie and her friends are sprawled in various positions at the far end of the room. I twist my head one way then the other. No log fire. No switchblades. No chain whips. Excellent. Frannie is off to one side, sitting in a chair by an open window.

"What's going on?"

I spin around, almost dropping the presents, to find Dad looking at me quizzically.

I recover my composure with impressive speed and say: "Go get Mum."

It hadn't crossed my mind that they might wish to witness the present-giving ceremony, but what the hell. Why not? Dad just stands there, alternately looking down at the gold-wrapped packages in my arms and up at my face.

"Dad," I plead, "go and fetch Mum, will you? And hurry – I don't want them to realise I'm waiting out here."

Finally, the penny drops, its descent presumably delayed by the after-effects of a fairly lengthy snooze in front of the TV, and he walks off into the kitchen. I turn and peer again through the crack between door and jamb.

Rosie's leaning back in one of the armchairs, with Mamta sitting at her feet. Occupying the settee are Dawn, Courtney Khan and the girl who was wearing the green and white checked dress at the party last Saturday. I now know that this is Cheyenne Chambers. Sitting in the other armchair, in front of Frannie, is Mei-Ling Jiǎng and kneeling on the carpet with her back to me is Saoirse McCormack, who's recognisable from any angle, and at any distance up to a couple of hundred metres, by the explosion of dark red hair sprouting at right angles from her head.

I am now certain, unless she's shoved it down between the settee cushions, that Dawn is not carrying a knife of any kind. Though, arguably, she could have a very small penknife, with which, let's be honest, she could still inflict a fair amount of damage. I could lose an eye, at the very least.

4Tune8's latest album is playing on the sound system so it would appear – and, patently, this is a double-edged sword – that their fifteen minutes are not yet up. I allow myself a small, though still slightly nervous, smile.

"What's all this about?" asks Mum.

I turn to find her standing next to Dad. She looks down at the presents in my arms then up again, appraisingly, at my face.

"These are for Rosie. I thought you and Dad might like to be there when I give them to her."

"What are you lot doing?"

Like the smell of a rank fart which you can't shake from your nostrils, Bennie is back. I frown, and rapidly calculate the relative merits of saying something caustic. Rosie's voice echoes in my head. 'Why can't you just be *nice*?" So, instead, I simply sneer. Dad explains the situation to the little toad.

I make sure I've got a firm grip on all the presents then walk into the lounge. Immediately, Rosie sees me. Saoirse, with her back to me, continues talking for a second or two before she notices that the attention of her friends is focused elsewhere. I'm conscious of Mum, Dad and Bennie filing in behind me. My heart is thumping. My throat feels like sandpaper. I feel a bit like I did when I walked on stage last night. This time, though, *I'm* the centre of attention, not Bass.

"Ah," I croak. "I've… I've got some presents," I say, walking toward Rosie. "For you," I add, redundantly.

I don't know why but I can't look at any of Rosie's friends. I steal a glance at Frannie, who's smiling, perplexed, which I take as a sign of encouragement. It can't be far from the door to the armchair in which Rosie reclines, but it feels like a marathon. I keep walking. In my head the citizens screech 'Shame!' as they spit and throw rotting vegetables at me.

I finally reach Rosie's chair then, bizarrely, some unseen force controlling my limbs, I kneel down and place my five gold packages in a line on the floor at her feet. Only when I look up at her does the peculiarity of my position occur to me. Why the hell am I kneeling?

Earlier, when planning all this, I'd assumed, that when I handed over the gifts, both Rosie and I would be standing, facing each other. Now, though, I'm the focal point of some weird tableau.

Here's Rosie, seated in the armchair like a queen on her throne, Mamta kneeling at her feet to one side like a lady-in-waiting with me directly in front of my sister like an explorer returned from distant lands with his golden treasure strewn on the floor before his beloved queen. I glance at Mamta, who's looking at me uncertainly, as though I might either collapse or explode. Rosie's other friends – Dawn, Courtney, Mei-Ling, Cheyenne and Saoirse – are arranged in twin arcs to either side. I twist to look over my shoulder, at Mum, Dad and Bennie. It's clear that, like everyone else, they have no idea what to expect.

I look up at Rosie again and lick my lips, suddenly unsure how to proceed.

Go with the flow.

Yeah, but what flow? Almost thirty seconds have passed since I kneeled down. I lick my lips again, then glance down at my presents. My hand hovers over the one containing the tee-shirts, the one I had planned to give her first, but then, as if controlled by an external force, it reaches out and grabs the box set, which I had intended to save until the end.

"Um, this is for you," I say, holding it out towards her.

She reaches for it but, at the last minute, I pull it away. I briefly catch sight of her frown before my gaze switches to her left knee, where it stays while I speak.

"Er, just before I give it to you, though, there's a couple of things I want to say – well, *one* thing, really."

I want to tell her how sorry I am. I want to tell her how sorry I am for being such a bastard to her for all these years. I want to tell her that I'm sorry I broke her tricycle on that Christmas morning when I was six and she was four and a half. I want to tell her that I'm sorry I've judged her friends while knowing nothing about them. Nothing other than a fantasy I've concocted in my head, that is. I want to tell her that I'm sorry I was such a *stupid fuck-face* last Saturday night. I want to tell her what a wonderful young woman she's becoming and that I'm glad she's my sister. I want to tell her how proud I am of her and that I love her.

"I really wanted to say..." I murmur, staring at her knee, "how much I... um... hope you have a very happy birthday."

I thrust the box set toward her, jerking my hand back as soon as she takes it from me, cursing my cowardice.

"Thanks," Rosie says quietly.

As I listen to her unwrapping it, I stare at Mamta's creamy milk chocolate thighs. For once, even though I'm staring, I'm not actually *seeing*. My gaze is fixed on Mamta's thighs but my attention is wholly consumed by Rosie. The rustling stops and there's a pause, presumably as Rosie identifies the gift.

"Wow," she says, and I can hear immediately that she hasn't been bowled over. "Look, it's a 4Tune8..."

Still staring at Mamta's thighs, I hear one or two breaths being drawn and the creak of settee springs as one of the girls sat thereon leans forwards to obtain a closer look.

"It's foreign, I think," says Rosie.

She doesn't know what she's holding, and she's disappointed. A sledgehammer pops into existence, hovering in the air above me, then swings down in an arc, slamming into my skull, driving bone fragments deep into my cerebrum.

Why doesn't she know what she's holding? Does she not know how much this cost me? Anger flares in my chest, the fades as fast as it appeared. It's my fault. As usual, the thing I'd built up in my head, the thing I'd spent hours constructing out of a thousand tiny mental Lego bricks, is just that – an imaginary *thing* in my head. Not reality.

Why would Rosie know anything about an imported Japanese box set? Why would she assign it any value? I only *thought* she'd go berserk when she saw it. I mean, I never heard her say: 'Gosh, I'd give *anything* for that Japanese 4Tune8 vinyl box set.' Oh no, it was me that *assumed* that the very thought of it would trigger multiple lady-rumbles.

"It looks Chinese," says one of the girls – Cheyenne, I think.

"Japanese," I murmur, but no one hears me.

"I wouldn't have thought they'd heard of 4Tune8 in China," says Mamta, pulling down the hem of her skirt. I guess she'd finally noticed me staring.

"Of course they have," says Saoirse. "They've played all over the world."

"Yeah, well, thanks, Atticus," says Rosie.

381

I summon the strength to look up and see her holding her Chinese box set, which she probably thinks I bought down the market for a couple of quid, looking at me, still with that damned uncertain smile.

"There's a few more things," I mumble, passing her the tee-shirt parcel.

Deciding to leave Mamta's thighs alone for the time being, I elect instead to see how long I can keep my eyes on Rosie. She slowly unwraps the package, then pulls out one of the tee-shirts. I notice that it's one with a full-colour head-shot of Rick, under which has been scribbled 'Hugs and kisses from Rick' with a black marker. I watch Rosie's eyes as she inspects the tee-shirt and I see them narrow as she looks down at the message, the possibility crossing her mind that it has been hand-written and not just part of the design. She rubs the fabric between her fingers and suddenly her eyes light up.

"It's been signed," she whispers, still not quite sure she can believe her senses.

"What?" asks Mamta, the only other person to hear her.

"It's been signed by him, hasn't it?" she asks, looking at me.

I nod. "They all have."

As Mamta snatches the tee-shirt from her, Rosie's mouth drops open, then she pulls out the next one.

"It has!" announces Mamta. "It's been signed by Rick."

"Let me see," say Cheyenne and Dawn together as they get up from the settee.

"They're not all signed by Rick," I say, apparently to myself as no one appears to be listening. "Some are signed by the others and there's one or two signed by all of them."

Apart from Rosie and Mamta, who remain seated and kneeling respectively, all the other girls are on their feet, inspecting the tee-shirts, holding them up against their chests, squealing and squawking to one another.

"Oh, look," says Courtney with breathy excitement, "this one says: 'Great big kisses from Gorgeous Geoff.'"

"And this one's signed by all of them!" shrieks Saoirse.

I look at Rosie again. She's sitting still, gazing in astonishment at one of the tee-shirts spread out on her lap. Without warning she crosses her arms and grasps the bottom of the blouse Frannie gave her earlier in the day then pulls it over her head. Underneath, she's wearing a grey Calvin Klein cotton bralet.

Embarrassed – a good sign, surely? – I look away.

Then I hear the springs of the armchair creak and Rosie is standing in front of me, modelling a tee-shirt, this one with a full-colour photograph of Luke's head. Her face is flushed and excited as she twirls around. I glance at the other girls' faces and see delight and – can I admit I find this gratifying? – a little jealousy.

"Mum! Dad!" squeals Rosie. "Look at this!"

I glance at my parents. They're nodding and smiling, obviously pleased. Rosie looks down at me, still kneeling on the floor. I can't recall the last time she looked at me with such undiluted joy in her eyes. Probably not since she was about three years old.

"These are absolutely brilliant, Atticus! Thank you so, so much!"

I shrug in a *Gee, it was nothing* kind of way, but inside I'm feeling as excited as she is, if not more so.

"And they're all for me?" she asks.

"Of course. Who else?"

Her gaze locks onto mine and, for a moment, I'm not sure what she's going to do. I don't think she knows, either. It crosses my mind that she's going to bend down and kiss me. Maybe it crosses hers, too. I don't know. What I *do* know is that the foundation stone of a bridge between us has been laid. At least I hope so.

"There's more," I say, while we're still looking at each other, "but you'd better sit down again."

I pass her the remaining parcels then get to my feet. I stand and watch as she opens the package containing the photographs, smiling contentedly as she registers the fact that they too are signed. Once again the other girl's flock around. I take my cue and move away, over toward Frannie.

"Where did you get all that stuff?" she asks.

I smile enigmatically.

"Well, you've certainly made her day, that's for sure."

"That was the general idea."

I glance back at Mum and Dad to see Mum scowling in our direction. Keeping my eye on Rosie and her friends as their excitement verges on near hysteria, I cross the room to stand next to Mum.

"Oh, wow!" squawks Mei-Ling, holding up a gigantic poster so that the others can inspect it. "Look at this! They've *all* signed it!"

"Why does she have to do that?" hisses Mum.

"What? Who?" I ask.

"Who do you think? Frannie, of course. She was smoking outside earlier. And I can still smell it, even in here, in my house. I don't understand why she has to do it."

384

"Probably," I say, "though I might be wrong, that's part of the reason *why* she does it."

"What? Just to wind me up? That's ridiculous. Pathetic."

"Mum," I say, putting my arm around her. "Don't fret about that now. Look at Rosie."

"How can I-"

"Come on, Elaine," says Dad, gently touching her arm. "Now's not the time. The boy's right. Look at Rosie. I can't remember when I last saw her so happy."

I watch Mum as she tears her gaze away from her sister and looks at mine. Gradually, annoyance gives way to pleasure. Feeling pretty damned satisfied with myself, I too turn to watch Rosie. She has returned to the armchair, still wearing the Luke-head tee-shirt, and is now scrutinising a handful of glossy black and white photographs. Dawn is perched on one of the arms of the chair, and Saoirse on the other, both smiling and laughing with Rosie as all three take turns pointing out various members of the hunky foursome we know as 4Tune8.

Everybody in the room seems to be happy – even Bennie, who I would have expected by now to have sloped off to his room, having become bored with the proceedings after three nanoseconds. Instead, he's leaning forwards over the back of the settee, as fascinated by the histrionic activity of the seven girls as he might be by a new PlayStation game.

"What's all the racket?"

I turn to see Zach standing in the doorway, staring in disbelief at the gaggle of larvae.

"Blame Atticus," says Dad, grinning.

"Eh?"

While Dad gives Zach a brief résumé of the proceedings so far, I pull out my phone. Quarter past seven. On cue, the door-bell rings.

"I'll get that," I murmur, making my way swiftly out into the hall. I open the door.

"Hi," says Apollonia. "Everything going according to plan?"

"Couldn't have worked out better," I answer, looking over her shoulder.

"Right, so what do you want me to do now?"

"Come into the lounge with me and wait by the door, then give me a few minutes because I want to say a few words beforehand."

"A speech, eh?"

"Yeah, something like that."

Back in the lounge, Rosie and her friends are still sorting through the 4Tune8 paraphernalia like demented shoppers at a Boxing Day sale. As I make my way towards Rosie I catch Frannie's eye again and raise my eyebrows, signalling that there's more to come. I position myself next to Rosie's armchair and cough loudly. Rosie's the only one that takes any notice of me. She looks up, face shining, smiling. I have to agree with Dad, here – it is a long time since she's looked quite so happy. Smiling myself, I reach down and gently grasp her wrist.

"Come on," I urge, tugging her arm. "Stand up."

She frowns, though still clearly happy, then complies. I feel the urge to put my arm around her shoulders but that seems, for now, like a step too far. Embarrassment. Self-consciousness. Whatever. Instead, I just stand next to her.

"There's something else," I say quietly then turn to address her friends. "Ladies!" I say loudly. "If I could just have your attention for a few moments."

Dawn, Saoirse and Cheyenne look at me. Mamta and Courtney remain engrossed by a signed CD and Mei-Ling is still carefully inspecting the poster she was holding up a few minutes ago.

I glance at Apollonia, waiting by the door. She smiles at me then, twitches her head and jerks her right arm up. For a second I think she's about to go into a full-blown grand mal convulsion, but then I realise she's actually telling me to put my arm around Rosie's shoulders. The woman is clearly psychic.

I quickly shake my head in response. *No way, lady.*

Apollonia frowns and looks disappointed. Zach clocks that something's going on and glances at Apollonia, who gives him one of her most captivating smiles. He turns back to look at me in amazement, as if to say: *What's she doing here?* All of this takes about five seconds. The larvae are still, in the main, ignoring me.

I grin at Zach. He realises that Apollonia's presence is somehow connected to me. And that, as you might imagine, makes me feel deliriously happy.

I clear my throat, pointedly staring at Mamta and Courtney until they look up. Once I've also got Mei-Ling's attention, I scan the room to make certain that everyone is looking at me.

"I just wanted to say a couple of words," I say, stiffly, "on this, Rosie's sixteenth birthday."

I'm feeling very awkward. Why am I talking like this? I glance at Apollonia, who's still encouraging me, with movements of her right arm, to put my arm around

Rosie's shoulders. I just can't do that. I turn and face Rosie directly.

"Um, look, I know I've probably not been a very good brother to you..."

Oh Lord, that's torn it. There's no turning back now.

"...and I know I've done some, you know, bad stuff in the past and... well, I know, I've not been very *nice*, but... ah... I just wanted you to know that I think you're a very special... um, person... I mean, sister."

I'm staring into her eyes so hard that I'm unaware of her expression and so I can't be sure what sort of an impression my clumsy words are making upon her.

"What I'm trying to say is that I think you're a very special young woman, and I also wanted you to know just how... er, proud I am of you."

I look away, down at the box set, discarded like an old pizza box at the foot of the armchair, then up at a framed photograph hanging on the wall of Zach, Rosie and I, taken before Bennie was born. The room is as quiet as a church. Everyone seems to be holding their breath. The only sound is that of the rivers of sweat running down my back.

"Look, I'm sorry – I'm not putting this very well," I mutter, still staring at the photograph.

"Sure you are," whispers Rosie.

I turn to find her smiling at me. A smile of happiness and gratitude. An encouraging smile. A smile full of all sorts of wonderful things I couldn't hope to describe. A smile into which I am, perhaps, reading rather too much. But, hey, you're not going to begrudge me that, are you?

"What I'm trying to say here is that I'm... well, just so very proud that you're my sister, and that I'm your brother."

Despite Rosie's beatific smile, my heart is starting to sink. What the hell is wrong with me? Why on earth am I so spectacularly incapable of articulating my feelings? I'm nearly overcome by the desire to bolt. But I stumble on.

"Look, I know I'm not making much sense, here..." I mumble helplessly.

Rosie's smile broadens, which I wouldn't have thought possible. Tiny tears are welling in the corners of her eyes. Good grief, the last thing I wanted to do was make her cry. Fate slaps me hard in the back, forcing me to press on.

"Anyway, I know how much you *love* 4Tune8, and I really hope you liked the presents I got for you, but there're just a couple more things."

I reach into the front pocket of my trousers and pull out a handful of tickets which I hold out for Rosie. Curious, she takes them from me then inspects them.

"Oh my God!" she squeals

"What?" hisses Dawn, sitting on the arm of the chair.

Mouth agape, Rosie holds the tickets up so that Dawn can see them. "For the concert tomorrow night!"

"Ten seats," I say. "Front row."

Rosie turns to face me again. "Atticus," she says, tears threatening at any moment to trip over her lower eyelids and spill down her cheeks. "Thanks. I really don't know what to say."

"You've just said it," I point out, chuckling. "You don't have to say anything else."

389

She looks at me for a second or two then lurches forwards, throws her arms around me and kisses me on the cheek. She pulls away, slightly breathless, and meets my gaze again. I can't quite decipher her expression but I'm going to take it as absolution. The lipstick at the corner of her mouth is now slightly smudged.

"One more thing," I say.

Rosie wipes her eyes with the backs of her hands then frowns, as though there couldn't be anything that would possibly top the concert tickets. That makes me smile.

"You've got the 4Tune8 posters, the 4Tune8 photographs, the 4Tune8 CDs, a rare *Japanese* 4Tune8 vinyl box set, and even ten tickets for a 4Tune8 concert, which leaves only one thing."

I nod at Apollonia then return my attention to Rosie because I want – more than anything else in the world at this moment in time – to see her reaction to what's going to happen next.

Rosie meets my gaze for a second or two and then looks toward the door. The muscles supporting her jaw relax and her mouth falls open. Then her eyes open a little wider and she draws a quick little breath. Her head snaps around to look at me again. I grin and nod then turn to watch Luke, Rick, Geoff and Alan walking towards us.

"Hey, Atticus," says Rick.

"Rick," I say, double cool with ice.

"And this must be Rosie," says Luke, smiling at her, eyes glinting. "Atticus, why did you not say that your sister was such a hottie?"

He moves right up close to her then reaches down and picks up her hand, which he lifts up to his lips. "*Enchanté*," he murmurs, his accent comically exaggerated.

Comedy, however, is the last thing on my sister's mind. To be honest, I'm not sure anything's on her mind, as she looks completely shell-shocked. For an instant, I worry that she might have stroked out, even though we don't have a particularly strong family history of cerebrovascular disease. Then, she giggles – a tinkling, coquettish, not unappealing sound – and reluctantly withdraws her hand from Luke's grasp. I feel a warm hand on my arm and turn to find Apollonia standing next to me.

"Better give them some room," she whispers, pulling me gently away from Rosie.

"Eh?"

"A little surprise. Just something I helped them work out on the way over here."

I follow Apollonia over to where Frannie is sitting.

Leading her gently by the arm, Luke helps Rosie to sit down in the armchair then joins the other members of the group, standing in a line facing her. Impulses cascade in my planet-sized brain and I realise that they're going to sing to her.

Geoff hums a note. I don't have perfect pitch, unlike Suzz, so I couldn't tell you which one. Like a barber-shop quartet, Rick, Alan and Luke hum the other notes in the chord. Then they start singing *Sixteen Candles*, an old doo-wop song from the late fifties, originally by a group called The Crests.

How do I know this? Long story. Suffice to say I was obsessed (which will come as no surprise) for weeks with an old doo-wop vinyl LP I found in a box in the cellar last year. Must have listened to that album fifty times. I'd like to know how it is that 4Tune8 know it, but, at the moment, that's immaterial.

391

For legal reasons, I'm pretty sure I can't reproduce the lyrics here. You'll just have to believe me when I tell you it's a rather pleasing, close harmony confection, with the lyrics expressing sentiments apposite to a girl's sixteenth birthday. Who'd have guessed?

What's more, I have to admit to being more than a little impressed by 4Tune8's interpretation. Being brutally frank, I didn't actually think they *could* sing. However, Alan, singing the baritone part, appears to be handling the *shoo-doop-a-doos* rather well, and Luke's lead vocal seems a lot stronger than it does on their hits. Rick and Geoff cope with the harmony admirably well. All in all, as I said, very impressive. Unless it's just the very favourable acoustics in our lounge.

I scan the room, checking the various reactions. Rosie, as you might expect, is in seventh heaven. Her face, initially beetroot red, now looks fetchingly flushed. The other girls are similarly entranced. In fact, everyone is spellbound by the performance, including myself, though I'm sentient enough to feel a tingle of pleasure as Apollonia loops her arm in mine.

4Tune8 finish the song then, one by one, lean down and kiss Rosie on the cheek, wishing her a happy birthday.

"Anyone want more autographs," asks Luke, grinning at the girls, "or have you got enough already?"

As a bees and honey pot situation rapidly develops, I turn to Apollonia and smile. "I think Rosie enjoyed that."

"I think you're right."

"Yeah, it all worked out pretty well."

Apollonia fixes me with her gaze. "Rosie's very lucky to have a brother like you."

Aw, shucks.

"Yeah, well... I... er... if you say so."

She laughs then releases my arm. "I think your brother wants a word."

I turn to see Zach glaring at me. He jerks his arm, beckoning me over to him. I watch Apollonia join the throng then walk over to him.

"Enjoy that?" I ask, my eyebrows raised impudently.

"Did you organise all this?" he asks, more agitated than I've seen him in a long time.

"Yeah."

"How? Do you know them, or what? And what are they doing here? And what's with you and Apollonia Wallace? What's she doing here? And how did-"

"Zach, Zach, Zach," I say. "Calm down. Never mind all those questions. Chill out. Go with the flow."

His mouth snaps open then slowly closes again. Gradually, a smile of grudging acknowledgement creeps onto his face. "I don't know *how* you did it but... well, I'm impressed. Bloody impressed."

After Dad and Frannie have congratulated me, Mum gives me one of her patented *You may not be the perfect son but you've done all right today* looks, hugs me and plants a big, wet, sticky kiss on my cheek, then goes off to organise some *refreshments*. I turn to watch all the fuss at the other side of the room. Geoff is sitting on the armchair, signing something for Mei-Ling. Inadvertently, he kicks the box set then reaches down and picks it up. He scrutinises it for a few seconds then hails Rick, who takes it from him, nodding his head admiringly. I'm gratified that at least someone realises it's value. I spot Rosie, facing me, listening intently as Alan regales her and Dawn with some fascinating anecdote. She looks up and, seeing me watching her, smiles. As a warm sensation floods my body, I realise

I've wet myself. Well, no I haven't, but I do feel warm and happy and... oh, I don't know... *nice*, I guess.

[32] Armageddon

It's almost nine o'clock and I'm back in my bedroom, trying
to decide what to wear for Red's party. I step into a pair of
jeans Mum bought me a few months ago. I can still
remember her horrified expression when she discovered
me, a couple of hours after she'd given them to me,
laboriously picking holes in the legs. 'It's what everybody
does', I told her, then immediately felt stupid for giving her
an excuse to launch into her *If everybody jumped off a
cliff...* mode.

    I open the wardrobe and run my finger across the
hanging shirts. I remain elated. It really couldn't have gone
any better if I'd planned it – which is a pretty idiotic thing
to say, seeing as I *did* plan it. You know what I mean. But
it does remind me of yet another one of my myriad faults:
emotional inarticulacy. Bzzzt! Irony alert! Oh, sure, I can
be quick on the draw with the odd quip, the cutting remark,
and so on, but when it's important, when I *really* want to
say something significant, I get completely tongue-tied.
Case in point: my ludicrous attempt to tell Rosie how I feel
about her. Even though I *knew* I was coming across like a
gibbering madman, I couldn't do anything about it. I think
the basic problem is that I can't express something fluidly
and clearly to someone else if I'm incapable of doing so to
myself. Hey, it looks like I'm not so special, after all –
Atticus William Blake Childress: Crazy, Mixed-up Kid.

    I've narrowed it down to either a baggy red and
white striped shirt with no collar or a black tee-shirt with
the message *Nuke the Whales* emblazoned across the front,
a present from Zach last Christmas. Zach's sense of
humour is rather twisted, to say the least, mutated by too

many hours spent slumped in the back of Transit vans. I suspect more people would be offended by the shirt than would find it amusing. And I'm aiming to please tonight, not provoke. The stripy shirt it is.

4Tune8 left soon after eight o'clock.

I'm only telling you in case you were thinking they were still downstairs, watching *Championship Ice Rounders* on *Sky Sport 13* with my father. And they're not coming to Red's party either. I mean, come on, this is real life, not some wish-fulfilment, half-assed piece of meta-fiction. Why on earth would 4Tune8 want to come to Red's pathetic party? Exactly – they wouldn't, and they're not. Back in your box.

But they didn't leave without bidding me farewell. As we shook hands, I told Rick that I didn't think I'd be at their concert tomorrow night. I said I was sorry, and all that, but that I didn't want to risk eardrum perforation, caused by ten thousand screaming larvae, or be trampled underfoot as they mounted repeated attacks on the stage. To be killed by hordes of rampaging teenaged girls is not the end I had envisaged for myself, even though it might be called a *Fortunette* death.

Just before he climbed into their monstrous black limousine, Luke pulled an envelope from his pocket and pressed it into my hand. 'A special present for Rosie,' he said, looking over my shoulder and winking at her as she stood on the front door step. 'Give it to her tomorrow.' I opened it a few minutes later, when no one was watching, and discovered ten after-show passes.

I walk across to the mirror and button up my shirt. The music is on random and *Without You I'm Nothing* by Placebo is playing. 'Every time you vent your spleen, I seem to lose the power of speech. You're slipping slowly from my reach.' I feel you, Brian, I really do.

I can feel my mood dipping. Not sad/unhappy, just coming down after all the earlier excitement. Entirely understandable, surely. I guess I'm just metabolising endorphins, or something. I grab a comb from the top of my chest of drawers and run it through my hair. Then I sit down on the bed and pull on a pair of basketball boots. As I lace them up, I realise I'm coming down a bit more than I'd like. For reasons unknown, I'm beginning to feel distinctly unsettled. Cyclothymia: it's not just for Christmas.

Maybe it's the music. I flip through the songs on my phone, looking for something to lift me up. Ah, some old school 80s rock, that'll do! David Lee Roth's *Skyscraper.* That should do the trick. DLR's *party hardy* offerings usually make me feel brighter. On this occasion, though, even Steve Vai's guitar histrionics aren't making me smile.

Suddenly, I realise that not only can I not be bothered to go to Red's party, it's actually the last place on earth I want to be. The realisation that I don't want to go settles on my shoulders like some mythical winged beast, all fanged mouth and taloned feet, it's beady eyes darting from side to side, it's massive weight crushing me. Never mind the black dog of depression, try having a 100kg cockatrice sitting on your back.

Why, oh why, do I have to feel like this? Tonight, of all times? Just when I was feeling happy. I curse my hormones. I scream oaths at my psyche. I hurl stones at my melancholic essence and daub rude slogans on the door of my Weltschmerz. And do you know what really pisses me off the most? I'll tell you. I knew – just *knew* – that I should have ended this bloody story at the end of the last chapter. I was feeling pretty good... no, I was feeling on top of the bloody world. I'd given my sister the best birthday present she'll probably ever get and I was feeling good about myself and about my nearest and dearest.

But no, I *had* to carry on, didn't I? I wanted to cap things off with a few pages of the witty repartee I was anticipating would occur at Red's party. I wanted to let you know how things were going with the two loving couples. Unfortunately, that's exactly what's now pushed me over the edge – the prospect of seeing Red and Bass with their respective *girlfriends* (God, right now, I hate that word) – and I'm now free-falling in the abyss of despair. Abandon hope all ye who drop down it.

The thing is, I thought I'd be able to handle it, but I know that now to be a simple delusion. I thought I'd be able to behave graciously, to smile and nod politely as Red and Chelsea engage me in conversation, their arms wrapped around each other's waists, smiling demurely at each other in that irritating fashion found only in those couples still in the throes of infatuation. I thought I'd be able to sit there calmly, suavely inspecting the pile of CDs adjacent to Red's father's high-end hi-fi, while, not two metres away, Bass and Suzz are writhing around on the settee, all wet sucking sounds and groping fingers.

Until now, whenever I've attended a party, it's always been as part of a trio. Me, Bass and Red. The Three Musketeers. Though some might suggest we were more like The Three Little Pigs. Haters gonna hate. With ne'er a girlfriend to cloud our saintly minds, we were always free to ridicule the happy loving couples. We could laugh at the lads trying to get their tongues down the girls' throats, or scoff at their feeble attempts to slip their hands up their consorts' shirts.

But the tables have turned now, haven't they? I don't want to sneer, I want to participate.

I tell myself to get my finger out, to pull up my socks, to shake myself out of this mood, to strap on... oh, I don't know, some sort of strappy-on thing.

"Get a grip, Atticus," I mutter to myself, and I don't often mutter to myself. Not out loud. My internal monologue is usually loud enough, thanks very much.

But it's no good – I can't. I'm a lily-livered Milquetoast, a cream puff, a spineless knucklehead. I lay back on my bed, staring at the ceiling, ignoring David Lee Roth telling me it's *just like paradise*. Yeah, right, pal. Maybe in Malibu in 1988.

My phone buzzes but I can't be arsed to even look at it to see who's calling. They can leave a message. Maybe it's Red, ringing to tell me that the party's off, seeing as Chelsea's told him she's willing to consummate their relationship and he needn't bother with the party. Or perhaps it's Bass, wanting to let me know that his parents have asked him if he and his friends want to go to their cottage in Wales next weekend. He'll tell me that Suzz, Red and Chelsea have agreed to go and he'll ask me if I want to join them. And I'll be able to tell from his tone that none of them really wants me to be there. What was 3 is now 4+1.

Screw it. I'm going to go to this damned party. And I'm not going alone either. A very good friend of mine will be more than happy to be my guest for the evening. My trusty friend, Miss AK-47, and I will have such a good time, filling all those lovebirds with lead, and watching their fat heads exploding in showers of bone and gristle.

There's a knock at the door. "Atticus?"

It's Rosie, probably come to tell me she still thinks I'm a loser. 'It was all a big joke, Atticus. I *knew* what you were going to give me. We all did. And I knew 4Tune8 were coming, because Apollonia told me. Didn't you know we were good friends? Oh yes, she told me what an immature cockroach she thinks you are, so we formulated this brilliant plan. We decided to play along with your little game, but once you'd gone upstairs we all laughed ourselves senseless. And that so-called speech you gave? What a hoot! I nearly pissed myself. Is English your second language or are you just incapable of stringing two words together? Anyway, I'm just off to Red's party now, me and all my *larval* friends, and I can't tell you how much I'm going to enjoy telling all *your* friends what a smelly turd you are, as if they didn't know already. Oh, and by the way, that was Red trying to get through to you. He's messaged me and asked me to tell you not to bother coming to the party, because you don't really fit in with that crowd anymore, seeing as you haven't got a girlfriend. The last thing they want is Johnny the Gooseberry hanging around, dragging everybody else down.'

"What?" I grunt.

"Can I come in?"

I want to tell her to go away. If there was any justice in this world, my bed would swallow me up like something out of a tacky horror movie. Realising this is not very likely, I reluctantly get to my feet, shuffle across to the door like a medicated mental patient, then open it a few inches.

The first thing I notice is that Rosie's head is a good few inches higher than where it should be. Immediately I look down at her feet to see a pair of ankle boots almost identical to the ones Suzz was wearing last night. My sister in five-inch heels – I can almost hear the opening seconds of *The Twilight Zone* theme playing. *Deedle-eedle, eedle-*

eedle. She's wearing denim leggings and the signed Luke-head tee-shirt. So far, so fair enough. When I look up and see what she's done to her face, I scowl. What the hell?

Rosie's face is almost unrecognisable beneath a thick layer of foundation. Her lips are so dark that she looks as though she's just guzzled her way through two kilogrammes of blackberries and – trapped between black mascara, black eye-liner and (almost) black eye-shadow – the whites of her eyes look like... well, two white things surrounded by a lot of black stuff. If it wasn't for the tee-shirt, I would have serious reservations about swearing in a court of law that this was, in fact, my sister. When I first opened the door she was smiling, but now her lips are pursed and her brow is creased.

"You all right?" she asks.

Sure, the birds are singing, God's in his heaven and all's right with the world. The fact that I'm a sad, introspective, unattached tea-towel has got nothing to do with it.

"Never better."

She stares at me, her eyes narrowing, or at least I think they are. It's tough to tell with the garish slap.

"Dominic's just messaged me. He says you're not replying to him. He wants to know if you're still coming to the party."

"Why wouldn't I be?" I ask, irritably. My nose twitches. I smell cigarette smoke. It's my turn to narrow my eyes. "You've not been smoking, have you?"

Rosie scowls. "Don't be an arse, Atticus. It's Frannie. She's in my room, with me and Dawn."

"I thought she went back to her flat."

"She stayed to help Dawn and I get ready for the party."

401

Which presumably explains the greasepaint. I want to ask why the pair of them need help preparing for a stupid party.

"Mum will go berserk when she finds out Frannie's been smoking in your bedroom."

"She's been leaning out the window."

"Right, that clearly makes *all* the difference," I point out then glance down again at Rosie's boots. "Where did they come from?"

I didn't intend to ask that. I mean, I was *thinking* it but I didn't plan to actually ask her. The question fazes Rosie not one iota.

"Suzz let me borrow them," she says, smiling in a manner I find rather disquieting.

I wait a few seconds to see if she wishes to elaborate, but she seems to be waiting for me to request elaboration. As you know, though, I'm not feeling in tip-top form and the last thing I want is to be reminded about Suzz.

As Rosie realises our conversation has drawn to a conclusion, she turns and starts walking back to her room. Scrutinising Suzz's boots, I notice – with no small amount of pride, though it has diddly-squat to do with me – that Rosie is a natural. Not a trace of wobble. Good on you, lass. Just as I'm about to close my door, Rosie stops.

"Oh, I almost forgot to tell you," she says without turning to face me, as if she knew that I'd been watching her. When she does turn, the stiletto heel of the right boot catches on the carpet and she almost loses her balance. Giggling, she looks down at the boots as though she'd forgotten she was wearing them.

"Oops," she says coyly, grinning.

Almost a natural.

"Dad said he'd drive us."

Us? What does that mean? Even if I was going to the party, which I'm not, does she think I'd want to be seen arriving with my sister and one of her larval friends? She must mean Dad's going to drive her and Dawn over there, though I suppose I'd better clarify the situation.

"Drive *who*?"

Frowning, she runs her hand back through her hair. I notice her cerise fingernails.

"You, me and Dawn, of course. Who did you think? So, be ready in about ten minutes."

Good Lord! She's taken leave of her senses. A multitude of sarcastic comments rush like lemmings to the tip of my tongue. But hang on, it's her birthday, give her some slack. I remind myself I'm trying to be nice and I try to recall how good I felt earlier, only a couple of millennia ago.

"It's all right, I'm not going until later on. I'll walk. You and Dawn go with Dad."

As I close my bedroom door I catch a brief glimpse of what appears to be disappointment on her face. With all that make-up, though, who knows?

Skyscraper is still playing, but I'm now finding David Lee Roth's bonhomie grating. I turn down the volume. My head is spinning again. Questions, riddles, conundrums.

Why would Rosie want me in the same car with her and Dawn? A big part of me doesn't want to go to the party, but a small part still does. If I don't go, I'll have a barrage of questions to face from Bass and Red, and my phone will be buzzing all night. I could turn it off, I suppose. Ha! Who am I kidding? Turn off my phone? LOL. JK. YOLO.

403

On balance, then, I'll have to go, but that doesn't mean I have to stay long. Put in an appearance, bugger off. But if I'm going, why would I want to go in the same car with my sister and her pal? It'll be embarrassing on the way, and even more embarrassing if someone sees me getting out at Red's house. But I got the distinct impression that Rosie *wanted* me to go with her and Dawn. What the hell is that all about? Does it matter? It's still her birthday. I've done some good work today. *Good job, Atticus!* Why ruin everything?

That's it then. I'm going, *with* Rosie and Dawn. Decision made.

What I need now is something to properly buck me up. Amphetamines are obviously out of the question. I used the last of my stash the other day, and my dealer's on holiday until next week. Music has rarely let me down in the past. I just need the right song. A nice uplifting anthem of some sort. I skim through the songs on my phone but nothing's leaping out at me.

On the floor at the side of the dresser is a stack of old vinyl LPs. I found them in a box in the cellar. The same box in which I found that album with *Sixteen Candles* by The Crests on it. The LPs belonged – well, still belong, technically – to my father. Various progressive rock albums from the 70s. I've listened to most of them, on a turntable I bought off eBay for £30 and hooked up to my sound system. Most of the albums are shite, to be honest, and some of them are the worst sort of shite imaginable, but some of them aren't *terrible*.

Suddenly, I know exactly what I want to listen to. I flick through the LPs until I find *World Record* by Van Der Graaf Generator, recorded in 1976. Don't laugh. The lyrics are mostly pseudo-intellectual claptrap and the music is angular art rock with parping sax. But I really like one song: *A Place to Survive*. I withdraw the disc, place it on the turntable and get everything set up. Side one, track two. It's just the ten minutes long. Short and to the point, it's not. I line it up and lower the stylus.

I stand in the middle of my room, eyes closed, and concentrate on the lyrics. I wish I could reproduce them but those damned copyright laws rear their ugly mugs again. Basically, the singer, Peter Hammill, is telling the listener to quit bitching and get on with it. Forget your troubles – they're only obstacles to be surmounted – and press on with your life. Don't look back and don't look for others to show you the way. However much pain and suffering one must endure, it'll be worth it in the end.

I certainly bloody hope so.

As I listen to Hammill belting out the last chorus, I lace up my boots again. I determine to follow the song's advice, for tonight at least. I will stand as straight as possible, look into the future, and get on with my life, even if it means having to watch Red suck Chelsea's face off. I lift the stylus clear of the disc and switch everything off then walk out into the corridor. To the sound of much giggling coming from Rosie's room, I walk downstairs to await my travelling companions.

Dad's in the lounge, lolling on the settee, watching some dreadful war film. I slump down into an armchair and fold my arms.

"Ready?" asks Dad.

Champing at the bit.

I sigh. "Waiting for Rosie and Dawn."

Five minutes pass, then another five. I'm starting to get involved in the film, which irritates me.

"Where are they?" I mutter as I get to my feet.

Dad looks across at me. "Where are you going?"

"To see what the heck they're playing at."

"Sit down."

I sit down.

"It's no use trying to hurry a woman when she's getting ready to go out," he says to the television. "You'll just waste time arguing and she'll still take as long as she wants."

We watch a group of American soldiers attack a group of German soldiers.

"So, what kind of party is this going to be?"

"I don't know. Just a party."

"How many are going to be there?"

"No idea."

"Do the Killingtons know about it?"

"I suppose. Look, I don't know, do I?"

"Just asking."

This is typical of my conversations with Dad. I always get the impression that I'm expected to work out what it is he's driving at and I always end up divulging more information than I'd planned. Like now, for instance. He's obviously concerned that his sixteen-year-old daughter is going to a party at one of my friends' house, but he won't come out and say so directly. He's not going to ask: 'Will Rosie be safe tonight? She's not going to be molested, is she?' Although this is exactly what he wants to know, or so I assume.

"There's no need to worry."

"I'm not worried."

"No, but all the same, you can rest assured that nothing's going to happen to Rosie."

"I should hope not."

"Look, I'm going to be there, aren't I?"

"She wouldn't be going otherwise."

I frown then smile as I realise that he's manipulated me into agreeing to *look after* Rosie. I don't know why he couldn't have just asked me in the first place. I decide to let him know I'm on to his little game. And another penny drops. I now see why Rosie was so keen to make sure I was going to be at the party. Without me there, she wouldn't be allowed to go. Luther has nothing on me.

"*I'll* look after her."

"I'm sure she'll appreciate that," he says, without batting an eyelid, and I am reminded that it's from him that Rosie gets her poise.

Eventually, half an hour after she told me to be ready in ten minutes, Rosie appears in the doorway. To say that she's undergone a transformation would be... well, it would be inaccurate, because she hasn't. Ha-ha-ha. Sorry, I'm just being silly. Thankfully, however, it would appear that she's toned down her make-up, slightly. The skim of foundation has disappeared and her eyes no longer look like white things surrounded by black stuff. I would imagine that after thanking Frannie for her *help*, she decided to apply her make-up unaided. She's still wearing Suzz's amazing boots, leggings and the Luke-head tee-shirt.

"We're ready, Dad."

I lean forward slightly, in a covert attempt to see what Dawn's wearing, not that I'm interested, of course. Not really. But she's standing behind Rosie, and I can see only her face.

Dad looks at me as he gets to his feet. "Coming?"

"I thought you said you weren't going until later on," says Rosie.

"Changed my mind. Is that a problem?"

"Not for me," she says over her shoulder as we all head for the front door.

With Dad and Rosie between us, I still can't see what Dawn's wearing.

I stop in the hall to check myself in the mirror. When I get out to the car, Rosie and Dawn are already in the back seat. I try to peer through the windows at Dawn as I walk around to the passenger door but it's too dark to see anything. This is becoming a bit ridiculous.

Rosie and Dawn spend the few minutes it takes us to drive to Red's house whispering to one another. I consider twisting around to look at Dawn but I'm unable to concoct a believable excuse for so doing and, anyway, I can't really understand why I'm so interested. Dad pulls up in the street, a few metres from Red's house – he knows better than to drop us off at the door.

"What time shall I pick you up?"

"It's all right," I say, "we'll-"

"About half past twelve?" suggests Rosie.

I scramble out of the car and quickly walk around to Dad's side so I can finally see what Dawn's wearing. Unfortunately – or fortunately, I can't decide which – it's nothing special. She's wearing a baggy black tee-shirt and a long black skirt which hangs almost to the pavement, so I can't even comment on her choice of footwear. She looks at me as she climbs out of the car and then smiles, which is bloody strange, bearing in mind the fact that she's done nothing but scowl malignantly every time she's set eyes on me in the last week. Her hair has been pulled back from her face and gathered into a pony-tail at the nape of her neck.

"'Bye, Dad," says Rosie, waving at him. "See you later."

The three of us walk up the drive. I can hear the steady thumping of loud music and the clamour of excited voices. It would appear that there are far more people at the party than I had expected. Even more unexpected is Rosie's arm looping through mine as we walk, and yet more unexpected than that is my acceptance of the situation.

If you'd told me a week ago that I'd be walking up the drive to Red's house, arm in arm with my sister, I'd have advised you to reduce your consumption of illegal substances. Now, however, it somehow feels... right – *nice*, even. Well, to be honest, it feels kind of surreal, but in a nice way.

Sandun Wiratunga opens the door, a can of strong lager gripped in his hand.

"Hey, Johnny! How's it hang-"

He spots Rosie and Dawn.

"Well, hello, ladies," he says, then bows low, spilling lager in the process.

Behind him, the Killingtons' spacious entrance hall is packed with people, many of whom I've never seen before. Where on earth have they all come from? Knowing Red, he's probably been promoting the blowout all over social media for most of the day. I certainly wouldn't put it past him. Rosie releases my arm then, with Dawn sticking close beside her, moves off into the crowd. Sandun pulls me to one side.

"What's all this with your sister?"

I stare at him.

"Couldn't you find anyone else?"

"Kiss my arse."

He emits a low moan. "Touchy."

A few hundred more obscenities spring to mind but I opt not to waste my breath. Instead, and against my better judgement, I decide to seek out Bass and Red. As I may have already mentioned, Red's house is huge – twice as big as Apollonia's – and every one of the umpteen ground floor rooms is as stuffed as the entrance hall. The whole of the St. Mick's student body seems to be here – from the fifth form up – and everyone seems to have a drink in their hand. I haven't got the foggiest how Red's managed to obtain such large quantities of liquid refreshments. I add this question to the list I construct as I wander from room to room.

After almost quarter of an hour, I still haven't found either of my chums, although I have been accosted a dozen times and congratulated regarding Bläck Gläss's performance. Finally, in the kitchen, I discover Bass. He's holding court, surrounded by half a dozen male fifth-formers. While I wait for him to notice me, I listen to the sad little geeks quizzing him about the gig.

"But what did it really *feel* like?" asks one.

"It must had been frickin' gnarly," says another who's obviously been watching too many US teen dramas.

"Your version of *Smells Like Teen Spirit* was fuckin' A," says a tall, thin lad wearing an Arsenal shirt. He may or may not be Anouk Johannes's younger brother.

Bass's face lights up when he spies me. "Got to go, guys," he says then shuffles over to me.

"Hey, Bass, you're looking totally gnarly tonight," I say, grinning.

Smirking, he grabs my arm then pulls me toward the back door. Outside on the expansive terrace, we are alone apart from a couple sitting on a bench who appear far too busy sucking the life out of each other to take any notice of us. I follow Bass to the edge of the terrace. Before us stretches a few million acres of landscaped gardens, maintained at considerable expense by a team of gardeners – oddly enough – referred to by Red as *my mother's little helpers*. Bass turns and looks at me expectantly.

"Well?"

"Well, what?"

"Haven't you got something to tell to me?"

There are a couple of hundred things I want to tell him, but none I suspect he'd like to hear.

"Such as what?"

He sighs. "Such as an impromptu appearance by one of our country's finest vocal groups, for instance."

"Oh, that."

"So, how did you arrange it, then?"

"Even if I told you, you wouldn't believe me."

"Oh, come on! You can't leave it at that!"

"Later, maybe," I murmur, glancing over at Romeo and Juliet, sitting on the bench.

Bass frowns but realises the subject is closed. Watching Romeo's hand massaging the back of Juliet's neck, I am reminded of my earlier concerns about attending the party.

"So, where's the delectable Suzz, then?"

"Last time I saw her she was talking to some friends in the snooker room."

"Yeah?"

Bass nods. "Some girls from the upper sixth."

"Really?"

"Yeah."

For the first time in my life I am struggling to make conversation with one of my best friends. As you can imagine, this does not please me.

"So, how's it going then?"

"What?"

"You know, between you and Suzz."

"Oh, all right, I guess."

"Good."

"Yeah."

The back door opens and three fifth-formers rush out, laughing and shouting. I watch them run past us and into the garden.

"Lot of people here, aren't there?"

Oh Lord, now I'm reduced to making small talk. We'll be gibbering about the weather soon.

"Yeah, there are."

"Where have they all come from?"

"I'm not sure. We'll have to ask Red."

"I suppose. Any idea where he is?"

"I think he's upstairs."

"With Chelsea?"

"Um, yeah, possibly."

"Oh, I think he's found himself a cheerleader."

Bass chuckles.

Next time I see a 'Well, that got awkward' meme on Facebook, it's going to be a photo of me and Bass stood here. Can someone not just put us out of our misery? If only I *had* finished the story at the end of the previous chapter, I wouldn't have to cope with this intolerable situation. This story is turning into the literary equivalent of an ageing rock-star – still plodding on, even though there's no point. Except I don't even have any old hits to churn out. Hey, I promise I'll stop as soon as I can.

"Do you want a drink?" asks Bass.

"Why not?"

We make it about half way back to the house when Suzz emerges through the back door. She's wearing a simple black sleeveless dress and black Doc Marten's.

Despite her pallor, she looks radiant. Despite my glum mood, I feel glum.

"There you are," she says, waiting by the door until we reach her. "I want you to come and meet my friends."

The local chapter of the Addams family, I would imagine. Or the cast of *Twilight*. She slips her arm around Bass's waist then regards me. I suppose it could be my despondency interfering with my perceptive abilities but I'm sure she's looking at me with a combination of pity and vague distaste.

"Hey, Johnny."

"Suzz."

"Having a good time?"

"Anticipate the worst. Enjoy a pleasant surprise."

We look at each other during one of those pauses with which I'm becoming increasingly familiar, having just endured three or four with Bass.

"Right," she says with admirable resoluteness.

"Right," I echo.

"Come on, then," she says to Bass, pulling him through the door.

"See you, Johnny," says Bass.

I wait until the doors swings shut. "Not if you can help it."

This is going well. I can't face returning to the house just at the moment. I look over my shoulder at Romeo and Juliet and realise I can't stay out here either. A rocky thing and hard thing scenario, to be sure. I step to one side to allow a group of inebriated revellers egress then watch them cavorting on the terrace for a minute.

Go with the flow.

Shut the bloody hell up!

I'm fed up with this 'go with the bloody flow' crap. I've tried as hard as I can and look where it's got me!

I make a decision. I'm not going with any damned flow, or riding any bloody tide. I'm going to do what the hell I want, and right now I want a drink. I grab the handle and jerk open the door then stamp inside and head for the kitchen. Am I being stupid? Possibly. Misguided, even? Damn straight. Am I taking the first step on the slippery slope of... something? So what? I'm sick to the back teeth of pondering the uselessness of existence and fed up of mulling over all my puerile problems. In fact, I'm weary of thinking – full stop. I snatch a six-pack of something from the kitchen table then stride purposefully back out onto the terrace. Romeo and Juliet are still hard at it, which really ticks me off. I walk over and tap Romeo on the shoulder. He pulls his leech-like face off Juliet's and looks at me. I've never seen him before.

"Uh, Quentin, isn't it?"

"Justin, actually," he gasps.

"Yeah, right. Figures. There's someone at the door, asking for you."

He pulls a face, as though such a thing could only happen in a parallel universe, not in this one.

"Sounded important," I prompt.

He gets to his feet and the pair of them straighten their clothes. I watch them walk toward the house. The hem of Juliet's mini-skirt is tucked into her panties. Under normal circumstances I'd probably find this both comical and arousing. As it is, I couldn't care less. Frankly, I'm surprised she's still got her panties on. I slump down onto the bench – still warm – and open the first can. Some kind of trendy fruity cider. African cucumber and dragon fruit.

Ten minutes – and two cans – later, I'm feeling a little better. Well, that's not quite true. The thing is, I'm not really *feeling* much of anything, apart from comfortably warm, slightly numb and pleasantly dizzy. You'll have gathered that my tolerance for alcohol isn't exactly the stuff of legend. I decide not to open another can. As far as I'm concerned, the party is bad enough without me turning it into an event people will remember for the rest of their lives as the one at which Atticus 'Upchuck' Childress puked his guts out all over the kitchen floor.

Instead, I decide to just sit here, on this bench, until it's time to go home. I've not forgotten my promise to Dad. I won't leave Rosie here. I presume, at some point, she'll come and find me. If not, then I'll just sit here until morning, or until I have to go and take a leak, whichever occurs sooner. In years to come, when acquaintances think back to this night, they'll say: 'Hey, Atticus, wasn't that the night you sat on that bench for several hours, all on your own?'

Well, I might be sitting alone but there's certainly a lot of activity on the terrace – enough, I hope and pray, to keep my mind off my problems for a couple of hours. Already, about ten couples have come out of the house and wandered off into the gardens. I haven't seen any of them come back yet so either they're having some kind of bacchanalian orgy in the middle of a moonlit glade or there's an unmarked quicksand pit somewhere just out of sight. I suspect the former but hope for the latter.

Another group of fifth-formers bursts out of the back door, spraying each other with shaken cans of cola. Alice Burton and Amy Harrison, both in the upper sixth, saunter out. They frown at the fifth-formers then start walking across the terrace. Amy lights a cigarette. Neither of them notices me or if they do, they certainly don't let on. Alice is wearing an ankle-length dark skirt, split at the front almost up to her crotch. I watch her long, pale left leg intermittently flashing into view as she walks. Behind me, someone opens a window and the sound of 4Tune8's latest hit fills the evening air. I spend the next ten minutes surreptitiously watching Alice Burton – or rather, watching her legs. She's sitting, legs crossed, next to Amy on the low wall that surrounds the terrace. Her skirt keeps falling open, revealing a tantalising expanse of thigh, and she keeps folding it back over her knees again. Why bother, lass? I'm only looking.

Amy tosses her butt onto the terrace then stands and grinds it out. Alice pushes herself up off the wall. I get a final glimpse of pale thigh then they walk back to the house. After a few minutes I realise I'm going to have to empty my bladder. No doubt there are queues for the toilets inside so the garden looks like my best bet, despite the very real possibility that I may stumble across a couple coupling in the undergrowth. Well, it would serve them right, wouldn't it? 'Hey, Atticus, wasn't that the night you let rip all over Connor and Jasmine?'

As it turns out, I return to my bench, bladder empty, having discovered no one. Perhaps there really is a quicksand pit out there.

I listen to the monotonic paean to homo-eroticism blasting out through the window behind me and look down at the four remaining cans of kiwi and kahikatea cider. One more wouldn't hurt, would it? I dislodge a can from the six pack ring and I'm about to snap it open when Rosie wanders out through the back door. She flicks her hair away from her face and scans the terrace.

She spies me and starts walking in my direction. My gaze flips to Suzz's boots then back up. Once more, I have to grudgingly – and silently, of course – congratulate my sister on her mastery of the art of walking in heels. Very impressive. I'm not sure I'm quite so keen on the fact that they make her so tall, *almost* as tall as me, but, as I'm sitting down, I really don't care.

"What are you doing out here," she says, standing in front of me, "all on your own?"

Of the many reasons for my isolation, there isn't a single one that I'm prepared to explain to Rosie. Instead, I smirk. To my surprise and slight disappointment, in lieu of a scowl, which is her usual response to such a gesture, Rosie smiles at me as if I was a mental midget who doesn't know any better. In other words, it's patently obvious that she knows exactly why I'm out here on my own, although God alone knows how she came by such knowledge. Unless, hang on, I've got it! Somehow, I've had an electrode implanted in my brain and it's transmitting my thoughts to anyone who has the necessary app installed on their phone.

"It *is* awfully hot in the house," she says.

On the other hand, she may know nothing of the sort.

"Er... yeah. Whatever. If you say so."

I snap open the can in my hands then look up to see Rosie staring hard at me. She looks away, toward the open window, through which the sampled beats of yet another current hit are booming. The Auto-Tuned-to-hell-and-back wailing of some nubile popstress grates at the edges of my alcohol-fuddled brain.

Unless I'm very much mistaken, which, as always, is a real possibility, my sister has something on her mind. I take a sip of kumquat and mangosteen cider, scrutinise her pensive profile and assess my options. I could come right out with it and ask her if there's something she wishes to say to me. Alternatively, I could hold my tongue and wait for her to make the first move. Or I could walk off into the garden and try to find a writhing couple over which to urinate.

"They suit you," I say.

Splendid, Atticus, old boy! Straight to the point!

"Eh?"

"Suzz's boots. They suit you."

Rosie looks down at them, then up at me and, after she's decided I'm not being facetious, she smiles. It's obvious that she doesn't quite know what to say to that.

"They make you look taller."

"Yeah, I suppose so," she says, shifting her weight from one foot to the other. "I just wish Suzz had told me how much they bloody kill your feet."

"Not something about which I'd have any personal experience."

Rosie looks appraisingly at me once again then sits down on the bench. Together, we watch another couple head off into the garden. Rosie crosses her legs then slips a finger down inside her right boot to scratch the side of her ankle. I can smell her perfume – Kenzo Flower. It's Mum's favourite and I know that Rosie likes to wear it too. She turns to face me and opens her mouth to speak. I hold my breath then, as she closes her mouth and looks away, exhale loudly.

"Out with it."

"What?" she asks, looking at me as if there was nothing more on her mind than the price of nail varnish. Then she purses her lips. "Promise you won't go mad?"

"Depends."

She frowns.

"I mean, not if you're just going to tell me you're pregnant or something trivial like that. If you're going to confess to using the last of my zit-cream, on the other hand, then, well, I'd be forced to slap you around a bit, but nothing more than that. A few welts and bruises – nothing to write home about."

Rosie sneers at me then looks away, again, over her shoulder.

"OK, look, I promise I won't get irate. Spit it out."

"I wanted your advice, really," she says, apparently peering at the kitchen window.

I bite my lower lip. "Really?" I ask, once the urge to burst out laughing has passed.

"I've got this friend who really fancies this boy," she says then turns to gauge my reaction.

I dare not risk opening my mouth. I mean, I thought they only said things like that on television, not in real life.

"But he doesn't seem to be interested in her at all."

"I see," I murmur, proud of my self-control. I may as well go along with this. Whatever *this* is.

"What do you think she should do?"

I take another sip of nungu and miracle fruit cider.

"Hey, look, I'm very flattered, you know, that you've decided to confide in me but... ah... I've got to ask… Why?"

"What do you mean?"

"Why ask *me* of all people? Your friends must be able to give you better advice.... I mean, give your *friend* better advice. Or Frannie. She'd be a much better bet than me."

This seems to flummox her, but only for a few seconds.

"I wanted to get a male perspective."

Colour me impressed. And flattered. I suppose it had to happen sooner or later. Rosie, as I've been noticing, is definitely growing up, and it would be churlish of me not to accept that, as part of that process, she was eventually going to develop feelings for someone. Why I'm involved in any of this, though, is completely beyond me.

"Well, I'd need to know a few more details about the two of them. Your friend. The boy."

"Like what?"

"Oh, like how old they are, what they like to do, that sort of thing."

It's Rosie's turn to bite her lip.

"They're about the same age as us and... I'm not really sure what they like to do."

"Not very helpful."

"Well, she likes to do what most girls like to do, I suppose."

"Clothes, make-up and boys?"

She smiles. "Um, yeah, I guess."

"And what about him?"

She starts scratching her ankle again. I'm beginning to enjoy this.

"So it's a purely physical attraction then? I mean, if she doesn't know anything about his habits, interests and so on."

"No," she says quickly, "it's not like that."

"I see."

"She knows quite a lot about him, really."

"But *you* don't?"

"Er... no..." she murmurs, scratching her ankle so vigorously I imagine she's down to bone, "...well, yes, but nothing specific." We're going to need a first aid kit soon.

I starting to feel sorry for making her feel uncomfortable.

"You're not really giving me much to go on, here."

"Yeah, I know but..."

"Right, then, so your friend fancies this boy something rotten but he doesn't want to know. Is that right?"

She nods.

"Does she know for certain?"

"Know what?"

"That he's not interested."

"No," she says slowly, "not for absolute certain."

"Well, there you are then. That's the first thing to find out, isn't it?"

She frowns. "But that's what I'm asking *you*. How's she going to find that out?"

"Ask him."

"She can't just go up to him and ask him that."

"Why not?"

"What if he tells her to..."

"... go jump in the lake?"

"Well, yeah."

"At least she'd know for sure."

"Yeah, but what if she's too shy?"

I think for a second or two. "Get a mutual friend to ask him."

She considers this for a few moments, her hand hovering at the top of her boot. "But what if there isn't anybody who could do that for her?"

I feel like walking over to the house and repeatedly banging my head against the wall.

"Look, if she can't bring herself to just go up to him I think she'd be better off looking elsewhere. No bloke's worth all that trouble."

I think Rosie senses my exasperation.

"But what I wanted was a male perspective, like I said. I mean, what do *you* like about a girl?"

There's a loud *thunk* and half way down the garden, twin spotlights illuminate a giant billboard. It's a cartoon drawing of a very large tin can, full of worms.

"What do you mean?"

"You know, what is it that attracts *you* to a girl?"

"Is that relevant?" I ask, stalling outrageously.

"I don't know. Maybe."

"Well..." I murmur. Another mouthful of cider goes down the hatch.

"I mean, I know boys like the way a girl *looks,* but surely not all boys are *only* interested in looks. What about personality?"

"Oh, a combination, obviously."

"But which is more important? For *you*?"

"Depends."

Does it? I ask myself. Does it, really? I think we all know exactly what you're more interested in, Atticus Childress. And it ain't a sweet disposition.

"Yes," I say, "it definitely depends."

I can see we're both fed up of this circular discussion and I'm on the verge of asking Rosie outright exactly *who* it is that she's interested in. If I know him, I can offer specific advice. Probably along the lines of: 'I wouldn't touch him with a cattle-prod if I were you.' Come to think of it, this is probably precisely why she's being so vague.

"Look," she says deliberately, "what I want to know is this: if this boy doesn't appear terribly interested in my friend then do you think he might be interested if she looked different?"

"In what way?"

"Oh, you know, wore something she thought he'd like. Something like that?"

"I don't think that would be right, though."

"What do you mean?"

"Well, then he'd like her just for her looks, not her personality."

"But he might like her after he'd got to know her."

"Possibly, but you couldn't count on that happening."

"No, I suppose not, but at least she'd have given it a go."

"Well, yeah, I guess so."

"Right, then."

"Right, then," I echo. I'm getting good at this.

"That's what I'll tell her to do."

"Your friend?"

"Of course."

"But don't tell her I said so, will you?"

"No, don't worry, I won't"

With that, Rosie uncrosses her legs, stands up and returns to the house.

Our conversation starts to replay in my head. Did I really tell her that it wouldn't be *right* if she wore something just because she thought it would make her more attractive to this bloke she fancies? Hang on, let me just look back at what I wrote.

Yup. Thought so. Astonishing! What a tightly knit, reverse split, travel kit hypocrite!

What I just told Rosie is diametrically opposed to the creed by which I lead my (interior) life. In my head, I am constantly dressing up women of all ages in outfits and footwear that make them more appealing to me. But when Rosie asks me if *she* should dress up for her inamorato-to-be, I tell her that it wouldn't be *right,* that he should be attracted to her because of her *personality,* not her looks, or how short her skirt is.

I would imagine you're reading this now, shaking your head, and you have every right to be doing so. I can't blame you. I'm doing the same. Literally. I'm sitting here, staring down between my knees, slowly shaking my head, shocked by the depths of my hypocrisy.

Yes, I know there are, by now, more than a few units of alcohol coursing through my cardiovascular system, but, even so, I am stunned. Flabbergasted.

My thoughts turn to the identity of the object of Rosie's unrequited love. I can't picture him – probably some steroid in the 1st XV – but I hate him. I slowly start to transfer my self-loathing to him. Why is he making my sister get so twisted up? Why is she thinking of turning herself into something she isn't, just to please him? Knowing at some deeper level that I really want to punish myself, I start thinking about what I'd do to this creep that's bamboozled my sister. I'll smash his face into a bloody pulp – after I've drawn and quartered him and wrapped his intestines around his scrawny neck. Unless he's bigger than me, or he's with all his rugby mates.

Romeo and Juliet emerge from the house, give me a black look – presumably for sitting on *their* bench – then head off into the garden. 'Oh Romeo, look! That horrible

Atticus Childress is sitting on *our* bench.' 'Never mind, Juliet, my little bundle of hormones, let's take a walk in the garden and perchance we should happen upon a quiet glade, or even an isolated area of scrubland, we could lie down and proceed to snog each other's fucking heads off.'

I resume replaying my conversation with Rosie but the persimmon and pomegranate cider is exerting its effects and I'm struggling to keep my train of thought on the tracks. I give up and close my eyes. The night is warm. The music from the house throbs almost pleasantly. I find I can almost think about what Red and Bass are undoubtedly doing at the moment without my heart rate rising above one hundred and fifty.

Ten minutes pass, or maybe fifteen. I'm not sure. I'm on the fourth can. My vision is markedly blurred at the edges. Half a dozen girls come tumbling out onto the terrace, or it could just be three. I think Courtney and Saoirse are among them although, for all I know, it could be James and Lars, from Metallica, in drag. The girls come nearer my side of the terrace. I can see now that my first impression was correct – there are six of them – and I don't think the twin driving forces behind Metallica are among them.

Following a brief lull, the percussive introduction to another current dance hit erupts through the open window behind me and Saoirse and a girl with an even more unruly mass of curly hair start dancing. Either the alcohol has caused a significant phase shift between my hearing and my eyesight or the pair of them have got no sense of rhythm whatsoever. I consider introducing them to the hemiballismic fifth-formers who were in the front row last night.

A girl in an extremely short, ruched dress lights a cigarette, blows out a cloud of smoke, then passes it to a girl in a dark mini-skirt whose massive shoes make her slim legs look like pipe-cleaners. Another girl, with pale blonde hair and long, tanned legs, has completely lost control of her right arm. She's waving it around at no one in particular and certainly not in time with the music. Out of the corner of my eye I discern movement and reluctantly shift my gaze away from the lissome girl with a serious neurological disorder to watch a couple returning from the garden, the first that I've observed so doing since taking up my current position. I scrutinise them as carefully as my condition allows for evidence of recent carnal activity – ripped hosiery, unbuttoned shirts, smeared make-up, and so forth – but can find none. Perhaps I'm doing them a disservice. Maybe they did nothing more than take a pleasant stroll. Or possibly they were warned about the psychopathic killer reputedly stalking the grounds, relieving himself on his victims before slaughtering them mercilessly.

Can you slaughter someone mercifully? I don't think so.

When I look back at the group of girls, I see that the long-legged blonde has stopped waving and is now walking toward me. As she draws nearer I see that it's Cheyenne. I scold myself for not recognising her earlier, especially as she's wearing the same green and white checked dress she wore at our party. I presume she's broken the prime directive of fashion etiquette because of the exceptionally appealing way the short hem-line shows off her faultless thighs, away from which I am unable to tear my gaze – until she stops a metre or so from me. Some of these larvae are definitely turning into butterflies. I look up to find a puzzled smile.

"Hi, Atticus."

I nod.

"What are you doing out here, all on your own?"

Good Lord, can't a young man enjoy a bit of peace and quiet without constant interruptions by nubile young women questioning his motives?

"Oh, just enjoying the view," I mutter.

Cheyenne's smile broadens and, although the light out here isn't what one might term good, I think she blushes. The fact that she thinks I was referring to her, or her legs, catches me slightly off guard. Why's she blushing? Does she think I fancy her? Does she fancy me? *Do* I fancy her? She sits down next to me and crosses her legs. My guts do a double flip and the cider in my stomach – a considerable amount, let's not forget – almost ends up splashed between my feet.

"You don't mind, do you?"

I presume she means her sitting next to me and shake my head. I look down, supposedly at the can I'm balancing on one knee. Actually, I'm surreptitiously admiring her legs. Extraordinary at any distance, they are even more alluring at close quarters. I am suddenly struck by the urge to reach out and touch them, to stroke her lustrous flesh, to feel their warmth. In response to this compulsion I take another sip of snow berry and star apple cider. When I think I've regained my composure, I look at her face again.

"Nice dress."

Hot damn! What a star! Why don't I just go all the way: 'Hey, Cheyenne, I think you've got a great pair of legs. Would you mind if I stroked them for a little while? Don't get me wrong, though. I'm not a pervert or anything like that, if that's what you're thinking. No, I'd just like to

427

touch them, then, if it's OK with you, I could maybe kiss your toes and work my way up. So, what do you say?'

"I'm sorry, I didn't mean..." I mutter, shaking my head, not knowing exactly what it was I didn't mean.

"That's all right," she says, laughing. "I'm glad you like it."

"Yeah, I think it's great, darling. Though it could look better, maybe tossed in a heap on the ground."

Except I don't say that, clearly. Instead I mumble: "Yeah, well, er..."

Which is more or less the same, isn't it?

"Have you known them long?" asks Cheyenne, clearly, thankfully, unaware of my internal monologue.

"Who?"

"4Tune8, of course."

"Oh, them," I murmur, the capacity to speak clearly having temporarily evaporated.

"I thought it was brilliant when they sang that song to Rosie."

Her eyes are glittering with such undiluted excitement it's almost sad. I let my head drop again and steal another lingering glance at her thighs. It occurs to me that, were I in possession of a certain type of manipulative personality, I could quite easily take advantage of Cheyenne's euphoria: 'Hey, Cheyenne, sweetheart, I know where 4Tune8 are staying. I could take you there, if you like. You would? Oh, how wonderful! Yes, that's right, it's just a short walk from here, down through the gardens. And if it's too dark, I could always hold your thigh... I mean, hold your hand.'

"We're all going to see them tomorrow, you know?"

I look up again. "Yeah? That should be fun."

At the sound of a raised voice I look over at the remaining girls to see Saoirse leading them over towards Cheyenne and I.

"Look, it's Rosie's brother, the one who knows 4Tune8," she squeals.

The five girls gather around the bench, twittering excitedly to each other.

"It was absolutely brilliant," says Courtney.

"Oh, and Luke," says Saoirse, "he's just *so* handsome."

"And Geoff's eyes were so blue," says Cheyenne. "Much more blue than they look in photos."

"I *wish* I'd been there," says the girl with the pipe-cleaner legs, handing the cigarette to the girl in the red dress.

And so it goes for the next few minutes. As none of the larvae seems remotely aware of my presence, despite Saoirse drawing their attention to me, I let my glance flip from one to the other as they speak while I sip at the fourth can. Miss Red Dress drops the cigarette end, daintily places the toe of a red patent leather court shoe over it then twists her foot back and forth, grinding it out. I watch her leg muscles contracting and relaxing and conclude that, while she wins the maximum exposure award, the Most Shapely Legs prize remains with Cheyenne. While I'm busy staring with consternation at Miss Pipe-Cleaner's choice of footwear, one of them addresses me.

"Eh?" I grunt, looking up.

"Can you get any more tickets?" asks Miss Red Dress.

"For the concert tomorrow," adds Saoirse.

I am saved from further torture by Rosie as she pushes past Courtney and grabs my wrist.

"Come on," she urges, pulling me to my feet, "there's someone I want you to meet."

As Rosie drags me off toward the house, I hand the almost empty can of walnut and wolfberry cider to Saoirse, who is smiling at me *very* strangely.

"Where are we going?" I demand as we walk through the kitchen. God, I hope she's not going to introduce me to her new boyfriend. If he's bigger than me and I'm forced to fight for my sister's honour, this could end very badly. For me.

Rosie, who still has a firm grip on my hand, does not answer. She leads me down a short corridor and into the entrance hall. Then we're into the crowded lounge and I start to feel slightly dizzy. I'm pulled into another corridor, and I'm dimly aware of brushing past Romeo and Juliet, tongues still jammed down each other's throats. They must be back from their garden excursion. I think about telling them their bench is now free. Maybe it's not the same Romeo and Juliet. Maybe they're breeding, or being cloned, or I'm the middle of some weird experiment. Rosie pulls me onward. I stumble and nearly fall. But she won't let go of my hand. Onwards, onwards.

Now we're in the snooker room. "Rosie!" I whine.

She shows no sign of slowing down. I'm dizzy and starting to feel sick. I pull up then jerk my hand from her grasp. She turns to face me, scowling.

"What?"

"Where are we going?"

"I told you," she says, glaring at me, "I want you to meet someone."

"Who?"

There are four lads from the upper sixth playing snooker – doubles, I assume – and they're all staring at

Rosie and me. There must be another dozen people in the room. Most are watching and listening.

"Just someone," hisses Rosie.

I stare at her, or try to. The room is slowly spinning around me and a familiar feeling is blossoming in the pit of my stomach. I swallow hard, determined not to embarrass myself. Rosie misinterprets my expression.

"Look," she says quietly, "don't be so bloody childish."

I can feel sick coming up into the back of my throat. I gulp it down. "I'm not-"

"This is important to me," she says, her voice a stage whisper, "so don't muck it up, OK?"

I meet her gaze as steadily as I can, biting my lower lip, then surrender. She grabs my hand again and pulls me onwards. Everything is whirling around me so violently that I become almost completely disorientated. I've only had four cans of exotic fruit cider. Can't hold my ale. Sad but true. The deep bass thudding of dance music becomes louder as we walk through another room, which I think might be the library, then into another corridor. The music is very loud here. Rosie pulls up and tugs me closer.

"How much have you had to drink?" she asks, sniffing my breath.

"Three... four cans, I guess."

"What, you mean you don't know?"

Hello, Mum! Didn't recognise you there for a moment. Have you had some Botox? You look a lot younger.

"Four. I've had four cans."

She winces, then shakes her head. "Listen, I want you to be nice, OK? You hearing me? Just be NICE!"

"I'm always nice."

431

"See, that's what I mean. Just keep your big trap shut."

"Hey, don't speak-"

"Promise me," she interrupts, "that you'll keep it zipped."

"What, you mean I can't say anything?"

"You know what I mean."

"No."

"Yes you do, so promise me."

Rosie hasn't released my hand. In fact, she's gripping it tighter than ever. Even in my muddled state I can see and feel how anxious she is.

"OK, OK, I promise."

She opens the door behind her then pulls me into a long room. The music – a raucous dance hit from last summer – is almost deafening. The room is packed with people, all gyrating to the cacophonous beat. Rosie drags me right through the middle of the crowd, across and then along the side of the room.

We pass a couple of open windows, through which a lovely cool breeze blows. As we pass, I look out, and can see the terrace again. What the hell? We could have got here from where we started in about thirty seconds. So why did Rosie lead me that merry dance through the house. I am now feeling very, very sick, and I am going to hurl spectacularly at any moment.

Then Rosie stops, but I don't and I stumble into her, nearly sending both of us clattering to the floor.

"Watch it!" she hisses as she grabs onto a nearby chair to stop herself from falling.

"Sorry," I slur.

I look around, expecting to see the apple of my sister's eye, that upper sixth bloke who looks a bit like a young Johnny Depp (in the right light), some acne-ridden fifth-former, or maybe someone in my year. The room tilts suddenly, and nausea blooms in the pit of my stomach. "Whoa…." I mumble.

The room returns to its normal orientation. The nausea subsides a little. I look around and realise that Rosie and I are standing in the middle of a ring of people. The music has been turned down – or my auditory nerves have been affected by alcohol poisoning.

I glance at Rosie. She's smiling at me very strangely. I look over her shoulder and see Bass and Suzz. Standing with their arms around each other's waists, they are also smiling. I slowly turn my head to see Red and Chelsea standing next to them. Chelsea is giggling to herself and Red is grinning like an idiot. I'm am now feeling very peculiar, and I don't think it's anything to do with the black sapote and conkerberry cider.

Next to Red, Mamta is watching me, her eyes wide with expectancy. When I see Cheyenne standing next to her my heart skips a beat then begins to accelerate. How did she get in here so quickly? And, more to the point, *what* is she doing here? My gaze flips to her legs then back to her face in time to see her glance at something to my left. I turn to look but only see a knot of girls talking to one another. I return my attention to Cheyenne and then, as a siren in my head starts to shriek, look once again at the group of girls.

There are four of them, but I can only *see* one.

With her back to me, I can't tell who she is. Everything in the periphery of my vision becomes fuzzy, but the centre of my field of vision becomes pin-sharp. I can see everything about this beauty before me in crystal clear detail. I wonder if I'm getting a migraine, or I'm about to have a convulsion. I can't remember my vision doing anything like this before.

I can see everything about this girl in exquisite detail. Top to toe, side to side. Nothing escapes my gaze. Not one square millimetre.

Her blonde hair is tied back in a high pony-tail. I can see the musculature of the back of her neck. Dangling from each earlobe are earrings which look like miniature dream-catchers, long enough to almost brush her shoulders. She's wearing a long-sleeved cropped top, grey with black block detail to the arms and neckline. The top clings so tightly that, although her arms and upper torso are covered, very little is left to the imagination. Her lower back is bare, gleaming dully, and I'm momentarily overcome by the urge to walk across and very, very gently run my fingers down the lower ten inches of her spine.

My breathing is fast and shallow as I look down at her feet. She's wearing ankle boots, black leather, with four-inch block heels which seem to have some sort of mirror finish. Six-inch stilettos they are not. But they look fabulous.

I look up again, leaving the best for last. She's wearing the most stunning pair of silver leggings I have ever seen. Sorry, I'll rephrase that. She is looking absolutely stunning in a pair of silver leggings.

But 'silver' doesn't cover the half of it. For a start, they're not actually silver. I think my eyes are playing tricks on me. Or my brain. Or something. From my extensive online research, I think these belong to that sub-genre of shiny leggings called 'liquid', for obvious reasons. But these aren't *just* silver, liquid leggings. After a moment, I realise that my eyes are working just fine. The leggings are actually *shimmering*. The material is holographic, iridescent, dancing with tiny rainbows, mirroring light.

The dizziness, which seemed to have subsided, returns with a vengeance as my gaze travels up one leg to her bare lower back then down the other, then back up the first and down the other again – round and round and round, up one glistening leg and down the other, over the gentle roundness of her calves, back and forth across the mesmerising swell of her arse, up and down the fullness of the backs of her thighs.

I think I'm going to faint.

There are so many thoughts careering around my head, I can't keep track of them all. I feel sick and dizzy and happy and dopey and enthralled. My heart's beating like a jackhammer. Sweat's seeping from every pore as if I were a sponge being squeezed. I feel icy cold and fever hot at the same time. My legs feel numb and there's a distinctly uncomfortable feeling in my groin.

My fingers are tingling and there's a tremendous feeling of pressure in my right hand, so much so that, with superhuman effort, I peel my gaze away from this vision of loveliness before me to find Rosie's hand still gripping it.

She's pulling me again, this time toward the girl. I want to resist, to stand here and stare at those gleaming legs until I pass away – even if I only last another few minutes – but I can't. I allow myself to be guided closer and closer to her.

My gaze is riveted to those legs and, as I approach her, they fill my vision. They fill *me*. I am consumed by them. I consume them. They are me and I am them. I am talking utter nonsense. I *am* utter nonsense. I don't know *what* I am any more. I don't care what I am any more. All I care about is these two legs before me, these lustrous twin towers.

When I have been led to within a metre of them, and my chin is on my chest – so reluctant am I to look at anything else – their owner begins to turn to face me, and my desire to gaze upon them forever is nudged out of its dominant position by that to learn the identity of the girl to whom they belong.

I allow my gaze to travel slowly upwards, over her sleek, shimmering thighs and across her hips, over her taut, pale belly, the knot of her umbilicus, over the hem of the cropped top, over what look like the most perfect breasts imaginable, into the shallow triangle formed by the top of her breastbone and her collar-bones, then, finally, up her neck to her face. Her lips are parted slightly, painted crimson and coated with gloss. Above her blushed cheeks her eyes meet mine. Her lashes are thickened with black mascara and dark grey shadow fades up toward the twin charcoal arcs of her eyebrows. Never mind brows on fleek, this is woman on fleek. In the centre of her green irises her black pupils are contracting and dilating slowly as she scans my face.

"Hello, Atticus," says Dawn.

Aaaaarrrrrgggggghhhhh!!!

The exclamation mark is, apparently, the most abused form of punctuation. Seemingly, it's usually quite unnecessary. There are, it is argued, always more elegant methods of conveying strength of emotion, excitement, whatever. The exclamation mark belongs only in advertising copy. Final Reduction! All Stock Must Go!! Last Two Weeks!!!

Allow me, therefore, to rephrase.

The tone of the siren shrieking inside my head becomes more strident, more urgent, as I realise that the femme fatale standing before me is none other than Dawn Ferner. My heart is beating like that of a small rodent. Sweat is running down my body in rivers, coursing down my legs and spilling out over my basketball boots to form a lake of salty fluid on the floor. If I was hooked up to a polygraph, the pens would be oscillating wildly, like things possessed.

Dawn bloody Ferner! This pulchritudinous, wet-look-clad nymphet, this alluring, block-heeled seductress, this paragon of glossy lasciviousness, is one of my sister's larval friends!

The realisation hits me like a nuclear wind, whipping me, beating me, ripping away my flesh, tearing out my soul. A scream starts to build within me, rising up from the centre of my being, growing louder and louder. My mouth opens in anticipation but every drop of saliva within has evaporated and my throat is a hollow husk. The primal scream, sensing a dead end beyond my vocal cords, hangs a left and sprints up to my brain. As I stare silently at Dawn the scream erupts in my mind, a long, terrifying howl of desolation.

Or, as I said before: Aaaaarrrrrgggggghhhhh!!!

Dawn says something else. I know this because I saw her glossy, crimson lips move, but I certainly heard nothing – something to do with that desolate howl I mentioned. I can no longer feel my heart beating in my chest, and the possibility that it may have stopped flits across my consciousness like a small bird spied from a great distance. In fact, except for sight, all my senses have deserted me.

A few seconds pass, or a few decades. I know not which. Time has lost all meaning. I see Dawn's brow crease and then her lips move again. My hearing begins to return, and the strains of a chart-topping *power ballad* seep into my head. I mention this only because the song has been a constant source of irritation to me over the last few months. Perhaps, though, I shouldn't feel so ill-disposed toward it as it may well be that the female singer's strident – and, in my opinion, quite characterless – tones are bringing me out of my fugue-like state, just as repeated playing of a comatose patient's favourite song may revive them.

Don't muck it up, OK?

Rosie's words echo in the misty canyons of my mind.

Now, listen, I want you to be nice, OK?

"I'm sorry," I whisper, my voice little more than a croak, "I didn't catch that."

"Do you want to dance with me?" she asks.

I smile, grateful that I can at last hear Dawn's words, though they are still not synchronised with her lips. Even more out of step, however, is my comprehension. Such a long time passes before I understand her question that there seems none left to consider my response.

"Sure," I hear myself saying.

Dawn takes a step toward me then lifts up her arms and places her hands on my shoulders. Through the thin – and damp – fabric of my shirt I can feel her hot fingertips. I couldn't even estimate the number of times I've envisaged myself dancing with a girl – locked in each other's embrace, swaying in time with the music – but now that's it's actually about to happen (with me and the girl from Clapham) I realise I've never actually worked out the mechanics of the situation. I am suddenly struck by the realisation that I have no idea where I should put my hands, or how much pressure I should apply, or whether I should pull her towards me or leave a polite distance between us, or... or anything, really.

Then, without conscious effort on my part, my hands move forwards and around her waist. My fingertips meet and I allow my hands to rest gently in the small of her back. I can feel the waistband of the leggings under my fingers and warm bare skin of her lower back beneath my thumbs. She begins to move, rocking gently from side to side, barely moving her feet, lightly transferring her weight from one mirror-finish heel to the other.

At first, I just stand there, gazing into her eyes, but then I too begin to sway and rock. Her hands start to move, slipping off the tips of my shoulders and sliding down over my shoulder-blades. I feel the pressure under her fingertips increase as she pulls herself closer to me.

My senses have returned completely, their acuity increased beyond all reason. I can smell her perfume, a heady musky fragrance, and beneath that I can smell *her*. I breathe in her scent, and it's the most wonderful sensation I've ever experienced. More than anything I can feel her body heat. I can feel the warmth radiating from her bare belly but I can also feel – or I am aware of – the heat generated from her face, chest, hips and thighs. It feels so good, having her so close to me, holding her in my arms. It just feels *right*, somehow.

It occurs to me that I should check the reactions of the circle of friends around us but I can't peel my gaze away from Dawn's glistening eyes. All my troubles seem so very far away – cue pastoral acoustic guitar – that I can't remember very clearly what they are, or were. Except one. Insistently tapping away on some internal window is my shame at what Dawn heard me say about her to Rosie a week ago.

"I want you to know that-"

"Shhh," she whispers, eyes hooded.

"No, I think I should-"

"Atticus," she says firmly as her eyes open wide to fix my gaze.

"What?"

With her right hand on the nape of my neck she pulls my head forwards then whispers in my ear: "Shut the fuck up and kiss me."

[33] Epilogue

Twenty years have passed since those eventful two weeks.
Dawn and I have been happily married for the last fourteen
years and, as each day passes, my love for her grows ever
deeper. We have three children, Laura, aged six and a half,
Jane, who's just turned four, and baby Benjamin who, at
this very moment, is sleeping in his cradle at the side of my
desk. Yeah, right, I know what you're thinking. Benjamin?
What can I say? It was Dawn's choice and, hey, how could
I argue with the woman I love?

After St. Mick's, I read politics and sociology at
one of the northern Russell Group universities then, after a
few traumatic months living at home and off my parents, I
got a job in the marketing department of a multinational
pharmaceutical company. The work maybe isn't what I
would have chosen but, hey, I'm (very) slowly climbing the
corporate ladder and it pays for the roof over our heads and
the food on the table.

To close the circle, I would love to have been able
to tell you that after getting a first in fashion, and then
paying my dues for several years earning next to nothing, I
finally got a break and I'm now one of the most successful
women's fashion designers in the UK. I could link you to
my website where a pair of Atticus Childress molten lead
leggings could be yours for just under £700.

The truth of it is that my fashion fetish, my
obsession with objectification, was just a phase, just a
chapter, albeit a long and introspective one, in the book of
my life. Don't get me wrong, I'm a heterosexual male and a
good-looking woman in a flattering outfit will still press
my buttons. But that stage, when I was seventeen, came to

an end soon after I started going out with Dawn. Thankfully.

So, where once my head was full of latex leggings, crop-tops and stilettos, it's now full of the usual stuff. Did we pay that last electricity bill? When's the MOT due on Dawn's car? Can we afford a holiday abroad this year? Am I getting a gut or am I just *a little thicker around the middle* than I used to be?

Red broke up with Chelsea a few weeks after his party. A succession of girlfriends followed, each of them with fewer neurones than the last. Although we're still Facebook friends, and we sometimes exchange Christmas cards (if Dawn's doing them that year), I kind of lost touch with him after he went up to a university in Scotland. Last I heard, he'd set up a company that churns out semi-pornographic, sexual technique, virtual reality videos. Someone has to, I suppose.

The other weekend, Dawn, the kids and I went down to London to visit Bass and Suzz. They're living in a rambling semi-detached house in Herne Hill. Bass's grandmother was loaded – who knew? – and left him enough money to buy the house outright. He's a freelance trumpet player – so, a pig in shit, basically – and Suzz works for a design company that specialises in trendy websites. They've no kids and they're not married – an *archaic* institution as far as Suzz in concerned – but they are very happy.

Rosie married Derek a couple of years after Dawn and I got hitched. Yeah, I know, it was as much of a shock to me, but they too seem quite happy. They have two kids, so I am Uncle Atticus to Logan and Ava Childress-Westbrook.

Little Bennie is no longer so little. He grew almost nine inches in the fifth form and now, at six feet five, towers over everyone, including me. He's a programmer, writing stock-control software, and is engaged to Asya Malhotra, Mamta's younger sister.

None of us know where Zach is from one week to the next. After many years as a roadie he started a transportation company with a couple of friends which quickly grew into a fairly big business, offices in Europe, and so on. But as my brother was never one to be satisfied with an office job he decided to work *out in the field*, as he likes to put it, and he now spends his time flying around the world, coordinating the tours of some of the biggest names in rock.

And that's about that, really. I don't think I've left anybody or anything out.

Oh, except for one thing.

Just one tiny, little, almost insignificant fact.

All of the above is complete rubbish. I just made it all up. Actually, it's only two weeks since Red's party. But I had you going for a minute there, didn't I?

It's quarter to nine on Sunday morning and I'm lying in my bed, thinking things over, which will come as no big surprise, I'm sure. However, there was an element of truth in what I was saying – those two weeks certainly were the most eventful of my life to date. The Childress Summer Saturnalia, Bläck Gläss's début performance, Apollonia and 4Tune8, Rosie's birthday surprise and, not least, Red's party. Each one an adventure which I'm sure I'll never forget.

One thing, though, that will definitely remain forever etched on my mind is the moment I first laid eyes on Dawn at Red's party. Those boots, her legs and arse

443

sheathed in liquid silver holographic leggings, her bare belly and lower back, the muscles in her neck standing out, her blonde hair, those funny dangling dream-catcher earrings.

It's Frannie I have to thank for all of this, apparently, although I've not yet had the chance to express my gratitude. It was to her that Dawn confided her attraction to me and it was she who, having been filled in by Rosie about my clothing-related obsessions, suggested the plan of action. It was Frannie who went shopping with Dawn and Rosie one evening before Red's party and helped to pick out the outfit. And it was Frannie who convinced Dawn that the way to a man's heart was not through his stomach but – at least in my case – through his obsessions.

Rosie was involved throughout every stage of the plan and latterly everybody but myself was in on it. That very strange conversation with my sister on the terrace was, evidently, a result of both Dawn and her getting cold feet at the last minute. But thankfully, their scheme worked out perfectly. I mean, normally I would feel more than a little annoyed at being so blatantly manipulated but, well, why look a gift-horse in the mouth? Or, more appropriately, why check to see if a woman's platform boots are leather or man-made?

I suspect, if you're of a certain disposition, you're wondering what happened after Dawn so politely asked me to kiss her. Well, you can rest assured that I did the gentlemanly thing and snogged her bloody head off. Ha-ha-ha. No, I didn't. That came later. I've got zero intention of relating, blow by blow, exactly what we did get up to so let's just say that we enjoyed each other's company for the rest of the evening, and have done so on a number of

occasions since. We've not consummated our relationship –
as the song goes: 'You can't hurry love' – but my first-hand
knowledge of female anatomy is growing at a steady, and
extremely pleasurable, rate. I've tried to persuade Dawn to
wear those leggings again but she keeps telling me that
she's waiting for a *special occasion*. I wonder what she
means.

Regarding the effects on me of those two weeks,
well, I think I've changed – hopefully, for the better – but
it's difficult to tell. I mean, I still feel like the person I was
before, only slightly different, if you see what I mean. Over
the last two weeks, since I've been seeing Dawn, I think
I've become a little more relaxed, a little more able to go
with the flow. This may have something to do with the fact
that, for the first time, I'm happy with the direction in
which the flow is moving. I'm not fooling myself, though. I
don't for one minute believe that things will always be thus.
Take yesterday afternoon, for instance.

Dawn and I were in town, just casually strolling
down the high street, as you do when you're a teenage
couple in lust. We weren't looking to buy anything in
particular, or even go anywhere specific. We were both
content to hold hands and amble aimlessly along the
pavement. Now and then, Dawn would pull up in front of a
clothes shop and point out a blouse that took her fancy or a
ludicrously expensive pair of jeans or a particularly ugly
pair of shoes. And I would smile or laugh or scowl,
whichever seemed appropriate. We chatted about this and
that, about the film we were planning to see that evening,
about Bass's increasing devotion to Suzz, about what will
happen when Red meets Chelsea's best friend, Georgia,
again (as, at some point, he must) and other inconsequential
matters.

445

Then, as we were hovering outside a clothes shop called, for reasons known only to its proprietors, *Pineapple Paradigm*, with Dawn's attention apparently riveted to a pair of brown leather calf-length boots with no heels and mine wandering haphazardly over the milling shoppers, I felt Dawn withdraw her hand from mine.

Now, you might consider this to be a trivial matter, an insignificant incident, but I felt as though my arm had been severed at the shoulder which, if nothing else, should indicate the order of magnitude to which, by this stage, my affection for her had developed.

I swivelled around, removing my gaze without difficulty from a young mum wearing a pair of flesh-coloured leggings, to see Dawn looking off to one side. I followed her line of sight to discover Mason Morgan and Rob Willems walking in our direction. Mason and Rob are in the upper sixth and considered, so I've been led to believe, to be the most handsome, the most desirable, the most *primo* boys at St. Mick's, an opinion with which they themselves wholeheartedly agree.

It's completely beyond me why anyone would be attracted to two such arrogant, self-satisfied anabolics. I suspect, however, that my sexual orientation (and copious amounts of self-delusion) may be interfering with my assessment because Dawn, so it appeared, did not share my views.

As the two muscle-bound lumps of manhood swaggered towards us, Dawn stood a little straighter and pulled a wayward strand of hair away from her face. Then, much to my annoyance and disappointment, a coy smile curled across her lips as they passed. She scrutinised their denim-covered buttocks for a second or two then returned her gaze to me, smiling as if nothing had happened.

I kept quiet and tried to keep my expression as blank as possible. In fact, I even managed to return the slight squeeze she applied to my fingers as she took my hand again.

Yesterday evening, in the cinema, I found myself continually thinking back to that incident. I kept trying to see it from Dawn's point of view.

How would I have behaved if a pair of libidinous vixens had been strutting towards us? And if I'd released Dawn's hand and ogled their jiggling Christmas baubles then turned to admire their firm buttocks and long, slender legs, how would Dawn have reacted? Would she have taken it as a sign that my devotion was not perhaps as strong as I'd led her to believe? Would she have slapped my cheek and stamped off in a huff? Would she have withdrawn snogging privileges until I'd seen the error of my ways? I don't know and I hope I don't find out.

So, I can't really say whether Dawn and I will still be together twenty years from now. If we are, though, and if we have a son, you can bet your bottom bitcoin he won't be called Benjamin.

The End

For my wife and children, without whom this book would have been completed and published a long time ago, in a galaxy far, far away.

Note from Phil Trum:

Thanks very much for reading *My Circus, My Monkeys*. I enjoyed writing it. If you've the time and inclination – and, when you think about it, how important is it *really* that you check out that new *Epic Fail* compilation on YouTube – could I ask you, politely and with a hint of desperation – to leave a review on the Amazon page. Feedback on the Facebook and Goodreads pages would also be appreciated. If you leave a five-star review I will email you some information that will, truly, blow your mind. I promise.

I lied. I won't email you anything. We clear? Cheers.

Goodreads:

https://www.goodreads.com/book/show/30834343-my-circus-my-monkeys

My Circus, My Monkeys Facebook page:

https://www.facebook.com/MyCircusMyMonkeysNovel/

Phil Trum Facebook page:

https://www.facebook.com/philtrumEU/

Printed in Great Britain
by Amazon